IN NORTHERN SEAS

IN NORTHERN SEAS

BY

PHILIP K ALLAN

WWW.PENMOREPRESS.COM

In Northern Seas by Philip K. Allan
Copyright © 2019 Philip K. Allan

ISBN-13: 978-1-950586-23-3(Paperback)
ISBN :13: 978-1-950586-24-0(e-book)
BISAC Subject Headings:

FIC014000FICTION / Historical
FIC032000FICTION / War & Military
FIC047000FICTION / Sea Stories

Cover Illustration by Christine Horner
Edited by Chris Wozney

Address all correspondence to:
Penmore Press LLC
920 N Javelina Pl
Tucson, AZ 85748

DEDICATION

To my dear brother, Fairley

Acknowledgements

Success as an author requires the support of many. My books start with my passion for the age of sail, which was first awakened when I discovered the works of C. S. Forester as a child, and later when I graduated to the novels of Patrick O'Brian. That interest was given some academic rigor when I studied the 18th century navy under Patricia Crimmin as part of my history degree at London University.

Many years later I decided to leave my career in the motor industry to see if I could survive as a writer. I received the unconditional support and cheerful encouragement of my darling wife and two wonderful daughters. I first test my work to see if I have hit the mark with my family, and especially my wife Jan, whose input is invaluable. I have also been helped again by my dear friend Peter Northen.

One of the pleasures of my new career is the generous support and encouragement I continue to receive from my fellow writers. In theory we are in competition, but you would never know it. When I have needed help, advice and support, I have received it from David Donachie, Bernard Cornwell, Marc Liebman, Jeffrey K Walker, Helen Hollick, Ian Drury, Chris Durbin and in particular Alaric Bond, creator of the Fighting Sail series of books.

Finally, my thanks go to the team at Penmore Press, Michael, Chris, Terri and Christine, who work so hard to turn the world I have created into the book you hold in your hand.

CAST OF MAIN CHARACTERS

The crew of the frigate *Griffin*

Alexander Clay—Captain RN

George Taylor—1st Lieutenant
John Blake —2nd Lieutenant
Edward Preston—3rd Lieutenant
Thomas Macpherson—Lieutenant of Marines

Jacob Armstrong—Sailing Master
Richard Corbett—Surgeon
Charles Faulkner—Purser
Nathaniel Hutchinson—Boatswain
Able Sedgwick—Captain's coxswain
Sean O'Malley—Able seaman
Adam Trevan—Able seaman
Samuel Evans—Seaman
William Ludlow—Landsman

Also on board the *Griffin*

Nicholas Vansittart—A diplomat
Joshua Rankin—His valet

Isaiah Hockley—A ship owner
Sarah Hockley—His daughter

In Paris

Napoleon Bonaparte—First Consul

Louis Alexandre Berthier—A general and Minister of War
Charles Maurice de Talleyrand—Foreign Minister
Pierre Alexandre Laurent Forfait—Minister for the Navy

In Lower Staverton

Lydia Clay—Wife of Alexander Clay
Francis Clay—Their son

In Copenhagen

Count Andreas Bernstorff—Chief Minister
Anders Holst—A naval captain

William Drummond—British Ambassador to the Danish Court

In St Petersburg

Paul I —Tsar of Russia
Grand Duke Alexander—His son and heir

Levin von Bennigsen—A general
Count Peter von Pahlen—Military Governor of St Petersburg

Lord Charles Whitworth—British Ambassador to the Russian Court

Others

Earl George Spencer—First Lord of the Admiralty

Sir Hyde Parker—Admiral in command of the Baltic Fleet
Lord Horatio Nelson—His deputy

CONTENTS

PROLOGUE

The candle flames trembled as Napoleon Bonaparte, First Consul of France, slammed the flat of his hand down on the table.

'No, gentlemen, it will not do!' he exclaimed. 'Glorious France, held at bay by a nation of shopkeepers? It is intolerable! There must be a way to defeat these damned English!'

'But First Consul, we just cannot come at them,' protested General Berthier, the curly-haired Minister of War. He pointed towards the huge map of Europe painted across one wall of the stateroom. 'We have tried everything! We have built an armada of boats to invade across the Channel, sent men and arms to ferment rebellion in Ireland, even made an attack on Egypt to get at their possessions in India. But always we are thwarted by their damned ships.'

'Alas, you have the truth of it, General,' agreed Napoleon. 'The moment the sea wets the boots of my soldiers, there I find them, waiting for me.'

'How can the elephant fight with the whale?' asked Charles Maurice de Talleyrand, leaning back in his chair and placing both manicured hands behind his head. 'Is it not the most delicious of paradoxes, my friends? Socrates himself would have appreciated it.' Napoleon pushed back a strand of hair that had fallen across his face, and turned his dark eyes on his Foreign Minister.

'And might we trouble you for an answer to this paradox, monsieur?' he asked, his voice dangerously low.

'No, of course not, sir,' smiled Talleyrand. 'If it had an answer, it would no longer be a paradox.'

'Have you been drinking again?' demanded Berthier.

'I have dined well, it is true,' conceded the Foreign Minister, 'but I am merely articulating the problem that we face. Our army crushes all opposition by land. Their navy does the same at sea. So I repeat, how can the elephant fight with the whale?'

'If I could be master of the Channel for six hours, I would slay your whale quickly enough,' growled Napoleon. 'What solutions do you have to offer, Monsieur Forfait?' All eyes turned towards the last man seated at the table. The Minister of the Navy blinked from behind his spectacles and cleared his throat.

'We are building ships as quickly as we are able, First Consul, as you have ordered, but alas, the English fleet grows even swifter.'

'Impossible!' exclaimed Napoleon. 'I have given you control of every shipyard from Venice to Amsterdam! How can they possibly be out-building us?'

'Timber, labour, money we have, sir,' explained Forfait. 'What we lack is tar for our hulls, hemp for our rope and canvas for our sails, all of which must come in ships from the Baltic. As long as it is the English who control the sea, it is to their dockyards these supplies go.'

'How splendid!' enthused Talleyrand. 'Surely we have yet another paradox? Because we have no supplies, we have no ships, and because we have no ships, we have no supplies!' Napoleon rounded on his Foreign Minister, his face scarlet, but before he could vent his anger he felt a hand on his arm.

'A moment, First Consul,' urged Berthier. 'I believe the minister may have just given us the solution.'

'I have?' said Talleyrand, sitting upright.

'He has?' queried Napoleon. 'I am not sure that I follow you, General.'

'Does the Foreign Minister's paradox not work in reverse?' explained the Minister for War. 'If there are no supplies for the English, it will be *they* who cannot build or repair their ships, no? So if we can stop this Baltic trade from going to them, will we not have solved our problem?'

'He is right, First Consul,' said Talleyrand. 'Clever Berthier! It is by suffocation that the elephant defeats the whale. While Forfait here builds our fleet, the English ships will founder for lack of tar, their torn sails un-mended, and they will have to choose between hanging their criminals or replacing their rigging. Conquer the Baltic, as you have conquered Italy, and you shall have your victory over the English.'

'But, gentlemen, how am I to conquer the Baltic?' protested Napoleon. 'Think what you are asking! It would mean fighting Prussia, Russia, Demark and Sweden, all at the same time as England. France is not strong enough for such a war.' The four men turned to stare at the wall above them and looked at where the countries he had listed crowded around the shores of that northern sea.

'Very well, gentlemen,' said Talleyrand. He pushed his chair back from the table. 'If you men of blood cannot shut the Baltic to the English with your armies, I shall have to do it for you.'

'And how will you achieve that, Foreign Minister?' asked Napoleon. Talleyrand rose to his feet and placed a hand over his heart.

'The enemy may have more ships, First Consul, but it is France that has the best diplomats.'

CHAPTER I

TRIALS

The great cabin of the *Namur* was ablaze with lanterns to combat the gloom. Autumn rain swept up the Solent, splattering against the row of glass windows at the back of the cabin, and making the big three-decker rock and fret at her moorings. The light fell on a long baize-covered table that ran in front of the windows and was strewn with books and documents. It glittered on the full dress uniforms of the officers, seven captains and an admiral, who sat in a row behind the table, and it caught in the seed pearls and gold that decorated a beautiful sword resting on the cloth in front of them.

To one side of the table was a double row of chairs. Some of these were occupied by more junior naval officers in less elaborate uniforms, and one had been pulled a little apart from the rest. In it sat a well-dressed civilian from London in a pale blue coat and buff-coloured britches. He was of medium height and had the young face of a man in his mid-thirties, although his thinning hair made him appear older. He sat very upright with both his gloved hands resting on a silver-topped cane, intently watching proceedings.

On the opposite side of the cabin was a single chair in which sat another naval post captain. He was a tall, lean man in his early thirties with curly chestnut hair and pale grey eyes that were fixed intently on the sword. Captain Alexander Clay was remembering the day that it had been promised to him. It had been two years ago, and he had just been presented to the king in Weymouth, after he had returned home with Admiral Nelson's despatch on the Battle of the Nile. How things have changed, he thought to himself. Both of them had been riding high then. Now Nelson had been censured for his behaviour during the French occupation of Naples, and for the open affair he was having with another man's wife. My situation is hardly better, reflected Clay. Here I sit, facing a court martial for the loss of my beloved frigate *Titan*. Is this where my brief career as a naval captain ends? His attention returned to proceedings as the admiral beckoned someone forward from amongst the witnesses. A solid-looking naval captain with a bald pate rose from his place and stood in front of the table.

'Gentlemen, this is Captain West of the frigate *Leda*,' explained the admiral to his fellow judges. 'Would you be so kind as to tell the court how it was that you learned of the loss of His Majesty's ship *Titan*, Captain?'

'By all means, Sir Thomas,' replied the officer. 'The *Leda* was hove to off the Brittany coast, with Cape Penmarc'h bearing north three miles. At four bells in the afternoon watch, I was summoned on deck by a report that smoke had been sighted due east of us. Upon my word, I thought at first, a damned volcano had erupted, there was such a column rising apparently from out of the sea. I proceeded eastwards to investigate, and on approaching the Glenan Isles became aware that a large frigate had been beached and set on fire.

By the time we reached the spot, there was precious little remaining of the ship, but signals were made to us to the effect that the crew were Royal Navy and in need of rescue.'

'How was such a signal made, if the ship was destroyed?' asked one of the judges, a portly captain with the ribbon and star of the Order of the Bath across his chest.

'A naval ensign had been draped over a prominent cliff, and various signal rockets, Red Bengals and the like, were being fired off,' explained West. 'I sent in our boats and recovered Captain Clay and his men, some of whom were badly wounded, together with sundry items that had been brought off from their ship.'

'And what did you then do, Captain West?' asked the admiral.

'From Captain Clay I learned that he had recently been in action with a ship of the line, close to the port of Quiberon, Sir Thomas. The wind being favourable, I thought it my duty to investigate further. The following morning the *Leda* approached Quiberon, where I found the French national ship *Argonaute* of 74 guns, moored in the harbour. She appeared to have considerable damage aloft, and had lost her foremast together with much of her bowsprit.'

'Good show, by Jove,' muttered one of the naval officers seated behind the table.

'Having made that observation, I returned to rejoin the fleet and report,' continued the witness.

'Are there any questions for Captain West?' asked the admiral, peering at his fellow judges over a pair of spectacles pinched onto the bridge of his nose. 'No? Then the witness may stand down, and I shall summarise what the court has now learned. We have had testimony from all the officers of the *Titan*, whose accounts agree well with the ship's log, and with Captain Clay's written report. We have also heard of that frigate's most unequal battle with a French ship of the line on the night of the tenth of August, subsequently identified as this *Argonaute*. We have learned of the handsome manner in which Captain Clay and his men fought their way clear, having sustained considerable damage and over a hundred casualties. Then we heard from her first lieutenant, Mr... eh... Mr Taylor, as to the desperate condition in which she found herself the following day, holed between wind and water, with both her pumps failed, and how she subsequently came to be beached. Perhaps we might now proceed to question Captain Clay on any points that remain unclear to the court?'

Everything sounded so reasonable, thought Clay, as he rose from his seat and stood before the line of judges. From the admiral's account, mere ill fortune had been behind the loss of the *Titan*. No mention of the warnings of betrayal he had received, but ignored. No hint that the encounter with the big French ship was not chance, but a well-sprung trap that he had failed to see coming. No mention of Major Douglas Fraser, who had fooled him with such ease, with dreadful consequences for his ship and crew. As he stood in his place Clay could sense that all eyes in the cabin were on him, but he found he was particularly conscious of the gaze of the civilian with the silver-headed cane. The portly captain who had spoken earlier was the first to ask a question.

'I believe we all understand that there was an urgent need to beach the *Titan* when the second pump failed,' he said. 'But why did you feel obliged to set fire to your deuced ship, once she was safe?'

'We had run ashore on a French island,' said Clay. 'In consequence I was fearful that she might fall into the enemy's hands. It was also the speediest way of signaling to Captain West and the *Leda* of our presence. I was mindful of my duty to the wounded. My surgeon was concerned as to their prospects if we were not promptly rescued.' There was a mutter of approval from the line of captains at this, and several jotted down notes. Keep it simple, he urged himself. No need to speak of the release he had felt as the flames whooshed higher, seeming to burn away all trace of that night's many mistakes.

'Captain Clay, could you explain how exactly you came to be caught by this *Argonaute*?' asked another of his judges. 'Surely as a frigate, the *Titan* was the swifter vessel?'

'They surprised us on a dark night, hard against the coast, sir,' replied Clay. 'We were only in such a false position because we were obliged to wait for the return of our ship's boat, which was conducting a mission ashore—' A cough sounded from behind Clay's right shoulder. He glanced that way and saw the civilian from London looking significantly at the admiral.

'Ah, indeed,' said the flag officer. 'I am mindful that the court should remain focused on the issue of the loss of the *Titan*. There is no cause for a more general inquiry.'

'But Sir Thomas,' protested the questioner, 'if the *Titan* was engaged in contact with the shore, we need to hear the particulars. In my experience the French only hazard their ships with some object in mind. Perhaps there was more to the appearance of the *Argonaute* than—'

'And perhaps you are straying into areas that are best not discussed so frankly,' warned the admiral. 'Kindly desist, sir.' Clay caught the briefest nod of approval in the corner of his eye.

'Might I ask a question concerning this Major Fraser, who

appears in so many of the reports, Sir Thomas?' said another of the captains.

'No, sir, you may not,' said the admiral, after a glance towards the man in the pale blue coat. 'We must keep our enquiry pertinent to the fate of the *Titan*. Are there any questions of that nature for the captain?' A few of the officers behind the table exchanged glances, and others shifted in their seats, but no one spoke. 'No? Then perhaps we can now move to consider our verdict. Master at Arms, pray clear the court.'

There was a general tide of movement out of the cabin and Clay found one of the *Namur*'s lieutenants at his elbow.

'Would you be so good as to accompany me, sir?' he asked, leading Clay towards a separate door. Outside was an empty corridor lined with cabin doors, one of which the officer opened. The room beyond was only furnished with a cot, a small desk and a chair. To Clay it seemed troublingly close to a prison cell.

'If you could wait in here, sir,' said the lieutenant, standing back from the door to let him enter. 'Can I offer you any refreshment? Perhaps a copy of the London papers?'

'Nothing, I thank you,' said Clay as he entered the cabin. He pulled the chair from under the desk and sat down.

'Very well, sir,' said the lieutenant. 'I shall return when the court has reached a verdict. I don't imagine the deliberations will be very long.'

The moment the door was shut behind him, Clay was on his feet once more, trying to pace up and down the tiny space. It was very unsatisfactory, with barely two of his long strides between the door and the blank oak side of the ship. He considered asking to be allowed to walk on the *Namur*'s quarterdeck, but quickly rejected the idea. Striding in the pouring rain would hardly be seen as the action of a guiltless man, and it would probably mean that he would have to encounter some of the witnesses. He did not want to face his former officers, or Captain West, until he had been acquitted and could look them in the eye. Assuming that he was to be acquitted, he reminded himself, turning around at the door. The sound of the *Namur*'s bell rang out from somewhere forward.

He went over the details of the trial as he walked, trying to gauge how the discussion amongst his judges might be going. It was hard for him not to be pleased with the testimony he had heard. George Taylor and John Blake, his first and second lieutenants, and Jacob Armstrong, the *Titan*'s American sailing master, had all given their evidence with an enthusiasm for their captain that had at times touched on hero worship. Then there had been the letters of support from former commanders, such as Sir Edward Pellew and Lord Nelson, all fulsome in their praise. If it were not for the awful consequences of a guilty verdict, Clay might have enjoyed that part of his court martial.

But there had been other currents running in the room. Several of the judges had seemed suspicious of the simple narrative presented to them. He had felt their penetrating gaze on him and sensed the doubt in their minds. What had the *Titan* been up to that night? Who was this Major Fraser who featured in so many of the reports? Was he connected with this mysterious French ship that had appeared on that stretch of coast, at that precise time? Clay knew it was the major who had betrayed them to the French, and had bled to death that night on the beach for his treachery. It was a tale that in part could exonerate him, and yet the admiral and the mysterious civilian seemed determined it would not be discussed. He lifted his arms in frustration as he turned in the narrow space once more.

What would happen if he were found guilty? It was hard not to dwell on the awful consequences of such a verdict. If he were censured by the court, he was realistic enough about his lowly connections to believe that he would be on the beach for life. And then there was the nagging feeling in the back of his mind that he deserved to be found guilty, for the way he had failed his men. He had been given plenty of warnings not to trust Fraser, but had failed to heed them.

There was a knock at the cabin door just as Clay turned away from it. He quietly returned to the chair, pulled his coat straight and settled into what he hoped was the position of an innocent man who had been seated the whole time. 'Come in,' he called. The door opened to reveal the same lieutenant as before.

'Would you accompany me once more, sir?' he asked. 'The court is ready for you.'

The same great cabin, the same grey sea outside, the same witnesses and observers sat to one side, and the same line of judges behind their table. All these thoughts came to Clay as he stooped to pass through the open cabin door with the practiced ease of a tall man who had served at sea for the last two decades. Then he saw that something had changed in the cabin. His sword had been turned around on the cloth, so that the hilt now pointed towards him. The admiral waited until Clay stood in front of the table before picking up a sheet of paper. He carefully re-attached his pince-nez and began to read.

'Captain Clay, it is the finding of this court that you are not answerable for the loss of his majesty's ship *Titan*,' he read. 'Furthermore your engagement with the French national ship *Argonaute* is considered to have been in the best traditions of the service. In consequence you are most honourably acquitted. Perhaps you will permit me to be the first to offer you my congratulations?'

The cabin seemed to disappear into a swirl of movement around him. In a daze Clay exchanged formal handshakes with the post captains behind the table, and more enthusiastic ones from a grinning Taylor, whilst Blake pummeled his back, and Armstrong scooped up his sword from the table and tried to buckle it around his waist. All the time he was conscious of the civilian in the pale blue coat, still sitting in his place and looking on with approval.

******

While Captain Clay was being congratulated by his friends aboard the *Namur*, four of his former crew were seated around a table in a Bristol tavern. The Anchor was a modest establishment, with loose reeds scattered over the floor, a low ceiling of dark oak beams and rows of solid tables, each flanked by a pair of elm-wood benches. But the beer was plentiful and cheap; the location convenient for both the docks and a nearby cock-fighting pit, and the serving wenches appeared comely, at least in the feeble light supplied by the tallow reeds on each table. In consequence it was popular with sailors.

'So what we doing in Bristol again, Sean?' asked Sam Evans, by far the largest of the four, a six-foot six-inch giant who retained the build of the prize-fighter he had once been. The dark-haired sailor seated opposite him took a pull of his beer before he answered.

'Now we've been paid off, we can't be hanging around Portsmouth any,' explained Sean O'Malley, his accent broad

Irish. 'Will you look at us, at all? Adam and I with fecking pigtails down to our arses, you with your tattoos, even Able here looks more sailor than slave these days. The press gang would sweep us up quick as quick. No, we needs to steer clear of Pompey until Pipe has his next barky, an' then we can go and volunteer for that.'

'But that'll not be until after his trial, like,' observed Adam Trevan, anxiety in his clear blue eyes. 'You reckon he'll be getting a new ship?'

'Course he bleeding will,' said Evans. 'He'll be free before you knows it. A frigate against a seventy-four! That'd be like Adam here milling with me! There ain't no disgrace in the *Titan* losing, no disrespect there, mate.' He patted the Cornishman on the arm.

'I see how we can't stay in Pompey, but why Bristol?' said Trevan, ignoring the huge Londoner. 'I wants to get back home to my Molly, now she's expecting a nipper.'

'Aye, and I does needs to get back to Pipe,' said Able Sedgwick, a well-built, handsome man. He had joined Clay's ship as a run slave in Barbados years before, and had been his coxswain throughout his time on the *Titan*. 'He's given me a few weeks liberty, but I need to return to Lower Staverton afore long, so come now, Sean. Why are we here?'

'Wouldn't it be grand to give your Molly a proper purse of chink to see her through, Adam?' said O'Malley. 'And we all lost a deal of stuff when the ship got burned.' He gestured for the others to move closer. 'Gather round, shipmates. We're here to make ourselves a fecking fortune!' The others exchanged wary glances.

'This ain't like that time you had us digging up half of St Lucia looking for bleeding pirate gold, is it?' demanded Evans.

'That was a mistake any fecker could have made,' protested the Irishman. 'No, ask yourselves. What touches at Bristol every month, lads?' The others looked blank.

'A convoy from the Caribee!' announced O'Malley. 'Even as we sit on our arses here, a fleet of West Indiamen will be a heading up the Bristol Channel, and every last one is a chance for us to make a fortune. Because what have those feckers got onboard?'

'Sugar?' offered Trevan.

'Rum, logwood?' suggested Sedgwick.

'Aye, all of that, to be sure,' said the Irishman. 'But what else?'

'Molasses?' said Evans.

'Parrots!' corrected O'Malley. 'Every tar on board will have bought a parrot. You'll remember how you could get a beauty on the quayside in Bridgetown for a penny?'

'In truth I was stuck on the bleeding barky at the time, for fear of the traps, but I remember some of the lads bringing them on board,' said Sedgwick.

'Right you are,' said the Irishman. 'Well, them as bought one will have been keening and cuddling them birds the whole voyage home. Learning them some blarney, and all manner of tricks. And then they arrive in Bristol, get paid off, and there's not a boarding house in the city as will let you keep a beast in your room. So we meet them jacks as they land, offer them a fair price for the fecking birds, say a tanner, and then it'll be us as has them.'

'I still ain't seeing it, Sean,' said Evans. 'So I am now up a parrot, down six pence, and I can't return to me boarding house, on account of this fowl. Where's the sense in that?'

'Do you know what folk will pay for a talking parrot in Gloucester up the fecking way?' asked O'Malley. 'Your parson as wants one for his daughter, the doctor buying something special for the wife? Ten fecking guineas, that's what!' The other sailors exchanged glances.

'When does this bleeding convoy get in?' asked Evans, his eyes alight with avarice.

******

At first glance the oak planking beneath his feet seemed to be smooth enough, running in long parallel lines across the room. But his limited experience had taught him that life was rarely so simple. He viewed the surface with suspicion as he stood, clinging to the side of the chair and testing the floor with one foot. He took a final look towards his destination, fixed his face into a look of determination and set off to traverse the gap. The moment he released his grip, the planking was on the move, tilting first one way and then the other, as if a considerable sea was running. After a few tottering footsteps, he collapsed forwards onto all fours, and then rapidly crawled the last few yards towards the extended hands of his father.

Alexander Clay swept up his son and held him at arm's length in front of him. Both grinned at each other, in expectation of what was to follow.

'Oh!' cried Clay, as he let Master Francis free-fall towards the wooden floor of the nursery, catching him a foot from disaster and lifting him back up again. His son shrieked with delight and kicked his plump legs in the air, prompting Clay to repeat the drop, with much the same reaction.

'Have a care, Alex,' warned his wife, Lydia, from the door. 'He has not long had his pap. Such exertion so soon after he has eaten cannot be good for his constitution.' The words may have been reproving but her tone was one of pleasure at catching father and son together.

'Your pardon, my dear,' said Clay, promptly dropping Francis once more and hauling him back aloft, accompanied by yet more squeals of delight. 'It is such a pleasure to engage with him. When I last left him he was a swaddled baby, but now he is so much more animated. Isn't that right, Master Francis?'

'Da!' yelled Francis in agreement, reaching forward for the loose end of Clay's neck cloth. His father dropped him once more, and was rewarded by more delighted laughter that ended when his son was sick across the sleeve of Clay's coat.

'Did I not caution you?' scolded Lydia, coming towards him, but the nanny was quicker. She crossed from her place by the nursery window with a square of muslin in her hand and collected the baby from his father's arms.

'There, there, little man,' she said, as she bore him away, leaving Clay contemplating the puke on his clothes.

'Oh Alex, it is so good to have you home,' said Lydia, mopping with her delicate lace handkerchief at the stain.

'And it is wonderful to be home,' said Clay. He caught her around her waist with his clean arm and drew her close.

'But how long will it last, now that you have been acquitted?' she asked, continuing to daub at his sleeve, while enjoying the feeling of her husband's closeness.

'That I cannot say, my darling,' said Clay. 'I have written to the Admiralty twice now, but have had nothing more than acknowledgements. I start to wonder if Sir Thomas did not include some hint of disapproval in his report on my court martial.'

'Surely there can have been no grounds for censure?' she asked. 'Your poor ship was roughly handled by a superior vessel, and you did your best to save her.'

'Yes, you are right, my dear,' he said. She turned within his arms, looking up into his pale grey eyes and he bent forward to kiss her. Her lips parted under his, and she started to melt against him. Then her eyes opened wide and she pushed him away.

'My dress!' she exclaimed, pulling the material out into a fan to search for any evidence of her son's lunch. Finding none, she resumed her mopping of his sleeve. 'It may be selfish on my part, but I would urge them to not be overly hasty in their deliberations, if only for myself and Francis's sake. No, it is no good. It requires a proper sponging. You shall have to shift this coat for another.'

By the time that Clay was changed, his son was fast asleep in his cot. He kissed him gently on his head and slipped from the nursery to re-join his wife in the drawing room at Rosehill Cottage, just as the front door bell rang.

'Were we expecting callers this afternoon, my dear?' he asked. 'I know that it is too early for my sister.'

'Indeed so,' confirmed Lydia. She looked towards the door as the maid came in and curtsied. 'Who is it, Nancy?' she asked.

'Beg pardon, madam, but there is a gentleman at the door asking to see the master. He's come in a handsome carriage, with horses and a footman an' all. He asked me to give you this, sir.' The maid offered a silver tray on which a calling card rested. It was thick and embossed, and carried the faintest trace of cologne.

'The Honourable Nicholas Vansittart, King's Counsel, and Member of Parliament for the Borough of Hastings,' he read. 'Who the deuce might he be?'

'He is no acquaintance of mine,' said Lydia. 'No, wait,

Vansittart you say? I believe my aunt may have mentioned him. If I recall correctly, he has excellent connections. She said that he was a close friend of Pitt's and has a finger in most of the government's pies.'

'A man of some consequence, then,' said her husband. 'Kindly show Mr Vansittart in, if you please, Nancy.'

The pale blue coat had been replaced by one of plum-coloured broadcloth, but the silver-topped cane was unchanged, as was the intent expression on the face of the man who had attended his court martial.

'Captain Clay, I do hope you will forgive my intruding in this way,' he said. 'It is impertinent of me, I know, particularly as we have not been formally introduced, but I was almost passing your door, so I thought that I would avail myself of the opportunity it presented.'

Clay and Lydia exchanged glances. The village of Lower Staverton was ten miles from the nearest turnpike, and their house was on a lane that ended in Farmer Grey's yard.

'You are of course most welcome, sir,' said Clay, shaking their visitor's hand. 'May I present my wife, Mrs Lydia Clay.'

'Your servant, ma'am,' said Vansittart, bowing low over her hand and brushing it with his lips.

'Please do take a seat, Mr Vansittart,' she said. 'May we offer you some refreshment?'

'My thanks, but mine is but a brief visit, I fear,' said their guest, glancing over her shoulder towards the case clock that stood against the wall. 'I am expected back in town this evening. But there was a matter of some delicacy I was hoping to discuss with your husband, before I depart.'

'Of course,' said Lydia, getting up from the sofa with a swish of satin. 'I do have some other matters to attend to. Would you excuse me?'

'Most obliged, Mrs Clay,' said their guest, bowing once more. When the door of the drawing room closed, he straightened up and turned towards Clay. 'Good. Now, to business.'

'By Jove, sir, but you are very forward!' exclaimed Clay. 'Perhaps you might start with an explanation for your behaviour. First attending my court martial, and now appearing unannounced in my home to chase my wife away with the barest civility. Who are you, sir, and what are you to me?'

'You are quite right, Captain, my manners have been deficient,' said Vansittart. 'The only excuse I can offer is that I am to sup with the Prime Minister tonight, and he is most particular about punctuality. I might add that if your residence were but a little easier to find, I could have gratified you with a more fulsome display of courtesy towards the mistress of this house.'

'If you had given me notice that you were coming at all, I would have sent someone to guide your coachman,' said Clay. 'But no matter, you are here now, although I am still no clearer as to why.'

'My first reason is to offer you an apology,' said his guest. 'It was on my recommendation that Major Fraser was assigned to your mission to the Royalist rebels in Brittany, and so I am in some part to blame for its failure and the loss of your ship.'

'I see,' said Clay. 'Well, in truth you were not alone in being made a fool of by that gentleman. I was quite taken in, although he failed to deceive my lieutenant of marines, Thomas Macpherson.'

'Is that the case?' said Vansittart. 'He must be a shrewd cove. Macpherson, you said his name was?'

'A very talented officer,' confirmed Clay. 'Was it your interest in Major Fraser that occasioned your presence at my court martial?'

'In part it was,' conceded the diplomat. 'The government was anxious not to have the major's activities brought to the attention of the public. Missions like his are best conducted in the shadows, what? But courts martial can be uncertain affairs. I was also there to ensure that the correct outcome was reached.'

'Was that wholly for my benefit, or was it to spare the administration any further embarrassment?' asked Clay. 'I imaging that a nice, uncomplicated version of events, for which no one need be blamed, was preferable to a close scrutiny of the shambles left by the major?'

'Pon, my word, sir, I can see you are no fool either,' his guest chuckled. 'You are wasted in the navy. You should try your hand at politicking. In truth I had aimed at achieving both ends.'

'And what happens to me, now that I no longer have a ship, Mr Vansittart?' asked his host.

'That deficiency can be swiftly remedied, Captain,' said his visitor. 'The navy is launching new ships all the time. I understand there is a rather handsome eighteen-pounder frigate named the *Griffin* that is just now being completed at Woolwich. She is a thirty-eight, so a little larger than the *Titan*. Would that be of interest?'

Clay felt a surge of pleasure at the prospect of command, compete with the dread at leaving his young family again, and irritation with Vansittart. Why was he being offered this ship by a damned lawyer, instead of the Admiralty, he wondered, and how is it he seems to know so much?

'Is such a thing truly in your gift, Mr Vansittart?' he

asked. 'Should it not come from my superiors within the service?'

'Oh, we are only speaking informally here, Captain,' said his guest. 'But I have discussed the matter with the First Lord. It was he who gave me the particulars of this ship. I make no doubt that if you want her, she is yours.'

'What will become of the surviving crew from the *Titan?*' asked Clay.

'You are more expert on such service matters than I, but I would imagine that as the *Griffin* is but recently launched, there will be vacancies for them all. If the handsome manner in which your officers gave testimony at your trial is typical, they would doubtless welcome the opportunity to follow you again.' Vansittart smiled at Clay, and then his face fell as he caught sight of the clock.

'Damnation! Can that truly be the time?' he exclaimed, jumping up. 'I must be away. I will let George—that is, the First Lord of the Admiralty—know that you will accept the *Griffin.*'

Clay rose to his feet, and found his hand grasped between both those of his visitor.

'My dear sir, your record as a captain is commendable, and I hope you observe that you are not wholly without friends, you know? Your efforts this past year have not gone unnoticed. An officer of your undoubted ability cannot be left idle at home in these dangerous times. I give you joy of your new ship, and I fancy that our paths may cross again before too long, Captain Clay. *Adieu* for now, as the French have it!'

It was only after Vansittart had rushed from the room and the front door had slammed shut behind him that it occurred to Clay that he hadn't actually said yes to his offer.

CHAPTER 2

HMS GRIFFIN

It was market day in the city of Gloucester, and close to the looming bulk of the cathedral a small crowd had gathered in a side alley off Westgate Street. On a grey day, the profusion of large, brilliantly coloured birds in cages that filled a handcart had aroused considerable interest. Hardly less exotic amongst the soberly dressed burgers of the city were the sailors who manned the stall. All four were in their shore-going attire of high-waisted trousers, shirts decorated with ribbons, short blue jackets and broad-brimmed hats. Several passersby were examining the birds, and one gentleman, dressed in the black suit and white neck cloth of a clergyman, appeared to be contemplating a purchase. He brought his face close to the bars of a cage that Evans was holding towards him so as to inspect the blue and yellow macaw within.

'Tis a Bengal Blue, yer honour,' announced O'Malley. 'Isn't he a beauty?'

'Bengal, you say?' queried the Reverend William Medley. 'But surely that is in the Indies? I understood you to say that these birds were all from the Americas?' The parrot blinked, as if it too was momentarily confused, before it resumed preening the feathers of one wing.

'Eh, did I say Bengal?' said the Irishman, tugging at the gold ring that dangled from his ear. 'I was after saying Bermuda. I am always getting them two confused. Lucky it ain't me as navigates the barky, eh?'

'Indeed,' said Medley, returning his attention to the parrot.

'Ain't he a wondrous creature?' enthused O'Malley. 'Tame as a dove, and prattles on like nobody's business, so he does.'

The clergyman tapped the bars of the cage with his finger. 'He doesn't seem very inclined to speak at present,' he observed, looking towards the other birds. 'What about that green one over there, with the rose coloured face?'

Evans was about to return the macaw to the hand cart, when its occupant deigned to speak.

'Coil that line, shipmate!' squawked the parrot.

'Oh, how charming!' exclaimed one of the bystanders.

'Bless my soul,' said the churchman. 'Why, it is conversing just like a little sailor! Mrs Medley will certainly find him most diverting. Was it ten guineas you said?'

'Aye, it were, sir,' said O'Malley, rubbing his hands together. 'I am robbing myself, in truth, but as you can see you have me at a disadvantage, with so many birds to shift.' The clergyman pulled out his purse and began to count out the money.

'Avast there, you poxed son of a whore!' ordered the parrot. Medley looked around.

'What did that bird just call me?' he demanded.

'Oh, t'was nothing, your honour,' said O'Malley, positioning himself between his customer and the parrot.

'He's just after forgetting where he is, amongst the genteel, like.'

'I have to consider my position,' said the clergyman, juggling the gold coins in his palm. 'It would never do to have lewd speech in my home, even from one of God's lesser creatures.' The Irishman stared at the money as it sparkled in the light. It was so close he could almost sense the weight of it in his palm.

'He may have picked up the odd word of sailor talk, that's all, your honour,' he explained. 'But once you get him home, amongst the society of respectable folk, he will be singing psalms afore you know it.'

'I bleeding won't, damn your eyes!' offered the parrot. The macaw's sudden garrulousness seemed to encourage the other birds to speak.

'Shift your arse!' demanded a plain green one.

'Bugger me,' offered another.

'That rope be slacker than a whore's—' The rest of the bird's offering was mercifully lost in a roar of laughter from the less reputable members of the crowd. The Reverend Medley's face turned crimson.

'These creatures are an absolute disgrace!' he roared, returning his money to his purse. 'How dare you offer such wicked fowl for sale to honest folk? I have a good mind to have your privilege to trade revoked by the magistrates.' The Irish sailor shifted from one foot to another, and exchanged glances with Trevan.

'You do have a market day license, I take it?' persisted the clergyman.

'Ah... a license is it?' queried O'Malley, patting down his pockets. 'I am sure as we do.'

'Constable!' called Medley, striding down the alley. 'I

24

need a constable, here!' The small crowd were now looking on with considerable interest.

'Have you got this here license, Sean?' asked Sedgwick from the side of his mouth.

'Course I ain't got no fecking license,' whispered the Irishman.

'Course I ain't got no fecking license!' repeated the macaw.

'Oh blimey! That ain't good at all,' offered one of the crowd, with obvious satisfaction.

'Did they transport the last bloke they caught without a license, Bill?' asked another. 'Or did he spend a day in the pillory?'

'Twas the pillory,' said his friend, making himself comfortable on an upturned box. 'Shocking state he were in, when they finally let him go.'

'We best bleeding scarper, afore the tipstaffs show up,' urged Evans.

'But what're we to do with all these fecking birds!' wailed O'Malley.

'I could let you stow them in my barn,' offered Bill, 'for a price, like. Could only be for a few hours, mind.' Sedgwick and Evans each grabbed one shaft of the handcart.

'Lead on, mate,' said the Londoner.

'Damn your eyes!' exclaimed a large red bird.

'Course you has to keep them quiet,' said Bill, looking at the parrot. 'While the traps are scouring the streets, looking for'ee.'

'Aye, all right,' said Trevan. 'I has a notion how we might do that.'

******

It was quiet in the office of Earl Spencer, First Lord of the

Admiralty. The tall windows faced towards the inner courtyard of the building and away from the blustery east wind. Although the Admiralty Building was in the heart of London, the cry of hawkers and the clop of passing carriage horses in the nearby streets barely registered over the steady tick of the carriage clock that stood on the mantelpiece. Beneath it a glowing fire of sea coal filled the grate. Lord Spencer looked up from the pile of dispatches on his desk in response to a knock on his door.

'Come in,' he said, returning his pen to the ink stand. A bewigged clerk entered and came partway across the carpet.

'Captain Clay is waiting in your anteroom, my lord, and Mr Vansittart has just now arrived.'

'Capital,' said the earl. 'Do show them in, Higgins, if you please. Oh, and kindly serve the superior Madeira.'

He waited until his clerk had bowed his way out of the office, then rose from his chair to examine his reflection in a mirror positioned on the wall to one side of the desk. Having checked his teeth, he tweaked his neck cloth a little straighter and turned back towards the door, which opened a moment later.

'Gentlemen, thank you both for coming to see me,' said Earl Spencer. 'I believe you may already be acquainted? Captain Alexander Clay, this is the Honourable Nicholas Vansittart.'

'Mr Vansittart did me the honour of calling at my house in the autumn, my lord,' said Clay. He bobbed his head towards the other visitor. 'Your servant, sir.'

'Delighted, I am sure,' said Vansittart.

'Excellent,' said the First Lord. 'Do please be seated.'

Higgins slid forward and held a silver tray between them. 'Some Madeira, sir?' he murmured. 'And for you, sir?'

'Is all well at Lower Staverton, Captain?' asked their host. 'Mrs Clay and the child are in good health, I trust?'

'Both were fine when I last saw them, my lord, although fitting out a new warship affords me little leisure to visit them at present,' said Clay.

'How is the *Griffin* coming along?' asked Vansittart. 'I passed her on the river a few weeks back, and she had hardly any of those ropes and sticks you naval coves are so deuced fond of.'

'She resembles a King's ship a little better now, sir,' said Clay. 'Her masts are rigged and she has her eighteen-pounder cannon aboard, although there is still much to do.'

'How soon before you will be ready for sea?' asked Spencer.

'I have a deal of fitting out to complete yet, my lord,' he explained. 'Almost all of the available *Titans* have volunteered for her, which is a blessing, but that still leaves me short by eighty men. Fortunately the bulk of my former officers were able to follow me.'

'Even young Lieutenant Preston?' queried the First Lord. 'Surely he lost an arm in your action with the *Argonaute*, not three months back?'

'He assures me that he is recovered, and able to perform his duties, my lord,' said Clay. 'It was his left arm, so in that respect he is better placed than some. Lord Nelson, for example.' The steel-grey eyes betrayed no hint of the painful visit Preston had made to him, pleading not to be left on the beach. He had still been weak and pale from loss of blood. Clay remembered the tears in the young man's eyes, his right arm animated as he argued, in strange contrast to the empty sleeve pinned across his chest.

'Rather you than me, Captain, but I am sure you know

best,' said Spencer. 'I receive no end of petitions from disabled officers applying to me, very few of whom I am able to find ships for.' He pulled a sheet of paper towards him, and picked up a pencil. 'So, you have your officers, I collect. What else do you need, beside men, to complete the *Griffin* for sea?'

Clay pulled a leather note book from his coat pocket, opened it on his knee and ran his finger down a page.

'Carronades for her quarterdeck and forecastle, shot and powder, all manner of gunner's stores, a spare foretopsail yard, four anchors, three hundred fathoms of cable, all our ship's boats, carpenter's tools, boatswain's stores, our sails, a forge and anvil for the armourer, thirty stands of muskets, fifty of pistols, boarding pikes, five dozen hammocks, provisions of all kinds—'

'Damn well everything then,' interrupted Spencer, laying down his pencil.

'—and I have yet to be allocated any marines. If my crew and stores could be completed promptly, I could have her ready for a trial sortie into the German Sea by the middle of January, my lord.'

'That may serve,' conceded the earl. 'I take it you would like Lieutenant Macpherson to command your marines again?'

'If you please, my lord.'

'Macpherson?' mused Vansittart. 'Weren't he the cove you mentioned last time we met? The chap who smoked what that damned idiot Fraser was about?'

'The very same, sir,' confirmed Clay.

'Very well,' said Spencer. 'Macpherson is yours, and I shall ask the port admiral at Woolwich to give you the cream of the press to bring you up to compliment. Let Higgins know the particulars of what stores you need on your way out, and I shall see that they are provided. You might want to add warm clothing for the crew and extra firewood to your list. I need you ready to sail by the beginning of February.'

'May I be told what commission the *Griffin* is required for?' asked Clay. In answer the First Sea Lord turned towards his other guest, who drew a newspaper from out of his coat pocket and passed it across.

'This is a recent copy of *Le Moniteur*,' he explained. 'How is your French, Captain?'

'I can converse tolerably, sir,' replied Clay.

'The article you are after is on the bottom right.'

Clay read it, but although he could follow the gist of what was said, he found that he was none the wiser. 'This seems to be an account of the return of some Russian prisoners of war to their homeland, sir,' he said. 'How might that concern us?'

'It concerns us because Boney don't do prisoner releases,' explained Vansittart. 'He holds that the able bodied will simply come back to attack him again. And it ain't just a few he has let go—over four thousand of the blighters, captured in the Low Countries a few months back. They've been cleaned up, given fresh uniforms, the officers entertained in style by General Berthier himself, and then sent back home.'

'Hmm, so am I to take it he wishes to ingratiate himself with the Russians?' asked Clay.

'You certainly are, Captain,' confirmed the politician. 'It's a damned shrewd move. Tsar Paul may be a simpleton, but the way to his heart is through his soldiers.'

'It is not just the return of these prisoners, Clay,' said Spencer. 'That devil Talleyrand has his diplomats swarming over every court in the damned Baltic. Fleas on a badger ain't in it! In consequence, the northern states grow resentful of

us, just like they did during the American War. They have
started to resist having their ships searched. Remember that
damned impudent Danish frigate that fired on the *Nemesis*?'

'The Tsar is leading the charge. He has never liked us, but
it is the damned Frogs who are behind it,' said Vansittart. 'I
am hearing rumours from St Petersburg that the Russians
will presently close their ports to our shipping. Of course, it
makes damn all difference now that winter is here, but it
needs to be resolved before the ice melts in the spring.'

'I don't need to tell you how vital the Baltic is to the navy,
Captain,' said Spencer. 'Half the items on that list of yours
come from there. No Baltic trade means no ships in the
Channel to keep the Frogs on their side of it.'

'I understand, my lord,' said Clay. 'What measures does
the government intend to take?'

'Any required to keep the flow of naval stores coming,'
said Spencer. 'And I do mean any. The Cabinet are quite
resolved. If it means war, then so be it. A fleet will shortly be
assembled in Great Yarmouth—with enough ships of the line
to offer battle, bomb vessels to pound the shore, and plenty
of smaller vessels. Sir Hyde Parker will be commanding.'

'Sir Hyde, my lord?' queried Clay.

'Do you have an objection to Admiral Parker, Captain?'
asked Spencer, his eyes penetrating.

'No, of course not, my lord,' said Clay. 'I would never be
so presumptuous.'

'I fancy the captain is surprised we're entering an old nag
such as Parker into a race, when we have a thoroughbred like
Lord Nelson in the stable, what?' suggested Vansittart.

'I would never put it like that,' said Clay. 'In fairness to
Sir Hyde, I am not well acquainted with him, but his
reputation is that of a cautious man. From your remarks, my

lord, I had imagined it to be a situation where bold measures may be required.'

The First Lord exchanged glances with Vansittart.

'Lord Nelson is available,' said Spencer. 'Between us, he will be promoted to vice admiral presently, and will go with Sir Hyde as his deputy. But I will be damned if he will be in command. He would be a liability if any diplomacy was required, which is passing likely. Look at the hash he made of matters in Naples. Besides, his private life is an utter disgrace!'

'Isn't he cuckolding poor old Sir William Hamilton?' remarked Vansittart. 'I heard Lord Nelson had moved into his house, borrowed his wife, and the husband appears perfectly content with the arrangement! Dashed odd, if you ask me. Meanwhile, Lady Nelson moons around Piccadilly, weeping on any shoulder she can find.'

'As I said, Lord Nelson's private life leaves much to be desired,' said Spencer. 'But I agree with you, Clay; he is the best fighting admiral we have. Sir Hyde can be his nursemaid, and ensure that matters do not get out of hand, while Lord Nelson will take charge if battle looks likely.'

'Now I come to think of it, ain't Hyde Parker just got hitched to some slip of a girl forty years his junior?' asked Vansittart, holding a manicured hand aloft as he tried to remember. 'Miss Onslow! That was her name. Lady Minto was telling me that she leads him around like a keeper with his bear. God bless my soul! Is there something in sea water as makes your admirals randy, George?'

Lord Spencer pulled at the lace cuffs of his shirt and glared at the politician. 'Pray, can we attend to the matter in hand, and leave your more lascivious observations for another occasion?' he demanded.

'As your lordship wishes,' said Vansittart, bowing low in his chair.

'Will the *Griffin* be part of this fleet, my lord?' asked Clay, keeping his face wooden as his fellow guest chuckled to himself.

'My thanks for showing the gravitas these matters deserve, Captain,' said the First Lord. 'I will need you to go ahead of the other ships. I want you to be first in that sea when the ice starts to break. You are to assist Mr Vansittart here on a diplomatic mission to the Baltic. The government will be entrusting him with full powers to treat on their behalf, which makes him very much our superior, Clay. It is hoped that you gentlemen may succeed in averting war, but if you should fail, then Parker and Nelson will do the rest.'

******

His majesty's frigate *Griffin* was a fine sight as she rode at her moorings, just off the bustling shipyard that had built her. Already the slip where she had taken shape had started to sprout the outline of a new hull, the frames curving up from the keel like the fossilized ribs of some huge, long extinct creature. The *Griffin* was newly painted; a broad stripe of yellow followed the line of her gun ports along her sleek black hull. Beneath her long, tapering bowsprit a bronze-coloured griffin crouched, its wings partly open and its beak gaping wide to reveal a bright red tongue. Above the deck rose a dark mass of masts and rigging, soaring high into the pale sky. Most of her yards were crossed and bore furled sails, as if she might leave on the next tide; but above the flowing brown water of the River Thames, a broad strip of copper gleamed in the winter sunshine to show that her hull was still half empty. In her wardroom, close to the waterline, four of her officers were enjoying lunch.

'This pigeon pie has an unusual savour to it,' said George Taylor, the grey-haired first lieutenant of the frigate. He prodded a piece of meat onto his folk and held it up for inspection in the light of the lantern.

'Too gamey for pigeon, I should say,' said John Blake, the ship's young second lieutenant. 'Could it be partridge?'

Jacob Armstrong, the *Griffin*'s American sailing master, sniffed at his food, then scratched at the periwig that encased his large bald head. 'I can barely smell my vittles over all the new oak and tar hereabouts,' he pronounced, waving towards the freshly painted cabin doors that lined the sides of the wardroom.

'Do you miss the stench of bilge water and rats already, Jacob?' asked Blake. 'They will return all too soon, I fear, and the frigate will stink just like the old *Titan* did.'

On the far side of Armstrong sat Richard Corbett, the frigate's naval surgeon. He slit open the pastry and teased the crust apart with care, as if about to operate. A waft of steam briefly misted his round spectacles as he examined the meat in the pie.

'From what anatomy has survived the cooking process, I would say that the origins are certainly avian in nature, but from a rather larger bird than a partridge, Mr Blake,' he said. He drew out a strand of muscle and held it up for inspection. 'With long wings, I should say. Where did you come by it, Britton?'

'It were given to the wardroom with the compliments of some of the newly arrived crew, sir,' said the steward. 'All former *Titans* just back from Gloucester, and grateful to be amongst shipmates. It were Adam Trevan what brought it. They gave another pie to the gunroom.'

'And did he say what was in it?' asked Taylor.

'That he didn't, sir, and I ain't had no occasion to ask, not wanting to seem ungrateful like,' said the steward. 'Would you like me to enquire, sir?'

'Not on my part,' said Armstrong, helping himself to another slice. 'Now that the surgeon has confirmed it is not rat or dog, I am content. I find it quite excellent.'

'Have you ever eaten dog or rat, Jacob?' asked Blake.

'Not to my knowledge, John,' said the sailing master. 'But then, how would I know, given we are so uncertain about this dish?'

'Is Charles still ashore, George?' asked Corbett.

'Mr Faulkner?' said Taylor. 'Yes, in pursuit of all manner of worsted clothing for the crew. Waistcoats, undergarments, gloves and the like. Who would be a purser, eh?'

'Are we off to seek for the Northwest passage then?' asked Blake.

Armstrong snorted. 'You know the Admiralty. A guinea says we shall be despatched to the Caribbean the moment Charles takes delivery of his last woollen mitten.'

'The Baltic is where I would put my money,' said Taylor, leaning forwards and lowering his voice. The sailors serving behind each chair leant forward too, anxious not to miss anything. 'I met up with a friend of mine last night, Sam Harper, who is third in the *Saturn*.'

'She's a seventy-four, isn't she?' asked Armstrong.

The first lieutenant nodded. 'He told me they've been ordered to join a fleet gathering at Great Yarmouth. Now, you only assemble there with one of two objects in mind—to fight the Hollanders or to sail for the Baltic. With Admiral Duncan having thrashed the Dutch back in ninety-seven, it doesn't require much figuring to see where we shall be bound. It would also account for the sudden shortage in woollens.'

'I have never had occasion to sail in those waters,' said Blake. 'Have you done so, George?'

'Some years ago I did,' said Taylor. 'When I was in the Whitby coal trade, before the war. It can be indifferent sailing, being so shallow in places, and the want of salt means the sea freezes with ease in the winter.'

'No salt in the sea!' exclaimed Corbett. 'Why the devil not?'

'On account of the entrance being so narrow, and no end of big rivers draining into it,' explained the veteran first lieutenant. 'It is barely above a big estuary, in truth. I should say it is no more brackish than the river water over the side.'

'I will take your word for that, sir,' said Armstrong, turning behind him to have his glass refilled. 'Still, a frozen sea may make an agreeable composition for one of your pictures, John.'

'It will indeed,' said Blake. 'I shall bring some extra canvases with me.' The officers all sat quietly for a moment, sipping at the wine and contemplating a voyage to that northern sea. After a few moments Taylor waved Britton forward to clear away the food. The surgeon indicated the unused plate next to him.

'Who was this extra place for?' he asked. 'Was Lieutenant Macpherson meant to be present?'

'No, Tom is still marching his marines across from Plymouth,' said Taylor. 'It was for Mr Preston, who I had hoped would join us. He is expected any day.'

'Ah, poor man,' said Armstrong. 'Is he truly recovered sufficiently to resume his duties? That was a fearful injury.' Taylor and the sailing master exchanged glances, remembering when the young lieutenant had fallen, his arm ripped open by a dagger of oak, his face pale in the moonlight.

'It was certainly a considerable wound,' said Corbett. 'But I was able to amputate quickly, and there was sufficient flesh in his upper arm to produce a satisfactory stump. He is young, and there was no putrefaction to complicate matters.'

'Would you care for some cheese, gentlemen?' asked Britton.

'Ah, not for me, I thank you,' said Blake, his appetite vanishing as he eyed the pale yellow cylinder on its wooden board, just the size and shape of his friend's stump. It was only the surgeon who took some, carving into the firm cheese with relish.

'The captain has seen him and pronounced him ready,' said Taylor. 'Let us hope his judgement is sound. I daresay Lieutenant Preston has been delayed on the road south from Yorkshire, and will be with us tomorrow.'

But Taylor was wrong about the ship's third lieutenant. He was in Woolwich already, within sight of the frigate as she pulled and snubbed against the tide in the river. He was looking at the *Griffin* at that moment, through the small window of his room under the eaves of the Star tavern. Edward Preston stepped back from the little panes of glass and, in the weak light that came through them, tried once more to button up his shirt, determined to succeed this time. He pushed a button towards the next slot in the linen with the fingers of his right hand, while his tongue slid from between his teeth and a frown appeared between his dark, sunken eyes. His left shoulder rounded forwards, the nerves in the stump tingling painfully as they tried to move a phantom arm to help. After a few moments of concentration, the button slipped through the hole. Motes of light came and went in the air around the young officer, and he sat down on the bed to regain his breath. Christ, but I am weak as a kitten, he thought. His pale face was covered with pearls of sweat, in spite of the chill in the room.

'Come now,' he urged himself. 'I'll have young Dray to help me once I am onboard, but I'll be damned if I will appear before the general gaze ill dressed. How hard can this be?'

But the answer to his question seemed to be, very hard. His body was still weak from loss of blood and shock. It was only as the pale winter sun, empty on any warmth, sunk behind the reek of London that Preston emerged from the Star and walked down towards the wharf. At his heels came the inn's ostler, singing to himself as he wheeled the officer's sea chest along in a barrow. In truth his britches were still too loose and his white waistcoat concealed a largely open shirt, but his dark blue uniform coat was buttoned up over all of that, and his neck cloth was tied correctly. Down by the river it was growing dark, with the sulphur wash in the western sky reflected back as amber from the surface of the water. The ostler stopped his singing for just long enough to let out a piercing whistle, and in response a river boatman came alongside the steps to take Preston across to the *Griffin*. He hunched a little deeper into his coat against the cold as he watched his possessions being loaded into the boat and tried to stop himself from shivering. He looked across the few hundred yards of water to the dark silhouette of the frigate, and smiled. Strange, he thought, I have never set foot on that ship, and yet it feels like I am coming home.

CHAPTER 3

COLD

The start of February found the *Griffin* out at sea and heading northeast, away from the English coast. She had a complete crew, a full hold, and a set of new sails in which to gather the keen north wind. The sky overhead was the colour of pewter and the sea all about her was rolling slate flecked with white where gusts tugged at the wave crests. The frigate surged forward, beating up into the wind and cutting a diagonal path across the heavy swell. She rose up to each successive wave, her hull creaking in protest, twisted over the summit and then plunged down the far side. White water flew back from her bow as she cut into the next wave, and the cycle repeated itself.

'How do you find the ship, Mr Preston?' asked Clay, as he came on deck in his heaviest coat, with a muffler around his neck.

'Very tolerable, sir,' replied the officer of the watch, touching his hat. 'The dockyard have handed her over in a good state. Mr Taylor and the boatswain had to renew some of the brace pendants on the foremast earlier, but otherwise the rigging seems sound. Perhaps not as swift as our old *Titan*, who was uncommonly fast, but very handy in stays.'

'She does have fine lines, and new copper of course,' said Clay. 'And not too wet, I think. We have a ship to be proud of, which is most welcome. And how do you fare, Mr Preston?'

'Well, I thank you, sir.' The young lieutenant's reply was clipped, and his chin jutted in a set way above his scarf.

I have not seen young Preston look at me like that before, thought Clay, as he searched the pale face and hollow cheeks and wondered again if he had made the right decision. The ship rolled more extravagantly to the next wave, and Preston staggered a little against his captain, but managed to keep his footing.

'You must be growing weary of everyone enquiring after your health, Mr Preston,' he offered. He was rewarded with a grin, much more reminiscent of the teenager he had witnessed grow into the man.

'In truth it can be a little trying, sir,' he replied. 'Tom Macpherson holds I shall blow away if I do not feed myself up. I bear the questioning by reminding myself that it is motivated by kindliness.'

'Quite so,' said Clay. 'We feared we had lost you when you were struck down, Edward.'

The young officer shrugged. 'Is that not the lot of a king's officer in time of war, sir? I recall the surgeon in despair when that musket ball entered your shoulder back in 96. Yet here you are.'

Clay instinctively rolled his shoulder inside his uniform, feeling the scars tighten as he did so, and then smiled at the young man. 'Well spoken, Edward. You and I have enjoyed good fortune. Let us be content with that, and speak of it no more.' He flogged his body with his arms, and then exclaimed, 'Goodness, but it's cold! And we have a good way farther north to go this voyage.' He looked up into the low grey sky and saw the lookout at the fore masthead, his clothes flapping around him in the strong wind. 'While we are discussing kindly acts, Mr Preston, pray see that the lookouts are relieved every hour, and that they are given a place by the galley fire to thaw out. In fact, I shall add that to my standing orders, while this chill weather lasts.'

'Aye aye, sir,' said Preston.

'Has Mr Vansittart settled into the wardroom satisfactorily?' continued the captain.

'He seems an amiable enough gentleman, although when I left him earlier to come on duty, he was finding the motion of the ship troubling, sir,' said Preston. 'He was also a little shocked at the size of the accommodation on offer. I believe he thought he was being made sport of when he first saw his quarters. Tom Macpherson had to show him all the other commissioned officers' cabins before he was satisfied that his was indeed the largest by a good two inches. It did make me wonder how his valet is managing. Mr Taylor has added him to your coxswain's mess on the lower deck, but twenty-eight inches in which to swing a hammock will come as a shock for a pampered servant.'

Clay laughed at this, his breath a trail of smoke, whipped away over his shoulder by the keen wind. 'Sedgwick will see he comes to no harm,' he said. 'But stay; is that not him over there? On the windward gangway?'

Preston followed the line of his captain's arm, and saw the man. He was swaying in time to the ship's motion with only one hand resting lightly on the rail, although he was certainly not dressed like a sailor. Stockings and heavy buckled shoes showed beneath his coat, and he had a short round hat on his head. He was a heavily built man of medium height, with a deeply tanned face and long black sideburns. When he saw the two officers watching him he raised his hat, and dark curly hair whipped around his head in the breeze.

'The valet seems rather more at his ease than the master,' said Clay, touching his own hat to acknowledge the compliment. 'Do you know his name?'

'I believe Mr Vansittart said it was Rankin, sir,' said Preston. 'Joshua Rankin.'

'Rankin,' repeated Clay, continuing to watch the man. Just then the thin figure of his own servant appeared, wearing no coat, and trying hard not to hop from one foot to the other. 'What is it, Yates?' he asked.

'Harte s... sends his c... compliments, sir,' stuttered the youngster through chattering teeth, 'and he s... says as h... how vittles is ready, and Mr V... Vansittart will arrive presently to d... dine with y... you, sir.'

'Tell him I shall come directly,' said Clay. 'Now get yourself below, lad, before you catch a chill. Carry on, Mr Preston.'

'Aye aye, sir,' said the lieutenant.

******

'Ah, Mr Vansittart,' said Clay, rising from his place at the table to greet his guest. 'I trust I find you well, sir?' The diplomat looked anything but. He was wearing his light blue coat once more, but it hung a little askew, and the garment's bright colour only served to heighten the pallor of his face, with its distinct shade of green.

'In truth I do not feel at all well, Captain,' he said, walking into the cabin and extending his hand out to grip that of his host. The frigate heeled over to the next wave, sending the guest careering past, and it was only by grabbing an arm that Clay was able to stop him fetching up against the windows that ran along the back of the great cabin. The steward rushed forward to take Vansittart's other arm, and between them they escorted him to his chair at the table.

'Thank you, most obliged,' he gasped, once he was wedged in place. He mopped his face with his napkin and then waved an arm towards the windows. 'Tell me, Captain, when do you expect this gale to desist?'

'Gale, sir?' queried Clay, settling down opposite him. 'This is only a little above a topsail wind. The northeast course we are obliged to follow makes the swell troubling, I grant you, but the conditions are quite normal for the German Sea in February. I daresay the Baltic shall prove more agreeable, when we should get there later in the month, although it will be damn cold. Would you care for a glass of wine?' He waved Harte forward with the decanter.

'I thank you, but no,' said his guest, placing a hand over his glass. 'Might I trouble you for a warm beverage? A pot of hot chocolate, perhaps, or a dish of tea?'

'Of course,' said his host. 'Kindly see to it, Harte.'

'Hot drink, sir!' exclaimed the steward. 'But I shall have to go to the galley to prepare one. The vittles will be sadly overcooked, sir.'

'Oh, I don't think you can overcook a good fatty piece of mutton,' said Clay.

'Aye, aye, sir,' said the steward, his face stone. He left the cabin, closing the door with a little more force than was strictly necessary.

'Mutton,' groaned the diplomat. His eyes rolled upwards

at the prospect, and then became mesmerised by something over Clay's shoulder. The captain looked around to see the cabin's lamp, swinging backwards and forwards on its hook above them. He returned his attention to his guest.

'I am not a sufferer from the sea sickness myself, sir, but I believe the best remedy is to eat a little, even if one is not inclined to do so, and to concentrate on something other than the motion of the ship,' he said. 'Should that fail, my privy is beyond that door behind you.'

'That does sound like tolerable advice,' conceded Vansittart, wrenching his gaze away from the light, and searching the cabin interior for something more solid. 'That is a fine likeness of Mrs Clay,' he said, pointing towards the bulkhead. Clay looked at the portrait of his wife. It showed her full length in a blue satin gown the exact colour of the eyes that looked back at him.

'It is a fine picture, sir,' he agreed. 'I was most fortunate that it survived the loss of my last ship, with no more than a little staining at the back. Lieutenant Blake was the artist responsible for it.'

'Blake!' exclaimed Vansittart. 'Can you mean the young gentlemen who resides in the monk's cell next to mine, and whose slumbers I can hear so distinctly at night?'

'The very same,' said Clay. 'He has considerable talent in that regard, although he only does it for his own amusement. As for your accommodation, I should observe that it is quite normal in size for a King's ship. A frigate is regarded as spacious when compared with the sloop of war that was my first command.'

'So I am told,' said his guest, his eye becoming a little less dull. 'Although I note that size of cabin, like so much in life, depends on rank.' He waved an arm to take in the cabin around him. 'The navy appears to have an exalted view of the accommodation required for its captains. Daylight? Book shelves? Why, this cabin must be over thirty feet wide! Can all this space truly be for just one man?'

'Eh... it is, sir,' said Clay. 'Together with my sleeping quarters and coach. Of course it is very much a working space, you understand? So I can converse with my officers with some degree of privacy. That was my object in inviting you to dine with me. I thought we might discuss our activities over the next few months.'

'A shift in the tone of the conversation worthy of a politician, Captain,' chuckled Vansittart, 'but a capital idea, notwithstanding. Let us leave a comparison of our cabins for another occasion.' He leaned forward with his elbows on the table. 'What we are facing in the Baltic is nothing short of a return to the same Northern League of Armed Neutrality as we faced in the American War. Back then we could do little about it. We were so busy fighting the Yanks, whilst trying to stop the bloody French and Spanish fleets from sailing up the Channel, that we were obliged to yield to the bastards.'

'And if I recollect, the members of this league are Russia, Prussia, Sweden and Denmark, sir,' said Clay.

'That's correct,' said Vansittart, his face already taking on more colour. 'But the Frogs are behind it.'

'I see, sir. So how do we proceed with breaking up this alliance?'

'You can ignore the Prussians,' explained his guest. 'They have damn all ships, and only go along to keep the French happy. No, it is Tsar Paul who is the chief mover in all this. Talleyrand has got to him, which was hardly difficult. His Imperial Majesty has never liked us, ever since we persuaded him to send some of his precious soldiers to an ignoble defeat in Flanders. Do you know much about him?'

'Only the little I have read in the papers, sir,' said Clay.

'Well, you may meet him soon, and count yourself blessed at the shortness of the acquaintance, by Jove!' said his guest. 'I have met him a few times, and he is quite the maddest member of a demented family.'

'Your hot chocolate, sir,' said Harte, appearing at this side.

'Do you know, Clay, I believe you were right,' said Vansittart. 'All our talk has quite driven away the seasickness. I declare my appetite may have returned. Could I trouble you for a glass of wine, after all?' Harte's jaw worked noiselessly, and for a moment Clay wondered if his steward was about to empty the pot of chocolate over Vansittart's head.

'Of course, sir,' he said. 'Kindly attend to it, Harte, and you can serve dinner now. So tell me of Tsar Paul?'

'His mother was Catherine the Great, who had more balls than the rest of the Romanov family put together,' explained his guest. 'She murdered her mad husband, Tsar Peter III, over thirty years ago, and ruled in his stead. Damned good ruler too, but wicked as they come. She brooked no opposition and rutted with any of her ministers that she fancied.'

'But surely then, Paul should have succeeded his father to the throne, not his mother?' said Clay. 'Yes, I will have some of the potatoes, Harte.'

'He should, but the lad was only eight when his father was killed, poor mite,' said Vansittart. 'Before he was out of small clothes, Catherine had married him to some Kraut princess she had selected to spy on him. Then she locked him away in the middle of Russia with nothing but his toy soldiers to play with. When he did have a son, Alexander, the boy was whisked off by Grandmother Catherine, and raised as her own. Alexander, at least, seems to have come out of life with the Romanovs reasonably sane. Meanwhile, Catherine ruled on and on, but even she couldn't live forever, although I dare say she tried. Three years ago she finally croaked, and out from his prison, blinking in the light, came Paul to find he was Tsar of all the Russias, but with no clue what he was about.'

'And it is this Tsar Paul that the French have persuaded to establish the League of Armed Neutrality you spoke of, sir?' asked Clay.

'Regrettably so,' said Vansittart, wiping his mouth with a napkin. 'See, if you can catch Paul's attention at the right moment, you can persuade him of anything. He can be as feeble as they come one day, and ranting fit for Bedlam the next. It drives our poor ambassador at St Petersburg to distraction. In three short years he's banned foreign books, stopped Russians travelling abroad, and turned half of the nobility against him. Not bad for a simpleton, what?'

'If he is such a fickle ruler, why are the other Baltic powers going along with his madness, sir?' asked his host.

'Fear of the Russian bear,' said the diplomat. 'A madman with a huge army ain't a neighbour you want to gainsay, what? Our aim shall be to try and reason with them, naturally. But if things cut up rough, and that don't answer, we shall have to make them fear us more than they fear Paul. That is where the navy comes in.'

'If it should come to fighting, the various fleets don't pose too much of a threat,' said Clay, sipping his wine. 'The Swedes have about a dozen ships of the line, the Danes much the same, while the Russians can put to sea with two dozen.

Things could turn ill if they were to combine, but fought separately, Sir Hyde and Lord Nelson should have their measure.'

'But before we mill with them, we must try persuasion,' said Vansittart. 'Starting with the Danes.'

'So we are to make for Copenhagen then, I collect, sir?'

'If you please, Captain, although not directly,' said his guest. He fished out a note book from one of his pockets, and pulled out a strip of paper which he passed across the table. 'I would first like you to visit this place on the Danish coast. I believe it to be a remote spot.'

'Very well, sir,' said Clay, glancing at the slip. 'What is our object?'

'To land my valet.'

'Your valet?' exclaimed Clay. 'The fellow I observed earlier, taking the air on deck?'

'The very same,' said Vansittart.

'Why on earth would you wish your valet to be landed in Denmark, sir?'

'To make contact with certain persons who are of our way of thinking, and to see how the land lies,' said Vansittart. 'Have no fears on Rankin's part, I pray. He is a resourceful enough cove to make his way across the country and rejoin us in Copenhagen.'

Clay waited for more of an explanation, but for once the garrulous diplomat was silent. He found his gaze held by his guest's dark eyes, quite devoid of any trace of seasickness.

******

When eight bells rang out from the belfry on the forecastle, the watch changed over. Moments after the sound of the final chime had faded away, there came the squeal of the boatswain's pipes and the thunder of feet on the ladder ways deep in the ship, as those who had been sleeping below came rushing up on deck. But as they emerged from the cattle shed warmth of the lower deck and out into the open, their pace slowed. Many paused to pull their jackets tighter around their bodies against the cut of the wind. Those waiting for them on watch hopped from foot to foot or flogged their arms, all the while breathing clouds of steam over their clenched hands.

'Move your arse, Pickford,' protested Evans as he watched his relief trudge along the gangway, winding a red woollen scarf around his neck. 'I wouldn't be surprised if me bleeding fundament had come adrift. I got a soaking earlier, and I ain't felt nought below me belt this past hour.'

'Aye, his ivories have been a-chattering away fit to raise the dead,' confirmed Trevan.

'Skeletons pleasuring themselves make less racket,' added O'Malley to general laughter.

'All right, I am here now, ain't I?' said Pickford. 'Christ, but 'tis cold!'

This last remark was directed at the backs of the three seamen as they hurried below. The lower deck of the *Griffin* was certainly warm, but it was also damp. It was placed just above the waterline when the frigate was level, and frequently beneath it, as now, when she was heeling over in a stiff breeze. In consequence the only natural light and ventilation were what filtered down through the gratings and hatchways from the world above. Lines of orange lanterns provided some illumination through the fog of moisture that filled the space. It rose like steam from the wet garments of those coming off watch. It ran in beads down the oak walls of the ship, and dripped from the beams overhead. But it also rose from the steaming bowl of burgoo that was set down in front of each sailor.

'Holy Mary, but that be fecking better,' sighed O'Malley, as he scraped the last of the hot food from his bowl.

'Bit sharp up top, then?' queried Sedgwick, who had yet to venture out.

'Devilish cold, so it is,' confirmed O'Malley. 'And like to get colder, according to Gustavsson. He was saying how even the sea freezes over in the Baltic proper, if you'll credit it.'

'Fancy that,' marvelled Sedgwick, shaking his head. 'I am a long way from Barbados now.'

'Who's the extra porridge for?' asked Evans, pointing to the last bowl on the table. 'Coz if it's spare, I don't mind stowing it in the hold, like.'

'You leave well alone, Sam Evans,' said Trevan, who was responsible for their food. 'That be for that new bloke's flunky, what'll be messing with us.'

'All right, but if he don't turn up sharpish I'll have it,' said the big Londoner. 'No call for wasting good honest vittles.'

'That weren't what you was saying about my parrot pie,' said Trevan, exchanging a wink with his mess mates.

'That were different,' protested Evans. 'Don't seem natural to eat them as can answer back. Anyhow, does this new bloke have a name?'

'He's called Joshua Rankin,' said Sedgwick.

'Josh Rankin, did you say?' queried Evans. 'Bleeding hell! It can't be!'

'You be all right, our Sam,' queried Trevan. 'You look proper spooked.'

'Aye, it'll be no more than hazard,' said the Londoner, with a shake of his head. 'I knew a bleeder of that name, back home like, but that don't mean nothing. There must be no end of folk with that name.'

'Well, it could be him,' said Sedgwick. 'He do sound a bit like you, now I come to think on it.'

'Another fecking Londoner?' protested O'Malley. 'Jesus, that's all we need!'

'No, it can't be him,' declared Evans, folding his arms.

'Really?' queried the Irishman. 'So how many fecking Joshua Rankins from London have you heard tell of, then?'

'Only the one, in truth,' said Evans. 'But he weren't the sort as would end up as no gentlemen's flunky. He were a right vicious bastard. Worked as a trap for some nasty blokes, squeezing them as couldn't pay up. When a couple of folk he'd been seen with turned up in the river with horseshoes for lockets, he had to scarper before the tipstaffs caught him. That were years back, mind.'

'I reckon we be about to find out, Big Sam,' said Trevan, looking over his friend's shoulder. 'If I ain't deceived, that be him a-coming.'

'Is this the bleeding muck we are obliged to break our fast upon?' said Joshua Rankin, taking his place at the table and peering at his bowl. 'While in the wardroom, the gentlemen tuck into mutton chops and salt bacon. Well, perhaps it's better than it looks.' He dropped his face to sniff at his bowl and then stopped when he caught sight of the big sailor opposite him. 'I know you, don't I? Your pa was a Welshman. Jones? Or Williams, maybe?'

'Evans,' corrected the Londoner.

'That's it! Evans! Sam Evans!'

'Hello, Josh,' said his fellow Londoner.

'You're a bleeding long way from Seven Dials, Sam, ain't you?' said Rankin.

******

The following morning Clay was awoken by two competing sounds, one familiar and a second that was not. The first was the musical gurgle of water being poured into his metal-lined washstand by Yates. The other sound was a persistent scraping on the deck above his head. While he tried to place the noise, he lay a little longer in the warm cocoon of his bed, aware that the air in the cabin was chill and uninviting. He looked at the hot water steaming in the basin and reached back into his years at sea for clues as to what the other sound might be, but without success.

'What the devil is happening on the quarterdeck, Yates?' he demanded.

'That will be the afterguard shifting all the snow what fell in the night, sir,' said the teenager, his eyes alight. 'Mr Hutchinson issued them with the shovels he uses to move ballast in the hold, but it don't answer any. More of the stuff just keeps on coming. Me and some of the other lads was fighting with snow grenades earlier, until Mr Taylor made us quit. There must have been a good foot of it lying on the deck at four bells.'

'Snow!' exclaimed Clay. 'At sea, and settling on the ship, you say? Is there no wind to drive it away?'

'Only enough to give us steerage way, according to Mr Armstrong, sir,' said Yates. 'It's a rare sight, an' no mistake.'

'Then, upon your recommendation, I shall go and see for myself,' decided his captain, swinging himself out of his cot and pulling his nightshirt over his head. He washed and shaved quickly, and laden with every item of warm clothing Yates could find, from sea boots to sou'wester, he left the cabin.

Snow on snow greeted Clay when he came out onto the

quarterdeck. The sky was full of tumbling, silent white. Over the side it vanished the moment it touched the dark green sea, but where it fell onboard it added to what was already there. It lay thick over the quarterdeck carronades, like the dust-sheets covering furniture in some long abandoned country house. The rail beside him had a soft layer four inches high on top of it. He swept a section clear with his gloved hand, the black painted wood startling amongst all the white, and watched as fresh flakes settled to repair the damage.

'Good morning, sir,' said Taylor, one of the dark figures that stood by the wheel. 'Thick as goose down in a plucking shed, I am afraid. I have the hands at work trying to shift it, but it returns the moment they move away.'

'It's extraordinary!' exclaimed Clay. 'I have never encountered anything above sleet or hail at sea before.' He looked up towards the rigging, blinking as flakes of snow landed on his eyelashes. Just beyond the rail at the front of the quarterdeck the solid column of the main mast rose up like a forest tree, but then vanished into the blizzard of white. Above the main yard, the upper two thirds was invisible.

'What is the state of the rigging, Mr Taylor?' he asked.

'The men have brushed much of the snow away, but some of the yards are frozen solid, sir,' reported the first lieutenant. 'So are a few ill-greased blocks, and as for the sails, sheet tin would be easier to handle. Fortunately we were already carrying the right canvas for the conditions when it began.' Clay next looked forwards. The ship ahead of him was shrouded with white, in spite of the best efforts of the crew to clear the snow away. The foremast was barely visible, while beyond it the ship vanished into a world of swirling flakes.

'I cannot see beyond the forecastle,' said Clay. 'Can you?'

'No, sir,' said Taylor. 'I have stationed extra lookouts in the bow. Fortunately we are barely making a knot.'

'How sure are you of our position, Mr Armstrong?' Clay addressed the frigate's sailing master, who came over and touched his hat, dislodging a little snow that had settled there.

'As sure as dead-reckoning can make it, sir,' said the American. 'I took a fair sighting at noon yesterday, and we have made limited progress overnight. I mark us at least fifty miles from the coast of Jutland.'

'Let us hope it clears a little before we are obliged to close with the land,' said Clay.

Were it not for the slight gurgle of water from over the side, Clay might have thought the *Griffin* was stationary. The ship was whispering onwards through a close, silent world of falling white. And then a flat boom sounded from somewhere in the blizzard.

'What the hell was that?' exclaimed Clay.

'Sounded like a cannon firing, sir,' said Armstrong. 'There it is again. Off to larboard?'

'No, I marked it from astern,' said Taylor.

'Mr Preston!' called Clay. 'You have the youngest ears. Where was that gunfire from?'

'In truth I thought it was ahead of us, sir,' said the officer of the watch.

'Deck there!' yelled the lookout from somewhere above. 'Firing a point off the bow!'

'What can you make of the ship?' yelled Clay, cupping his gloved hands around his mouth and bellowing.

'Can't see no ship, sir, begging your pardon,' replied the unseen voice. 'Only the flash as she fires. There she goes ag'in!' Another series of flat booms echoed off the sea. Staring ahead Clay thought he could see a little orange glow amongst all the white.

'Have the watch below turned up and the guns manned, if you please, Mr Taylor.'

CHAPTER 4

FIRE

The *Griffin* sailed on across an ever-renewing circle of dark water, through a world of falling white. Somewhere towards the south, the pale winter sun would be continuing to climb above the horizon, but no trace of its warmth could be felt on the deck of the frigate. Now all her guns had been manned and run out. Glancing over the side, Clay could see the wide, black barrels and raised gun ports providing new surfaces for the snow to accumulate on. The quarterdeck snow had been swept from around the big carronades, and trampled down by their crews. Red-coated marines lined the bulwarks between each gun, and stared out into the blizzard, searching for an enemy. Another cannon boomed out, closer now, the glow of orange ahead more intense.

'It may be lifting a touch, sir,' said Preston. 'I fancy I can see a little of our headsails now.'

'I believe that may be so, Mr Preston,' said Taylor, shielding his eyes with the flat of his hand. 'The light grows brighter, too.'

'Still pretty thick, mind,' grumbled Clay. 'I would dearly

love to know what lies ahead of us.'

'Firing must mean at least one friend and one foe, sir,' said the first lieutenant. 'Perhaps more will be visible from the masthead.'

'I dare say it will,' said the captain, staring ahead through his telescope. 'Mr Preston, would you kindly take a glass aloft and tell us what you see?'

It was only the length of pause before Preston acknowledged the order that made Clay realised what he had just asked.

'Aye aye, sir,' said the young officer, touching his hat.

'My dear sir,' exclaimed Clay. 'What can I have been thinking of? Forgive me, but of course you cannot go. Let Mr Russell take your place.'

'With respect, sir, but I must go,' said Preston. 'If I might be accompanied by one of the top men to carry the spy glass, I will manage well enough.'

'I am not sure that is prudent,' said Taylor. 'Some of the ropes are very icy.'

'Then I shall take extra care, sir,' said the young lieutenant. 'I gave the captain my word that I should be able to carry out all my duties. I will not be found wanting on the first occasion it is put to the test.'

He walked swiftly away down the weather-side gangway before he could be called back. When he reached the bottom of the main mast shrouds he looked upwards. The thick lines of black hemp rose above him, steep as a ladder, until they disappeared into the falling snow. The hum of sound from the main deck seemed to fade, and when he looked for the reason he became aware of the eyes of the gun crews beneath his feet, watching him.

'What's he about?' muttered one sailor to his mate,

unaware how far his voice carried. 'Surely he ain't going aloft with just the one fin, like?' Preston breathed deep to try and slow the banging of his heart. Then he reached above his head, scrambled up into the main chains, and started to climb.

'Easy there, sir, beggin' your pardon like,' said Trevan, jumping up beside him. 'I were up there first thing to clear the yards, and it be proper treacherous in parts. Here, let me get a safety line around you. Ain't no dishonour in that. All us top men be using them in this frost.' Preston felt the Cornishman's arms encircle his waist with the line, and the rope drawn tight as he knotted it. 'There, that be better. Up you goes, now. I'll follow astern, and I got your spyglass, like.'

'Thank you, Trevan,' he said, noting the concern in the sailor's piercing blue eyes. Then he resumed his climb.

At first it was hard to get into a rhythm. Before he would have run up with confidence, arms and legs moving in tandem, but with only one arm he found his progress strangely jerky. He had to pause every two ratlines while he threw his hand like a claw up above his head, aware that for a horrible instant, it was only the soles of his shoes on the snow-covered rope that was keeping him from a plunging fall. As he rose up the mast he felt the emptiness growing behind him. The ship-board sounds faded away, to be replaced by silence. The snow dropping past him seemed to want to draw him down with it. He was midway through circling his arm upwards again, when one of his feet slid free of its hold, and time froze as he lurched outwards from the shrouds. For a moment he hung in balance, motionless with fear. Then he felt a hand on the back of his leg, tipping him forward and away from the void.

'Steady now, sir,' said Trevan, once the officer's flailing arm had grasped hold. 'Let's get you set ag'in.' He felt his foot guided back onto the ratline, and he drew icy air deep into his lungs.

'My thanks, Trevan,' he gasped.

'No call for thanks, sir, you be doing just fine,' said the Cornish sailor. 'Why, look'ee aloft! The maintop be just above us now. And what with all this snow, no one on deck will mark us if we use the lubber hole. Shall I go first, sir?' Without waiting for an answer Trevan scampered ahead, up the last ten feet of the shrouds and disappeared from sight. Then Preston felt the safety line tighten, drawing him upwards. Trevan was right, he concluded. The futtock shrouds, which leant backwards at a steep angle, would be impossible for him. It was normally considered a disgrace for a sailor to use the convenient hole cut in the maintop that the shrouds passed through, but now Trevan had done so with the line, he was obliged to follow. He joined him on the main top, crawling onto the platform, his legs weak with the effort and his right shoulder aching.

'Ain't no race, sir,' said the Cornishman, squatting down beside the officer. 'Let's catch our breath here afore we climbs the next bit.' Preston set aside the temptation to rest a little longer and pushed himself back up to his feet. What sort of an example are you setting, he scolded himself. You're a damned officer. Act like one.

'I am quite recovered now,' he lied. 'Let us climb the last part.'

If the main mast shrouds were pitched at the angle of a ladder, those of the main topmast were like the sides of a steeple. Trevan went first this time, keeping a gentle but constant pressure on the line to reassure the officer.

Preston's arm was trembling with the effort being asked of it, and the ratlines beneath his feet were now marbled with ice. A combination of fear and effort made Preston's breath blow in clouds around him as he made his way up towards the crosstrees, where an anxious Trevan awaited his arrival. At last, with one final heave he was there, sitting on the tiny perch and clinging to the slim topgallant mast beside him. They were a hundred and thirty feet above the surface of the sea, and yet were lost in a private world. In every direction, lines of rigging curved away from them and vanished into the snow storm.

'Now, sir, I been doing some reckoning, begin' your pardon like,' said Trevan. 'There be no way you can hold the mast and your glass with the same arm, so I thought if I was to make you fast with this here line, you would be free to see what was what.'

Preston sat unresisting as a child, while Trevan worked away, passing the safety line around the officer and knotting it to the mast. He looked down, beyond his feet as they dangled in the air, but the frigate was lost in the falling snow beneath them. And then, slowly, the shape of the hull began to emerge.

'I reckon it be clearing a bit, sir,' said Trevan, as he finished the last knot, and then passed across the telescope. Preston hesitated for a moment, then released his grip on the wooden spar beside him and took the instrument. He swayed a little against the ropes, testing their hold, and then caught the cold brass eye piece under his chin and extended the tube. The snow storm ahead was lit by an inner flame, close to the water, and a rumble of sound echoed up to them.

'Deck there!' called the lookout at the top of the foremast. 'More firing, dead on the bow!'

Preston focussed on the point where the firing had come from. All he could see were swirling motes of white. His eye latched onto the mesmerising points, as they filled his view through the telescope. Come on, he urged, what else is there? He forced his eye to slide a little out of focus, and then he saw it. There was something behind the snow, like the faint stroke of a pencil on a sheet of paper. He concentrated on that line, and as the frigate sailed closer he realised it was the mast of a ship. Now he had something solid to focus on, other details appeared around it. A second mast behind the first, yards and sails, the web of black tarred rigging. Beneath that was the loom of a low hull, next to a much larger shape. A square of bright red flashed and went, appearing and vanishing like the beating wing of a bird. It took Preston a moment to register that it was the fly of a big flag, the rest of the colours lost from view. A line of fire erupted down the side of the smaller ship, illuminating the blank hull, close alongside. A single tongue of flame answered.

'Deck there!' he yelled. 'Two ships five cables ahead. One looks to be a small warship, a sloop perhaps. I believe she may be showing French colours. The other is a large trading brig, armed with a single cannon.'

Clay's reply was distorted by a speaking trumpet. 'Do you suppose the brig to be a merchantman with a carronade, Mr Preston?'

'Like enough, sir, but I cannot be certain,' replied the lieutenant.

'What course should I follow to come up on the disengaged side of the Frenchman?'

'A half point to starboard should do it, sir,' bellowed Preston. 'But I only glimpsed a red fly through the snow. It could just as readily be the ensign of a Danish ship.'

'Then she has no business attacking a merchantman,' replied his captain. 'Very good, Mr Preston. You may come down now.'

'Aye aye, sir,' replied the lieutenant, passing the telescope across to Trevan.

'Ah, getting down,' muttered the Cornishman, pulling off his hat and scratching at his blond hair. 'In truth, I hadn't thought that far ahead, sir. I daresay sliding down the backstay one-handed will not answer, which do leave us with a bit of a poser.'

******

The *Griffin* swung onto her new course and sailed towards an ever-retreating veil of snow. From the quarterdeck there was still no clear sight of the ships ahead. Clay stood by the rail, leaning out over the side and staring into the curtain of flakes, when a hail came from the bow.

'Ship ahoy! Ship off the larboard bow!' Clay crossed to the front rail and looked down into the body of the ship.

'Ready the larboard guns, Mr Blake,' he called, although he could see that the big eighteen-pounder cannon were already run out and manned. The gun crews crouched a little lower around their weapons, while those on the opposite side of the deck stood up and relaxed. The frigate's second lieutenant turned and touched his hat towards him.

'Aye aye, sir,' he replied, and then, 'Stand by, larboard side!' Each gun captain took up the slack of the firing lanyards, checked all was as it should be, and raised an arm to show his piece was ready.

'Where the hell is this damned ship of Preston's?' queried Taylor, from beside Clay.

'There, sir!' said Armstrong from his other side, pointing.

Something tall and dark was emerging from the white, like a sea cliff through fog, a little to the left of the frigate's bowsprit. Then a broadside was fired ahead and in that flash of brilliance, a whole scene appeared. Two ships were locked in combat. One was a low, sleek privateer, with a big French tricolour at her mizzen. She was a sloop, with a half dozen small cannon per side, and was trying to close with and board a larger trading brig beside her. One of the merchantman's twin masts was down, and the sloop was sliding closer to her victim. In the moment before the image vanished, Clay saw boarders massing in the Frenchman's rigging, the flame of the guns twinkling off polished steel. Then the light was gone, and he was looking at shadows in the snow once more.

Almost immediately Clay heard a hail from the Frenchman's masthead, the words unclear but the tone piercing and urgent. A series of alarmed orders followed.

'I believe we may have been noticed, sir,' said Armstrong.

'I believe you are right,' smiled Clay, imagining the panic aboard the privateer at the sudden apparition of a large frigate a few hundred yards off their stern. As the *Griffin* swept on, the grey mass ahead resolved into a complete ship. He could see her stern, outlined in settled snow, with a line of dark windows staring back at him. Below was her name, *Hirondelle,* in thick white letters across her counter. Above that her rigging was alive with crew swarming aloft to set sail. The angle was changing quickly as the frigate overlapped the sloop. He could see open gun ports along her black hull, each with a little six-pounder in it. He turned back towards the wheel. 'Bring her up into the wind and hold her thus. Back the topsails, if you please, Mr Taylor! Mr Blake! Open fire as the guns bear.'

A moment of calm, as the *Griffin* drifted to a halt amongst the falling snow, and then a sharp order from Blake followed by the roar of her broadside. Fire and smoke filled the space between the ships, and Clay heard a long series of crashes as eighteen-pounder balls struck home. Beneath his feet the gun crews flew through the stages of reloading, while from across the water he heard cries of panic mixed with the screams of the wounded. The privateer started to inch forward as her first sail was sheeted home, but she would still be comfortably within his frigate's broadside when the guns were reloaded. One more hail of fire like that should induce her to strike, he concluded. Then he became aware of Taylor, trying to attract his attention.

'Sir! Look at the merchantman! She has taken fire!'

Against the white of the snow, there were flames of red and yellow now. The wreckage of the brig's fallen mast had flared up like a torch. Tongues of red had spread onto the hull of the ship, flickering across the wood. As Clay looked a stream of flaming balls raced up the tarred rigging of the one remaining mast. Several of her crewmen were waving a union flag to attract his attention. For a moment Clay was back on the Brittany coast, watching his last ship being consumed by fire. He was frozen to the spot, unable to decide what to do. Sweat beading on his forehead, in spite of the cold. He wrenched his gaze away from the burning ship and back to the privateer, at his mercy but starting to move away through the water. What to do? he asked himself, for once unsure. He felt numb at his lack of decision. Then he looked back at the merchant ship. The volume of fire had doubled in moments, and beneath the coiling black smoke the flag was being waved with increased desperation.

'Damnation!' exclaimed Clay. Then he took a deep breath

and forced himself to decide.

'Cease firing, Mr Blake,' he ordered. 'Secure the guns, if you please.' Then he turned away from the privateer and towards the stricken brig. Behind him came the sound of orders on the French sloop, growing fainter as she gathered way. From the stricken trading brig he could hear the crackle and bang of burning wood. He could feel the heat of the flames as the forepart of the merchantman swelled into a volcano of fire.

'Upon my soul!' exclaimed Taylor, who was looking at the blaze through his telescope. 'I do believe there is a woman onboard!'

'Mr Armstrong, bear down on that merchant ship,' he yelled. 'Swiftly now!'

'Aye aye, sir,' replied the American, turning away to issue orders.

'Mr Hutchinson!' called Clay towards the forecastle. 'Have the pumps manned and the fire hoses rigged. And I want the red cutter in the water to take off the crew. They will have to do so by the stern.'

'Aye aye, sir,' came the boatswain's deep bass as he hurried down onto the main deck.

'I will get Mr Preston to arrange for a party of men to line the side, ready to boom us off if we should drift too close, sir,' said Taylor. He closed his telescope and looked around. 'Now, where the devil is Mr Preston?'

'Here, sir,' said the breathless lieutenant, running up. 'My apologies, but descending the mast proved a deal more challenging than climbing it.'

Clay ignored the flurry of activity that now engulfed the frigate, and stared after the departing French ship. The *Hirondelle* was no more than a grey shadow as she made good her escape. A sudden flurry of thickening snow masked all trace of her, and when it cleared she had vanished.

******

'She was the *Fair Prospect* of Whitby, sir,' reported Taylor, from his chair on the far side of Clay's desk. 'Three days out from Hamburg with a cargo of timber, which accounts for how readily the fire took hold.'

'By Jove, ain't that the truth!' exclaimed Vansittart, who sat on the lockers that formed a bench seat beneath the cabin's windows, nursing a glass of Clay's Madeira. 'I never saw such a damned blaze! If I hadn't witnessed the highly creditable way you naval coves acted, I wouldn't have believed it possible to rescue a soul.'

'Thank you for your good opinion, sir,' said Clay. 'We do practice fighting fires regularly, and the men treat it with a deal more seriousness than most of our drills. Perhaps being obliged to serve on a wooden ship, stuffed tight with powder, concentrates the mind wonderfully. Yet for all our efforts, we could not save the vessel. How are the crew that we did rescue, Mr Taylor?'

'Mr Corbett does not hold out much prospect for the three that were most badly scorched, sir,' reported the first lieutenant. 'He has dressed their wounds with goose fat, and given them sufficient rum and laudanum to ease their suffering. The others are in a better state. The ship's master is named Isaiah Hockley. He was only slightly hurt, and his daughter was unharmed. Three other crewmen have minor wounds, from which they should recover presently.'

'At which point you will doubtless press them into the navy?' chuckled Vansittart. 'Out of the fire, but perhaps back into the frying pan, what?'

'Three prime seamen that are now without a ship, sir?' said Clay. 'I would be disappointed in Mr Taylor to find they were not on the *Griffin*'s books already.'

'Your clerk read them in an hour ago, sir,' confirmed the first lieutenant, rubbing his hands. 'Two able seamen and a carpenter's mate. If we have concluded, Mr Hockley desires to see you. Shall I have him shown in?'

'If you please, Mr Taylor,' said Clay.

Isaiah Hockley proved to be a small, sprightly man, with grey hair and a pronounced Yorkshire accent. Apart from a sizable burn in the sleeve of his coat, and dark smuts on his britches, he seemed otherwise unharmed as he came into the cabin. When Clay stood up and held out his hand, he grasped it with both of his.

'Bless you, sir!' he exclaimed. 'I was praying hard for deliverance when those French devils were firing into my poor *Prospect*, and praise the Lord, there you were, appearing out of the snow storm, like an avenging angel!'

'Eh... indeed,' said Clay, trying to rescue his hand. 'It is very good to make your acquaintance, sir. Mr Taylor, my first lieutenant, you will have met, I don't doubt. May I also name the Honourable Nicholas Vansittart? He is one of the members of parliament for Hastings, and is travelling aboard this ship.'

'Good seaport is Hastings,' said Hockley. 'I am very glad to meet your honour.'

'Likewise, I am sure,' said Vansittart, eyeing the burnt sleeve.

'Apologies for my state of dress, gentlemen,' said the merchant captain. 'I regret my sea chest went down with my ship. If I had been able, I would have shifted my coat at least.'

'No matter, sir,' said Clay, showing him to a seat. 'I am sure we all quite understand. May I offer you some refreshment? A glass of something?'

'I am not a drinker, sir,' said Hockley. 'But I would gladly take some tea.'

'Of course,' said Clay, glancing at his steward. 'Would you oblige the captain please, Harte?'

'Aye aye, sir,' said Harte. 'Hot tea it is. Fetched from the galley.' He departed with an audible sniff on his journey through the ship.

'And how is your daughter bearing up, after her ordeal?' asked Clay.

'Sarah? Oh, I have no concern on her part, sir. We breed our lasses to be hardy in the North Country. Not that she doesn't possess all the accomplishments that a young lady should, mind, but she has travelled with me many a time since my wife passed away. She has endured no end of storms and such like at sea, without complaint, so I daresay she will do very well.'

'That must be a comfort for you, Captain,' said Clay. 'Might I trouble you for the particulars of your encounter with the *Hirondelle*, so I can conclude my report to the Admiralty?'

'Now, let me order my thoughts,' said Hockley, passing a hand through his thin grey hair. 'We left the estuary of the Elbe River three nights back, and were heading for home. Then last night the snow started to fall, until it were that thick it might as well have been fog.'

'We encountered much the same from four bells,' said Clay.

'Aye, that would be about right,' agreed the Yorkshireman. 'The *Fair Prospect* is... your pardon, was... a swift enough ship, so I generally sail alone and hope, with the help of the Good Lord, to stay clear of trouble. If that doesn't answer, I also carry a brace of big carronades up on the forecastle to keep ne'er-do-wells at bay. I had ordered the bell to toll and the gun to fire each ten minutes or so, being fearful we might run onboard another ship in the snow. I suppose the clamour we were making was how that cursed privateer got wind of us.'

'Doubtless so,' said Clay, making a few notes. 'Ah, here is your tea.'

'Which it may be tepid, havin' come so far, sir,' muttered Harte as he handed it across.

'Most welcome, smiled the merchant captain, spooning sugar into his cup and then taking a sip. 'Now where was I?'

'The privateer was about to attack?' prompted Taylor.

'Aye, so she was,' said Hockley. 'They appeared out of the snow to starboard, coming straight for us. I dare say she hoped to board before we knew much about it, but my lads were having none of it. Thanks to my orders to fire that regular warning shot, the carronade was manned already. My first mate was a former quarter gunner in a John Company ship, and a couple of my people had served in the navy, so they knew how to handle themselves, thank the Lord. First shot took a cracking great lump out of the Frenchman's foremast, after which she drew off to batter us a little first.'

'That was handsomely done, by Jove!' exclaimed Vansittart. 'I do wish that more of our commerce would show such pluck.'

'Perhaps if the navy refrained from pressing so many of our people, we might be able to, sir,' said Hockley, looking at Clay. 'I dare say you'll have already taken those of my lads that survived?'

'As the law of the sea requires,' said Clay. 'Pray continue with your account, sir.'

'We were giving those devils as good as we got, but it was one piece against six. Two of my crew were killed outright, and then our foremast came down. I had just resolved to surrender, but no sooner had I ordered our colours to be struck, when out of the snow came salvation in the form of your ship. After which, I believe you know the rest.'

'Not quite,' said Clay. 'How was it that your ship took fire?'

'It began close to the bow,' explained Hockley. 'Given that is where the mast came down, I suppose some of the wreckage must have got in the path of our carronade. The flame from the barrel could very easily have set it ablaze. None of my men survived from that part of the ship, so I can offer you nothing more definite.'

'Even so, I dare say your conclusion is correct,' said Clay. 'Thank you for assisting me. I just regret that we were unable to save *The Fair Prospect*.'

'My ship's boat was destroyed by a shot from the *Hirondelle* early in the engagement, sir,' said Hockley. 'So we were left with no means of escaping the flames. In rescuing my daughter, you recovered what was most precious to me onboard, for which I will forever be grateful.' He held his hand across the desk, and shook that of Clay's once more. Vansittart blew his nose loudly on a large calico handkerchief.

'It occurs to me, Mr Hockley, that you and I may be of similar stature,' he said, returning the cloth to his coat pocket. 'Would you do me the honour of accepting the loan of some of my clothing?'

'That is very obliging of you, sir, but I do not envisage being long in your company,' said Hockley. 'A fine ship like this could make Hamburg swiftly enough, from where I can get new clothes and a passage home. I can shift into seamen's slops until then.'

'I am afraid there is no question of our diverting to go there,' said Vansittart, before Clay could say anything. 'This ship is on urgent government business. In a few days' time we shall be undertaking a mission on the Danish coast, after which we must make haste to enter the Baltic.'

'Would Copenhagen serve as a place for us to set you down, Mr Hockley?' said Clay. 'I daresay clothes and a passage home can be secured from there.'

'Do I have a choice, sir?' asked the merchant captain.

'None, I fear,' said Vansittart.

'Would you kindly extend the hospitality of the wardroom to the captain and Miss Hockley, Mr Taylor?' said Clay. 'At least for the next week or so.'

'It will be a squeeze, sir,' said Taylor, blowing out his cheeks. 'We already have Mr Vansittart, and I am not sure we can provide accommodation suitable for a lady.'

'Have no fears about Sarah,' said Hockley. 'She is quite accustomed to life afloat.'

'I will have the carpenter reduce the size of the cabins, sir,' concluded the first lieutenant. 'I am sure we shall manage.'

'Capital!' muttered Vansittart. 'Smaller bloody cabins!'

CHAPTER 5

JUTLAND

The following evening the wardroom of the *Griffin* had been transformed, so that it managed to look both magnificent and distinctly cramped. It had been decorated with one of the frigate's smaller naval ensigns. What was a modest looking flag when aloft, was in reality an enormous and stubborn bolt of material that had been dragged down two flights of ladders and squeezed through the cabin door. A small portion of it had been pinned across the stern bulkhead, while all the remaining swathes were heaped on the deck beneath. In addition to the flag, ribbons of red, white and blue now decorated the door handles of the officers' cabins. Other ribbons had been woven in a crisscross pattern around the solid column of the mizzen mast that ran down through the middle of the room, and straight through the polished surface of the wardroom table. This had been laden with silverware, borrowed for the occasion from the captain's steward, glittering glass, and yet more ribbons. The warm light of candles played over it all, and winked back from the polished buttons of the officers as they awaited the arrival of their guests.

'Is dinner ready to be served, Britton?' asked Taylor of the wardroom steward.

'Aye, that it be, sir,' he confirmed. 'Biggest fishermen's pie you ever saw. I had all the hands from Brixham casting lines off the bow through the forenoon watch. I pledged a tot of rum for each tub of fish, which answered a deal better than I reckoned on.'

'Good, so we have plenty of vittles,' mused Taylor, returning his attention to the table. 'Will we truly be able to accommodate everyone? With a servant behind each chair, we shall be packed closer than meat in a pie.'

'The captain is a tall man, I grant you, but fortunately Mr Vansittart, Mr Hockley and his daughter are all small persons,' observed Charles Faulkner, the frigate's aristocratic purser, who regarded himself an expert on matters of social etiquette.

'If it helps with the seating arrangements, I could sit next to wee Miss Hockley,' said Lieutenant Thomas Macpherson, pulling his marine officer's tunic a little straighter, and giving a final twist to his glossy black sideburns.

'No, Tom, as an artist, I believe I am best equipped to converse with her on the finer accomplishments,' said Lieutenant Blake. 'She is our guest, so we surely want to put her at her ease.'

'In which case I should sit beside her, John,' said Richard Corbett. 'It is with me that she is best acquainted, since I have treated both her and her father as a physician, you will recall.'

'She will not want such unpleasant memories stirred up, man,' protested Blake.

'If it's the finer things you wish for, what could be more

diverting than my tales of life in the Highlands?' asked Macpherson.

'We are in the German Sea!' protested Blake. 'She has only to look over the side to observe the fog and sleet of your damned Highlands!'

'What a pity l am shortly to be on watch,' observed Armstrong. 'I shall miss you all squabbling to catch her eye, like roosters in a barnyard.'

'Roosters in a barnyard?' queried Macpherson, his face colouring.

'Gentlemen, calm yourselves, please!' said Taylor. 'Less of this unseemly tumult, I pray! I have already determined the places at the table, and I have no intention of changing it now. Miss Hockley will be seated here, between myself and Mr Preston.'

'Next to you!' exclaimed Blake. 'But you're old enough to be her father, George!'

'Exactly,' said Taylor. 'Which makes me a much more suitable chaperone for her than any of you satyrs! May I also remind you that her actual father will be present?'

'I must say, she does look rather fetching in the sailor's clothes I provided for her,' said Faulkner. 'There is something about a filly in trousers. It ain't quite proper, of course, but even so...'

The talk in the wardroom faded as the officers all toyed with the vision presented by the purser. In the resulting quiet a series of bell strokes sounded through the ship.

'I must relieve Mr Preston on watch,' announced Armstrong, buttoning up his pea jacket, and heading towards the door. 'Shall I tell the lucky dog who his companion at the table is to be?'

'If you wish,' said Taylor. 'Now, our guests will be here

presently. To your places, gentlemen!'

No sooner had Armstrong departed, than there was a knock at the door, and in came the guests. First into the wardroom was the object of the officer's discussion. Miss Sarah Hockley was an attractive young lady, as tall as her father, with a pleasant smile and hazel eyes. Her rich brown hair was piled up onto her head, with a few curls allowed to trail down one side of her face. Only on close inspection could it be seen that her hair was pinned in place with the thinnest copper nails owned by the ship's carpenter. Disappointingly for her many admirers amongst the frigate's younger officers, she was dressed once more in the pale yellow frock she had worn when she left the burning *Fair Prospect*. She was followed in by her father, looking a little stiff and awkward in Vansittart's fifth best coat, followed by its owner, impeccable in the height of fashion. The final guest was Clay, in the full dress magnificence of a post captain of the Royal Navy, all dark blue broadcloth, white silk and sparkling gold braid. During the flurry of introductions, Lieutenant Preston managed to squeeze in behind him and make his way to his place at the table.

'Your pardon, Miss Hockley,' he said. 'I barely recognised you out of seamen's clothes.'

'In truth, Mr Preston, it is something of a relief,' she said. 'Your sailmaker did his best to tailor them for me, but they still fit very ill. But I will admit that trousers are much superior to skirts for moving around a ship.'

'They most certainly are,' agreed Preston. 'Sailors abandoned britches and stockings for them long ago. Although I did notice on my last visit home that the fashion for trousers had spread ashore. Is that not so, Mr Faulkner?' The purser considered this for a moment from his place across the table.

'Amongst the flashier sort they might, I daresay, but I can't imagine them catching on in the ranks of the superior classes,' he offered. 'My father will go to his grave in britches, I have no doubt. Ah, here comes the wine at last. I confess to being quite parched.'

The volume of conversation around the table dropped as the servants behind each chair, ship's boys for the most part, stepped forward to pour the wine.

'Come now, Rankin,' said Vansittart quietly. 'You know better than to pour from the left.' His valet squeezed his bulky frame round to the other side of his master's chair.

'Your pardon, sir,' he muttered.

'So I understand you to have invited us all here to celebrate a notable date, Mr Taylor,' said Hockley, indicating the flag and ribbons. 'What, pray, is the significance of the fourteenth of February?'

'Surely every unmarried person, at least, will be familiar with that date,' said his daughter, colouring a little. 'A date connected with a certain saint beginning with "V"?'

'I should certainly hope so, Miss Hockley,' enthused the first lieutenant. 'Only four years have passed since the navy defeated the Dons off Cape St Vincent. It was the most splendid of victories, and was fought upon this very day.'

'Then let that be our first toast, gentlemen,' said Vansittart, raising his glass. 'The Royal Navy and their noble victory off Cape St Vincent.' Glasses were drained with enthusiasm, and calls of "Hear him!" rang out. Several of the officers drummed their hands on the table.

'You seem disappointed, Miss Hockley,' said Preston. 'Did you have another saint in mind?'

'Are you seeking to tease me, sir?' she demanded, noting

the twinkle in his eye.

'A little, perhaps,' he smiled, before leaning closer to whisper in her ear. 'I knew all the time the true significance of the date.'

'I am pleased to hear it,' she said, appraising him over the top of her wine glass.

'Of course... how could I forget that it is also the anniversary of the fall of Yorkshire's very own Captain James Cook?'

'Well remembered, Edward,' said Taylor from Miss Hockley's other side. 'Splendid man that he was, and an excellent seaman. Lanced by savages in a dispute over a stolen jollyboat, I believe.' Preston exchanged glances with Miss Hockley, and both burst into laughter.

'I am not sure it is the occasion for mirth,' said the first lieutenant, before turning away to talk to his other neighbour.

'I trust you do not mind being made game of a little, as one Yorkshire born to another, Miss Hockley,' said Preston. 'My sisters do the same to me when I am at home, and I miss it, in truth.'

'I thought your accent was familiar,' she said. 'You're not from the coast, though, that at least is plain. Vale of York perhaps?'

'You have a good ear, Miss Hockley,' he said. 'My people are from Ripon.'

'Which is quite some distance from the sea,' she observed. 'How came you into the navy, Mr Preston?'

'That happened very much in opposition to my parents' will. My father wanted me to follow him into the wool trade, which would doubtless have happened, had an uncle not given me a copy of *The Life and Adventures of Robinson*

Crusoe one Yuletide. After reading that, I became quite determined to go to sea.'

'Were his experiences as a mariner not off-putting?' she queried. 'Shipwrecked and then left for years on a deserted island, if I recall.'

'True, but what grand adventures followed that unpromising start, Miss Hockley,' said Preston, his eyes alight.

'On the subject of matters that are grand, here comes our fishermen's pie,' said Taylor.

As promised, the pie was indeed a huge creation, several feet across, with a raised pastry top that towered up in a golden wedge. Steam rose through holes in the side like smoke from the vents on a volcano. Its arrival, borne by two seamen, was greeted with acclimation by the hungry guests.

'Is there some significance in the shape of the crust, Britton?' asked Clay, who had noticed the look of pride on the wardroom steward's face. 'The Rock of Gibraltar, perhaps?'

'Not the Rock, no, sir,' he explained. 'It be formed in the shape of the Cape St Vincent headland itself, leastways according to how she is set down on Mr Armstrong's chart, and the best recollection of Gonzales in the larboard watch.'

'How splendid!' said Taylor, over the general rumble of approval.

'So was this battle of particular note to you gentlemen?' asked Hockley, as the pie was being served up. 'Were you all present?'

'In truth no,' admitted Clay. 'I was convalescing at home at the time. Mr Macpherson and Mr Preston here were returning from the West Indies, and I believe the rest of these gentlemen were serving in the Channel Fleet. But we were all at the Battle of the Nile the following year, as marked by the medals we bear.' He pointed to the gold disc at his throat, and indicated the silver ones the officers had. 'Everyone present that night received one, even the seamen, who were given a bronze version. It was a splendid idea, which I hope may be repeated for future engagements of note.'

'Then we have a further toast to drink,' said Vansittart. 'To the victors of the Nile, with a bumper if you please, gentlemen!' Again the glasses were drained. The combination of the packed numbers in the wardroom together with the strength of the wine began to flush faces around the table, apart from the teetotal Hockley. When the food arrived in front of Miss Hockley and Preston, she looked at the lieutenant with concern.

'It had not occurred to me until this moment, but I have not yet witnessed how you manage at the table,' she said. 'With your injury, I mean. If you need assistance, I will happily help.' A flicker of sadness passed across his face, and she reached out and touched the right hand that rested on the table next to her. 'I am sorry, Mr Preston. I hope that my foolishness has not offended you. Was I wrong to mention it?'

'By no means, Miss Hockley,' he said. 'It is I that am being foolish. I was so enjoying our discourse, I had quite forgotten my want of an arm. But you need have no fear on my part. Fish pie will present little difficulty for me; besides, I have this.' He held up his fork, one tine of which had been replaced with a blade.

'How ingenious,' she said. 'That will serve you very well.'

'It is modeled on one that the captain observed Lord Nelson using in the Mediterranean, and was fashioned for me by Mr Arkwright, our Armourer. It performs thus.' He sawed a piece of fish in two, spiked one half, and popped it into his mouth. With his rival unable to speak, Blake took his opportunity to join the conversation from across the table.

'How are you finding life aboard, Miss Hockley?' he asked.

'Very agreeable, I thank you, Lieutenant,' she replied. 'My cabin is a little snug, but perfectly dry and comfortable for all that.'

'Upon my soul, ain't snug the word,' muttered Vansittart, a little louder than he intended.

'And what of the society of sailors?' added Macpherson, whose face began to mirror the scarlet of his tunic.

'I have travelled a little with my father, so I am not wholly unfamiliar with life afloat,' she said. 'I can report that the officers of this ship, at least, seem to be perfectly civilised and refined.'

'What, even young Preston, who has been shamelessly monopolising you this past half hour?' said Faulkner, to general laughter.

'Even he,' continued Miss Hockley. 'I had been warned that Royal Navy sailors can be very forward, with the reputation of having a sweetheart in every port, but I have seen little evidence of such vice.'

'Ah, but you have yet to witness the hands ashore,' said Corbett. 'More drunkenness and whoring than Babylon in its pomp. The weeks after are my busiest, although my Hippocratic Oath forbids me from sharing more of the particulars.'

'I should hope so, too,' protested Blake. 'We are still eating!'

'I am pleased to hear your report that the behaviour of my

officers, at least, is quite honourable, Miss Hockley,' said Clay. 'I have long despaired at restraining Jack ashore, but their conduct is often better than the lewdness reported of sailors more generally in the popular ballads.'

'Although such tales are not wholly without foundation,' added Faulkner. 'What about the case of Lieutenant Carmichael, of the *Majestic?*'

'Ah, yes,' agreed Blake.

'The old hound,' added Corbett.

'Whatever did he do?' asked Miss Hockley, her hazel eyes wide and innocent.

'Nothing but rumours while he lived,' said Faulkner. 'But after he fell in battle no less than three wives approached the Navy Board to claim their widow's pension, every one of them armed with a valid certificate of marriage.'

'Poor ladies,' said Miss Hockley, underneath the laughter of the officers.

'Try not to judge us too severely,' said Preston. 'We are obliged to spend too much time away from the civilising influence of ladies. Most wardrooms are like this at sea. Young men, living together, with the prospect of death or injury just beyond the horizon. It makes us bawdier than we would be in other circumstances.'

Miss Hockley placed her hand on his again. 'I do understand that, Mr Preston, and I am not in any way distressed,' she looked around the room of flushed faces and animated chatter. 'In many ways I feel privileged to have been invited to share in a world that is so different to my own.' She looked back at him, her eyes straying to the empty sleeve of his coat, and then to his face, still pale and thin. In her eyes he read compassion, laced with something warmer.

******

Forward from the bright candlelight and wine-fuelled jollity of the wardroom, a more restrained atmosphere prevailed on the lower deck. The men had eaten their evening meal earlier, and now the watch below took their ease at the mess tables. The third one along on the larboard side was a scene of companionable industry. Sean O'Malley, who was comfortably the frigate's best musician, at least in his own opinion, was fitting new strings to his fiddle. Trevan was carving a tracery of flowers into the handle of a small wooden comb he had made, while Evans held an oil lamp close above the table surface, to help him see clearly. Sedgwick was resting with his back against the ship's side reading from a slim leather volume that he had angled towards the light. They all looked up as the door of the wardroom swung open. A burst of light and laughter flowed out, followed by the captain and Vansittart loudly thanking their hosts.

'Pipe and the Hollander sound more pissed than a brace of parsons,' observed Evans.

'Bout fecking time they finished their carousing,' said O'Malley, a trace of envy in his voice. 'Aren't we a warship, sailing into danger, at all?'

'That mate of yours will be along soon, Sam,' said Sedgwick.

'He ain't no bleeding mucker of mine,' growled Evans. 'You couldn't touch his sort back home. He worked for them as ran most of the gin shops and bawdy houses.'

'But he ain't in that world no more,' said Sedgwick. 'Now he's in ours.'

'Ha!,' snorted Evans. 'How you bleeding figure that? He's working for the Hollander, ain't he? Who has the ear of the Prime Minister his self, if you'll credit it. We got more chance of making post than getting one over the likes of him.'

'Hold steady, there, Sam,' protested Trevan. 'You be shaking that lamp like a wrecker trying to beach a galleon. I can't see bugger all.'

'Sorry, mate,' said the big Londoner. The lamplight steadied and Trevan picked up his knife once more. 'Nice bit of wood, that.'

'Aye, slice of elm, this,' agreed the Cornishman. 'Boxwood's better for fine work, but this be coming out all right. The carpenter gave me a few off cuts as was bound for the galley fire. I've fashioned some bits from them.' He pulled a small wooden rattle and a beautifully worked spinning top from a cloth bag that lay beside him on the deck. Evans spun the top between finger and thumb and watched as it ran with barely a wobble on the table top.

'You got a proper talent when it comes to shaping lumber, Adam,' he said. 'You going to flog this stuff?'

'No, the comb's a gift, and them toys is for the nipper,' said Trevan. 'My Molly's due any day now.'

'What you hoping for?' asked Sedgwick.

'I wants a boy, but Molls reckons that'd be too raw for her, what with losing our little Samuel so young,' said Trevan. 'In truth, her and the babe coming through safe would do me just fine.'

'Fecking strange, ain't it, lads,' observed O'Malley, almost to himself. 'Adam being a father an' all.'

'You could be one, if you fancied it,' said Sedgwick. 'What became of that girl you promised to wed?'

'Back in Drumgallon?' said the Irishman. 'Lovely colleen, so she is. I'll return for her, when I've done with roving, and saved enough chink.'

'Sometime around 1840, then,' observed Evans.

'Now ain't this a scene of domestic bliss,' said Rankin, appearing out of the gloom and sitting down heavily at the table. 'Music, reading, polite conversation? I daresay you ladies will start chanting psalms presently.' He swayed in his place a little more than the easy motion of the ship required, and then belched against the back of his hand.

'You been at the fecking grog, Josh?' asked O'Malley.

The new arrival tapped his nose. 'That's a flunky's privilege, my Irish friend,' he explained. 'Whisk away the bottles with a gill left in and replace them with fresh ones. Once the Grunters are past the first remove, they never bleeding notice.' He favoured the table with a broad smile, and then settled his attention on Sedgwick.

'Read, can you?' he observed. 'Or is you just pretending?'

'I can read well enough,' said Sedgwick.

'Able ain't just got his letters,' said Evans, glaring at the new arrival. 'He's only been an' wrote a book, with no end of pages an' all.'

'A blackamoor with schooling,' marvelled Rankin. 'Best watch out, lads, case the savages become the masters and we end up as slaves, eh?' He laughed uproariously at the thought, his mirth loud in the silence around the mess table.

'So what you reading then?' he resumed. Sedgwick held up the title page for inspection. '*The Bramptons of Linstead Hall*, a novel in three volumes, by a Lady,' he read aloud. 'What's that all about, then?'

'Pipe's sister writes too, and this here is one of hers,' explained Sedgwick. 'In truth I ain't entirely sure what be going on. Miss Brampton is hot for this young buck, but he be more interested in the squire's daughter, and no end of dancing and turns about the garden seem about to put it right.'

'Not unlike what were going on in the bleeding wardroom with the Hockley wench,' said Rankin, pointing with a thumb over his shoulder.

'She be a comely piece, and no mistake,' said Trevan, laying aside his knife. 'Not a patch on my Molly, of course, but handsome enough.'

'There's a few of the Grunters what would agree with you there,' said the valet. 'Why, they was swarming about her like flies round a chamber pot. We nearly had a mill over whose arse was to sit beside her.'

'Was she sweet on any of them?' asked Evans.

'Oh, aye,' confirmed Rankin. 'She and that Grunter what's shy of an arm were close as thieves. Her father was proper vexed by it all. Odd her choosing to favour him over the others.'

'Young Preston?' said Sedgwick. 'Good for him. He deserves some luck, after what he's been through.' There were mutters of approval at this from those at tables nearby who listened on. O'Malley shifted on his stool.

'How will he fecking manage, I wonder?' he asked. 'With the one fin, like, when they wants to, you know... do it, like.'

'It's his arm as is missing, not his bleeding Thomas!' protested Evans. 'He climbed the main mast in a blizzard. I dare say he'll manage, when the time comes.'

'Aye, it be no different from you, Sean,' said Trevan. 'How many times have you been in a bawdy house, too pissed to stand? You lies back, and so long as you can raise your topgallant mast, the wenches can generally do the rest!' Once the roar of laughter that greeted this image had subsided, Evans turned back to Rankin.

'I don't remember you being no scholar, Josh,' he said. 'Back home like, yet you read Able's book brisk enough.

84

Where'd you get your letters?' The valet's dark eyes became thoughtful as he regarded Sam.

'There's plenty about me what you don't know, Sam lad,' he said. 'Much of which had best stay that way. But to answer you straight, it were John Company what gave me my schooling, back in Madras. That's where I fetched up, after I had to scarper.'

'Bleeding India?' said Evans. 'What you been doing out there?'

'Soldiering, for the most part,' said Rankin, 'amongst other stuff. There's no end of work for them with a talent out there. But one answer deserves the same. How'd you end up being a tar? I had you marked for a prize-fighter, when I left home.'

'I was, right enough,' said Evans. 'A bleeding good one an' all. I even beat that Jack Rodgers, the Southwark Butcher.'

'I'm impressed,' said his fellow Londoner. 'So why did you quit?'

Evans shrugged his shoulders. 'Turns out my old man had pocketed a deal of chink from the bookies for me to take a drop against Southwark Jack,' explained Evans. 'Only I never saw it that way. I don't need to tell you what a bastard an angry bookie can be.'

'Aye, worked for a few of them in my time,' said Rankin. 'No wonder facing bleeding cannon balls seemed the safer place to be. You and I have a lot in common, Sam lad.'

'If you say so,' said Evans, without any trace of a smile.

******

Dusk was gathering around the frigate as she sailed beneath a blanket of low cloud. The faint drizzle that had fallen for the last hour had soaked the deck and silvered the ropes. The green sea darkened to grey as the light faded, and the chill wind became fitful with the approach of night. To one side of the *Griffin* was the North Sea, wide and empty in the last of the evening light, while on the other side was the low coast of Jutland. It was a drab, flat land. An endless beach of promising white sand gave way to low, scrub-covered dunes, treeless and dotted with the occasional sheep.

'It's little more than a long finger of land with a saltwater lagoon and a deal of marshland behind it, sir,' reported Armstrong. 'The only settlement of note is a fortified village at the far end, named Thyboron, that commands the entrance. I believe I may be able to see the place now.'

Clay followed where the American pointed with his telescope. The sun had almost set now, but as it dipped to the horizon a few rays slipped beneath the cloud and lit up the land. Clay saw the grass-covered embrasures of a gun battery, with a red Danish flag stirring over it. Beyond it were the grey roofs of a settlement and the haze of wood smoke from its chimneys. The beach ended at a stone breakwater, behind which could be seen the masts of fishing boats. A line of birds flew in front of the village and faint over the water came the mournful honk of a goose. Then the sun vanished, and it grew dark. Soon the village was only visible as a cluster of yellow points in the night. Clay closed his telescope.

'A bleak spot, Mr Armstrong, and yet it is undoubtedly the right place,' he said. 'Heave too, if you please, and call away the blue cutter.'

'Aye aye, sir,' said the American. Clay turned to a slight figure standing next to the wheel.

'Mr Todd, kindly go below and give Mr Vansittart my compliments,' he said. 'Inform him that we have reached our destination.'

'Aye aye, sir,' said the youngster, touching his hat.

As the midshipman departed, Clay heard a burst of laughter, quickly stifled, from the leeside of the quarterdeck. He walked in that direction to investigate and came across two figures standing by the rail. The taller of the two stiffened and touched his hat, while his companion, who was lost in a sailor's jacket many times too big, bobbed down in a slight curtsy.

'Good evening, sir,' said the first figure.

'Good evening, Mr Preston,' said Clay. 'Your servant, Miss Hockley. I trust you will not get a chill in the damp of the evening?'

'Good evening, Captain. You sound a little like my father. In truth it is delightful to be away from the stuffiness below. Besides, I doubt that a little damp is excessively injurious; else the world would have a deal less sailors, would it not? I trust we are not in the way here?'

'Not in the least,' said Clay. 'But I think I hear Mr Vansittart. Will you excuse me?'

When Clay returned to his place by the wheel, he found the diplomat in urgent conversation with his valet. 'Hansen will give you a horse, after which you must make contact with Captain Lindholm. Give him my note, and tell him the time has come for him to earn his stipend.'

'Yes, sir, I understand,' said Rankin. He stood dressed in a long coat above riding boots. With his hat pulled low little could be made of his tanned face, except for his eyes, which were bright with excitement. There was a solid confidence in the way he stood, rocking on his feet with the motion of the ship.

'Would you like me to send Lieutenant Macpherson with a file of his marines to secure the beach first?' asked Clay.

'Heavens no, Captain,' said Vansittart. 'We are not at war with Denmark, at least for the present. Lets us not provoke them with reports of redcoats wading ashore.'

'Have no fear on my part, sir,' added Rankin. 'I got me arguments ready, should they be required.' He plunged a hand deep into the coat's side pocket and drew out the rounded butt of a pistol.

'Cutter is over the side, sir,' reported Armstrong.

'Very well, Rankin,' said Vansittart. 'Best of luck to you, now. Captain Clay says it will take us a week to reach Copenhagen by sea, wind permitting.'

'I will meet you there, sir, have no fear,' said the valet, turning away towards the entry port.

'Unless you are dead in a ditch,' muttered Vansittart as his servant departed. Then he went to join Clay looking over the ship's side. In the gloom they could just make out the figure of Rankin as he clambered down into the boat and settled himself in the stern.

'Push off in the bow,' said the quiet bass of Sedgwick. 'Give way, handsomely now.' The dark mass of the cutter turned on the water and vanish into the dusk towards the beach.

Armstrong had remained at his place by the wheel, making sure his precious frigate came to no harm. It was almost entirely dark now, but he could sense the ebb of the tide beneath his feet, and the flow of the breeze as it pressed against the backed sails, holding the *Griffin* in position. He was concentrating so hard that it was only after a few minutes he became aware of another presence. He looked round and saw a small, wiry figure standing at his elbow.

'Good evening, Mr Hockley,' said the sailing master, touching his hat. 'Have you come on deck to see why we are hove to?'

'Nay, Mr Armstrong,' said the ship owner. 'It was my daughter I was looking for. I can't seem to find her anywhere. Is she here abouts?'

'Not that I am aware of,' said the American, moments before a laugh, obviously female, rang out from the back of the quarterdeck. Hockley stiffened at the sound.

'Have a care, Mr Armstrong,' he hissed. 'Deceitfulness is as wicked as any of the mortal sins.'

'If you say so,' said the American towards the retreating back. 'It's just good to see Edward happy again,' he added, to himself.

'What is the meaning of this, Mr Preston?' demanded Hockley as he approached the couple.

'Good evening, sir,' said the officer. 'I am not sure what you can mean? I was simply taking the air with Miss Hockley. She found it a little close below decks.'

'Mr Preston was telling me an amusing story, father, about a time when he was a midshipman and they captured some Italian musicians—'

'Now then, my dear,' interrupted her father. 'We mustn't intrude in the running of the ship. Besides, you will get a chill, exposing yourself to the night air in this fashion.'

'Oh, but it is so pleasant out here,' she protested.

'I am sure a little longer would not be injurious to Miss Hockley,' said Preston.

'That's as may be, but Sarah will be returning below with me,' said Hockley. 'Good evening to you, Lieutenant.' He took his daughter by the arm and guided her back towards the ladder way.

'Good evening, sir, good evening, Miss Hockley,' said Preston. He was rewarded by the flash of a smile before the two figures disappeared, leaving him alone with his thoughts. He didn't notice the clatter of the returning cutter or the noise of the frigate getting underway. Instead he stared out over the dark water, to where two stars had appeared through a break in the cloud, rising high above the sea.

CHAPTER 6

COPENHAGEN

A week later the *Griffin* had entered the Baltic. A driving north-easterly wind had pushed her across the shallow waters of the Kattegat, flinging showers of sleet against her reefed topsails to slither down onto the heads of the crewmen beneath. Last night she had ridden to her anchor as the wind eased, waiting for first light to run the Sound, the narrow strip of sea that divided Denmark from Sweden. At dawn she had passed the grey walls and gun batteries of the Danish fortress at Elsinore, wondering if war had been declared and the cannons would burst into life the moment they were in range. But they had remained silent, and now the frigate was approaching the Danish capital from the north. Long fingers of fog clung to the chill water, but from the extra height of the quarterdeck Clay had an uninterrupted view over the mist towards the shore on both sides.

The low winter sun had left the Swedish half of the channel in shadow. Opposite him a slope of dark trees led down towards a little fishing village that stood on a promontory. He could see a line of gaily painted boats on a shingle beach. The men grouped around them paused to stare at the big frigate for a moment, before returning to their work. Nothing to trouble us there, concluded Clay, taking his telescope from his eye, and walking across the deck to examine the Danish coast.

Here the ground sloped up more gently and was a patchwork of brown ploughed fields and orchards with lines of skeleton trees above yellow grass. A cluster of stone buildings with steep pitched roofs marked where a farm lay, while at the top of the ridge the sails of a windmill turned languidly. Clay concluded that there must be a track running parallel with the water, to judge from the horse and cart he could see moving along it. Ahead of the frigate was a lone trading brig on the same course as them. A blue and gold Swedish flag flapped at its mizzen peak.

'Very little shipping, I note, Mr Armstrong,' he said to the sailing master, who was conning the frigate. 'That must be the first vessel above a fishing boat I have seen this morning.'

'The ice will only just be starting to break up at the head of the Baltic, sir,' said the American. 'Return in a month, and the Sound will be busier than the Pool of London. But it is fortunate that the Swede is here to guide us. Unless I am sadly out in my reckoning we are in the fairway to Copenhagen, but I'll be damned if I have seen a single buoy yet.'

'No, we are close, right enough,' said Taylor, who was studying the shore too. 'I delivered coal from Whitby to Copenhagen before the war. When we clear that point ahead, we should see the city.'

'Deck ho!' came a shout from the masthead. 'Boat ahoy! Fine off the starboard bow!' Clay and Armstrong walked back to the ship's side. Ahead was a trailing serpent of fog, with a dark shape at its heart. As the frigate approached it resolved into a large rowing boat. In the middle was a group of men hauling in on a weed-encrusted cable, while the rest of the crew braced their oars flat on the surface of the water. The cable stiffened into a solid bar, there was a cry from the coxswain, and all the men heaved together. After a moment more of resistance the cable came surging up, leaving the boat rocking on the swell.

'That accounts for the lack of navigation buoys, sir,' commented Armstrong. He pointed to the centre of the boat, where several kegs were stacked, each with a painted pole on top and a coil of slimy green rope beside it.

'Can you hail them as we pass, Mr Taylor?' said Clay. 'Find out what they are about.' The first lieutenant bellowed across at the boat through a speaking trumpet, but received only a shrug from the coxswain. The rest of the boat's crew glared at the frigate, and someone shouted something in Danish.

'Shall I pass the word for Pedersen, sir?' suggested Armstrong.

'If you please, and we had best heave to,' said Clay.

'Aye aye, sir,' replied the American.

Pedersen was one of the frigate's lithe top men, his ash-blond hair in startling contrast to the mahogany tan of his weathered face. He wiped his hands on his trousers before accepting the brass speaking trumpet from Taylor.

'Ask them why they are removing navigation buoys, if you please, Pedersen,' said Clay. He watched as the sailor asked his question, noting the look of distain that accompanied the reply from the coxswain.

'So, they say it's none of your business, begging your

pardon, sir,' translated the Dane. 'Only with some Danish words as ain't polite.'

'Did they indeed, the blackguards!' said Clay, colouring. 'Kindly tell them that I have a perfect right to question a boat that I find to be acting suspiciously, and if they cannot give me a civil reply, I shall be obliged to assume they are up to no good. Mr Taylor! Have a brace of starboard guns manned and run out, if you please.'

Pedersen resumed his dialogue with his fellow countrymen. This time the reply was much fuller, the tone rising to one of panic as the two eighteen-pounder cannons rumbled out from the frigate's side and settled their aim on the boat.

'They say they are under orders of the harbour master, sir,' explained Pedersen. 'They ask you not to shoot, and also want to know why I am on an enemy ship.'

'That is how they named us?' queried his captain. 'They called us an enemy ship?'

'Aye, sir, they did.'

'And did they give an explanation as to why they are pulling up these buoys?' asked Clay.

'So, they say that they are preparing for war, sir,' replied the sailor. Clay exchanged glances with Taylor before returning his attention to his translator.

'Can you ask them if war has been declared?'

Pedersen shouted the question across, but there was no need for him to translate the shrug that accompanied the short reply.

'Not yet, sir.'

'Thank you, Pedersen,' said Clay. 'You may return to your duties. Mr Armstrong, kindly get the ship under way.'

'Aye aye, sir.'

'Mr Taylor, have the watch below turned up, and the ship cleared for action, if you please,' he ordered, 'and pass the word for Mr Vansittart, with my compliments.'

The *Griffin* left the Danish boat and resumed its course, the thunder of its marine drummer echoing over the calm water as the crew were summoned to their stations. As they approached the headland that Taylor had mentioned, Clay began to see a haze of smoke rising into the winter sunshine from the domestic fires of the city. Against the smoke several thin spires rose proud of the tongue of land, like dark warning fingers. He lowered his telescope as Vansittart appeared beside him, his dove-grey coat contrasting with the scarlet tunics of the marines that were forming up behind him.

'I see you are leaving nothing to chance, Captain,' he said, indicating all the preparations for battle being made around him.

'I have just had a rather frosty dialogue with a Danish boat, sir,' said Clay. 'We shall find out how the Danes will receive us presently, but if we should prove to be at war with them, I will not be found ill-prepared.'

'That is wise, but we must not be the ones that provoke matters,' urged the diplomat. 'Our mission here is to try and secure the peace, if possible. Perhaps you could avoid any of the more visible manifestations of being ready to fight? None of your marine sharpshooters aloft, and keep the guns run in, for example?'

'Make it so, Mr Taylor,' ordered Clay. 'Now, Mr Armstrong, tell me what to expect around this point.'

'The channel runs south from here into the Baltic proper, with Copenhagen on one side, the island of Saltholm ahead, and Sweden on the other side, sir,' explained the American.

'The water looks broad and deep enough, but pray do not be fooled. It is shallow as a pan within a few cables of the shore, while in the centre lies a bank of mud they name the Middle Ground. Fully three miles long and a half mile wide, without a trace of it to be seen above the waves, now the cursed Danes have pulled up all the marker buoys.'

'I trust we shall have the services of a local pilot, sir,' said the first lieutenant.

'I hope so, Mr Taylor,' said Clay. 'You have visited the city, I collect, during the peace?'

'Indeed, and found it to be very tolerable, sir,' replied Taylor. 'It lines the west side of this channel, all about an inlet that serves as the harbour. The entrance is dominated by a fortress they call the Kastellet. There's a ring of walls and ditches on the landward side, but little above a breakwater facing the sea. The fleet could pound the city something cruel from that side.'

'Let us hope that such a threat will aid in your negotiations, Mr Vansittart,' said Clay.

'Indeed so,' agreed the diplomat, peering ahead. 'Although the chance to plant my feet on God's honest earth is what I am chiefly looking forward to. How you mariners keep to the sea for months, without running mad, is beyond me.'

'Not long now, sir,' said Armstrong, turning to the men at the wheel. 'Come up a point, if you please, Amos.'

'Point to loo'ard, aye, sir,' repeated the helmsman, turning the spokes through his hands.

'Headsails, Mr Hutchinson!' roared the American towards the bow of the frigate. 'Ready about!'

The angle began to change as the frigate turned around the final headland, opening up a wide expanse of green, choppy water. The last of the morning mist had vanished now, although the air was still raw and cold. Clay swung his telescope towards the shore; there, sprawled along the edge of the sea, was Copenhagen. Images passed through the round circle of his telescope's view, lit by the winter sunshine behind his shoulder. More of the spires he had seen earlier, which he could now see were covered with weathered green copper. Steep-pitched roofs of grey tiles rose above the tall buildings, many with walls that had been painted white, ochre, yellow or pale blue. He could see the grey stone walls of the fortress Taylor had mentioned, crouched on the shore. Next to it was the entrance to a harbour that bristled with the masts of ships. All of this was what Clay had expected to see, but between him and the city lay something he had not.

Across the entrance of the harbour a huge wooden platform had been built, apparently floating on the surface of the sea. Through his telescope Clay could see that it rested on massive wooden pilings, many the size of tree trunks, driven down into the muddy sea floor. Thick beams of oak formed a wall, perhaps ten feet high, through which the muzzles of heavy cannon pointed out to sea beneath a fluttering, blood-red Danish flag. But this was just the start of the city's new defences.

Running south from the wooden battery was an almost continuous line of perhaps twenty warships of all shapes and sizes. There were ships with one gun deck and others with two; some with masts and yards, ready to sail; while others were little more than hulks with a single spar set up like a flag pole. What they all shared in common was that they were securely anchored in place, bristled with cannon, and every ship showed at least one big Danish ensign. Together with the battery, they presented a wall of oak and artillery to any ship approaching from the open sea.

'Good heavens!' exclaimed Taylor. 'There must be over a hundred cannon in that floating battery over there!'

'And many hundreds more in the ships,' added Clay.

'They are not yet content, either,' added Armstrong. 'Direct your gaze towards all those lighters around the third rate with the red strakes. I fancy I can see workmen armouring the seaward side with extra timbers.' As the frigate sailed on, the faint sound of hammering came over the water.

'Mind, I would still place my faith in our three-deckers over any number of Danish hulks,' said Taylor. 'Admiral Parker has the *London*, and Lord Nelson the *Saint George,* do they not?'

'They do, although vexingly the water close in is too shallow for anything above a third rate to float,' said Armstrong. 'The Danes have chosen their ground with care.'

'So not quite as open to the bombardment of the fleet as we assumed,' observed Vansittart. 'Splendid! I can see my negotiations may prove a little more challenging.'

Clay was silent as he looked across at the Danish defences, his heart sinking at how formidable they seemed. There was something familiar about the line of moored warships. He looked around and caught sight of Macpherson, immaculate in his uniform at the head of his marines. Against the scarlet broadcloth of his tunic glistened the silver disc of his Nile medal, hanging in the sunlight on its blue and white ribbon. Suddenly he was back in the Mediterranean, on a sultry night in August, leading Nelson's fleet towards a similar line of anchored warships.

'No more formidable a position than we faced at the Nile, gentlemen,' he said. 'And we won through that night.

Besides, we are not at war with the Danes, yet. Mr Armstrong, kindly heave to here, if you will. Let us await their pleasure.'

'Aye aye, sir,' said the American, stepping away from the ship's side.

'Mr Taylor, that is a Danish National flag flying over the Kastellet fortress. Kindly clear away a bow chaser, and start firing the salute.'

'Aye aye, sir.' The lieutenant touched his hat, and then hurried away. The first gun of the salute was returned from the fortress wall, the puff of smoke visible long before the sound of the cannon reached them. Clay breathed a sigh of relief.

'Secure the guns, and dismiss the watch below,' ordered Clay, as the salute continued to bang to and fro between the ship and the fortress. Then he turned to the man standing next to him. 'From the courtesies being exchanged, it would seem that we are not at war yet, Mr Vansittart,' he observed. But before the diplomat could answer, a hail came from the masthead.

'Deck there! Boat putting out and heading this way! Danish colours!' Clay looked towards the city. Sailing out from the shore was a large gaff-rigged cutter.

'That vessel seems a little grand for a harbour pilot,' he observed. 'I suspect we are going to have a visitor. Man the entry port, if you please, Mr Taylor.'

'Aye aye, sir,' said the first lieutenant.

Clay's hunch proved correct. The cutter swept up alongside in smart fashion, dropping its main sail at the last moment. The first man up the ship's side, dressed in a simple blue coat and sea boots, was obviously the pilot, but he was followed by a naval captain in full dress uniform. A white ribbon edged in red lay across his chest and he had a glittering order at his throat. He paused in the entry port, with one gloved hand touching his hat to acknowledge the trilling boatswain's calls and line of saluting marines that greeted him, before approaching Clay.

'Welcome aboard, sir,' said the frigate's captain. 'My name is Alexander Clay, in command of His Britannic Majesty's ship *Griffin*. May I name the Honourable Nicholas Vansittart, Member of Parliament, who is here on behalf of his Majesty's government?'

'Pleased to make your acquaintance,' said the officer, his English excellent, with only the faintest of accents. 'I am Captain Anders Holst of the Danish Royal Navy. I am charged with ascertaining your intentions in visiting Copenhagen, gentlemen.'

'My orders were to bring Mr Vansittart here,' explained Clay.

'My credentials, Captain,' said the diplomat, pulling some folded documents from the inner pocket of his coat and holding them out. 'You will find I have a letter of introduction from the Court of St James to your Crown Prince, together with confirmation that I have been given full powers from His Majesty's government to treat on their behalf.'

Holst brought the heels of his shoes together with a click, bowed his head for a moment and accepted the documents. After a brief viewing he returned them.

'I take it from your presence that we are not yet at war?' he asked.

'We are not, Captain,' said Vansittart. 'That would be a very melancholy prospect between such friends. Denmark and Britain have always been neighbours and allies. It is only the meddling of that damned Corsican tyrant in Paris that has brought us to this sorry pass.'

'Yet we hear rumours of a large armada under your Admirals Parker and Nelson gathering on the other side of the German Sea,' said Holst. 'Hardly the action of a friend, but as you will have noticed, we are not wholly unprepared on our own part.'

'The state of preparedness for war on both sides gives urgency to my mission,' said the diplomat. 'When can I meet with the Crown Prince?'

'Alas, he is indisposed at present,' explained the Danish captain. 'But your ambassador warned us you would be coming. I am instructed to invite you to meet with his Chief Minister. I will return for you this afternoon.'

A slight frown of annoyance played across Vansittart's face, but he smoothed it away with a smile. 'Until later, then,' he replied.

'What of my ship, Captain?' asked Clay. 'I would like to replenish my water and firewood, and perhaps allow some of my men to go ashore.'

'As you are a neutral vessel visiting in time of peace, there can be no objection to that, Captain,' said Holst. He indicated the pilot, who was still waiting by the entry port. 'Give your requirements to my colleague, and he will make the arrangements. He will also guide you to the moorings for visiting warships. You have been allocated a place, next to the *Liberté*.'

'I beg your pardon?' queried Clay. 'What was the name of that ship?'

'The *Liberté*, Captain,' repeated Holst. 'She is a French National frigate of forty-four guns, so rather larger than your fine command. Of course, as Denmark is neutral, there can be no question of any conflict between you while you are both guests in Copenhagen.' The Danish captain held Clay's eyes for a long moment.

'Be assured we shall ignore them, like duelling rivals who chance to encounter at a ball,' said Vansittart.

'That is good to hear,' said Holst. 'Two ships, both here on diplomatic missions. I can scarce remember when so many of our friends wanted to visit us. Until later this afternoon then, Mr Vansittart.'

******

News that the frigate would stay in Copenhagen for a few days, and that shore leave might be granted, spread quickly across the lower deck. Soon a harassed Lieutenant Taylor was besieged by requests to go and sample what delights the city had to offer. Most he was able to grant. Once an anchor watch had been set, all but the most notorious deserters amongst the crew were allowed ashore. From their place by the forecastle rail, Edward Preston and Sarah Hockley watched the last of the boats pull across the choppy water to the stone quayside, full of noisy sailors all dressed in their shore-going finery.

'It is a pleasing prospect, seen from here, is it not?' said Preston, meaning the city, with its colourfully painted buildings, rather than the departing crew. 'Lieutenant Blake was sketching it earlier, with a view to producing a painting.'

'Is it the diverting architecture that is sending the crew ashore with such enthusiasm, then, Mr Preston?' she asked with a smile.

'I doubt that very much,' he said. 'They will run past any number of splendours to be first through the door of the nearest grog shop.'

'Were you not tempted by the city, Mr Preston?' she asked. 'Some of your fellow officers have gone. I was surprised to find you were not amongst the party.' He glanced at his companion. The wind had tugged streamers of rich brown hair free from under her bonnet, and was making her eyes sparkle with life.

'I find the company left onboard perfectly to my liking, Miss Hockley,' he said, and was rewarded by another smile. 'What progress has your father made with securing your passage home?'

'He will go ashore tomorrow morning and visit a shipping agent he has done business with in the past,' she said. 'I imagine we will leave the *Griffin* shortly thereafter.' Preston felt chilled at the thought of her departure. He looked across at her and sensed that she felt it too. The sound of the ship seemed to fade around them, as his hand crept along the rail towards hers.

'I would regret that very much, Miss Hockley,' he said. 'Although our acquaintance has only been brief, I feel as if I have known you much longer.'

'Ah, there you are, Sarah,' exclaimed Mr Hockley, striding along the starboard gangway. They separated with a start as her father came up.

'Good afternoon, Mr Hockley,' said Preston, touching his hat.

'And to you, young man,' said Hockley, without returning the salute. 'Now Sarah, I am quite certain that the lieutenant will have matters he needs to attend to.'

'As it happens I am not required to be on duty before the end of the second dog watch,' explained the young officer.

'How fortunate,' said Hockley. 'In that case, perhaps you would walk with me a while, Mr Preston? There is something

I wish to discuss with you.' Without waiting for a reply, he turned to his daughter. 'I need to speak with the lieutenant, Sarah. Perhaps you could go below, and pack your things for tomorrow.'

'I have so few possessions, father, that will hardly detain me long,' she said. 'Could I not stay on deck a little longer?'

'Do not defy me, girl!' barked her father. 'Go below, I say.' Sarah's face coloured at the rasp in his tone, but she dropped her eyes, bobbed a quick curtsey, and made her way towards the aft of the ship. Hockley started pacing along the gangway, gesturing for Preston to walk with him.

'I can assure you that nothing of an inappropriate nature was taking place, Mr Hockley,' said Preston, as he fell in step beside the older man.

'And can you also assure me where matters might have ended if I had not happened upon you?' demanded Hockley. 'I am not generally thought of as a fool, young man. I have seen how you have attended to my daughter this last week. Mooning around her, every idle hour of the day.'

'I will not deny that I enjoy her society,' said the lieutenant. 'But what is so strange in that? Your daughter is a very accomplished young lady.'

'Aye, she is an exceptional lass,' said Hockley with pride. 'Which is why I need to have a care as to who she is associating with. You know of what I speak, Mr Preston. The reputation of a young lady can be lost in an instant.'

'But I would never do such a thing!' protested the lieutenant. 'I have sisters of my own. I very much admire Miss Hockley, but in a natural and honourable way.'

'And do you suppose that she returns your admiration?' said Hockley. 'My daughter has a very caring nature, sir. Pray do not mistake her sympathy for your condition for something more.'

'My condition?' said Preston, bridling. 'What has that damn well got to do with it?'

'Pray do not blaspheme in my presence, sir,' warned Hockley. 'Damnation is a punishment meted out by our Saviour, not by the likes of you.'

'The likes of me?' spluttered Preston. 'What do you mean by that? I am an officer and a gentleman!'

'I do not wish to quarrel with you, Lieutenant, but you must understand how precious my daughter is to me. When she came into this world, it was at the cost of my darling wife, and I prize her above everything.'

'That I can quite understand,' said Preston. 'But surely a father's love does not preclude her placing her affection elsewhere?

'What has happened, sir?' demanded Hockley, his eyes narrowing with suspicion. 'Have you reached some understanding with my daughter behind my back?'

'No, in truth I have not, Mr Hockley,' said Preston. 'My comments were of a general character.'

'Good, because tomorrow Sarah and I shall leave this ship and return home, and that will be an end to it.'

'I would still wish to maintain you and your daughter's acquaintance, when I am next in Yorkshire,' said Preston. 'May I have your permission to at least do that?'

'Let me be frank with you, Mr Preston,' said Hockley. 'I know my Sarah will leave me one day and that on that day I shall gain a son. But I have decided views about the person best suited to that role. Probably he will be another merchant captain, or the like. Someone skilled in business, able to take over my affairs when my time comes.'

'Would a sea officer in the King's service not be eligible?'

asked the young lieutenant.

'Not to my mind.' There was finality in Hockley tone which made Preston smile bitterly.

'Are you quite certain that you are choosing on your daughter's part, and not your own?' he asked.

'Don't be impertinent!' roared Hockley, white with anger. 'I have never heard of such presumption!' He leant towards Preston, so close that the younger man felt spittle touch his face. 'I can tell you this much. The man she weds will be whole, not some cursed cripple!'

******

At first the four sailors enjoyed the simple pleasure of being off the frigate as they walked from the quayside along the cobbled streets of the city. They were surrounded by sights that was quite new to them. Arched stone openings led off into courtyards lined with workshops, where the sound of hammering rang out, or saws rasped through wood. Copenhagen was laid out in a grid pattern, but occasionally the streets opened up into little squares, some dominated by a church, others with a fountain or a bronze statue at their hearts. Tall buildings lined the roads, some of plain stone or half timber, just like home, but many were more exotic. At first they had laughed and pointed at the coloured walls, painted with trailing leaves or lines of flowers across their render. But as they penetrated deeper into the city, they began to notice the stares that were directed towards them. There were soldiers grouped at most intersections, their blood-red coats a deeper shade than British scarlet, who eyed them with suspicion as they approached. Then there were the citizens who stepped from their path and then stared after them, some with folded arms, while others shook their heads. Behind them they began to hear the occasional call in Danish, few of which sounded welcoming.

'Surely any bleeding grog shop will do us, Able,' urged Evans, as the coxswain paused at the intersection of two streets and looked up at the road names painted on the wall.

'Afraid not, Sam,' replied Sedgwick. 'It has to be the one as Pipe said. Why does every street in this cursed place end with bloody "gade"?'

'These here Danes be an inquisitive lot, and no mistake,' observed Trevan. 'I never seen such a deal of staring.'

'Perhaps they ain't never seen a negro before,' offered Evans. 'No offence, Able, but we've not passed a soul as weren't pale as a sheet. Not so much as a mulatto.'

'Or could be that we're keeping company with a giant,' suggested Sedgwick, looking up at the tall Londoner.

'Nah, 'tis scorn in their eyes I am after seeing,' announced O'Malley, with satisfaction. 'I am telling yous, it's not just the Irish as hates the fecking English. Any right-thinking foreigner does the same.'

'I reckon the tavern could be this way,' said Sedgwick, pointing down a street. 'Let's push off sharpish, before them lads over there summon up the pluck to start a mill.' The others looked at the shadowy group that had formed in a doorway a few houses down, one of whom had a club and seemed to be urging the others on.

The sun was sinking lower now, and all around them people were hurrying past, while the soft light of candles and oil lamps began to spill out from windows. Several intersections farther, Sedgwick looked up at the road names, and let out a sigh of relief.

'Rosengade,' he said. 'Not afore time, neither. Now, the tavern we're after has a fish with a crown on its head painted over the door.'

Once they had found the right street, it was easy to locate their destination; an old half-timbered building three stories high that leaned out over the pavement. The sailors pushed open a studded wooden door, black with age, and found themselves in a large, stone-flagged room. Above their heads the beams had been painted burnt ochre, which contrasted pleasantly with the strips of yellow plaster ceiling between them. At one end of the room a cheerful blaze of logs filled a substantial fireplace, above which hung a row of polished copper pots. Wooden booths lined the walls, each equipped with a table and benches and lit by oil lamps. Several were occupied, and the buzz of conversation mingled with trailing wisps of pipe smoke that drifted through the air. Directly opposite the door a lively card game was in progress, while from somewhere deeper in the room came the sound of a German flute being played.

'My, this is a bit bleeding grander than your regular grog shop,' exclaimed Evans, hurrying forward into the warmth. His words might have been the incantation of some powerful spell, so rapid was the change that followed them. The flute stopped mid-note, the conversation ceased, the card players turned to stare at the newcomers, while more faces appeared around the other wooden partitions. The dry crackle of the fire was all that could be heard in the silence of the room.

'Evening, lads,' said Trevan with a friendly wave of his hand. No reaction.

'This one here is empty,' said Sedgwick, pushing his friends towards the nearest booth. The sailors crowded in and sat down around the table.

'So why was it this bleeding tavern in particular we had to find, Able?' asked Evans.

'Was it the warmth of the fecking locals, you was after?' added O'Malley.

'Aye, we might be safer drinking with the others, down by the fish market,' added Trevan, tamping tobacco into his pipe, and standing up to suck it alight from the lamp that hung over the table.

'It were all that cursed Hollander's fault,' whispered Sedgwick, leaning forward. 'When I asked Pipe for leave to go ashore, he were in the cabin too. "*Do you know your letters*?" says he, and when I says how I does, he got me to cast this place to memory. We're to meet with his flunkey and smuggle him back on board.'

'Josh bleeding Rankin!' exclaimed Evans. 'I might have know that arse would be at the bottom of all this! Why's he so special, then?'

Sedgwick shrugged. 'According to the Hollander, it be proper important. He even gave me some chink, in case we needed it.' He dredged a couple of guinea coins from his pocket.

'Yellow boys!' exclaimed O'Malley. 'Well what are we fecking waiting for!' He let out a piercing whistle, which silenced the room once more. After a long pause, a serving girl appeared at the end of the table. She wore a flared skirt and an embroidered linen blouse, the whole gathered in by a tight red bodice that showed off her figure well. Blonde plaits framed a heart-shaped face devoid of any welcome.

'*Hvad?*' she barked.

'Four mugs of your best fecking ale, my pretty colleen, with more beer, bread and cheese alongside it,' said the Irishman. 'After which you can take your ease on my lap.' He patted the top of his thighs in invitation, and favoured her with what he imagined was a winning smile. The girl regarded him with distain, before repeating herself.

'*Hvad*?'

'We should've fetched Pedersen along with us, I am after thinking,' observed Sedgwick, while the others tried to mime what they wanted. The girl waited, her face stone, until they had exhausted their full repertoire of dumb-show. Then she turned away from the table with a shrug of her elegant shoulders.

'They does breed their wenches surly hereabouts,' observed Trevan. 'Comely too, mind, but that look she gave Sean would have pickled an egg. You reckon she knows what we wants?'

'Just so long as we gets the beer,' said Evans. 'I'm bleeding parched with all this walking, and I still ain't fathomed what's so important about that Rankin.'

'Your mate's been spying and the like, I am after thinking,' said O'Malley.

'For the last bleeding time, we ain't muckers!' protested Evans.

'Perhaps not, but I reckon you has the truth of it there, Sean,' said Trevan. 'But hush such talk, now! Here comes the wench.'

'Hah, she don't speak no bleeding English,' scoffed Evans. The serving girl approached the table again, making light work of the heavily laden tray that was balanced on her hip. On it was everything the sailors had asked for.

'You lads make better players than I reckoned,' said Sedgwick, looking at the spread on the table as she transferred it across.

'Two crowns for the meal,' said the girl, in accented but understandable English, 'but if you give me the gold piece, I will also tell you were you can find your friend.' The sailors gaped at her.

'Why didn't you bleeding say as you understood us plain?' demanded Evans.

'You didn't ask,' said the waitress. 'So, do you want to know?'

'Aye,' said Sedgwick, handing over the coin. 'Where is he, then?' She tested it between her even white teeth, and then slipped the guinea into a pocket.

'He eats in the booth nearest the fire,' she said and promptly turned away. O'Malley's hand shot out and grabbed her wrist before she could disappear.

'Not so fecking swift,' he said. 'Now you've got yourself a month's wages for so little, be a love an' show your man over,' he said. He released her arm and went to pat her behind, but she swayed clear of his clumsy lunge and sashayed away towards the fireplace.

'Easiest chink that wench has ever earned,' observed Trevan.

'Why didn't that arse come over when he heard us come in?' demanded the Londoner.

'Coz I hadn't finished my stew, Samuel Evans,' said Rankin, appearing around the end of the partition and sitting down at their table. 'And what Mr Vansittart will make of how you've been chucking his bleeding gold about, I daren't consider, blackamoor.'

His coat was travel-stained, splashed with mud beneath the waist, and his hair was a little more dishevelled than when they last saw him a week ago, but otherwise he seemed unchanged. He helped himself to some of their beer, drank deeply, and then wiped his mouth.

'Nice of you all to show, at last,' he observed. 'So what instructions from his nibs?'

'I'm to get you back to the *Griffin*, in one piece,' explained Sedgwick.

'Too bleeding right, but not until it is fully dark, nor by the front door,' said Rankin. He nodded in the direction of the serving girl. 'Clara can show us out the back way, when the time comes.' The sailors exchanged glances.

'I ain't sure as how you needs us, Josh,' said Sedgwick. 'You seem to have matters down pat.'

'Wouldn't exactly say that,' explained Rankin. 'I have been through the odd mill, and I lost my pistol three days back. But getting clear from here should be easy enough. It's at the other end I shall chiefly need you boys. Them bleeding Danes will be watching the *Griffin* closer than a miser does his cashbox. If I was to show up alone, I wouldn't get within a hundred yards without having my collar felt. But if I pitch up in the midst of a party of returning tars, no one need be any the wiser.'

'Hiding a tree in a wood, like,' said Trevan

'Or a turd in a privy,' muttered Evans.

'First I'm an arse, then I'm a bleeding turd?' queried Rankin. 'I am starting to think we ain't friends, Big Sam, which would be a shame. Coz you really don't want to be my enemy.' He smiled at his fellow Londoner with his mouth, but his eyes were ice. Then they flicked away from Evans towards a group of locals who had appeared at the end of the table.

'You not welcome, Englanders,' snarled the leader, a big man with bare arms and the leather apron of a blacksmith. The others arranged themselves behind him, fingering various weapons and glaring at the sailors. From the far side of the partition came the sound of the bar's other customers leaving. There was no sign of Clara the serving girl.

'That's a bleeding pity,' said Rankin calmly. 'See, I likes this place, with its fine ale and friendly punters. So I shan't be going nowhere until I choose to.' There was a pause while the man in the leather apron translated the gist of this to his companions, who all growled in response.

'We fight,' declared the blacksmith, stepping back from the table and inviting his opponent forward.

'If we must,' sighed Rankin. He turned to the other sailors. 'Looks like you're going to be needed after all, lads. Hope you're up for it.' He drained his mug, rose to his feet and stepped out of the booth, with the sailors crowding forward at his back. The blacksmith bunched his huge hands into fists, but Rankin turned away and walked towards the fireplace. The Danes exchanged looks of surprise.

'What's he bleeding playing at?' whispered Evans.

'I ain't sure,' said Sedgwick, 'but the bastard's got some bottom, I'll grant him that.'

Rankin seemed to be ignoring them all. He reached the end of the room, pulled off his coat, and hung it on one of the metal hooks set into the wall beside the chimney breast, all the time with his back to the Danes. The leader shrugged at the others, then rushed at the Londoner. Just as he neared his helpless opponent, Sedgwick realised that he could see multiple versions of Rankin's face, watching the man's approach in the polished bottoms of the copper pans above the fireplace. As the Dane drew back his fist to deliver a swinging blow, Rankin snatched the nearest pan from the wall and whirled around, light as a dancer. He swept it two-handed into the blacksmith's face with a clang that reverberated across the room. The Dane crashed down as if he had been shot.

'Clever bastard!' marveled the coxswain.

'Watch your fecking self, Able!' warned O'Malley. With bellows of rage, the blacksmith's companions launched themselves at the sailors, and a general melee broke out.

Although the seamen were veterans of many a tavern brawl, things started poorly. Evans, who was by far the most formidable fighter amongst them, found himself cornered in the booth, facing a Dane armed with a battered sabre. Unable to close with his opponent, he was reduced to parrying the weapon using a large pewter jug he had swept up from the table. The blade screeched and clashed off the dull metal, leaving silver gashes in the surface.

One of the other men rushed at Sedgwick, his club swinging through the air. The coxswain sprang inside the blow, which thudded across his shoulder, and he crashed into the chest of his opponent. His momentum carried both men into an empty booth on the opposite side of the bar, where they flailed and grappled on the floor.

This left O'Malley and Trevan to fight the three remaining Danes, all of whom had heavy sticks and cudgels. By ducking and weaving, they managed to avoid the heaviest hits, but it could hardly last. Eventually the Irishman, while avoiding a savage blow from one enemy, stepped into the path of a thrust from another. It caught him full in the stomach, and he sank down to his knees with a groan.

Then the fight started to turn in the seamen's favour. Evans realised that though his opponent was the best armed, he had little training in how to use a sword and was tiring fast. The big sailor pretended to slip, watched his opponent's eyes light up in triumph, and side-stepped his clumsy lunge with ease. The man stumbled forward and received a crashing left jab on the point of his chin. The right hook that followed it would have felled an ox, but the Dane was already on his way to the tavern floor, and it buffeted off the top of his head. Evans vaulted out of the booth into some clear space at last, swept his left foot forward and dropped into his prize fighter's stance. Then he advanced on the three Danes that had Trevan cornered by the door.

The first man never saw the blow that crashed into the side of his head, plumb on one of his ginger sideburns. The second managed to turn towards Evans, but was too slow to parry the volley of punches that rained in on him. With both his colleagues prostrate, the third opponent stared with horror at the huge sailor in front of him. A gust of chill air made him look around, and he saw that Trevan was holding the door of the bar open. The long ash handle he had been using as a weapon clattered onto the stone floor as he fled out into the street.

'You all right, Adam?' asked Evans, coming out of his crouch. He pointed to his own cheek. 'You got a bit of claret on you, just there.'

'It only be a scratch,' said Trevan, wiping a sleeve across his face. 'How's Sean?'

'Fit to puke,' gasped the Irishman, getting shakily to his feet. 'An' my fecking nose is bust—again.' Sedgwick crawled out of the booth where he had been fighting, wringing one of his hands. A pair of motionless boots, proud of the partition, was all that could be seen of his opponent.

'How's Josh?' he asked, looking towards the fireplace.

Rankin seemed quite unharmed by the fight, but the same could not be said for the blacksmith. He knelt on the floor, clawing at his neck with terror in his bulging eyes. A length of silk cord was wound around his throat, biting so deep that it was barely visible. His blue tongue lolled out from a foam-speckled mouth. Behind him stood Rankin, one end of the cord wrapped around each fist, his face contorted with fury as he garrotted his victim.

'Jesus, let the fecker go!' yelled O'Malley.

'You're going to killing him!' warned Sedgwick.

'No more than the bastard deserves,' snarled Rankin, jerking the cord a little tighter.

The sailors ran over. Sedgwick grabbed one arm while Trevan pulled at the other, but Rankin shook them off.

'Too bleeding slow,' announced Evans. He paused for a moment to set himself, and then sent his right fist crashing, hard and full, into the face of his fellow Londoner.

CHAPTER 7

FLIGHT

Lieutenant Edward Preston stood by the quarterdeck rail of the frigate, contemplating the waters of the Sound as they slopped against the side of the ship. The wind had dropped as the short day moved towards evening, and the green water was darkening in the fading light. The sea was dotted with floating detritus. Two gulls were squabbling for possession of a large clump that drifted off the frigate's beam.

'What in all creation is that damned smell?' exclaimed Thomas Macpherson, who had come up on deck to take the air.

'The contents of Copenhagen's many privies, I fancy, Tom,' replied Preston. 'All coastal cities discharge their filth into the sea, but with the breeze no longer playing it's part and no tide to speak of in these parts, it is refusing to disperse.'

'No tide?' queried the Scot.

'Not above a few inches,' confirmed his friend. 'There will be even less as we proceed deeper into the Baltic.' Macpherson wrinkled his nose.

'No wonder the Danes insist on pickling their fish before consuming them,' he observed. 'So it is not the odour of our neighbours?'

Preston looked across at the big French frigate that was moored parallel to the *Griffin*, between the Royal Navy ship and the steep stone walls of the Kastellet fortress. She was a fine-looking vessel, with a hull that was significantly longer than that of her rival. Her lofty masts soared high into the evening sky, a good ten feet above those of the *Griffin*. The black hull of the *Liberté* was split by a broad white stripe that followed the line of her gun deck, from her figurehead of a bare-breasted woman brandishing a sword to the gilded figures clustered around her stern. The two men found themselves looking across at a matching pair of French officers, who leant against the rail of their ship and stared back at them. One of them raised his hat, revealing the blond curls of someone barely out of childhood, and after an awkward pause the British officers did the same.

'She looks a fine ship,' remarked Macpherson. 'I am no expert, but her lines seem sharper than ours.'

'Yes, she'll be devilish fast,' agreed Preston. 'French ships are often built to be quick. It gives their commanders the option to fight or flee, should they find themselves embarrassed by one of ours.'

Macpherson considered this for a moment. 'Why are our ships not built to match them, then?' he asked.

'Because swiftness comes at a price,' said his friend. 'Those same lines will make her a deal less weatherly. A very wet ship in a blow, I make no doubt. No, I would sooner be aboard our *Griffin* if any sort of sea was running.' He patted the oak rail beside him, as if reassuring a nervous horse.

'You hold ours to be the better ship, then, not least for the company aboard,' said the marine, looking significantly at him. 'I notice that in spite of her father's keenness to be away, Miss Hockley is still gracing us.'

'She is,' said Preston. 'But that can be no concern of mine.' He continued to stare at the oily water, the broken reflection of the French ship wavering on its surface.

'What?' exclaimed Macpherson. 'But surely you have won that particular race? Half the wardroom wanted to enjoy her society, and yet she shows a clear inclination for you.' He stroked one of his bushy dark sideburns. 'It is a mystery why, I grant you. Perhaps those delightful eyes of hers are weak? Mind, they do say that love is blind.'

'She may be partial to my acquaintance, but her father has made his views as to my suitability very plain.'

'And what is it he objects too?' demanded the Scot. 'You are more of a gentleman that he is.'

'Look at me, Tom,' said Preston. 'I am hardly much of a catch.' Macpherson did as he was asked, taking in his friend's handsome face, still pale and gaunt, the dark eyes haunted by pain, and the empty sleeve pinned across his chest.

'Fine, regular features,' listed Macpherson, 'together with an open countenance. No trace of any conceit, yet a cheerful disposition, considerable intelligence and notable courage. I know of nothing in your character that you should not be proud of, Edward.'

'I am in want of an arm, for God sake!'

'Which makes your appearance superior by at least an eye over that of Lord Nelson,' observed the marine, 'and he seems to have little problem attracting the attentions of the fairer sex. He has to beat them off, if half the rumours are true.'

'Lord Nelson!' exclaimed Preston. 'Why does everyone try

and compare me to him!' He spun away from the rail, but his friend caught his arm and drew him back.

'Your pardon, Edward,' he said. 'It was ill-judged of me to speak lightly of such a grave matter. It is just my way. Will you forgive me?'

'There is nothing to forgive, Tom,' said Preston. 'You find me low in spirits, because I admire Miss Hockley but I cannot think how to win her in the face of the implacable opposition of her father. And time is so short! They will leave the ship soon, returning home, while we are bound for God only knows where. I am not sure how I shall bear it.' Macpherson looked at his friend with pity in his eyes. The young man's voice was cracking with the depth of his emotion.

'You know, Edward, your situation reminds me a wee bit of the captain's courtship,' he said.

'How so?' asked Preston.

'He fell in love with a woman of a superior rank to his own,' explained Scot. 'He was forbidden to meet with Miss Browning, as she was then, and yet in spite of all, they are now man and wife.'

'But he is a post captain,' protested his friend.

'Not when they met. He was only a lieutenant, just as you are,' said Macpherson. 'Consider your many advantages over his position. The captain was divided from the object of his affection by many thousands of miles, she having accompanied her family to Bengal.'

'He wasn't a cripple,' said Preston quietly.

'Leave it be, Edward!' urged his friend. 'It's clear to all that your want of an arm means nothing to Miss Hockley, so why the devil should it prove a bar for you? Declare yourself to her, man! Tell her how you feel, before she leaves the ship and it is too late.'

'And what of the objections of her father?'

'He loves his daughter above all else,' said Macpherson. 'That is plain to see. If she truly cares for you, she will find a way to persuade him.'

******

'Still breathing,' pronounced Sedgwick, kneeling low to bring his cheek close to the Danish blacksmith's mouth. 'Let's hope we can say the same for Rankin, after you lumped him, Sam. You do know we're to see him back to the barky in one piece?'

'It did make him bleeding stop, mind,' said Evans, who was standing over the recumbent valet. 'Felt good, an' all. I've been wanting to do that since I was a youngster.' The serving girl appeared beside him, leant forward and spat on the unconscious Londoner.

'*Dit svin!*' she hissed.

'Aye, you tell him, Clara,' agreed Evans, patting her on the back.

'What manner of neck cloth be this, lads?' queried O'Malley. He pulled a rope of twisted red silk from Rankin's unresisting grip, weighted at each end with a round knot. 'Sort of thing a fecking Turk would use.'

The blacksmith made a gasping cough, and his eyes started to flutter open. At the same time the Dane who had fought with Sedgwick groaned and shifted in the wrecked booth, while from out in the street came the sound of distant shouting.

'The one you let go!' exclaimed Clara. 'He will have called out the watch! Quick, you come with me!'

The four sailors picked up the unconscious Rankin and

followed the serving girl down a hallway that led towards the back of the building. There were doors on either side; one opened into a kitchen lit by the glow of a fire, the next had stone steps, leading down, but Clara pressed on to the passageway's end. She pulled open a big door and stood aside, urging them through it. They hurried into the cold night, and found themselves in a narrow, dark passageway that ran between the buildings. The moment they were outside, Clara slammed and bolted the door behind them.

'What the feck do we do now?' said O'Malley, looking each way along the alley.

'Back to the barky, sharpish,' ordered Sedgwick. 'You and Adam lead off, Sam and I will lug Rankin.'

'Back to the barky, your man says,' muttered the Irishman to himself, as he led the way forwards. 'Now, which fecking way might that be?'

When the sailors had walked through the well-ordered streets of Copenhagen earlier that evening, they'd had only a little difficulty in finding their way. En route they had passed the odd shadowy archway, or entrance to an alley, but had not imagined the labyrinthine world that existed behind the elegant stucco frontages of the buildings. It was fully dark now, and what little light the night sky had to offer failed to penetrate the warren of narrow passages. High stone walls fenced them in on both sides. In some places the first floors of buildings had been constructed over the top of the alleys, turning them into echoing tunnels. There were unseen boxes and stacked lumber to trip them up, and dank puddles of water or worse that lay amongst the slippery cobbles. It would have helped if the way had at least run true, but instead it branched repeatedly, crossed other alleys and made abrupt turns of ninety degrees around the outer walls of buildings. Stray cats hissed with venom at them from the tops of walls, while guard dogs snuffled and barked from behind the doors and gates as they hurried past.

'This way for certain, lads,' announced O'Malley, after quarter of an hour of fruitless wandering. He indicated a passage that ran off to one side.

'You sure this be right?' asked Trevan, peering down it. 'Not another of them dead ends you seems to favour?'

'I thought Seven Dials were a bleeding warren, but this place takes the pudding,' puffed Evans, who was carrying Rankin's shoulders. 'Can we grab a breather?' They propped up their burden in a doorway and his head slumped forward.

'Is he still alive?' queried Trevan.

'Aye, the Devil cares for his own, seemingly,' said Evans. 'He started to come round earlier, so I clonked his head on the wall in passing.'

Sedgwick, who was looking back the way they had come, suddenly stiffened.

'Get under way, lads,' he said. 'Someone's coming.' The others looked around to see light reflecting off the wall of the alleyway. From behind them came the faint patter of footfalls. The sailors picked up Rankin again and stumbled after the Irishman.

The alley bent around a corner and then ran straight for a while. It grew wider, and better flagged underfoot. Up ahead light glowed through an arch with some sort of road beyond it. A carriage pulled by two horses clattered by, the lantern mounted next to the coachman flashing towards them as it passed.

'Told you it was the right fecking way,' said O'Malley. 'That's a proper Christian street, to be sure.'

'Not before bleeding time,' muttered Evans.

'I ain't sure if we wants to break cover just yet,' said Sedgwick. 'Streets is where the tipstaffs will be. Remember all them Lobsters we saw earlier?'

They reached the end of the passageway, and peered out onto the main road. Large buildings fronted it, many with light spilling from their windows. Locals in hats and coats walked along the pavements. On the far side of the road was a matching alley to the one they were in, while away to their left the street opened onto a small square, dominated by a splashing fountain. At the corner glowed a brazier, with a group of soldiers warming themselves around it.

'No good for us, lads,' whispered the coxswain, as he ducked back into cover. 'Too open by far.'

'Stopping here's no bleeding good, neither,' protest Evans, pointing back the way they had come. 'Them bastards with that lamp are right up our arses.'

'Oh, my b-bleeding head,' groaned Rankin, stirring at last and holding a hand up to his temple.

'Shhh, Josh,' urged Trevan. 'Quiet now.'

'Shall I clonk him again?' suggested Evans.

'W-why am I c-c-covered in blood?' asked Rankin in a conversational tone. A man walking past on the pavement slowed to look at them, and the sound of footsteps quickened in the alleyway behind them.

'Let's chance it,' decided Sedgwick. 'Sean, take his other side. Come now, Josh, let's get you into your hammock.'

'That do sound g-good, my sooty friend,' said Rankin, patting Sedgwick's shoulder. 'But I needs to get all this blood off me b-before I sleep. Ah, that fountain will serve.' He took a few halting steps towards the square.

'No!' exclaimed O'Malley. 'This way mate. There be plenty of water back at the barky.' Between Sedgwick and the

Irishman they half carried, half dragged him across the cobbles, with Trevan and Evans following them.

'Don't be looking towards them Lobster, lads,' hissed Trevan through the side of his mouth.

'I still reckon it would be easier if I silenced him,' offered Evans.

'So how did we come to leave that bleeding bar then?' asked Rankin as they plunged back into cover. 'And why does my jaw hurt so much?'

'No time for that now, Josh,' said O'Malley. 'Some of them fecking Danes jumped us. We managed to get you clear, but the hue and cry is hard astern. Might help if you could walk a touch yourself?'

'That's r-right!' declared Rankin. 'I remember I clonked one of the bastards with a bleeding skillet!'

The alleyway turned around another corner and widened into a small cobbled yard. Two other passageways crossed at this point, one with a gurgling open drain running alongside it.

'Easy all,' said Evans. 'We got to make a stand, lads. Crossing that street ain't shaken them blokes off, and they're closing fast.' A glance behind showed he was right. The light from a lantern glowed from farther back down the alley, and in addition to footsteps they could now hear voices.

'Here be as good as any place we passed through,' announced Trevan, indicating the dark corners to either side of the alleyway's opening.

'Some lumber here, lads,' said O'Malley, picking up a stick from a pile. He flexed it between his fists and it promptly snapped.

'Sam, you and Sean hide on that side!' ordered Sedgwick. 'Adam and I'll take this.' Left without any support, Rankin wobbled a little, and then sat down heavily on the ground.

No sooner had the sailors hidden themselves than spears of light shone down the alleyway, glittering on the wet cobbles. Approaching footsteps echoed in the confined space. Evans and Sedgwick bunched their fists and couched either side of the entrance.

The leading man, the lantern swinging from his hand, trotted into the courtyard and was neatly tripped by Sedgwick's foot. His light smashed down onto the cobbles and erupted as flaming oil spilt across the ground, illuminating the little yard. Following the first man were two others in long coats. One received a swinging hay-maker from Evans, delivered with every ounce of his hefty frame behind it, while Sedgwick leapt at the second man. There was a deafening explosion and a tongue of flame as the two men came together.

'Able!' yelled Evans, leaping over his victim towards the two bodies on the ground. One picked himself up, while the other continued to lie prone.

'I-I think I'm all right,' said the coxswain, leaning against the wall and shaking his head to clear the ringing from his ears. 'Bastard must have been carrying a shooter on full cock. Is he all right?' Evans dropped down beside the body.

'Out cold,' he pronounced. 'He looks to have cracked his bleeding nut on the stones when you bundled into him. I wonder where the ball went?'

'And the other?' asked Sedgwick.

'He'll soon be fecking trussed up tighter than a Christmas goose,' announced O'Malley, who was sitting on his chest with a knife against his throat, while Trevan used the man's belt and neck cloth to bind his hands and feet.

'This bleeder's got a pistol, too,' said Evans, who was

searching the pockets of the one he had hit.

'Better still, your man here had a flask of fecking grog on him,' said O'Malley, holding his prize aloft in the dying flames from the oil.

'Best be pushing off, lads,' said Trevan. 'That shot'll have every Lobster hereabouts on our trail.'

'But which bleeding way?' wailed Evans. 'I ain't got a clue where the barky lies.'

'That way,' said Sedgwick, pointing towards the alley with the drain. 'Grab Rankin, and follow the ditch. It's sure to flow downhill and fetch up at the sea.'

The open drain proved to be an inspired guide. In the dark of the alleyways, it could be clearly heard (and smelled) running beside the path. When it disappeared for stretches underground, the sailors paused to listen for its gushing and followed that direction until it reappeared. Eventually it was swallowed completely into a culvert, but by then the sailors needed no further guide. They could hear the sound of waves lapping against the shore ahead of them. They had left the residential part of the city behind and walked along the bottom of a dark canyon between lofty warehouses. A keen wind blew in their faces, redolent with wet kelp and sea mud. They soon reached a road that ran alongside the coast. The others waited in the shadows, while Sedgwick went ahead to scout along it. He soon returned.

'Do you want the good tidings or the ill?' he asked.

'Good first, Abel,' said Trevan.

'I knows where to find the barky.'

'Best give us the fecking ill then,' grumbled O'Malley.

'We be a good mile off and the way is thick with folk.'

'How we going to get him past that lot?' asked Evans, jerking a thumb towards Rankin.

'Well, you ain't going to bleeding lump me no more, Sam Evans, if you know what's good for you,' growled a voice behind them. The sailors turned in surprise, to see their charge in a sorry state. His long coat was smeared with mud, and one sleeve had been wrenched free from the rest, leaving a white flash of lining showing like a mouth at the shoulder. His face was caked with dried blood, and more was clotted in his hair, but all trace of confusion had left his dark eyes.

'Come now, Josh,' urged Sedgwick. 'If Sam hadn't done what he did, they'd be stringing you up for murder. Let's get you back to the barky, and let bygones go.'

'An' how you going to bleeding do that, blackamoor?' said Rankin, his arms folded stiffly. The coxswain looked him up and down.

'Can you act pissed?' he asked.

'If I has too,' said Rankin, 'and I don't need you clonking me nut, neither, Evans.'

'Sean, give us that flask you found,' said Sedgwick.

'Aye, a nip of grog will settle everyone's fecking nerves,' said the Irishman as he passed it across. Sedgwick pulled out the cork and poured the contents all over Rankin. A cloud of alcohol fumes, perfumed with herbs, engulfed the group.

'My fecking grog!' protested O'Malley.

'Here, what you bleeding doing?' said the valet.

'Saving your bloody arse,' said Sedgwick. 'Now, let's get under way, and remember, you're pissed.'

The road that ran along the sea wall was wide and well maintained. Even at this hour, returning revellers mingled with those taking the sea air as they strolled along the pavement. Carriages and carts rattled over the cobbles, taking citizens home to bed, or bringing provisions into the city for the morning markets. The sailors kept in the shadow of the buildings that faced the sea, ready to bolt into cover at the first hint of trouble. On the seaward side of the road, upturned boats lay in rows against the sea wall, or were moored in the shallows. In several places earth fortifications had been thrown up, facing the sea, with lines of cannon standing ready. A few hundred yards from the shore was the wall of anchored ships, the lights onboard winking off the dark water. Everywhere there were Danish soldiers, their coats black in the night, in contrast to the startling white of their cross belts. They stood guard over the guns and boats or patrolled the sea wall, and all seemed to eye the sailors with hostility.

'Mice must feel like this, scuttling past a basket of sleeping cats,' muttered Evans, as the sailors made their way along the road.

'Maybe we needs to seem jollier?' whispered Trevan. 'Give us one of your bawdy songs, Sean.'

'I can't,' said the Irishman. 'My tongue's drier than a Turk's sandal.'

'We be a good half way along this here line of ships,' reported Trevan. 'I can see the barky, moored ag'in that big fort over yonder.'

'Just keep going,' ordered Rankin, his head slumped forward, and his arms draped around Trevan and O'Malley's necks. Evans and Sedgwick brought up the rear, the Londoner staring ahead, while Sedgwick looked around him.

'You all right there, Abel?' asked Evans.

'I will be once we're back on board,' said the coxswain. 'I am just having a look at what the Danes is about, since we seem like to be warring with them soon. What do you reckon all them boats are for?'

'Fishing?' suggested his companion.

'No, they be ship's launches and the like for the most part; besides, why would Lobsters be guarding fishing boats?' said Sedgwick. 'I had thought to nick one and row back to the barky in it, but they're watched too tight. Strange they have so many, but I dare say there'll be some reason as I ain't fathomed yet.'

'All right, bleeding Nelson,' said Evans, saluting his companion as they walked. 'What else has your lordship observed?'

'That this southern end of the Danes' line of ships is a deal easier to attack that the northern stretch,' said his friend. He pointed to where the *Griffin* and the French frigate lay beside the Danish citadel. 'Up there you got a fortress with more guns than a first rate, that dirty big battery built on spars on the water, while down this end it be hulks, sixth rates, and only the odd proper ship. That might be worth knowing.'

'I suppose that makes sense,' said the Londoner. 'Given the fleet will be coming from up there.' He waved airily ahead, and then paused to grab his companions arm. 'Thank Christ for that—we're bleeding saved!'

'What?' queried Sedgwick. In response Evans put the circled fingers of one hand into his mouth and blew a piercing wolf-whistle.

'Shhh!' exclaimed O'Malley. 'What the feck are you about!'

'*Griffins* ahoy!' yelled Evans. 'Hibbert there!' The lead figure amongst a crowd that had spilt out of a side street looked around, then raised an arm towards them. He was surrounded by a large mob of sailors, many of them unsteady on their feet.

'Thank Christ for that!' exclaimed Sedgwick. 'Mix in with

our shipmates, lads. I reckon we're going to be all right.'

******

The following day the crew of the *Griffin* laboured to replenish their ship's stores. They were driven on by the officers, who were anxious both that their ship should not appear inefficient under the watchful gaze of the men of the *Liberté*, and to sweat out of the men the excesses of the previous day's run ashore. As evening approached, the frigate was replete once more, and Clay was working at his desk with his clerk, trying to make sense of the receipts in Danish submitted by the Copenhagen naval yard.

'Good to have the frigate full, with a possible war in the offing, Mr Allen,' concluded the captain as he dashed off his signature on the last indent. 'If war should be declared, we shall have to make shift for ourselves.'

'I daresay that is correct, sir,' said the clerk, blotting the entry, then gathering up the paperwork. 'Is war certain then? Only some of the Danish hands are a mite worried. They've been asking whether they will be required to fight or no.'

'In truth I don't know,' said Clay. 'Mr Vansittart and the ambassador have spent most of the day trying to prevent it, but with what result I cannot say.'

'Ah, well, doubtless you shall know presently, sir,' said Allen. 'I reckon I just saw the gentleman seated in the blue cutter what just passed beneath the stern.'

'Was that just now?' said Clay, turning in his chair towards the cabin's window lights. 'That is earlier than I would have expected, so perhaps all proceeds satisfactorily. In any event, you can tell Pedersen and the others that should we find ourselves fighting the Danes, I will see that they are only required to help Mr Corbett with the wounded.'

'Aye, that will be a comfort to them, sir,' said Allen, rising from his place in response to a thunderous knocking at the door. Harte came into the cabin, with a visitor doing his best to push past him.

'Ah, Mr Vansittart,' said Clay. 'Would you care for a little of this excellent coffee? That will be all, thank you, Mr Allen.'

'Coffee!' exclaimed the diplomat. 'I will need something a damned sight stronger than that!'

'Bring some madeira, if you please Harte,' said Clay. 'Now my dear sir, do take a seat and calm yourself, before you become ill. Whatever is the matter?'

Vansittart sat down and thumped the bottom of his walking cane against the deck.

'The impertinence of the man!' he cried, his face bright red. 'Yesterday he keeps me waiting for two whole hours. Today he refused my credentials, because they were not written in French, if you'll credit it! Once we got beyond that farce, would he let me see the Crown Prince? Oh, no! Me, a representative of the king himself! Told me his highness was too busy, which is an absolute lie, and that I would have to treat with him, the rogue!'

'Pray, who are we talking about, sir?' said Clay, bewildered by his guest's fury.

'The Danish Chief Minister, Andreas High-and-Mighty Bernstorff! He ain't even a Dane but a bloody German!' exclaimed Vansittart. 'Topping it the patrician, if you please, though he is no more than the ill-bred son a Saxon tinker! Of course, he's in the pocket of the damned French, which is the real problem.' The diplomat finally slumped back in his chair, breathless.

'So I take it that the negotiations did not proceed well then, sir?' asked Clay.

'Refused every proposal we made,' said the diplomat. 'Paris must have put the fear of God into him. Bill Drummond has never seen Bernstorff show such pluck.'

'That would be Mr William Drummond, our ambassador at the Danish Court?' asked Clay.

'He *was* our ambassador,' said Vansittart. 'But he will be asking for his passport tonight and will return to London to report. Fact is that Bernstorff is prepared to hazard all on us not having the bottom for war. He don't believe we have the nerve for it. It will presently be the turn of Admiral Parker and Lord Nelson to disabuse him of his view.'

'Have we failed altogether then, sir?' said Clay, twisting his glass between his long fingers. 'It is to be war after all.'

'War with the Danes, certainly, but the dashed ball ain't over yet, Captain, only the first dance.' Vansittart drained his glass of madeira and held it out towards Harte. 'You're forgetting the activities of my sadly battered valet.'

'How is he, sir?' asked Clay. 'Still in the sick bay?'

'He will live,' said Vansittart, 'although he was in a sorry state last night. Barely conscious, reeking of drink, and with his nose broke. He says that one of your crew was responsible.'

'The drink was poured over him by my coxswain, sir,' confirmed Clay, 'as a ruse to smuggle him past the soldiers who were patrolling the waterfront. Meanwhile, the most extraordinary rumours are circulating on the lower deck. There is talk of your man attempting to murder a Danish civilian by throttling him with a lanyard of some description. Did he mention that at all?'

'I am not in the habit of heeding idle gossip, Clay,' said Vansittart.

'Nor I, but the particulars seem so strange in this case,

sir,' continued the captain. 'I am used to hearing of fights with fists or cudgels, even knives on occasion, but strangulation? It is the sort of thing one thinks of happening at the court of some Oriental potentate. Not in a tavern brawl!'

The two men looked at each other for a long moment. It was the diplomat who broke the silence first.

'Perhaps we should let that particular hound continue to slumber, what?' he suggested. 'The main thing is that he has returned, with important intelligence for us.' He leant forward and dropped his voice. 'He made visits to several of our key adherents at court. It seems there is precious little support for Bernstorff's pro-French stance, but the Crown Prince is terrified by Russia. So that is where the solution to this sorry mess lies. If we can persuade Tsar Paul to abandon this ridiculous League of Armed Neutrality, then the Danes, Swedes and the rest will follow.'

'I see, sir,' said Clay. 'And how do we do that?'

'Why, we must make haste and proceed to St Petersburg,' said Vansittart. 'Russia is the trunk of this confederation. Hew that down, and all the branches will fall with it.'

CHAPTER 8

AURORA

'Is your ship some cursed prison hulk, where I am to be held until I have served my time, Captain?' demanded Isaiah Hockley, leaning across Clay's desk the following morning.

'No, of course not,' said Clay. 'And for my part, nothing would give me greater pleasure than to be rid of your damned impertinence! Prison hulk, indeed! I see that the unfailing gratitude you pledged when this ship was the agent of your rescue has now worn thin. But pray attend to Captain Holst, here. I have no part in this. It is the authorities in Copenhagen that will not allow you to leave the *Griffin*.'

The Danish naval officer was almost as brilliantly uniformed as during his last visit. Only the red and white ribbon and glittering order were missing.

'I regret the inconvenience to you and your daughter, Mr Hockley,' he said, 'but there is no question of anyone leaving this ship. The city is in uproar! British spies running through our streets, a patrol of agents assaulted in an alleyway, and an attempt made to strangle one of our citizens, all in a single night! The Chief Minister's instructions permit no exceptions.'

'You're quite certain that these sailors weren't from the *Liberté*, captain?' offered Vansittart. 'The damned Frogs will try anything to stir up ill feelings between those who should be friends, don't you know?'

'*Quite* sure,' said Holst. 'It is a group of five British sailors that are sought for in connection with these matters. They should be easy to trace. One is described as exceptionally tall and strong, and another is a negro. Does anyone from this ship match that description?'

'It could be any number of my men, I am afraid, Captain,' said Clay, his face a mask.

'How peculiar,' remarked Holst. 'A ship entirely crewed by blackamoors and giants. Very well, until they are found and handed over to the authorities, no one will be allowed to come ashore.'

'But... but my daughter and I must return home,' pleaded Hockley. 'It is imperative that we leave this ship! We took no part in the events of last night.'

'Imperative perhaps, but also impossible,' said the Danish officer. 'There can be no exceptions, sir.'

'As it happens, this ship will be departing Copenhagen in the next hour, Captain Holst,' said Clay. 'I was going to request a pilot, unless you have decided to replace the navigation markers?'

'I am sure that a pilot would be in order, sir,' said the Dane. 'I will have one sent across as soon as we have concluded here. I imagine that you will be returning home, via the Sound?'

'Not at all, we shall be heading east.'

'Further east!' groaned Hockley, sitting down and holding his head in his hands. 'Within the hour!'

'I am sure you know your business, Captain, but I must warn you that the sea in the eastern Baltic will only just be clearing of ice,' said Holst. 'Most of the coasts and ports there will be frozen for some weeks yet.'

'Nevertheless, that is where we must go,' said Clay. 'I also wish to remind you that as Copenhagen is still a neutral port, the rules of war do not permit you to allow hostile ships to depart within a day of each other.' Clay pulled out his watch, and flipped open the cover. 'If we sail a little after six bells this morning, can you assure me that the *Liberté* will be prevented from following us before, let us say, eleven tomorrow morning?'

'I will gladly pass on your request, Captain,' said the Dane, bringing his heels together. Clay looked sharply at him.

'I may have phrased it as a request, but surely there can be no question of Denmark not complying?' he queried. 'Or was I wrong in assuming Copenhagen to be still neutral?'

'It is, for now,' said Holst, extending his hand out to Clay. 'Have a prosperous voyage, Captain.'

'What am I to do?' said Hockley, as Harte escorted the Danish captain out of the cabin.

'What are you to do?' repeated Clay, rounding on the merchant. 'I daresay you will continue to enjoy the considerable hospitality that has been extended to you by the officers of this ship. I have never heard of such a damnable want of gratitude!'

'But my daughter, and Mr Preston...,' began the merchant captain.

'Your daughter will doubtless continue to be treated with the utmost courtesy,' said Clay. 'As for Mr Preston, he is a gentleman whose conduct has been beyond reproach, unless you have some accusation you wish to make?'

'I have no specific charge,' said Hockley. 'My observations were more of a general—'

'So nothing beyond a general dislike then?' said Clay. 'If you find the society of my officers so repellent, then perhaps I should have you set adrift as soon as we are clear of Danish waters, by God! Now get out!'

'New money,' observed Vansittart, as Hockley left the cabin. 'They may be able to ape the airs and graces of a gentleman for a while, but in time their behaviour betrays their origins. Anyway, now that dreadful man has left us in peace, perhaps we can converse with some degree of freedom. What was all that bandying with Captain Holst over the *Liberté*?'

'She is a swifter ship than the *Griffin*, sir,' said Clay. 'I wanted to secure a day's head start to prevent her from interfering with our mission. With time against us, the last thing we need is a battle with her. Do you believe the Danes will prevent her sailing?'

'Without me or Drummond here to watch them?' snorted the diplomat. 'I trust Bernstorff to defy Paris as I would an adder-fanged, as the Bard would have said.'

'In which case, we may well encounter them on the way, sir,' said Clay.

'Would you have the beating of her if you had to?' asked the diplomat.

'In my old ship I would say yes, for certain, even though the French have much the bigger frigate, sir,' said Clay. 'But the *Titan*'s people were all veterans who knew their duty well. A third of these *Griffins* have yet to taste a proper battle.'

'So the *Liberté* could win?'

'Nothing is certain in a sea fight, sir,' said Clay. 'And much depends on how you measure victory. She has only to knocked us about sufficiently to prevent our reaching Russia. We are very much on our own, now. If she brought down one of my masts, the nearest friendly port where I might find a replacement is back in England.'

'I suppose that is so,' mused Vansittart. 'How long will it take us to reach St Petersburg?'

'With a fair wind, and no ice, five days, sir,' said Clay. 'But the wind is more certain than the lack of ice. Holst was right, the open sea may be free here, but it will be very different farther east.'

'Their fleet in Reval will still be frozen solid for some weeks, but the Russians do try and keep some sort of channel open to their capital,' said Vansittart. 'It's quite a sight how they achieve it, with dashed great fires set on the ice, and no end of serfs all sawing blocks of the stuff to be dragged away.' There was a knock at the door, and a pleasant-faced midshipman entered in response to Clay's call.

'Yes, Mr Russell?'

'Mr Taylor's compliments, and a pilot has just now come on board, sir,' he said.

'Thank you,' said his captain, rising to his feet and taking his hat from Harte. 'Will you kindly ask Mr Taylor to summon all hands and prepare to weigh anchor. I will be on deck directly.'

******

The last of the clinging grey mud of Copenhagen had been scrubbed from the frigate's bower anchors, and the smell of the city had been left far behind them. The frigate sailed into a wide expanse of clean, cold sea, driven by a breeze blowing from the southwest. She could have been sailing across an ocean at the dawn of time, so empty was the sea around her. The air was cool, but not as chill as it had been, with perhaps a hint of spring to follow the long northern winter. Away to the south was the coast of Prussia: low, flat marshes and empty beaches, still gripped by the snow of winter. To the west was Sweden, a rockier shore of grey stone and black forest, its harbours choked with ice. The frigate made a long, sweeping turn towards the north, shaking out her topgallants as she did so amid a thunder of flapping canvas. Now she sped on, her big sails bulging scoops of white as they caught the wind, and the green sea foamed in a line behind her.

Lieutenant Edward Preston stepped out of the wardroom, with his pea jacket buttoned close and the cuff of his empty sleeve pushed deep into his left hand pocket. He climbed up to the main deck and returned the salute of the marine who stood guard beside the door to the captain's quarters. Then he set off up the next ladder way, which opened onto the quarterdeck. As his head cleared the level of the deck, the breeze pulled at his hat, forcing him to pause and let go of the rope handrail so he could jam it down a little more firmly. As he did so, he saw Sarah Hockley stood by the rail, her long mane of chestnut hair flying and whipping in the breeze and a look of delight on her face.

Almost before he realised what he was doing, he had turned around and run back down the steps, returning to the gloomy space beneath the quarterdeck. The marine guard gave him a quizzical look, unsure whether he should salute the officer afresh, having barely completed his previous one. Preston walked across the deck, then turned on his heel and walked in the opposite direction. In front of him was one of the frigate's main battery of bulky eighteen-pounder cannons. Aware of the marine's eyes on him, he made himself look over the guns breeching while he gathered himself. Out of the corner of his eye he could see two startled crewmen, who had been deep in conversation nearby, but now stood frozen in the presence of an officer.

Come on, he urged himself, she is only a girl! Why shouldn't he share the quarterdeck rail with her? Hadn't his friend Tom Macpherson not urged him to meet with her, and declare how he felt? Perhaps the crowded deck of the *Griffin* in the middle of the day was not the place for such a sensitive topic, but he could at least converse with her. He slapped the cold metal of the cannon with decision, and turned back towards the ladder once more. Through the slats he saw the bandy, stockinged calves and heavy buckled shoes of Isaiah Hockley climbing purposefully up to the quarterdeck. A less pleasant memory came back to him. Hockley, his face pinched with fury as he bellowed "The man she weds will be whole, not some cursed cripple!" He paused a moment longer, and then took the ladder that led back to the lower deck, and the sanctuary of the wardroom.

'He must have heard us, to be suddenly poking around here,' whispered William Ludlow, as he peered after the lieutenant's disappearing back. He was the smaller of the two men disturbed by Preston, a lithe figure, with gaunt features framed by bushy dark sideburns. Although dressed as a sailor, his lack of pigtail marked him as a recent recruit.

'No need to bleeding worry about that grunter, Bill,' said Rankin, the second person present. 'He were just looking over that there gun.'

'Pretending to, if you ask me, Josh,' said his companion. 'There was a deal too much staring into space, an' muttering to his self, for my liking. Proper spooked me, that did.'

'Well, he ain't here no more,' said Rankin. 'So do you want to earn yourself a bit of chink, or no?'

'Always up for that, Josh, as you'll recall,' smirked the landsman. 'What do you need fixing?'

'Not what, but who. Sam Evans is who needs fixing,' said the valet, his face hardening.

'Easy there, Josh,' urged Ludlow. 'You've picked the wrong bloke to mill with, mate. I ain't shy, but have you seen the bleeding size of him? Goliath ain't in it! Why's it got to be him?'

'Look at my face,' said his fellow Londoner. Even in the half light the bruising looked spectacular. 'Evans did this, and no one lays a bleeding finger on Josh Rankin and walks away.'

'But there you go, mate,' whined his companion. 'If he did that to you, what hope has I got?'

'I ain't expecting you to fight him,' said Rankin. 'Just a little thieving, like back in the old days. Pinch me some'it small, but worth a bob or two from a shipmate. A ticker from one of the Grunters, maybe? I'll stash it in Evan's dunnage, and then we shop the bastard to the traps.'

'I ain't sure about this at all,' said Ludlow. 'Folk don't take kindly to a cutpurse on a ship, an' lower deck justice can be proper savage.'

'Better and better,' smiled Rankin. 'So Evans might wind up getting a thrashing from his mates. I can't wait to see that.'

'But what if I gets caught?' hissed the landsman. 'Look around you! The barky's too tight for such stuff. We couldn't even have our bleeding chat, without some Grunter showing up.'

'You left your bleeding balls on the quayside, when you

came aboard?' demanded the valet. 'It were pretty close in Seven Dials. I don't recall that holding you back any. Besides, it'll be Evans as will be getting fingered.'

'I am sorry, Josh, but you got the wrong bloke,' said Ludlow. 'It ain't just Evans. He's a dumb ox, but he's got mates as is proper deep. That Able Sedgwick, for a start. The bloke's writ books an' the like. There ain't enough chink in the Tower of London as would make me run a risk like that.'

The sailor started to turn away, but Rankin grabbed a fistful of shirt and pulled the landsman's face close to his.

'That depends on what price you put on your fucking life, William Ludlow,' he snarled. 'You weren't just a snivelling little cutpurse, back in the day. There were no end of ill deeds you done for me, weren't there? How do you suppose your new friends will feel when they find they're sharing their mess with a murderer?'

'That were back then, Josh,' said Ludlow. 'I ain't like that no more. I left all that behind when I joined.' Rankin patted him on his cheek and then let his shirt go.

'I am your past, old cock, and I've just bleeding caught up with you.'

******

It was the knocking that first woke Preston. He emerged from a sleep filled with pleasant images of Sarah Hockley, and sat up in his cot. The cabin was dark and close, but light from the lantern in the wardroom shone through the slats in the door, illuminating the interior with lines of orange and black. The gentle sway of the ship made them flow across the bulkhead, like the pelt of a running tiger.

'Whose there?' he asked, but there was no reply. Then the sound was repeated, more of a muffled thump this time and coming from the curved outer wall of the cabin. He pulled himself out of bed, and placed his hand against the inner skin of the ship. The officers' cabins were down at the waterline, and he was used to hearing the gurgling rush of the frigate's wake surging past, but this noise was quite new to him. Through ten solid inches of oak he felt the tremble of another blow, accompanied by a grinding sound.

'What the devil can it be,' mused the lieutenant, as he reached for his britches and began to pull them on.

'Edward, are you awake?' whispered Tom Macpherson from beyond the door. The shadow of the marine showed against the slats.

'Only just,' replied Preston. 'I was woken by this peculiar banging against the hull.'

'Aye, it started a while back,' said the Scot. 'At first I thought it was in my head, occasioned by sharing a dram too many of Danish aquavit with Faulkner and Corbett last night. Surely the carpenter will not be working on the hull at this ungodly hour?'

'It is no shipboard sound that I am acquainted with,' said Preston, struggling with his clothes. 'I shall come as soon as I am able to dress, although it might be quicker if I had my servant to assist me.'

'Och, let the wee laddie sleep,' said Macpherson. 'Would you find it insupportable for me to assist you?' Preston was silent for a moment, weighing the humiliation of being dressed by a brother officer against a lengthy bout of one-handed fumbling with his clothes. Another bang, sharper this time, sounded behind him.

'Much obliged to you, Tom,' he said, pulling open the door. The marine was fully dressed, and stepped into the cabin. He took the britches from Preston's unresisting hands and dropped to his knees to hold them out.

'Tis no matter, Edward,' he said. 'I have served my father in the office of a servant enough times, when the whiskey has unmanned him. Now let's get that nightshirt off you.'

The young lieutenant turned his slim torso away from his friend, unwilling for him to see the hump of flesh lined with puckered scars that covered where his arm had once been. Only when his shirt was being buttoned up for him did he relax.

'I believe we might dispense with a weskit and neck cloth at this hour,' said the marine, 'but you'll be wanting your warmest coat and gloves.'

Once the lieutenant was dressed, the two men hurried through the sleeping ship and up onto the quarterdeck. Outside it was bitterly cold but calm with a gentle breeze pushing the frigate forwards. Overhead the night sky was a dark bowl, studded with an unimaginable number of stars. Blake, who was the officer of the watch, looked around from his place by the wheel.

'My, but my watch is getting popular,' he exclaimed, indicating all the shadowy figures that were lining the rails. 'And all come to admire a fine night, with a little ice in the water.' Preston and Macpherson found an unoccupied stretch of rail and looked out over the calm sea. For the most part it was a mirror for the heavens, a dark, endless carpet studded with reflected points of light. But dotted over the surface were numberless grey lumps that barely showed above the water. Most were small, but one piece of ice the size of a large barrel drifted close to the hull just beneath them. As the frigate hissed onwards it struck with a thump that sent ripples across the water, and set the stars to dancing. The ice slowly turned through the water, grating and knocking against the hull until it was lost behind them.

'Ice!' exclaimed Macpherson. 'Is that all that has occasioned such a disturbance?'

'I will have you know it can be very hazardous, Mr Macpherson,' said Taylor, one of the figures standing near them. 'A floating ice mountain can easily sink a ship, although I will own that this broken stuff should present little difficulty to a vessel built to resist cannon balls.'

'Aye aye, sir,' said the marine. 'I had not meant to make light of them, but down below the sound was distinctly menacing. I had envisaged Krakens rising from the deep to assault us, at the very least.'

'I am sorry to see you disappointed, Tom,' said Clay, who stood next to Taylor. 'For my part I shall leave you seeking your sea monsters and turn in. Keep our speed under two knots, if you please, Mr Blake. They will do little harm struck at that speed. I am to be called if the floes become any larger or more numerous.'

'Aye aye, sir,' said Blake, touching his hat to his captain. Others began to drift away, leaving Preston and Macpherson alone under the stars. After a while the older man began to speak.

'I hope you will not think me presumptuous, but I could not but note the reluctance you had to let your wound be viewed,' he said.

'It is a particularly ugly wound,' explained Preston, after a while.

'Aye, as are they all,' said the marine. 'But a wound suffered for your king is not without honour.'

'As everyone seems anxious to tell me,' said the Yorkshireman. 'But in my heart I sometimes wish that I had either been spared altogether or been slain outright. Life might be simpler now.'

Macpherson looked at his young companion with concern. 'Edward, laddie, you cannot truly mean that?'

'Perhaps not when I am sharing a fine night like this with you, Tom,' said Preston, 'but in darker times I come to think on it.' The ship sailed on, and another floe drifted close beneath them, but failed to make contact with the side.

'Do you remember when I was shot, back in ninety-six?' said Macpherson. 'Attacking that damned fort in St Lucia?'

'The bullet stopped by Miss Clay's book,' said Preston. 'How could I forget? It was the talk of the fleet.'

'Aye, it was much discussed, but that miraculous escape masked the truth,' said Macpherson. 'All my peers thought it a splendid matter, and everyone seemed much more concerned to view the wee book with the ball lodged within its pages, than to consider how I might be. For I was shot that day! I saw that damned French soldier aim his piece and pull the trigger. I was struck the hardest blow I have ever endured, and fell to the ground insensible.'

'You had a brace of bust ribs and a bruise the size of a dinner plate, as I recall.'

'That's right,' said Macpherson. 'And night terrors that came to haunt me long after that had faded away. When I next had to face the French, I found myself shamefully un-manned by what had passed. For a while, I, too, thought that it might have been simpler if I had not had the damned book upon me that day.'

'I recall that tremble in your hand, back aboard the old *Titan,* when we fought that Frenchman off the coast of Ireland,' said Preston. 'But you faced down your fears, as I recall.'

'I did, and I would council you to confront your own, Edward,' said the marine. 'You can be their master or their slave. I would recommend the former.'

Preston stared out over the dark sea in the starlight for a moment.

'So what should I do?' he asked.

'Be proud of your wound, knock down any fellow who speaks ill of it, and tell Miss Hockley how you feel towards her, before the poor lassie gives up on you entirely,' said the Scot. 'That should answer.'

'Are you now taking the office of my confidant, Tom?'

'Sooner that then your valet,' said Macpherson, turning his friend towards him. 'I fear I have buttoned your coat up very ill.' He corrected the misaligned buttons, his fingers quick and nimble.

'Much better,' laughed Preston, 'although being a valet doesn't seem a position requiring much in the way of deference or domestic skill, to judge from Mr Vansittart's man.'

'Aye, you have the truth of it there,' said Macpherson. 'I believe friend Rankin's abilities lie in a quite different direction, if you follow me.'

'That foray of his into Danish territory?'

'That, and these rumours of strangling a man with a silk cord,' said the marine. 'It put me in mind of a story told by a cousin who served in a John Company regiment out in Madras. They have some manner of Indian highwaymen in those parts, named Thugs, who murder their victim in just such a fashion.'

'Why do you suppose that a diplomat of the crown should travel accompanied by such a fellow?' asked Preston.

'Curious, is it not?' mused Macpherson, stroking at one of his sideburns.

******

148

The Scotsman had returned to the warmth of below decks, along with most of those who had come to investigate the strange knocking. The frigate had shouldered her way past the last of the ice, and was now sailing through the night across an endless expanse of dark water. Preston listened to the gentle creak of the rigging as the frigate's masts swayed across the vault of stars, and felt the whisper of the breeze against his face. Both seemed to urge him to sleep, but the young officer knew that he had too many thoughts whirling through his head for that.

He turned from the rail, and looked across the deck of the frigate. There was no moon yet, but the stars were clear above and the ship generated her own light. Grids of squares were projected onto the sails from the lamps hung beneath the gratings on the main deck. The faces of Blake, the midshipman of the watch, and the quartermaster at the wheel were lit by the oil lamps in the compass binnacle. The afterguard sat in shadowy groups around the quarterdeck, marked by their quiet talk, and shifting of position. The lights that hung beneath the quarterdeck and forecastle showed the rest of the watch at their posts. Only one figure seemed out of place — a slender looking seaman hunched in a coat several sizes too large, who was barely visible in the shadows behind the last carronade on the starboard side. He felt drawn towards the sailor, hoping it might be the person he had been thinking of.

'Good evening, Mr Preston,' said the figure, the warm voice accompanied by a cloud of breath. 'I had hoped to pass unnoticed here, and so enjoy a little more of this beautiful night.'

'Would my presence be unwelcome then?' said the young

lieutenant, hesitating to come closer. A trace of white glimmered in the night.

'By no means,' she said, making space for him at the rail.

'You need not fear my intervention, Miss Hockley' said Preston, taking a place beside her.

'True, but then you are not my father, come to fuss over my getting a chill.'

'That is so,' he said. 'Do you find his consideration for your welfare trying?'

Sarah Hockley let out a long sigh. 'He means well, and could not be more attentive, but sometimes I do find it confining,' she said. 'Take our voyage now, into the unknown. To my way of thinking it is an exhilarating adventure, but father only frets about how we shall get home, and how I might be ravaged by one of the young men aboard.' Preston laughed at this, a little abruptly. As it happened, ravishing Miss Hockley had featured in several of his more lurid dreams.

'Perhaps if I had been raised at home, in a more conventional manner, I could have been content with such attention,' she continued. 'But my mother passed away when I was but a child, and my father took me to sea with him to supervise my education. I fear he was not aware what an exhilarating schooling it would prove. Climbing the rigging; yarning with the hands; learning to hand, reef and steer; visiting all manner of foreign ports. I am quite the Amazon, you know, Mr Preston. Do take care!'

'It may be too late for that, Miss Hockley,' he said quietly.

She looked at him quizzically. 'And yet I feel that you have been avoiding me of late, Mr Preston,' she said.

'In truth, I probably have,' he said. 'Your father made his disapproval of me very plain.'

'He disapproves of most of the men who wish to befriend me.'

'Yet he also told me that I might be mistaking a women's sympathy at my condition for something more than it was,' he said. 'That you might, in reality, be repelled by my injury.'

She turned to look into his sad, dark eyes, and saw the longing in them. Then she leant towards him and touched his left shoulder, her hand gentle at first as it felt through the heavy broadcloth of his coat. He felt tears start in his eyes as she cupped her hand around the stump.

'Miss Hockley...' he began.

'Shhh...' she urged, 'call me Sarah, please.' He found that he had slipped his good arm around her waist and she drew close to him. Her face was just beneath his now, the eyes smiling, her lips slightly parted. He bent forward and gently kissed her.

******

The lovers were so wrapped in each other that the first flicker of green in the sky passed unnoticed by them. Together they had unbuttoned the front of Preston's coat, and she had pulled it around her to make a tent of shared warmth in the chill night. It was only the exclamations of surprise from those around them on the quarterdeck that alerted them to what was happening. Preston noticed with a smile that the afterguard had all moved themselves to the opposite side of the deck from him and Sarah, and that Lieutenant Blake stood with his back solidly positioned towards the couple. Then he gasped aloud too.

In utter silence a curtain of green had dropped across the sky, bathing the ship in a venomous light. The lower edge was sharp, coiling over and over like tumbling silk, while the highest part faded into crimson before vanishing altogether.

It hung like a translucent sheet, gossamer thin so that the stars behind it were still visible.

'What in the name of all creation...' breathed Sarah Hockley, standing close within the arc of his arm.

'Aurora,' he whispered by her ear. ''T'is the fabled Northern Lights come to bless our understanding.' She squeezed his arm, and then settled back against his chest. He drew the flap of his coat across her, and with the perfume of her filling his nostrils he watched as the first wash of light began to fade. Almost immediately a fresh swath of bright green appeared, stretched across a new part of the sky, to be greeted by murmurs of appreciation from the watching sailors. Now the light seemed shaped into a distant land of hills and vales, green and sunlit, glimpsed through a crack in the heavens.

High above the deck sat Harry Perkins, perched on the delicate royal yard with one hand gripping the topgallant mast beside him, and his feet dangling over the dark void. Like most of the watch he had been watching Preston and the girl. The young lieutenant was a popular officer with the men, and his terrible injury had caused much distress to his shipmates. But now he was mesmerised by the aurora, which he had the best view of in the ship. At first the lookout had been terrified. Nothing in his early life as a house slave in Jamaica, nor his time in the navy after he had escaped, had prepared him for for what he was seeing. He had cowered down against the mast when the poisonous green light had first appeared. Dim memories filled his head of the tales his African grandmother had told him, of evil spirits and the underworld. But slowly he had relaxed, reassured by the obvious awe and pleasure in the voices that drifted up from the deck below. Then he had sat back and enjoyed the extraordinary display in the sky.

Small wonder, then, that Perkin's duty as lookout quite left him for a while, and he failed to see the tiny square of grey that stood just proud of the horizon for fully half an hour. Had he seen it, he might have puzzled over it, until he noticed how the light of the aurora played across the sails around him, illuminating them, for once, in the dark night. Then he would certainly have realised that he was seeing the fore royal sail of a ship that quietly followed in the wake of the *Griffin* across this northern sea.

CHAPTER 9

ICE

As the *Griffin* entered the Gulf of Finland her pace slowed appreciably. The nights were still cold, and full of eerie spectral light, but the days were starting to grow at little warmer as the short northern spring developed. The green sea continued to be dotted with clumps of ice. Most were small enough to be pushed aside by the solid bow of the advancing ship, but others were bigger. The experienced whalers amongst the crew warned that when the part above the water was the size of the frigate's longboat, they were best avoided, for the part beneath the sea was always very much larger. Extra lookouts fed a constant stream of warnings back to the harassed officer of the watch as the frigate picked her way eastward.

'Deck ho!' yelled the sailor at the masthead. 'Fleet at anchor, two points off the starboard bow!'

'That will be Reval, sir,' said Armstrong. 'The Russians always moor up for the winter there. They move back to Kronstadt when the ice permits.'

Clay turned his telescope towards the south. A low island,

heavily forested with dark firs and rimmed with ice, blocked his view at first, but as the frigate sailed on he could see into the heart of a bay still choked with ice. At the southern edge were the hulls and lower masts of warships, while a little farther along the ice-bound shore he could see trails of rising smoke to mark where the city lay.

'Do the ships not suffer from the freezing of the sea about them?' he asked.

'I daresay they do in part,' conceded Armstrong. 'But when the frost becomes cruel they force no end of serfs out onto the ice to cut and clear it away.'

Clay turned his attention to Reval next. The city was surrounded by a stone wall with plentiful round towers, each topped by a witches' hat of red tiles. Behind the wall he could see lines of roofs, the grey bulk of a castle off to one side, and another group of smaller ships locked into the ice inside a breakwater. The sun glinted off something as he swept the port, and he retraced a little. A cluster of gilded domes, all shaped like onions topped the largest building. Clay smiled to himself at the exotic look of the cathedral. You're a long way from home now, Alex, he thought to himself as he closed his telescope.

'Mr Russell and Mr Todd, a moment, if you please,' he said, calling over the two midshipmen of the watch. Although they were dressed in matching uniforms, any similarity between the officers ended there. Russell was almost a man now, and he towered over the slight figure of his fourteen-year-old colleague, whose voice had yet to break.

'I have a task of high importance for you to perform,' he said gravely. 'We may presently be at war with Russia, and to that end I need to inform Admirals Parker and Nelson the exact force that may oppose them. Kindly take spy glasses and notebooks to the mastheads, and provide me with a detailed reconnaissance of the enemy fleet.'

'Aye aye, sir,' came the midshipmen's replies, a good octave apart, and they hurried away to perform their duty.

'What is it we are meant to do exactly, Rusty?' whispered Todd to his colleague.

'Pipe wants us to count the warships,' said Russell, as they reached the main mast shrouds.

'So why couldn't he just have said that, then?' asked the youngster, as they started to climb, 'Instead of all that guff about admirals and the like.'

'How long do you suppose it will be before the Russian fleet is able to sail, Mr Armstrong,' asked Clay. The American sailing master lowered his own telescope and considered matters.

'According to the sailing directions, the bay should clear of ice within two weeks, sir,' he said. Taylor, who was standing close by and also observing the fleet, snorted at this.

'Knowing the Russians, it will take them a few weeks more than that to raise a sail,' he offered. 'The officers will be carousing on their estates for a good while yet. I can't see that a single topmast has been set up, nor any yards crossed in the whole of their fleet, the lubbers.'

'So, they are no concern of ours on this trip, Mr Taylor,' concluded his captain.

'Not in my experience, sir.'

'Would you please excuse me, but I fancy it is close to noon,' said Armstrong. 'I know we are just off Reval, but my chart is an indifferent Swedish one. The entrance to the Gulf of Finland was set down very ill. With a fine sun like this to shoot, I should like to check our position.'

'Do carry on, I pray,' said Clay. Armstrong touched his

hat and went to pull his sextant from its place by the wheel. Then he stood behind the ship's compass rose to check if the sun was due south of the *Griffin*.

'Another few minutes yet,' he muttered, before turning to his master's mate. 'Mr Holden, would you oblige me and go and collect the boxed chronometer? I left it with the captain's clerk.'

'What orders, sir?' Taylor asked his captain.

'Once the young gentlemen are able to report their observations, I shall press on to St Petersburg,' said Clay. 'It can't be beyond a couple of days from here.'

'Will we be able to close with the shore,' asked Taylor, 'or will it be frozen solid like the Reval?'

'Mr Vansittart tells me the Russians maintain a clear channel through much of the winter,' said Clay.

'If they have made it wide enough,' observed Taylor.

'What is that young fool about?' said Clay, who had looked aloft to see how the midshipmen were doing. 'Mr Todd has his glass focused in quite the wrong direction.' Before Taylor could reply, a bellow of outrage sounded from beside the wheel.

'Gone, Mr Holden!' exclaimed Armstrong. 'How can a marine chronometer have gone?'

'Mr Allen says he hasn't seen it since first light, sir,' reported the master's mate. 'He says as how he thought you must have taken it back.'

'What seems to be amiss, Mr Armstrong?' asked Clay.

'The new chronometer, sir,' said the American. 'It seems to have been misplaced. It cost the best part of sixty guineas!'

'The latest model, too,' commented the first lieutenant. 'I trust it has not been stolen. It will be worth five times that price smuggled ashore in Russia.'

'Let us not talk of thieving yet,' said Clay. 'Not before a proper search has been made. It is much too large an item to simply vanish.'

'Aye aye, sir,' said Armstrong. 'If you will excuse me, I will go and look for it now.'

'Pray do so, Jacob,' said his captain. 'Ah, here come the young gentlemen. What have you to report?'

Russell pulled out his notebook and turned to the right page with the help of a wetted finger. 'We counted twenty ships of the line, sir,' he began. 'All two-deckers. Six looked to be smaller than the others. We thought they might be fifty gunners. Also a dozen single decked ships, sloops and frigates for the most part. Nothing appears ready to sail.'

'Thank you, Mr Russell,' said Clay. 'And what was of such interest to you, Mr Todd, away to the west?' The boy shuffled his feet a little and looked up at his larger companion.

'Well, sir, Rusty — I mean Mr Russell — couldn't see it, but I thought I saw a masthead, just proud of the horizon.'

'A masthead you say?' said Clay. 'Did the lookout see it?'

'No, sir,' said Todd looking down. 'Only me.' His captain regarded him for a moment.

'You did quite right to speak of it, Mr Todd,' he said. 'Always report truthfully on what you observe at sea, whether others are in accord or not. Now, do you suppose if you returned aloft with Mr Taylor here, and my best glass, you could show him in which direction you saw it?' The boy nodded.

'Aye aye, sir,' said the midshipman.

'You reply "yes, sir" to a question,' said Taylor, not unkindly, 'and "aye, aye" for an order.'

'Away with you then,' ordered Clay. 'I will slow the ship a little, to see if we can raise this masthead of yours once more.'

'Aye aye, sir.'

******

As the day wore on thin trails of cloud, high and wispy at first, but building steadily began to mask the Spring sun, until the frigate was sailing beneath a ceiling of grey. Deprived of its feeble warmth, the temperature fell steadily, conjuring trailing mist from the chill water. Fingers of white swirled between the floes of ice which dotted the sea around them. The *Griffin* sailed onwards, at times looking like a ghost-ship with her hull wreathed in tendrils of fog. The sun set at last, fiery red amongst the cloud, and the light faded steadily from the sky.

'It will be a black night, gentlemen,' said Clay to the officers grouped around him in the pale light from the ship's binnacle, 'with none of the aurora that Mr Preston and Miss Hockley seem to find so diverting.' There were several chuckles in the gloom, and Macpherson gave his young friend a gentle nudge.

'Perfect conditions for what we are about,' continued the captain. 'The *Liberté*, for I am quite certain it is she, is upon our coat tails. I don't doubt she has been there since we left Denmark. She has been wary, keeping out of sight for the most part, and closing on occasion to raise her lookout proud of the horizon to observe our progress. If Mr Todd did not have keen eyes, she might have remained undetected altogether. I daresay that she knows the import of our mission, and will stop us if she can.'

'Let them but try, sir,' growled Macpherson. The other officers muttered their agreement.

'Regrettably, more is at stake than just our ship, Tom,' cautioned his captain. 'In a stand-up fight we might emerge victorious, and yet still be so wounded aloft as to be of little further use to Mr Vansittart. Remember we are in hostile waters and far from any aid.'

'What do you believe we should do?' asked Taylor.

'Arrange a little ambush for the French,' said Clay. 'The enemy will have marked our speed and course, and we have not varied from it all day to make sure that he does. As soon as it is wholly dark, we shall clear for action, douse every light aboard, and hold our position. With no sail showing, and no wake to mark us by, it would be strange if we could not deliver some lusty blows before the French have left their hammocks. How are the gun crews, Mr Blake?'

'Tolerable, sir,' said the ship's second lieutenant. 'With so many new recruits, we have yet to reach the three broadsides in two minutes that the old *Titan* could fire, but I have worked the hands hard in training. We shall certainly not be found wanting.'

'Very good. Any further questions?' asked Clay.

'How will we guarantee the safety of Miss Hockley... and the other civilians onboard, sir?' asked Preston.

'Perhaps you would be good enough to escort Miss Hockley down to the cockpit before attending to your duties,' said his captain. 'Along with her father and Mr Vansittart, of course. They can assist Mr Corbett with the wounded while we are in action. Any more questions?' Clay looked around the group. 'Very well, let us precede, gentlemen. Have the ship cleared for action. We will douse all lights and haul our wind at two bells. Good luck to you all, and damnation to the French.'

Hands were shook across the binnacle and most of the officers hurried away. A few minutes later the rattle of a drum roared out on the main deck, followed by the sound of the watch below hurrying to their stations. Down in the wardroom the officers were making their own preparations.

'My pistol!' demanded Macpherson towards an open door, as he buckled his sword around his waist.

'Just checking the priming, sir,' reported his servant from within his cabin.

'Make haste, now,' said the marine. He slipped his hand into the basket guard of his claymore, reassured by the familiar touch of the hilt as it settled in his hand. Then he slid the blade out a few inches to check it was free.

'Do you not find that old sword a trifle long for use on a ship, Tom?' asked Armstrong, as he buckled on his own weapon. Macpherson accepted the proffered pistol from his servant and pushed it into the crimson sash around his waist before replying.

'On occasion,' conceded the Scot. 'But I have never found its equal for sharpness. My grandfather used to say that it was made from Toledo steel, recovered from the wreck of a Spanish galleon that foundered on the coast.'

'May it keep you safe, brother,' said Blake, shaking the marine's hand. 'Now, I must go and see to my guns.'

The second lieutenant left the wardroom and stepped out onto a deserted lower deck. Hammocks hung in rows, abandoned by their occupants. Beneath his feet he could hear the sound of sea chests being dragged across the planking in the cockpit to form an operating table for the surgeon.

'Precisely *how* long will I be obliged to spend down here, young man?' came the whine of Vansittart's voice from the deck below. 'The headroom in my cabin was challenging enough, but this is preposterous!' Blake smiled to himself at the thought of the elegant politician's discomfort, then he ran up the ladder way and out onto the main deck.

'Mind yer back, sir!' warned a voice from just behind him. He turned to see a portion of Clay's dinning room table coming towards him. The bulkheads that made up the captain's suite of cabins had vanished altogether, leaving the gun deck as one long continuous space, crowded with people.

Gun crews clustered around each of the frigate's huge eighteen-pounders, checking over equipment, rigging gun tackles, or winding their neck cloths into bandanas over their ears against the roar of sound that was to come. Sailors rushed to and fro, casting sand on the deck to give the bare-footed crews better grip, or bringing buckets of ice-cold seawater from the pumps for each cannon. Other figures were motionless, like the marines who stood guard over each hatchway, to prevent anyone fleeing for the safety of the hold. Blake walked to his usual place in the centre of the deck, just behind the main mast, where he could see the whole space. To someone unfamiliar with his world, the deck seemed in chaos, but he could see the underlying order that was there. A few moments later the swirling movement settled into a familiar pattern.

'Mr Todd,' he said to the midshipman beside him, once all was as it should be. 'Give my compliments to Mr Taylor, and would you tell him that the guns are now ready for action.'

'Aye aye, sir,' squeaked the boy, excitement glittering in his eyes.

'Remember to move at the pace becoming of a king's officer,' he added, as Todd made to sprint away. 'There is yet time.'

The youngster disappeared, only a little more slowly than he had first intended. Blake stood stiff and upright, rocking to the gentle motion of the frigate, aware that the eyes of many would be on him. His mind drifted a little, back to the last time he had been in action at night. The image of Preston came to him, pale and unconscious as he lay in the crowded sickbay of the *Titan*, his stump a mass off bandages, black with congealed blood. He opened his eyes wide in horror. Get a grip, man, he urged himself as he forced his face back into the stern calm required of him.

'Mr Taylor thanks you for your message, and would you kindly run out the guns on the larboard side, and then mask the battle lanterns,' said the midshipman, appearing beside him once more.

'Thank you, Mr Todd,' said Blake, grateful for something to do. He looked over the expectant faces turned towards him.

'Larboards!' he ordered. 'Up ports!' All along one side of the ship a row of squares appeared, opening onto dark water laced with sea mist. Cold air flowed in, displacing the warm fug of the deck. He waited for all to be still once more.

'Larboards, run out the guns!'

With a chorus of grunts, the crews threw their weight against the tackles, sending the heavy cannons rumbling across the deck to thump into position. Beneath his feet Blake felt the slight shift in the heel of the deck with the enormous transfer of weight. Silence descended once more.

'Petty officers! Shutter the lamps!' he called. The warm orange glow from the lanterns that swung between the guns steadily vanished, leaving almost complete dark. A murmur swept across the deck.

'Quiet there!' ordered Blake into the dark. 'They will be uncovered the moment you are required to serve your pieces. Take your ease now, but stay alert and await my orders.'

Not quite dark, thought Blake to himself, as his eyes adapted. Now he could see the faint glimmer from ice floes as they drifted past the open gun ports, and the glow of the linstocks in their tubs burning like so many devil-red eyes, along both sides of the deck.

******

'Mr Blake reports that the guns are run out and ready for action, sir,' said the first lieutenant to the shadowy figure next to him. 'And the ship is now dark.'

'Thank you, Mr Taylor,' said Clay, looking around the crowded quarterdeck. Above him the spreading cloud had emptied the sky of stars, and no moon would rise for many hours. He glanced over the side, onto a lake of pitch, with only the gleam of floating ice to show where the surface lay. 'Have the extra lookouts been positioned?'

'Yes, sir,' said Taylor. 'One at each masthead, all paired with a reliable hand to bring word back to the quarterdeck. I have another half-dozen men with night glasses manning the rail.'

Two bells rang out from the forecastle of the *Griffin*.

'Very well, bring her up into the wind, and take in sail, if you please,' ordered Clay. 'But keep the hands ready to set the topsails again, the moment I give the word. And let that be the last time the bell sounds this night, Mr Taylor.'

'Aye aye, sir,' said the first lieutenant.

The frigate lay silent and dark now, her hull black beneath her empty masts, crouched amongst the little bobbing ice flows. The night grew colder, with an icy wind blowing across the surface of the water. Clay felt his gloved hands ache where they gripped the cold brass of his telescope, and his eyes started to water with the effort of staring into the dark. He thought of ordering Harte to bring him a pot of hot coffee, but then remembered that dumping the galley fire over the side was almost the first thing done when a ship cleared for action. Instead he stamped his feet on the deck to get some life into them, and moved towards the ship's binnacle, the only light on board. He pulled out his watch and angled it in the faint glow.

'Barely ten o'clock,' he muttered. 'What time did you suppose the enemy might appear, Mr Armstrong?'

'They will have closed up a trifle at dusk, sir,' said the American, 'and we reduced sail considerably since then to allow them to draw near. Given that we have been stationary for the last hour, I reckon they should be up with us between one and two hours from now.'

'As much as that?' said Clay, wondering why he had cleared for action so long ago. He could have been taking his ease in his warm cabin now, and still have had plenty of time to prepare. 'Well, at least this cold will serve to keep us awake.'

Time seemed to stand still aboard the *Griffin*. The gentle tap of ice against the hull was like the slow strokes of a clock. A few stars broke through a gap in the clouds, bright as diamonds, before they vanished once more. In their light Clay noticed that the mizzen shrouds seemed to glow a little. He walked across and examined the surface of the ropes. They were white with frost. He had just turned away to remark on it to Taylor, when he heard the thrum of a descending body, sliding down the mainmast backstay, accompanied by a cloud of displaced ice crystals.

'There be a touch of topsail showing, maybe three mile off, sir,' reported a breathless figure. 'We saw the buggers when them stars was out just now.'

'Where away, Rogers?' asked Taylor.

'Two points off the stern to larboard, sir,' replied the sailor. There was a general movement of officers towards that side of the quarterdeck, while the messenger returned to the masthead.

Clay scanned in the direction indicated by the lookout. All he could only see was utter dark above the dotted pattern of ice floes on the water.

'Three miles off?' grumbled Taylor. 'Something should be visible.'

'I might have them, sir,' said one of the lookouts. 'Just abaft the last carronade. The wake of a ship, maybes?'

'Or the wind stirring the ice,' suggested Armstrong. Then he stiffened. 'No, I have it too. A bow wave for certain.'

Clay swept the surface of the sea, looking for something, anything. He locked onto a large ice floe, and as he focussed on it, it vanished. He blinked in surprise, then realised that something large was passing between him and it. Now he knew where to look, the elements of the image began to form. The ghost of a bow wave, moving steadily forwards. Trailing behind it was a line of silver where a hull moved through the water. Above it was the slight glimmer of canvas against the night sky. A haze of yellow hung above the ship's deck, as lamplight shone through the gratings. His memory of the large frigate that had been moored beside them in Copenhagen served to fill in the rest of the detail, until he was as certain of what he saw as if it were noon.

'The *Liberté* for sure,' he said. 'Coming rapidly up on the larboard beam.'

'Aye, blundering like a bear towards our trap,' enthused Armstrong.

'Mr Russell,' he called across to the midshipman of the

watch. 'Kindly tell Mr Blake to make ready, but he is to show no light until I give the word.'

'Aye aye, sir,' said the officer.

'Mr Taylor, we need to show enough jib to swing us a point to starboard,' said Clay. 'And have the hands sent aloft, ready to set topsails.'

'Jib and hands aloft, aye, sir,' repeated Taylor. 'I shall go forward to see it done.'

'Here she comes, sir,' reported Armstrong. 'A touch over a mile astern and coming on bold enough. She has not varied her course or speed that I can tell. Fifty guineas says she has no notion we are here.'

'How close do you think she will pass?' asked Clay. Armstrong looked up from his night glass to judge the angle.

'Within a cable, perhaps closer, sir,' he reported. 'Look, you can see light around an ill-fitting port lid, the lubbers.' The American was right. An angle of shining gold thread marked where the glow of a lamp leaked into the night.

'I fancy I can hear them now, too,' said Clay. Armstrong held his head on one side and opened his mouth a little. The crack of an ice floe against the *Liberté*'s hull sounded across the water, then the swish of her wake, and the creak of rigging as the big frigate came closer. All around them the carronade crews rose to their feet, stretching their chilled limbs and groping in the dark for their equipment.

'Corporal Edwards,' said Macpherson from somewhere behind him. 'Kindly make a tour of the men, and see they are all alert at their posts.'

'Aye aye, sir.'

Clay moved towards the front of the quarterdeck rail. From the dark pool beneath him came the clink of equipment and the sound of the gun crews shifting in the dark.

'Mr Blake!' he called.

'Here, sir!' came the officer's voice from the deep shadow around the main mast.

'The enemy will shortly pass within a cable to larboard,' he said. 'Give them a broadside and then keep firing. I will endeavour to hold us on their beam.'

'Aye aye, sir,' came the reply. 'We are ready when you give the word.'

Clay looked back at the enemy. Her mass of sail and rigging loomed up in the night, her hull a black space where she masked the ice flows. Her bowsprit was almost level with their stern.

'How have they not marked us, sir?' queried Armstrong, next to him. As if in response an urgent cry came from the *Liberté*'s masthead.

'Set topsails, Mr Taylor!' yelled Clay towards the forecastle. 'Uncover the battle lanterns, Mr Blake.

'Aye aye, sir.'

Warm light, like the glow from a fire, suffused the gun deck, spilling out over the sea in shards of orange through the open gun ports. In the aura of light, Clay could see the hands spread along the yard arms, wrestling with the furled canvas. The fore topsail was first to drop, and as it was sheeted home the *Griffin* began to move through the water. He returned his attention to the silhouette of the big French frigate a hundred yards off the beam. He could hear volleys of shouted orders, edged with panic at the apparition that had appeared beside them, and her ship's bell started to peal in warning.

'Open fire, if you please, Mr Blake,' he called down.

'Larboard side!' roared the lieutenant. 'Are you ready?' A

curved line of arms went up as each gun captain raised a fist aloft from his position crouched over his cannon. 'Open fire!'

In a lightning flash the night was swept away by the long tongues of flame that leaped from the frigate's side. Clay saw a world of black and white. Black water, covered with startling white ice floes, black masts with bulging white sails, and the long black hull of the French ship with its white stripe, unbroken by a single open gun port. White columns of water towered up along her side, showers of splinters rose behind them. Then a wall of smoke boiled up, and the dark returned, deeper and blacker than before.

'Not one darn shot in return, by God!' exalted Armstrong 'Not even a musket!' He banged the rail with his fist in delight. The two officers were at the calm centre of swirling activity. Ship's boys came running up from the magazine with fresh charges for the quarterdeck carronades. The marines who lined the spaces between the guns were busy spitting fresh bullets into their weapons and driving them home with their long ramrods. Clay had been so intent on watching his opponent that he only now realised the soldiers must have been firing all the time. The *Griffin* emerged from her bank of gun smoke, and he returned his attention to the enemy. The *Liberté* had moved a little ahead of her slower opponent, and the gap was widening all the time.

'Set the topgallants, Mr Taylor,' he yelled.

'Aye aye, sir,' replied the first lieutenant. Through the soles of Clay's feet he felt the tremble of gun trucks on oak, as the first cannons to be reloaded were run out.

'She had the look of a swift ship back in Copenhagen, sir,' commented Armstrong beside him. 'If she don't care to stay and fight, I dare say she can show us a clean pair of heels.'

'Not before we can land a few more blows,' said Clay. 'Up

your helm a point, quartermaster. Give her the same again as you bear, Mr Blake.'

'Point to windward, aye, sir,' replied Old Amos at the wheel. The *Griffin* turned a little, losing some way, but bringing every gun into action. The Frenchman was still very close.

'Open fire!' yelled Blake. A burst of brilliant light rushed away towards the distant horizon, painting every thread of their opponent's rigging in a tracery of gold, and the ship heeled away from the enemy as the cannon rushed back in board. The French ship's hull was pockmarked with damage from the previous broadside, marring the smooth perfection. Her foretop yard had been shot through and hung down in festooned ruin. Clay saw a section of her rail vanish in a fan of fragments, and then it was dark again. Still there was no return fire, only shouted orders and the groans of the wounded. The dark shape continued to outpace her tormentor, despite her damage aloft, and her silhouette seemed to shrink in length.

'She's turning away, sir,' said Armstrong. 'Cutting and running.'

'Another broadside, Mr Blake!' roared Clay. 'Get those cannons reloaded!'

'Aye, aye, sir,' replied the lieutenant. 'Almost ready!'

Their enemy looked quite different this time as she appeared in the light of the guns. She was stern on and growing ever more distant. Clay saw brilliant carved figures dressed in swirls of gold cloth, crowding around the run of glass windows across her stern and above them a huge tricolour, frozen in elegant folds before the light vanished once more.

Then she was gone, dousing all her lights, and sailing

away as fast as she could, chased by hoots of derision from the crew of the British ship. The sound of ice floes banging against her hull faded into the distance. The *Griffin* followed her for a few hours, but Clay was unwilling to charge through an ice field at night with the same recklessness abandon as their opponent. When dawn came, the frigate was alone once more, sailing over an empty sea.

CHAPTER 10

ST. PETERSBURG

The wide seas around the frigate had been narrowing steadily as they approached the eastern end of the Gulf of Finland, until at last they could go no further. Now a forested shore lay on both sides of them, close to the south and a more distant line on the horizon to the north. The grey walls of a fortress could be seen down near the shore, with cannon pointing towards them and a Russian flag fluttering over it. Ahead of them was a large fortified island, sitting in the centre of a narrow bay. Plenty of guns were on show here, as well as more Russian flags. Beyond the island the sea was covered by a thick sheet of ice, with a narrow channel of green water cut through it. Clay could see parties of men out on it, their heavy coats black against the white surface as they worked with long-handled axes and poles with hooked ends to widen the channel further. They were supervised by a few figures mounted on shaggy ponies. As he looked, Clay saw a sledge, pulled by three horses in a row, set off towards the shore, laden with slabs of ice. Apart from the grey stone

172

walls of Kronstadt Island and the men working, there was no sign of any city.

'Kindly heave to and anchor, Mr Taylor,' ordered Clay.

'Aye aye, sir,' said the first lieutenant. 'Bring her up into the wind! Anchor away!'

The *Griffin*'s best bower dropped from the starboard cathead amid an explosion of water. With a growling roar its cable, as thick as a man's thigh, sped through the hawsehole. A cloud of hemp fragments spiralled like chaff in the spring air, until the rate slowed as the anchor touched bottom. The frigate backed gently away, paying out cable as it did so.

'Holdfast!' bellowed Hutchinson to the anchor party. He stood with the sole of one shoe resting on the enormous rope, sensing what was happening on the seabed seventy feet beneath him.

'Another four fathoms of scope!' he ordered, and more cable was paid out. 'Easy there!' The angle at which the rope emerged from the water tightened, accompanied by a symphony of creaks as the anchor's fluke bit deep into the mud. 'Make fast and belay all!' he ordered. 'She's a-holding, sir!'

'The boatswain reports that the anchor is holding, sir,' repeated Taylor to the figure next to him, who would have needed ears of tin to have missed Hutchinson's shout from the forecastle.

'Thank you, Mr Taylor,' said Clay. 'Kindly get in sail and secure the ship.' He turned to Vansittart. 'We have arrived in St Petersburg, sir.'

'Have we, indeed?' queried the diplomat. 'Then where, pray, is the city?'

'I assure you it is close at hand, sir,' said Clay. 'It lies just beyond yonder ice field. The palaces and churches are quite clear from the masthead. No more than seven, perhaps eight miles away.'

'From the masthead!' exclaimed the diplomat. 'Eight miles away! Can you come no closer? Surely this breeze will serve to sail up that channel cut in the ice?'

'It may serve to bear us in, but it will be dead foul to bring us out again, sir,' said Clay. 'The safety of this ship is my concern. I have no intention of being caught in some narrow place, unable to manoeuvre, and dependent on the goodwill of Russians, who you tell me may presently be my enemies.'

'Quite right, sir,' agreed Taylor. 'Remember what happened at the Texel back in ninety-five.'

'And what did happen in ninety-five, Mr Taylor?' demanded Vansittart.

'Why, a Dutch squadron of warships was forced to surrender to French soldiers who came at them across the frozen sea,' explained the lieutenant. 'Imagine the disgrace! Bested by the bloody army!'

'Quite so,' agreed Clay. 'I have already lost one of his majesty's frigates this last twelve-month. I'll be damned if I shall lose another.'

'And how do you propose to get me ashore?' asked Vansittart.

'Oh, as for that, the longboat will be able to fetch you up that channel in no time, sir,' said Clay. 'Shall I order it launched?'

Vansittart looked over the side at the water. Tendrils of chill mist clung to the surface, in spite of the bright sunshine, and a slab of ice drifted past in the current.

'Of course, you will need to dress warm,' added the captain.

'Deck ho!' yelled the lookout. 'Launch be putting out from

the island with Russian colours, and there be another one coming up yonder channel.'

The Russian boat was the first to arrive. A well dressed naval lieutenant scrambled aboard to ask, in halting French, why a Royal Navy warship was anchored so close to his country's capital. Once Clay had explained the diplomatic mission they were on, and confirmed that no one onboard was suffering from any infectious diseases, the lieutenant departed again with a smart bow. By the time he had left, the second boat was less than a mile away.

'Deck there!' called the masthead once more. 'Strange to tell, sir, but I reckon that next launch be showing our flag.' Clay focused on the boat, a large affair with two masts that was approaching swiftly. A tall man in a scarlet coat sat in the stern sheets. Clay passed his telescope across to Vansittart.

'Tell me, do you recognise the gentlemen in regimentals?' he asked.

The diplomat studied the boat for a while. 'By Jove, he's stouter by a good few pounds since we last met!' he exclaimed. 'Doubtless been feasting upon diplomatic caviar and champagne, but that is Witless for certain.' He lowered the telescope and took in the blank look on Clay and Taylor's faces. 'Lord Charles Whitworth, our ambassador to his Imperial Majesty Paul, Tsar of all the Russias,' he translated. 'Sound enough cove, but not the sharpest mind in the diplomatic pantheon.'

'An ambassador!' exclaimed Taylor, coming to life. 'Then he rates as a vice-admiral! Side boys! Boatswain's mates! Call out the marine guard! Run, boy! Find Mr Rudgewick, and tell him I shall need a salute to be fired.'

The launch came alongside, and a man in the bow caught

onto the frigate's main chains with a boat hook. Lord Whitworth rose from his place, made his uncertain way to the steps built into the side of the frigate, and then climbed up to the entry port. He arrived just as the last marine was pushed into place by his sergeant, and the final pair of ship's boys pulled on their white gloves.

'Present arms!' ordered Macpherson, who had been sound asleep in his cabin moments earlier. The marines went through the evolution of their salute well enough, and the boatswain's calls twittered away as the ambassador stood rigidly to attention. If the boatswain's mates were a little more breathless than usual, or some of the marines' faces matched the scarlet of their tunics, Lord Whitworth gave no sign of having noticed. As the salute banged out from the bow of the *Griffin*, Clay took the opportunity to study his visitor. Whitworth was a large, middle-aged man, with a long face, brown curly hair that was growing thin on top, and thick ginger sideburns. When the echo of the final gun had faded, he stepped forward to shake his hand.

'Welcome aboard, your lordship,' he said. 'My name is Alexander Clay, captain of this frigate.'

'A pleasure, I am sure, Captain,' said the ambassador, looking beyond him.

'I believe you are already acquainted with the Honourable Nicholas Vansittart?' said Clay, following his gaze.

'Nicholas, my dear sir,' said Whitworth, pushing forward to grasp his hand. 'Thank God you're arrived at last! I flew here the moment your ship was reported in the offing!'

Clay exchanged glances with Vansittart. 'Perhaps you gentlemen would like to join me below for a glass of Madeira,' said Clay. 'We can converse with a degree of freedom in my cabin. Do please follow me.'

Once they were all settled, Vansittart turned to Whitworth.

'Now then, old boy, do tell us what has been happening?' he said. Whitworth pulled a handkerchief from out of his pocket and mopped his brow before replying.

'Where do I start!' he exclaimed. 'St Petersburg has been in uproar for much of the winter! Tsarina Catherine was a hard enough piece, with all of her whoring and endless favourites, but at least you knew where you stood. But Tsar Paul is madder than a sack of hares! Bedlam ain't in it, I tell you!'

'Calm yourself, George, and tell us what he has done,' said Vansittart.

'The latest outrage? Why he has only confiscated every British ship lying in a Russian port, of which there are several hundred. He's had all the crews rounded up, masters as well as men, and says he'll march them off to Siberia, just as soon as the snow melts! Of course it was all that damned Frenchman's doing, pouring poison against us into the tsar's ear.'

'The French ambassador?' queried Vansittart.

'Aye, Monsieur Barthélemy de Lesseps, the snake, with his tales of exotic travel from the far side of the world,' confirmed Whitworth. 'He has Paul feeding from his hand.'

'Lesseps, my lord?' queried Clay. 'Why is that name familiar to me?'

'Because he was the sole survivor of that French expedition to the Pacific, back before the war,' said Vansittart. 'The Frogs couldn't stomach our Cook gaining all the distinction, so they sent off a brace of ships of their own under that La Perouse cove. Naturally, it ended very ill.'

'That's right,' said the ambassador. 'He left them in the

Orient to return overland with the maps and logs and whatnot, while the rest of them pressed on to see what we were about in New Holland. They vanished just after leaving our colony in Botany Bay, so of course Napoleon says the perfidious English must be behind it, what?' He drained his glass, and held it out for Harte to refill.

'It would seem that the sooner I can meet with the tsar, the better,' said Vansittart. 'When can that be arranged?'

'I have tried everything to get you an audience, Nicholas old chap,' declared Whitworth. 'But Mad Paul is adamant. He refuses to even see you.'

'But I am the king's representative!'

'You could be the second coming of the Messiah, for all the tsar cares,' declared Whitworth. 'I tell you, the blighter won't shift. He is quite set on war, and nothing will persuade him otherwise. God knows I've tried.' Vansittart put down his drink, and laced his fingers into a steeple.

'That is vexing,' he said. 'Have you considered a more, shall we say, delicate approach to the problem?'

'What are you about, Nick?' said the ambassador, his brows coming together.

'Was his move against our commerce popular?'

'Good heavens, no!' said Whitworth. 'Most at court are involved in it to some extent, and stand to lose a ruddy fortune if trade with Britain should stop.'

'I see,' said Vansittart, 'and of course he was already disliked by the army, I collect?'

'Paul just can't stop himself,' confirmed Whitworth. 'The man's a dashed simpleton! He grew up in that ghastly palace his mother kept him in, with nothing but Prussian toy soldiers to amuse him. So the moment he came to power, he gave all the plum jobs in the army to Kraut officers, and got them to change everything. Prussian uniforms, Prussian musketry drill, even getting the poor blighters to goose-step, for all love! On top of that, he seems to regard his household troops as no more than a box of giant toy soldiers for him to play with! He has them parading for him at all hours, whenever the fancy takes him.'

'Hmmm, all very illuminating, George,' said Vansittart. 'What of his heir, Grand Duke Alexander? Is he of the tsar's way of thinking?'

'The son has little love for the father,' said the ambassador. 'Catherine made sure of that, raising him apart from Paul, very much as her creature. Now he, at least, is a rational man.'

'That sounds more promising,' said Vansittart. 'I had heard what a splendid fellow he was. I look forward to meeting with him, but first I wonder if you would invite a couple of other chaps to look over captain Clay's command, and perhaps stay for a little refreshment?' He passed a slip of paper across to his colleague, who glanced down at it.

'God bless my soul, you want to meet with these two?' he exclaimed. 'Are you sure?'

'Quite sure,' said Vansittart. 'Tomorrow would be convenient. It might be best if this was looked on as a private visit, independent of the government. Perhaps to help maintain that fiction, it would be best if your lordship was not one of the party?'

******

Lieutenant Taylor had always kept a smart looking ship, but the news that two important, but unnamed, Russian gentlemen would be visiting the frigate the following day prompted him to take matters to another level. As the *Griffin* was newly built, her hold had yet to acquire the richer odour of a mature ship, but still he ordered her gratings to be thrown open so that sunlight and cool sea air could enter into her mustier corners. While the hull was being aired, some of the crew were sent over the side with pots of fresh paint, to cover over the powder stains and cinder burns caused by the brief battle with the *Liberté*. Others busily scrubbed each of her decks to an even shade of grey. Every inch of her brass work was polished to the sheen of a mirror, and the boatswain led a party of veteran seamen in an orgy of rope weaving, decorating the ship with a profusion of Celtic knots and Turk's heads. It was a weary crew who gathered around their mess tables later that evening, once all had been stowed away and put back in place.

The clear sky above the frigate had filled with stars, and the gentle light of the moon brushed the rigging and upper works with silver. On her deserted orlop deck, only a modest scatter of white points had filtered their way down through the successive layers of grating. Even the stronger light from the few horn lanterns that swung on hooks beside the ladder ways served only to emphasize the many dark places all around. Joshua Rankin peered uncertainly under the low deck, with its scant five foot of headroom. The sound of the men's talk and the clatter of mess stools being shifted reverberated through the planking overhead. He unhooked one of the lamps and advanced into the dark.

'Here, Ludlow!' he whispered. 'Where you bleeding hiding?'

'In the cable tier, like what I said,' came a hissed reply from farther off.

'An' how am I expected to know where that is?' muttered the valet, as he crawled towards the sound of Ludlow's voice.

He sensed more than saw a black void that opened up beside him. Peering over the edge he found himself looking down into the hold. A row of huge barrels, all tightly wedged in place, were lined up just beneath him.

'Bleeding hell!' he exclaimed. 'You never said nothing about holes in the floor! I could have bust my neck!'

'Not so loud, Josh,' urged the voice. 'You're close now.'

Rankin crawled on, and soon the glow from his lamp began to flow over great columns of coiled rope, close on either side. Over the noise of the crew above came the sound of rapid scampering from the shadows on either side.

'Are there bleeding rats hereabouts?' he demanded.

'Course there'll be rats!' said Ludlow, seemingly from just ahead of him. 'You're on a bleeding ship, ain't you?'

Rankin turned around the last coil of rope and found the seaman, sitting cross-legged on a clear area of deck, with another lantern and a polished wooden box set out in front of him. The box was eight inches square and six deep, and looked to have been made with considerable care.

'I hope you ain't brought me down here on a fool's errand, Bill,' warned the valet, settling down beside his fellow Londoner.

'Nah, I got what you wanted,' said Ludlow. 'I risked me bleeding neck to get it, mind, but you said it had to be something worth a bit. Reckon this should answer.' He pushed the wooden box across the planking. It was made from rich brown mahogany that gleamed in the lamplight. A pair of folding brass handles fitted into recesses on the sides. Rankin pulled the box across towards him, surprised at first by its weight. The snugly-fitting lid swung open on well-oiled hinges to reveal an interior lined with baize. Mounted on a loop of brass was a large, beautifully crafted clock. Rankin tilted the box towards the light, and the chronometer pivoted silently on its gimbals so that it remained perfectly flat. He held his lantern over it and read the maker's name, painted in flowing script on the white enamel face.

'*Thomas Earnshaw of London,*' he said. 'What the bleeding hell is this?'

'It's like what you asked for,' said Ludlow. 'Some manner of ticker.'

'For a bleeding giant, maybe!' exclaimed Rankin. 'I said to pinch something small, like a pocket watch! How am I meant to slip this into Evan's stuff?'

'I just done the thieving, like what you said,' replied Ludlow, folding his arms. 'You wanted something valuable, and that's what I got you.'

'Aye, a bob or two I said, you arse!' exclaimed Rankin. 'Any fool can tell this is worth a bleeding fortune! Where did you come by it?'

'I were passing the clerk's cabin, and it were sat on the desk,' said Ludlow. 'The Lobster on guard were looking t'other way, an' no one else were around, so I nabbed it. Weighs a bleeding ton, mind.'

Rankin looked at him askance, then closed the box and pushed it away.

'It's got to go back,' he announced. 'Grunters were talking about this in the wardroom. This must be that bleeding chronometer-thing what the Yank's looking for. I didn't know what they was on about, but him and Taylor are proper hot over getting it back. When they finds it, some arse is going to bleeding swing.'

Ludlow gazed at the box in front of him, innocent-looking but suddenly full of menace.

'The chance I had to nab it ain't never going to come

round again,' he said, pushing the marine chronometer back towards the valet. 'Deals a deal. You said I only had to take it, and it were you as was going to stash it on Evans. It's yours now, Josh.'

Rankin stared at his fellow Londoner, taking in the firm set of Ludlow's jaw and the determined look in his eye, wondering how far he could push him.

'Fair's fair, I suppose,' he said at last. 'I can come and go pretty freely amongst the Grunters, so I daresay I might be able to think of something. Keep it for a little longer for me, Bill, while I works out how I can smuggle it back to the Yank.'

******

A deck above where Rankin and Ludlow were crouched, Sarah Hockley sat over a bucket of water in her tiny cabin. Her head was tilted to one side and her hair was gathered in a single, thick tress that she was pressing dry with a towel. The space was tiny, a mere six feet between two partitions of stretched canvas, with the ship's side at her back and the flap of material in front of her that served as a door. A drover in his tent must live like this, she thought, before correcting herself. No, he at least had the freedom to pitch his dwelling where there was sunlight, birdsong and the smell of crushed grass under foot. She, on the other hand, was in the dark, airless lower deck of a frigate, surrounded by the oath-edged talk of scores of sailors. But Sarah was content as she worked at her hair, the colour changing from the slick black of an otter to burnished chestnut as it became dry. The ship's bell struck seven times, making her smile. Only half an hour before he comes off watch, she told herself, and she started to sing gently.

'May I come in, my child,' said her father. He must have

been waiting outside for some time, she thought, for she had heard no footfalls approaching.

'Of course, please enter,' Sarah said, reaching for the elm wood comb with a tracery of carved flowers that some anonymous sailor had made for her. She had found it on her hammock one day, left as an act of kindness while she was on deck.

He came in, pulling the flap to behind him. Slight though they both were, between them they filled the tiny space. Sarah pushed the bucket to one side and rose to her feet, still combing her hair.

'You are making yourself beautiful, I see,' her father observed.

'Oh, it is such bliss to have clean hair!' she exclaimed. 'I begged for some fresh water when the frigate renewed its supply this morning, and the captain's steward was kind enough to spare me a little soap.'

'And do you pay such attention to your looks to catch the eye of Mr Preston?' he asked. Although he spoke calmly, she could see he was trembling with anger.

'I chiefly do so for my own part, Father,' she said. 'I had always understood cleanliness to be adjacent to Godliness. Did the Reverend Wesley not say as much?'

'I doubt very much that he was referring to the preparations of a jezebel!' exclaimed Hockley.

'Father!' said Sarah, colouring in her turn. 'How can you use such a word about me?'

'And what word would you prefer?' he hissed. 'Harlot, perhaps? Do you deny that you go to see that man?'

'I do not deny it, but I go only to walk a little in the evening air, and enjoy the diversion of his society,' she said, trying hard to stay calm. 'What on earth do you think I would be doing with Mr Preston?' She felt tears prick in her eyes, but she blinked them back. Neither of them had noticed that the sound of the lower deck outside had grown quiet.

'Disobedient creature!' exclaimed her father. 'Have I not forbidden such contact? I have never chastised you before, Sarah, but I am so vexed by your stubbornness in this that I could strike you now!'

'Not if you bleeding knows what's good for you,' growled a voice from beyond the thin canvas screen, together with a murmur of approval from the other listening seamen.

'Will you not interfere!' yelled Hockley turning towards the lower deck.

'Pipe down then, you arse, and don't you go a-threatening the little miss,' answered another voice.

'The impertinence of these sailors,' fumed Hockley. 'Listening to the private discourse of their betters. I have a good mind to report them all to Captain Clay!'

'Father, let us speak more softly,' said Sarah, catching hold of his hands and turning him towards her. 'You must know that I love you—'

'Then obey me, child, as the fifth commandment requires of you,' urged Hockley.

'I love you,' repeated his daughter, 'but matters have gone too far now with Mr Preston, for I also love him. As for the fifth commandment, it requires me to honour you, which I will always do, even if you seem to have such little regard for my future happiness.'

'But it is your future happiness that moves me to act as I do,' said Hockley. 'The station and character of the man that you marry will certainly determine that.'

'I agree with you wholeheartedly,' said Sarah. 'Mr Preston's station is of a gentlemen and officer, and if you would but converse with him a little, I know you would be quickly convinced of the agreeableness of his disposition.'

'Sarah, you are a very amiable and attractive person,' he said. 'You could have the pick of the merchant captains in Whitby.'

'Such as who?'

'John Wainwright, for one,' said Hockley. 'He has often spoken of you in the most favourable terms.'

'But I barely know the man!' she exclaimed. 'And he must be my senior by twenty years.'

'Not quite so many, and at least he is whole in body.'

The moment the words were out of his mouth, Hockley realised he had made a dreadful misjudgement. For the first time in his life, he saw contempt in his daughter's eyes.

'Whole in body?' she repeated. 'What are you saying? Is this how you judge the worth of a man?'

'No, of course not, but it is surely a consideration—'

'Was it a *consideration* for our saviour, when he tended to the sick and injured?'

'Sarah, please, I only want what—'

'What would happen if I wed Mr Wainwright and he was injured in an accident? Would you have me abandon him as no longer suitable?'

Of course not,' said Hockley. 'But that is not the same—'

'Then how can you ask me to disregard Mr Preston on the same grounds?' said Sarah. 'It would destroy him! If you truly think me capable of doing such a thing, then you do not know the daughter that you have raised. Now stand aside, sir, and let me pass!'

******

'It grows warm, does it not,' commented Clay the

following morning. He was standing to one side of the *Griffin*'s entry port. The Baltic sun was shining down on the dark blue of his heavy full-dress coat, and was strong enough to make him feel warm now, for the first time in weeks. It glistened on the tops of the ice flows that continued to bob all around the frigate.

'It does indeed,' agreed Vansittart, who was stood beside him in an elegant green coat of a much lighter weave. 'Why, the sea ice must have retreated a good thirty yards since yesterday.'

Clay looked at the channel of green water. It was ragged at the edges now, as pieces of ice broke free to join those bobbing past on their way out to sea. All the gangs of men who had been cutting it had also vanished.

'We shall have the Russian fleet at our rear presently,' said Taylor, who stood beside his captain.

'I daresay we shall,' agreed Clay. 'Have all the preparations been made, Mr Taylor?'

'They have, sir,' confirmed the first lieutenant. 'The ship is ready to pass an inspection from the king, bar the lack of ceremony when the gentlemen come aboard.'

'Precisely so,' said Vansittart. 'This is to be a strictly private visit.'

'Deck there!' yelled the lookout overhead. 'Boat putting out from the shore!'

'Any colours?' yelled Taylor.

'No sir, just a boat with a pair of gents in the stern.'

'So who are these Russians that will be visiting us presently?' asked Clay.

'General Levin von Bennigsen, hero of sundry wars with the Turks, much loved in the army, and summarily dismissed by Tsar Paul on a whim,' explained Vansittart. 'He is the thinner gentleman with the silver hair seated on the left. The man beside him in the white coat is Count Peter von Pahlen. Now he is a decidedly useful cove! A Baltic German, a life-long friend of General Bennigsen, and currently military commander in the city.'

The boat came alongside, and the two men climbed their way up to the entrance port. The first to arrive was the general, a tall, spare man with dark eyes and a prominent nose. He threw his arms wide when he saw Vansittart.

'Nikolai!' he exclaimed, pulling the startled diplomat close. 'It has been too long!'

'Quite so, General,' said Vansittart, as he wriggled free. 'May I introduce you to Captain Alexander Clay, who commands this ship?' Clay found his hand gripped firmly by the general. Although the soldier was twenty years his senior, and a few inches shorter, there was wiry strength in his lean frame.

'Pleasure to meet you, Captain,' said von Bennigsen, in reasonable, if heavily accented English. 'You have good Russian name, no? Alexander, just like son of our tsar, although what is "clay"?'

'Eh, it is a type of mud, used in the making of pots, sir,' he explained. 'Welcome aboard the *Griffin*.'

'Mud, you say,' said von Bennigsen, both eyebrows raised. 'Your name mud!' Then he roared with laughter, before lightly punching Clay on the shoulder. 'You English! Always you make good joke!'

'Would you honour us with an introduction to the count, General,' said Vansittart, indicating the second visitor from the shore, an aristocratic looking man who peered around the deck with obvious interest.

'Of course,' beamed the general, drawing his friend

forward by the arm. 'May I present Count Peter von Pahlen.'

'Delighted to meet you, Mr Vansittart,' said the count, in excellent English. 'Much obliged to you, Captain Clay.'

'Would you gentlemen permit me to name some of my officers to you?' said Clay. 'After which I wondered if you would care to inspect the ship?'

Once the Russians had shaken hands with the line of officers, they set off on a tour of the frigate, led by Taylor. Clay had arranged it this way so that he could stand back a little and watch the reactions of the two soldiers. He was unsure how familiar they would be with naval matters, but trusted that as fighting men they would be used to assessing the combat potential of what they were shown.

'Mr Harrison, kindly set the fore topsail, if you please,' ordered Taylor.

'Aye aye, sir,' said the boatswain, taking the silver call from around his neck and sounding a trilling blast. It was answered from the deck below, and the top men came flooding up onto the deck, to then race up the shrouds and out along the yard. Within moments, the huge sail was tumbling down above them to be sheeted home, pressing the frigate backwards against the pull of her anchor. Clay caught a glance of surprise between the two visitors at the speed with which the change had been made.

'Thank you, Mr Harrison,' he said. 'You can furl the topsail once more.'

'Aye aye, sir.'

'The blighters do it just as swiftly in a blow, though how quite defeats me,' commented Vansittart, as the party made their way up onto the forecastle. Both Russian's stopped in surprise at the sight of one of the frigate's huge carronades.

'This gun, very big,' said von Bennigsen, slapping the

breech with admiration.

'It's a thirty-two pounder, sir,' said Taylor. 'The men call them smashers. They are poor weapons at range, but answer very well close to.'

'Could such a cannon be used on land?' asked the count.

'I daresay it could,' replied Clay. 'They weigh little more than the twelve-pounder long guns they replaced.'

'Their manufacture is by no means straightforward,' said Vansittart. 'But I am sure our ironmasters could make some for export, for friends of our nation.'

The two visitors let the comment pass, and followed Taylor below deck. It was soon clear that neither man was familiar with life onboard a warship, if only from the repeated occasions that they struck their heads. But they took their buffeting with good humour, continuing to peer into each part of the frigate with polite interest.

'How many sailors does your ship have, Mr Taylor,' asked the count, as they stood in the middle of a lower deck packed with men taking their ease around the mess tables.

'Two hundred and fifty is our full compliment, your lordship,' said Taylor. 'But not above half are rated as sailors.'

'You surprise me, sir,' remarked von Pahlen. 'What can all the rest be required to do?'

'Forty are marines, that is a type of soldier who is trained to fight on ships,' he explained. 'Then we have the officers, of course, and the rest are what we name idlers. Cooks, armourers, carpenters, coopers, sail makers, gunners and the like. We are something of a floating town, you see, able to shift for ourselves, even when we are far from home.'

'Thank you, Mr Taylor,' said Clay, at the end of the tour. 'Would you care to follow me to my quarters for a little refreshment now, gentlemen?'

In Clay's cabin the table had been set for four. Through the stern windows, the Gulf of Finland opened between shores of fir on either side. The green water sparkled in the sunshine, dotted with ice flows to the horizon.

'I like your English navy,' announced von Bennigsen, accepting a glass of wine from Harte, and placing a hand on Clay's. 'You have good ship, I think.'

'The late Tsarina Catherine invited some of your brother officers to come and help train our navy before the war,' added von Pahlen. 'One Scottish officer, in particular, was very well received. Were you acquainted with the late Captain John Elphinstone?'

'Good man,' added his fellow Russian. He struck his other hand against his chest. 'Show our sailors how to be heart of oak. Catherine make him Russian admiral, and he kill many, many Turk.'

'I regret he served before my time in the navy, gentlemen,' said Clay, sliding his hand from beneath von Bennigsen's. 'But it is useful to be reminded of an occasion when our nations were on friendlier terms. Perhaps we might drink to their return?' The toast was drunk, and the glasses held out to be refilled by Harte.

'I understand you are Military Governor of St Petersburg, Count,' said his host to von Pahlen. Von Bennigsen laughed out loud, before his friend could reply.

'Now, yes, but next week? Who can tell?' he scoffed.

'Ah, I had heard that Tsar Paul's favour can be a little— shall we say volatile, Count?' said Vansittart. Von Pahlen shrugged his shoulders.

'Last August I was relieved of my duties,' he said. 'Then in October, the tsar chose to favour me once more.'

'That must be very vexing,' said the diplomat, 'having to serve a master with such a capricious nature.'

'Serving is always both an honour and a burden,' said the count.

'Quite so, although perhaps more of the later, under the present tsar?' asked Vansittart.

'Tsar is fool,' said von Bennigsen. 'Fool when he forced me from army, and more fool now.'

'Perhaps he compounds his folly by also leaving you at liberty to act, General,' said Vansittart. 'I believe it was Machiavelli who urged that, "*If an injury is done to a man it should be so severe that his vengeance need never be feared.*" Let us hope that those around the tsar are not urging him to apply those principles in your case.' Conversation dried for a moment, as Harte and his assistants served the first course and replenished the wine.

'Tell me, Captain, do you speak French as fluently as Mr Vansittart here?' asked the count.

'Not as well as that, but I can understand it tolerably,' replied Clay.

'Perhaps we could use it to converse, then?' asked von Pahlen. 'It is the language of educated Russia, and my friend here speaks it much better than English. It will also permit us to speak more freely.' The count looked significantly towards Harte.

'As you please, monsieur le comte,' said Clay, switching to the language.

'Let us be frank with one another,' said von Pahlen, adjusting the position of his plate a little. 'Impressive as your delightful ship is, Captain Clay, I have no doubt there was more than a desire to share it with us behind your kind invitation.'

'No indeed,' said Vansittart. 'I principally wanted to discuss the state of trade between our two nations.'

'Trade!' spluttered von Bennigsen.

'Quite so,' continued the diplomat. 'I was given to understand that many at court will be impoverished should trade with my country not restart in the spring, not least you two gentlemen. Ah, trade! It is such a vital part of making life civilised, do you not agree? So much of what one finds here in St Petersburg is provided by it.' Without waiting for a reply, Vansittart started indicating objects on the table. 'Porcelain plates; the wine in my glass; why, even the glass itself; this silver fork...'

'We have silversmiths aplenty in St Petersburg,' protested von Pahlen.

'And where, pray, do they get their silver from, Count? Like almost all of Russia's trade, it comes by sea. I trust your palace was kept warm this winter, General, with all the Whitby coal delivered last summer. Mind, stocks in the city must be running low now.'

'It is not only the English who have coal, you know,' said von Bennigsen.

'That is so, there are others who can supply you, at a price,' agreed Vansittart. 'And how will such coal ships arrive, when there is a British fleet in the Baltic, blockading your coast, General?'

'What fleet?' scoffed von Bennigsen. 'This little frigate?'

'We are but the advance party, sent ahead to help our many friends in Russia avoid a costly and needless war,' explained the diplomat. 'Be assured that should we fail, the fleet will follow. By now Lord Nelson will already be in control of the mouth of the Baltic as he approaches Copenhagen.'

'Nelson?' queried von Pahlen. 'The young admiral who won that victory in Egypt?'

'The very same,' said Vansittart. 'We take the threat of war very seriously, as you see, but I cannot but think that the whole prospect of war is unnecessary. We have no desire to fight you. We simply wish to buy, for a fair price, your tar and hemp, while you wish to continue to trade with the world. It is hard to comprehend why we should come to blows.'

'Your navy insists on stopping Russian ships,' said the general, pointing his glass at Clay.

'Only to ascertain that they are not bound for France, after which they are allowed to proceed,' said Clay. 'It is the right of any nation at war to do so.'

'The only person to gain from our falling out will be the Corsican tyrant in Paris, gentlemen,' continued Vansittart. 'I come here, in good faith, with complete discretion from my cabinet to negotiate an end to this folly, and your tsar will not even meet with me! What do you suggest I do?'

Clay watched the two Russians exchange glances across the table, and thought he detected the slightest nod from von Bennigsen.

'We, too, have no desire for war,' said von Pahlen. 'Tell me what is it you need from us?'

'I need to be able to negotiate with your tsar,' said the diplomat.

'But I understood you to say that he refuses to see you,' said the count. Vansittart rolled the wine around his glass for a moment before replying.

'That is so,' he said. 'Which is why I did not choose to name which tsar.' The silence that followed was so profound that Clay was aware of all the shipboard sounds around him.

A snatch of laughter from the wardroom beneath his feet, the slosh of a wave against the rudder, the hum of the wind through the mizzen shrouds. Then von Bennigsen cleared his throat.

'Have a care, old friend,' he growled. 'You speak treason.'

'Perhaps, but I believe you also know that I talk sense,' said Vansittart. 'Paul is not fit to rule a great nation like yours, and the late Tsarina Catherine never intended that he should. Why else would she have locked him away, all the time schooling his son, Grand Duke Alexander, to be tsar after her? The accession was a dreadful mistake. There is plenty of precedent in both our countries for those with power correcting such errors. We could even say that it is their duty to do so.'

'And how do you suppose that it will be done?' asked the count.

'I suggest nothing violent, of course,' said Vansittart. 'Simply that he must be persuaded to abdicate in favour of his son, and allowed to return to playing with his toy soldiers.'

'You think it will be so simple, Nikolai?' asked von Bennigsen.

'Oh, I have no doubt it will be anything but simple, General,' said the diplomat. 'But you have the confidence of the army, and the count here controls those who guard the tsar. Between you, I am sure you will find a way to persuade him, and of course the captain and I are here to assist you in any way we can.'

Clay tried to keep his face empty of his surprise at this announcement.

'The tsar is deeply unpopular, and there has been much talk at court along the lines you speak,' said von Pahlen. 'I myself have broached the matter, in private, with the Grand Duke Alexander. Nothing can be accomplished without his support, you understand. While I know him to be very much opposed to war with your country, he is also not yet persuaded it is his duty to replace his father.'

'Then he must be convinced,' said Vansittart. 'Tell him that Paul plans to move against him.'

'He will require proof.'

'So give it to him,' said the diplomat. 'Go and see Paul with rumours that his son is plotting to overthrow him and ask for permission to arrest him. Then you can show that order to Alexander.'

'Will it work?' asked von Bennigsen of his colleague. 'What if the tsar asks for proof of his son's betrayal?'

'I very much doubt that he will, General,' said Vansittart. 'There is only one thing you can be certain about a paranoid man. Tell him that his deepest fears are real, and he will always believe you.'

'The vengeance of a tsar can be awful,' said von Pahlen.

'True, but it is of Paul the Simple we speak, not Ivan the Terrible, gentlemen,' said Vansittart. 'If matters should go ill, which I very much doubt, find a way of coming aboard this ship. You shall be quite safe.'

'Simple for you to say such things,' muttered von Bennigsen.

'That is so, but if you fear Paul so much, you must certainly act against him,' said the diplomat. 'If he is truly the arbitrary and unreasoning person you fear, he will soon learn of your presence here and believe that you conspire against him, whether you do so or not.'

CHAPTER II

MIKHAILOVSKY

The letter had been delivered by a smart-looking naval launch that came alongside the frigate. The bearer was a young officer in a beautiful white uniform. His gleaming cavalry boots and trailing sabre had made climbing the ship's side a perilous struggle, and most of the anchor watch had been willing him to fall, but both he and the letter had eventually arrived dry. Clay flexed the thick cream paper between his fingers and then held the seal up to the light. A double-headed eagle with the elaborate arms of Imperial Russia was embossed into the disc of burgundy wax.

'Pass the word for Mr Vansittart, if you please,' he called towards the cabin door. He heard the marine sentry repeat the order to his colleague on the deck below, and a few minutes later the diplomat was shown in. Clay passed the letter across.

'An invitation, Captain,' said Vansittart, once he had opened and read the letter. 'Like all Imperial documents it is written in French, so they have made a sad hash of my name. No matter. We are commanded to attend a banquet with the

Tsar of all the Russias and his son, Grand Duke Alexander, at the Palace of Mikhailovsky tonight.' He tapped the letter with his long index finger. 'Now, I wonder what may be afoot?'

'You hold it to be something more than a courtesy, sir?' asked Clay.

'Naturally,' said the diplomat. 'I can't imagine that Tsar Paul wants us there, which means that someone else must be behind our invitation.'

'The gentlemen who visited us a few days ago, perchance?'

'Indisputably,' confirmed Vansittart. 'I am familiar with the Winter Palace and the Hermitage, but not with the Mikhailovsky, which is newly built. Still, it lies in the heart of the city, so we have a long boat ride ahead of us, Captain. In fact we are to go in the launch that brought the invitation. It states that it will return for us at five, whatever that may be in those bells of yours.'

'Two bells, sir,' said Clay. 'I must confess to being uncomfortable with attending. Admiralty regulations forbid me from leaving my ship in time of war, except when ordered to do so by a superior officer.'

'Well, that is easily done,' said Vansittart. 'You forget that I am a representative of the king with full powers to treat on his behalf. I can oblige you with that order if you require it of me, Captain.' He spread his arms wide. 'In any event, we are in Russian waters and in receipt of an Imperial command. I cannot see how it can be refused.'

'No, I daresay you are right.'

'Besides, I would value your council and support tonight. May I be frank with you, Clay?'

'I would like that above all things, sir.'

'My presence at your court martial was not wholly driven

by a desire to prevent an injustice, you know,' explained Vansittart. 'You were also marked as a man of discretion with some familiarity with the more clandestine side of warfare.'

'God bless my soul!' exclaimed Clay. 'You amaze me, sir. How have I earned such an unwarranted reputation?'

'From Lord Nelson, for one,' said the diplomat. 'He spoke highly of the manner with which you negotiated with the authorities in Naples on his behalf, back in ninety-seven. And then there were your activities in support of the French Royalists last year that were so unfortunately compromised by Major Fraser.'

'Heavens, is that how the Admiralty think of me?' said Clay, shaking his head. 'I will naturally assist in any way I can, sir. What do you suppose may occur tonight?'

'That I cannot say,' said Vansittart. 'Nine chances in ten it will be no more than a good dinner, but we must be prepared for all eventualities.' He looked across at the stoop-shouldered Harte who stood by the cabin door. 'To that end, it is customary for men of rank to attend such functions accompanied by a servant of some kind. I suggest you chose one who will be of value in case of need.'

'Then I will chose my coxswain, Sedgwick, sir,' said Clay. 'Discreet, intelligent and useful in the event of trouble.' Vansittart threw back his head and laughed.

'The negro? Goodness! It will be worth a guinea just to see what the Russians make of him,' he chuckled. 'For my part I shall take Rankin.'

******

The second stroke had just rung out from the belfry as Clay emerged from his cabin, once more in the glory of his full dress uniform. It was a cool spring evening, with a gentle breeze from the shore bringing the scent of pine forest, although the rain clouds that had been gathering for much of the day had begun to look threatening. Most of the crew were below, leaving the upper deck to the officers. Clay noticed Preston and Miss Hockley up on the forecastle, standing with their heads angled towards each other, while her father glared at them from the quarterdeck rail. I need to get a grip of that situation, before there is trouble, he decided, as his first lieutenant came over and touched his hat in salute.

'Fine evening, is it not, Mr Taylor?' said Clay.

'For now, although you may require your boat cloak later, sir,' replied the older man, eyeing the clouds. 'The Russian launch is on the larboard side, and Mr Vansittart and the others are waiting by the entry port.'

'Thank you, I shall go there directly. Do keep an eye on Mr Hockley, would you? He seems rather vexed by the attention Mr Preston is paying to his daughter. Try and see that nothing is said that might be regretted later.'

'Aye aye, sir. I shall do my best,' said Taylor. 'Would you care for some agreeable tidings?'

'Very much so. What do you have to report?'

'Mr Armstrong has his marine chronometer back, undamaged, and the ne'er-do-well who stole it is in the custody of the Master-at-Arms, sir.'

'Splendid!' enthused Clay. 'Who was the culprit?'

'William Ludlow, landsman in the starboard watch, sir,' said the first lieutenant. 'We received word anonymously that it was he. Apparently he was a notorious cut-purse before he joined the ship.'

'Word from one of the crew?' queried Clay. 'That is unusual. They generally resolve such matters without reference to us. But no matter, at least he has been apprehended. Now I must be away. It wouldn't do to keep the tsar waiting. You are in command until I return. If I am not back by dawn, you will find the ship's orders in the top drawer of my desk.'

'Aye aye, sir. And good luck.'

The boat was indeed the same launch that had brought the invitation. Clay and Vansittart settled into the stern sheets, while Sedgwick and Rankin went to join the Russian sailors in the bow. The diplomat nudged Clay, then looked towards the front of the boat, where the crew were shifting out of the way to make plenty of room for his coxswain. One seaman with a dark beard pulled a small icon from under his shirt and kissed the image, while the others observed the former slave with suspicion. As soon as they were all settled in place, the naval officer in charge barked an order, and the crew hauled a big lug sail and jib aloft to catch the evening breeze. The boat left the frigate's side and headed for the channel cut through the fast-disappearing sea ice.

The same officer who had delivered the invitation earlier was lounging in the stern sheets, still in his white uniform and gleaming high boots. He fell into an earnest conversation with Vansittart. Clay tried to listen to what was being said, but their French was too rapid for him to follow, so instead he sat back and enjoyed the view. The edge of the sea ice on either side was thin and broken now, with channels and fissures running through it. It had appeared white from the frigate, but close to he could see that the edge was like pale blue glass in places, where lumps had recently broken free. It was noticeable cooler on the water, and as the sun neared the horizon, the ice began to groan and crack. From out of the hushed conversation between Vansittart and the officer he distinctly heard the name 'von Bennigsen'. He forced himself not to look around, and instead watched the southern shore as it passed.

The wall of dark fir trees gradually thinned, to be replaced with areas of farmland. Brown earth, divided up into tiny plots and strips and dotted with wooden huts thatched in straw, stretched away from the coast towards the horizon. Bearded men, women in bright headscarves, and children at play paused to watch the naval launch as it sailed by, while chickens scratched around their feet. The number and density of dwellings grew as they sailed on towards the city. Soon the odd stone building appeared amongst those made of wood, and the dwellings began to line the sides of dirt tracks. As it became darker, orange light glowed in the occasional window, and they passed a little church with an onion dome. The clash of its bells sounded continuously across the ice as figures made their way towards its open door. As the boat came level, Clay glimpsed the glow of candles from deep inside.

The coxswain bellowed an order and the launch went about, following another channel in the ice, narrow and slanting towards the shore. Now the buildings facing the sea were bigger. They were all of painted plaster or brick, their facades full of tall windows. Clay realised that the beach of pebbles and drift wood had become a quayside. A frozen river led inland, and down it Clay glimpsed the span of a lamp-lit bridge. Ahead was what must be their destination. The slot of clear water through the ice led straight towards a landing stage projecting out from the shore. It was lit with strings of lamps, and thronged with soldiers. With a fresh volley of orders, the launch swept up to the jetty, dropping its sails as it did so. The last of the boat's way was sufficient to bring it alongside some steps, and a sailor with a painter jumped ashore and made it fast. Waiting at the end of the landing stage was a carriage, drawn by four sleek horses, with a bewigged coachman on the box seat and another holding the animals' heads.

'Welcome to St Petersburg,' said the young Russian officer, rising to his feet and indicating that they should step ashore. Vansittart led the way, followed by Clay and their guide. Trailing along behind came Rankin and Sedgwick.

On either side of the landing stage was a rank of soldiers in dark green who presented arms as they spotted the uniforms of the naval captain and their guide. Clay touched his hat in acknowledgement, and with a last look back towards the sea he followed Vansittart and the officer into the upholstered interior of the carriage. It swayed and creaked on its springs as Sedgwick and Rankin climbed onto the outside seat at the rear. Then, with the crack of a whip and a guttural order in Russian, the coach lurched into motion. They gathered pace to the sound of iron wheel rims and hooves on cobbles, and turned down a broad street into the city.

It was almost dark now, and Clay could only get a fleeting impression of St Petersburg through the carriage window. He saw other coaches, and people walking along the pavements. The row of buildings that bordered the street would occasionally give way to show an onion-domed church or brightly lit palace set back from the road. He felt the carriage start to climb, and looking out he could see the white ice of a frozen river beyond the parapet of a bridge. On the far side they passed through a torch-lit gate, guarded by yet more soldiers, and entered a small area of parkland. The softer crunch of gravel sounded from beneath the wheels. Black, leafless trees lined the drive, with a glimpse of empty flowerbeds and flattened grass beyond.

'These gardens must be magnificent in summer,' he said in French, indicating a little white temple that stood beside a frozen pond.

'Oh, they are, monsieur,' enthused the officer in white. 'You are seeing the palace at the worst time. The snow has almost gone, but nothing yet has begun to grow. In a few weeks from now it will be transformed. Our destination is just ahead.'

The carriage made a sweeping turn, and a tall building with a pitched roof of green tiles reared up beside them. The walls were of orange plaster set between gleaming white columns. More white stone surrounded each window and doorway, and there were many more soldiers in the same dark green uniform.

'Tell me, Lieutenant,' said Vansittart. 'Which of the Guard regiments is protecting the tsar at present?'

'The Preobrazhensky have that honour this month, sir,' said the young officer.

'Indeed,' said the diplomat. 'They are a very fine body of men. Did I hear that they were the late Tsarina Catherine's favourite regiment?'

'That's right, sir,' said the lieutenant. 'General von Bennigsen was their colonel for many years.'

'So he was,' said Vansittart, almost to himself. 'So he was.'

It was quite dark now, and cold rain had begun to fall, but the light from several thousand candles spilt out of the palace's numerous windows. The carriage came to a halt, and a footman in a long coat and powdered wig pulled open the door, while a colleague folded down the steps.

'Would you kindly follow me, messieurs?' said the officer. 'I am ordered to take you to see the governor first.' Clay hesitated at the carriage door, pulling his cloak close and settling his hat on his head. He saw Sedgwick and Rankin being led away towards a much smaller door. Vansittart and the Russian were already hurrying through the rain towards the palace, so he set off after them. As soon as he was out of the coach he realised that they had driven beyond the huge covered porch in the centre of the building's facade to draw up level with a lesser entrance. More soldiers presented arms at the door, and then they were inside. Clay surrendered his wet cloak to a footman, tucked his cocked hat under his arm, and set off down a wide corridor with a lofty ceiling that stretched ahead of them. The floor was of gleaming marble, slightly treacherous beneath his wet shoes. The walls were covered in a rich burgundy paper, and lined with gilt-framed pictures. Sets of double doors stood on either side, each with a footman standing by it, but they marched past these, deeper into the building, turning first one way and then another until they arrived at a door with two more sentries guarding it. The young officer in white knocked and immediately opened it, standing to one side and gesturing for them to enter.

Clay found that he was in a large, book-lined room, with a thick Persian carpet on the floor. There were small tables and comfortable chairs dotted around, and a painted globe on a stand in one corner. A bright fire burned in the grate, and its light sparkled off the uniforms and military orders worn by the men who stood around the fireplace, drinking champagne and talking loudly. Trails of blue cigar smoke drifted up towards a chandelier that hung overhead. As the group turned towards the door he saw it included both General von Bennigsen, in a much more elaborate version of the green uniforms worn by the sentries outside, and Count von Pahlen, resplendent in a white tunic covered in gold fogging. There were five other men with them, all in various military uniforms. Von Bennigsen broke off his conversation with a moustached hussar officer, and came over to embrace Vansittart.

'Nikolai, you cunning fox, you!' he exclaimed. 'We were just now singing your praises! I was explaining to Konstantin here the ruse you devised to bring Alexander to join our little conspiracy.'

'Have a care now,' urged Vansittart, looking at the group of men in alarm. 'I am not sure I entirely follow you. Have you been drinking long, General?'

'There is no need for fear, old friend,' explained von Bennigsen. 'These men are all patriots, sworn to aid us. They can be trusted implicitly.'

'And what of the servants?' asked Vansittart, indicating the footmen in the room.

'Each one is an army veteran, whose position I obtained for them in the palace,' said the general.

'Nevertheless, perhaps it would be best if the captain and I were not present,' said Vansittart. 'I think I heard you speak of conspiracy?'

'Don't be coy, old friend!' beamed von Bennigsen, drawing the diplomat towards the group. 'Von Pahlen here took your advice. He told the tsar that his son was plotting against him, and the fool was signing an arrest warrant before he had finished speaking!'

'When I showed the document to Grand Duke Alexander,' explained the count, 'he agreed immediately with my suggestion that his father was plainly mad, and should be required to abdicate in his favour.'

'Splendid, is it not?' beamed von Bennigsen. 'Bring

champagne for our guests here!' The two Englishmen found glasses pressed into their hands.

'That does all sound very satisfactory,' said Vansittart, sipping at this drink. 'Although I am surprised that you think I was in any way responsible for these events. The credit rightly rests with you gentlemen. However, I can assure you that His Britannic Majesty's government will be the first to recognise Tsar Alexander. I will, of course, need Russia to withdraw from this *so-called* League of Armed Neutrality, and restore all the merchantmen and crews seized by the former Tsar Paul to their rightful owners.'

'Agreed,' said von Pahlen. 'Both will be among the first actions of Tsar Alexander, the moment he is on the throne.' Clay and the diplomat exchanged glances.

'The moment that he is on the throne!' repeated Vansittart. 'Am I to understand that the abdication has not occurred yet? I thought, what with the champagne...'

'Oh, we always drink champagne, Nikolai,' explained von Bennigsen.

'Then when, pray, will Paul be, eh, asked to abdicate?'

'Tonight!' said the general, waving his glass towards the clock that stood on the mantelpiece. 'We will do it tonight.'

'Gentlemen, I am not sure it is wise for myself and the captain to be present during such events,' said the diplomat. 'This has to be a purely Russian affair.'

'Absolutely,' agreed Clay. 'We should return to the ship immediately.'

'Nikolai! This is your moment!' said von Bennigsen, throwing an arm around Vansittart's shoulders. 'Of course you must be here. Besides, if you leave now, it will arouse suspicion. Come, give my friend, and Captain Clay another drink, and let us toast our success!'

'Oh, very well,' said the diplomat, as his barely tasted first glass was replaced with a brimming second. 'So what is your plan?'

'The banquet tonight is a small, private affair,' explained von Pahlen. 'No more than a hundred of us. The tsar is the host, and Grand Duke Alexander the principal guest. Paul will retire early to his private apartments, which I have told him will be the signal for the arrest of his son. In reality it will be the moment for us to follow him there, and make him sign the abdication document that I have on my person.' He slid a hand into his tunic and drew out the corner of a thick piece of folded parchment.

'What of his guards, count?' asked Clay. 'Will they not try to stop you?'

'The Preobrazhensky Regiment are my children,' smiled von Bennigsen. 'They despise the tsar almost as much as they love me.'

'Does he have any servants, or Gentlemen of the Bed Chamber, who might intervene?' asked Vansittart.

'Maybe ten, maybe a dozen,' shrugged the general. 'The Preobrazhensky are eight hundred strong, and the count here has more soldiers close by, should we require them.'

'But let us not talk of violence, gentlemen,' said von Pahlen. 'A signature is all we require, nothing more than that.'

'We should join the others now,' said von Bennigsen. 'It will cause suspicion if we are late. Be strong, and know that we act for Mother Russia.' The other officers murmured their assent, drained their glasses, and headed out of the room.

******

'I am most uncomfortable with our being here, sir,' hissed

Clay, under the chink of spurs and the clatter of boots from the conspirators ahead of them.

'I am inclined to your way of thinking, but we can hardly withdraw now, Captain,' replied Vansittart, out of the corner of his mouth. 'I fear General von Bennigsen is right, that will arouse more suspicion than if we stayed. This is a most fortuitous turn of events for us, which it is our duty not to imperil. Stay alert, try not to show any agitation of spirits, and drink sparingly. Tonight may prove to be an interesting one.'

The corridor ended at last, opening into a substantial stateroom. High above Clay's head was a vaulted ceiling of painted panels set above a line of chandeliers. Their light was caught in the huge gilt framed mirrors that were built into the walls, and glowed off the polished wooden floor. Scattered across the room were perhaps fifty people bunched into groups, with more joining all the time. Many of the men were in uniform, the rest in formal black coats and britches. The women wore satin evening dresses of every colour. Wherever Clay looked he saw piled up hair, bare shoulders, bold dark eyes and the glitter of diamonds.

'*Du champagne, monsieur?*' murmured a voice at his elbow, and a footman extended a silver tray towards him. All the conspirators took a glass, then dispersed into the room, leaving Clay and Vansittart with von Bennigsen. The general introduced them to the members of the nearest circle of courtiers in rapid French. Vansittart managed to follow what was said, but to Clay it was a stream of titles and unpronounceable names. He did his best to make polite conversation with his immediate neighbours; but soon found that his lack of knowledge of Russia and their disinterest in the sea quickly exhausted his stock of small talk. Clay was at heart a shy man, and although his French was reasonable, he became tongue-tied and awkward. Fortunately Vansittart was at his urbane, gossipy best, which allowed Clay to step a little back from the group.

Was it his imagination, or was there a detectable tension in the air? He was taller than most of those around him, and this allowed him to survey the room. The mirrored walls brought images to him from all directions. He could see von Pahlen, in urgent conversation with a civilian who wore the star and ribbon of an order across his chest. The hussar officer Clay had met earlier was looking at his watch and chewing at the fringe of his drooping moustache. Another conspirator was giving instructions to a pair of young guards officers close to the door. Then a large, barrel-chested chamberlain, in a coat that seemed to be made entirely of braid, beat the point of his staff on the floor before bellowing something in French. The doors at the far end of the room were flung open and the conversation around Clay ebbed into silence. Everyone turned towards the pair of men who entered, both dressed in military uniforms.

Tsar Paul was a short, middle-aged man, with a shiny domed head above a pair of small dark eyes that shifted quickly about the room. They soon lighted on Clay, obvious thanks to his height and unfamiliar uniform, but then slid away just as fast. Beside him was his son, a taller man in his early twenties, with sandy hair already starting to thin to reveal the same domed head. Grand Duke Alexander seemed to be unsure what he should do with his hands, sometimes clasping them behind his back, and then letting them hang by his sides.

The two royals made their way around the room, their progress marked by a wave of curtseying women and bowing men. Tsar Paul exchanged the odd smile of greeting and occasional word as he went, but he pointedly didn't approach the group that included Vansittart and Clay. His son, on the other hand, did, and von Bennigsen made the introductions.

'My grandmother spoke very highly of your Royal Navy, Captain,' said the grand duke, in excellent English.

'I am delighted to hear you say so, Your Highness,' said Clay. 'Her friendship continues to be remembered with fondness in the service.'

'It is to be hoped that friendship between our nations has not wholly vanished, Your Highness,' added Vansittart.

'Indeed,' said Alexander. 'And how does a Dutchman come to be in the service of King George?'

'Dutch by name, but my family have been English this past century or more, Your Highness,' explained the diplomat. He extended a single buckled shoe in front of him. 'Been a while since this foot donned a clog, what?' There was polite laughter from the group, and a smile from the heir to the throne.

'I trust you gentlemen will have a pleasant evening,' he said, moving away.

'A *very* good evening, Highness,' growled von Bennigsen, somehow managing to make it sound like a threat.

Once the royal pair had completed their tour of the room, the chamberlain beat the polished floor with his staff again and announced that dinner would be served. There was a renewed hum of conversation, and the guests made their way through to another, equally huge room. This one was carpeted under foot, and had walls of lemon yellow set with classical columns in white and gold. Two large fireplaces dominated one side, with log fires burning in the grates. A long table bearing silver and glassware stretched across the middle of the room, with a footman behind every chair. The chamberlain faced the flow of guests, like a rock in a stream, telling those unsure of their place where they should sit. The British pair found themselves directed to the far end of the table, close to a set of much plainer doors, where Clay suspected the food would come from.

The meal proved a lengthy and dull affair, as an endless succession of dishes and wines appeared from over Clay's left shoulder, to be removed and replaced by the same route. Clay found himself seated between a very reserved, elderly lady, who seemed to be hard of hearing, and a Russian civilian whose French was so heavily accented that he could only understand one word in five. As the conversation faltered towards silence, Clay watched the opposite side of the table with growing envy, where Vansittart laughed delightedly with the pair of pretty young ladies who flanked him.

'Capital caviar, what?' the diplomat remarked to his fellow countryman, before returning to his flirting.

'A little salty for my liking, in truth,' muttered Clay, as he contemplated the pile of shiny grey spheres.

'Eh... pardon?' queried the dowager beside him, cupping a hand to her ear.

'Tres bon!' he said, smiling and pointing at his plate.

The ambiance of the meal was not helped by the atmosphere in the room. The fires made it warm and close, encouraging the guests to drink the chilled wine thirstily. The tsar radiated brooding hostility, glaring towards his son beneath furrowed brows. At one stage he made a pointed remark that hushed the conversation around them, and left Alexander red-faced. For his part, Alexander seemed preoccupied and quiet, barely touching his food. The

212

conspirators Clay had seen earlier all seemed nervous, apart from von Bennigsen who was loud, boisterous, and a fair way to being drunk.

After what seemed like hours, the tsar at last pushed back his chair and dropped his napkin down beside his place. His son rose to his feet and the chamberlain banged his staff once more.

'*Messieurs et madames, le Tsar!*' Alexander announced, holding up his glass.

'May the next cup of wine choke the wretch,' said Vansittart, in a stage whisper towards Clay. All rose to their feet for the toast. After it had been drunk, the Russian men turned as one towards the log fires and hurled their glasses into them. The two Englishman exchanged a look of surprise, then Vansittart shrugged his shoulders, and their glasses followed, into the heart of the nearest blaze.

Once the tsar had retired, the women all rose and in a river of colour left the room through a set of doors that stood between the fireplaces. Clay glimpsed a saloon beyond, with card tables and sofas, before the doors closed once more. He could not have sworn to it, but it seemed to him that they were pushed shut by the green clad arms of soldiers, rather than by uniformed footmen. Count von Pahlen rose from his place at the table, and looked significantly towards the others as he left the room by the exit that the tsar had used. One by one the other conspirators followed. Vansittart looked across the table at Clay.

'Best for us to stay put, I fancy,' he said.

'Where has Count von Pahlen gone?' demanded a large civilian, further up the table. 'Ah, perhaps this chap will know.' Clay looked around to see a guard's officer approaching. He came up to Vansittart and clicked his heels together.

'Would monsieur and the captain kindly join the general?' he said. 'There is a matter he would like to discuss with you.'

'If we must,' muttered Vansittart, rising to his feet. Clay stood up too, and followed the diplomat and officer, ignoring the puzzled looks on the faces of the guests near to him.

'What the devil does von Bennigsen want with those two?' demanded the civilian behind them. The last thing Clay saw as he left the room was Alexander's face, pale and drawn, watching him go.

The corridor outside was lined with Preobrazhensky guardsmen, each one with a bayonet fitted to his musket. Count von Pahlen was looming over the chamberlain, whom he had trapped in a corner. Their faces were very close together.

'If anyone asks, the tsar has been taken ill, and I have ordered them to stay put,' said von Pahlen, in slow clear French.

'But... but...' stuttered the man, his staff trembling in his grasp.

'Should anyone try to leave, the major and his men here will prevent them from doing so,' said the count, staring down the official. 'Is that clear?'

'*Oui...*' whispered the chamberlain. Von Pahlen held the man's gaze for a long moment, then smiled.

'Good,' he said. 'I am sure the Grand Duke will remember your loyalty when this is all over. Now, off you go.'

'General, Count, surely you cannot want Captain Clay and myself to attend your discussions with the tsar,' protested Vansittart.

'Of course we do, Nickolai!' exclaimed   von Bennigsen,

breathing alcohol fumes around him. 'This was all your idea, remember. Come and enjoy your triumph!'

'But do so swiftly,' said von Pahlen. 'We have wasted enough time already. Follow me, gentlemen.'

Vansittart shrugged at Clay as they joined the small group of officers, who set off down the corridor. General von Bennigsen gave a guttural order in Russian, and a dozen soldiers peeled off to follow in their wake. They hurried forward twenty yards, and then a staircase opened on one side. Von Pahlen led the way up, and turned along another corridor. As they pressed forward, they heard shouting from behind them. Looking around, Clay saw Sedgwick and Rankin struggling to get past the soldiers.

'Sir! Sir! It's us!' called the coxswain. 'We saw all these here Lobsters surrounding the place, so we figured you might have need of us.' Vansittart spoke rapidly in French and von Bennigsen grunted an order to the guardsmen, who stood aside to let them through. Then the enlarged group pressed on.

A turn down another short stretch of corridor and they found themselves in a small hall, with chairs pushed back against the walls on either side of a decorated set of doors. Above them a large double-headed black eagle with the arms of Imperial Russia had been moulded into the ceiling. Two more guardsmen stood in front of the entrance, but they stepped back when von Pahlen motioned them aside. The group pushed through into the anteroom beyond.

The lighting was much more subdued here. A small coal fire glowed in a grate; candles burned in a branched candelabra on the table. There were mirrors on the walls, and the eyes from stern family portraits glared down at them. Several doors opened off the room, and the conspirators paused in confusion.

'Ah, count, has the traitor been apprehended?' said a cultured voice in French, and a man in a military tunic, unbuttoned at the neck, strolled into the room. He froze when he saw the gleam of firelight on the polished steel of bayonets. 'Good lord, why have you brought soldiers with you?'

'If you know what is good for you, Vasilyev, you will take a seat by the fire, and not interfere,' said von Pahlen. After a moment's hesitation, the officer sat down as he had been ordered. Von Bennigsen gave a command and one of the soldiers took up position opposite him, his musket at the ready.

'Good,' said the count. 'Now which of these doors lead to the tsar's quarters?'

'What are you going to do?' said the officer, his eyes wide.

'Never you mind!' spat the hussar with the moustache. 'Just answer the question.'

'It is only a matter of signing some state papers,' said von Pahlen, holding up a hand to restrain his colleague. 'Which door did you say?' The officer pointed the way.

'Have a care, sir,' he said. 'His valets have yet to retire.'

They pressed on down a narrow passageway, with more rooms opening off it. Von Bennigsen led the way, shouldering each door open as he went. The first few swung wide to reveal bed chambers; all well-furnished, but unoccupied, and obviously not grand enough for a tsar. Clay followed in the general's wake, glancing into the rooms as they passed. One was entirely filled with racks of clothes, and was followed by another with lines of boots and shoes. From ahead came cries of protest, accompanied by a crash. Clay pushed forward and found himself in another salon.

It was a large, dimly lit but comfortably furnished room, full of sofas and tables. A coal fire burned in a grate, and lavish drapes had been pulled across the windows to shut out the night. In the centre of the room was a baize-covered table strewn with playing cards and glasses of wine. At the table sat two young men in waistcoats and shirt sleeves, their neck clothes discarded along with their coats on a nearby chaise long. A third man was standing beside an upset chair, confronting von Bennigsen.

'What is meant by this outrage, sir?' he protested.

'Sit back down, puppy, and tell me where the tsar is,' roared the general.

'The tsar has retired,' said the man, his look of pride turning to horror as the soldiers clumped into the room behind the conspirators. His mouth opened and shut for a moment, and then he turned towards the doors behind him.

'Flee, Your Highn— His cry was cut off by von Bennigsen's fist in his stomach. One of the other servants leapt to his feet but received the butt of a musket full in the face, and he fell senseless to the carpet, bleeding badly.

'You men, keep them quiet, and see we are not disturbed,' ordered the general. 'The rest of you, follow me.'

The doors to the tsar's bedroom were of heavy polished wood and swung open noiselessly. Beyond, the only light was a single candle that burned beside the bed, like a votive offering in a dark cathedral. In the flickering light a huge room could be guessed at, the flame sending shadows across the heavy furniture, and sparkling back from a distant mirror. It was dominated by a four poster bed, the drawn curtains of richly decorated cloth of gold. The Russian conspirators looked at each other, wondering what to do next. Von Pahlen pulled his coat straight, drew the abdication document from his pocket, and advanced on the bed.

'Your Majesty?' he said, peeling back one of the curtains. Then he started in surprise, and pulled the drape wide. 'By St Vladimir! The bird has flown!' He stepped back from the empty bed as the others rushed forward. The covers had been thrown aside, the sheets disturbed, and there was the imprint of a head on the pillow. Von Bennigsen slid his hand across the bed.

'He may have flown, but he cannot have gone very far,' he said. 'The nest is still warm.' A stifled whimper sounded from one of the room's darker corners. The general seized up the candle and headed towards the sound. A painted Japanese screen made from concertinaed panels appeared out of the gloom.

'Look,' whispered von Pahlen, pointing at a bare foot just visible under the bottom. He drew the screen aside. Behind was a cowering figure in an embroidered nightshirt, huddled against the wall with his arms wrapped around his legs. A tasselled nightcap covered the domed head of the Tsar of all the Russias and his little dark eyes were shut tight, as he rocked backwards and forwards.

Clay looked on in horror at the pitiful sight, until he felt Vansittart tug at his arm.

'We will leave you gentlemen to your business, and await you outside,' he said, drawing the naval captain away. Clay glanced over his shoulder as the diplomat closed the door. The last thing he saw was the childlike figure still rocking in the corner, surrounded by the boots and legs of the Russian rebels.

'Is there something to drink?' he asked. Vansittart patted him on the shoulder. 'I daresay there is, Clay. Damnable business, what?'

******

'How long does it damned well take to sign a document?' demanded Vansittart, as he paced up and down the salon carpet. 'We have been here bloody hours!'

'Almost an hour, sir,' corrected Clay, who was stood by the bedroom door. 'They have stopped shouting now, so perhaps that is progress.'

'Our Tsar will never sign,' said one of the valets, who sat under the watchful gaze of a guardsman. On his lap was the heavily bandaged head of his colleague who had been struck with the musket butt. 'You traitors will hang for this, even the foreigners!' The same guard's officer who had fetched them from the table came into the room.

'Where is the general, sir?' he asked. 'The Grand Duke wants to know what the delay is, and the major is not certain how long the men can keep the palace secure.' Clay knocked on the bedroom door, and after a pause the conspirators all came out.

'The stubborn fool won't sign,' declared von Bennigsen.

'What do you mean, he won't sign?' exclaimed Vansittart. 'He has to, damn his eyes!'

'God knows, we have been trying!' exclaimed von Pahlen. 'He is in the grip of some madness. All he does is rock to and fro like the damned movement of a clock, muttering prayers.' Vansittart resumed his pacing, waving his arms in frustration.

'And why pray, did you invite the captain and I to be part of this farce?' he demanded. 'In front of bloody witnesses, for all love!' he added, waving towards the valets.

'You encouraged us to do this!' protested the general.

219

'Paul the Simple, not Ivan the Terrible, you named him.'
Vansittart stopped at the window, ran his hands through his
hair and looked at the ceiling for a long moment. When he
turned around, there was determination in his eyes.

'General, I wish to speak freely with you gentlemen,' he
said. 'Might I suggest that the tsar's valets are removed, and
that your men withdraw. Rankin, Sedgwick, you as well.
Kindly wait outside.' Once the door closed behind the last
soldier, he rounded on the conspirators.

'Now, pray attend. The throne must be vacant before
Alexander can become tsar, yes?'

'Of course,' said von Pahlen. 'There can only be one tsar.'

'This night Paul is completely at your mercy, and you
have force to hand,' said the diplomat. 'A more favourable
opportunity will never occur for you to act.'

'We all know that!' exclaimed the general. 'What is your
point?'

'No more and no less than I have just said,' said
Vansittart, avoiding his friend's eye. 'He must be forced from
the throne, by whatever means are required.'

'Whatever means!' repeated the general. 'What exactly
are you proposing, Nikolai?'

'Are you suggesting that we harm the tsar, or even... kill
him?' said von Pahlen. 'Are you quite mad?'

'What are you saying, sir?' whispered Clay, but the
diplomat waved him away.

'We have all travelled too far this night to turn back now,'
he explained. 'Even the captain and myself are
compromised.'

'What—' began von Pahlen, but Vansittart spoke over
him. He pointed towards the bedroom door.

'We are obliged to resolve things now, this instant, or

accept the vengeance that creature in there will wreak on us all, my country included, when he finds himself no longer unmanned by fear.'

'No,' said von Bennigsen, backing away. 'We spoke only of him abdicating. I cannot do such a thing, nor order it done.' The other conspirators shook their heads, and the officer in the hussar uniform crossed himself. Vansittart looked around the room.

'The Tsarina Catherine showed greater resolution than your own when it came to dealing with Paul's father,' he observed.

'You ask too much of us,' said one of the conspirators. 'The tsar is anointed by God.' In the hushed silence that followed Vansittart looked at each man in turn.

'It is well that you have allies then, prepared to act for you,' he said. 'Kindly summon my servant.'

'What! Will your black devil do it?' said the hussar, his eyes wide.

'Ah... wrong devil, old chap,' said Vansittart. 'Rankin!' he called towards the door. The valet came into the salon.

'Yes sir?'

'Kindly go through to the bedroom. You know what needs to be done.'

'Yes, sir,' he repeated, his eyes blank as he advanced across the room. He extended one arm down by his side and shook it. From out of his coat sleeve, smooth as an emerging serpent, flowed a thick silk cord. He wrapped the ends around his hands, jerked it tight as if testing its strength, and then disappeared through the bedroom door.

Clay grabbed the diplomat by the arm, and whispered fiercely. 'What are you doing, sir! You surely cannot mean to have that poor wretch murdered?'

'Do not interfere, Captain. That is an express order,' replied Vansittart.

'I want no part in this,' said Clay, moving towards the door. 'This is disgusting! How can you be party to such a thing?' The naval captain felt himself pulled fiercely around by the arm.

'Don't you presume to sneer at me, Clay!' spat Vansittart, furious in his turn. 'Walking away from this mess, with no thought for the ruin to your country is the easy path! Staying to see it through, whatever the cost, that is hard! You imagine I relish this task?'

'But this is not how civilised nations should conduct themselves,' protested Clay.

'Know this, Captain,' said Vansittart, 'you and I slay our country's foes at the bidding of the same master. You military men may be granted the privilege of swaddling your actions in a flag, while I must content myself with life in the shadows, but there the difference ends. How dare you name what I do revolting, while claiming there is honour in your own actions! We are not so very different, you and I.'

The few minutes that Rankin was out of the room seemed to drag for an age. Little sound from the bedroom penetrated the heavy panelling to those listening in the salon. Instead, other noises filled the space. The patter of rain against the window, the dry rustle of the fire in the grate, the regular tick of a case clock that rested against the wall, and the heavy breathing of the conspirators as they stood, frozen in a tableau. At last the door swung open, and Rankin stepped through it. The silk cord had vanished once more. He stood close to his master and whispered in his ear. Vansittart turned towards the others.

'Gentlemen, the tsar is dead,' he announced. 'Long live Tsar Alexander Pavlovich!'

CHAPTER 12

LUDLOW

March was fast moving towards April, and with it had come more rain. Boiling clouds filled the sky overhead, and water thundered onto the anchored frigate, drumming on the upper decks and running in silver twists down the rigging. It hissed across the sea, foaming the surface, and poured in gushing streams from the last of the fast-vanishing ice. The walled island of Kronstadt was just visible through the curtain of water. Tendrils of low cloud seemed caught amongst the dark trees on the near shore, while the far coast had vanished altogether.

In his day cabin, Clay did his best to ignore the rain hammering on the deck just above his head as he worked at his desk. In front of him was the latest despatch from Lord Whitworth. The ambassador had achieved much, in spite of Vansittart's low opinion of him. From the moment they had arrived at his residence in the middle of the night, having rushed through the rain from the Mikhailovsky Palace, he had sprung into action. His contacts had smuggled them back on board the *Griffin* that same night, while under

Whitworth's urging, the new tsar was now busy reversing the policies of his father. Already he had lifted the ban on British merchantmen using Russian ports, and restored all the confiscated ships to their rightful owners. Now, in his latest letter, Whitworth wrote that Alexander planned to see the ambassadors of the other Northern League of Armed Neutrality countries to inform them that Russia would no longer be a member. All this good news, combined with the heated brick Harte had supplied for his feet, and the pot of hot coffee he had placed at his elbow, should have made Clay content. But whenever he paused to reflect on the events of two nights ago, he still saw the huddled figure in the candle light, the thin bare legs cradled within the circle of his arms, the night cap awry, gently rocking on the hard wooden floor.

As so often when he felt in need of comfort, his eyes travelled to the portrait of his wife, which hung on the bulkhead opposite his desk. Lydia gazed down at him, her eyes full of sympathy.

'What am I to make of such a beastly act, my dear?' he asked. 'It utterly revolts me, and yet that damned Vansittart seems to have been proven right.' He fluttered the ambassador's letter as evidence, as if the painted face could really see. 'With a single act, all is made satisfactory, while if Paul had lived we might well have had the Russians as implacable foes for years to come.' He rose to his feet and started to pace the cabin, leaving the heated brick and coffee to cool.

'But is it truly war, as that bloody man says?' he demanded. 'As valid as the fighting I am engaged in, or is it little better than the violence of the mob brought to serve the state? In which case, how are we any different from the French, with their Terror, and their summary executions?'

He spun around and started to walk back towards the painting. From this angle the face seemed different, the eyes held a hint of concern, together with urgency.

'You are right, my dear,' he sighed. 'Perhaps I should leave such speculation to our philosophers, for we must depart presently. Word of the tsar's death may well prevent a needless war. But there is another duty I must perform first.' He raised his voice sufficient to reach Harte in the coach next door.

'Pass the word for Mr Hockley, if you please, Harte. Ask him if he would care to join me.'

The merchant captain was shown in, and Clay came across to greet him.

'Good day to you, Mr Hockley. Do please take a seat. Would you care for some refreshment? The coffee is excellent.'

'No, thank you, sir,' said the merchant captain. 'I believe you wished to see me?'

'Indeed, I wanted to inform you of some excellent tidings,' said Clay. 'Our ambassador in St Petersburg tells me that Russian ports have now been reopened to our commerce, which means that you and Miss Hockley will be able to find passage home presently. The *Griffin* will be leaving soon. We need to rejoin the fleet with word of the change in regime here.'

'Murdered, was he not, sir?' said Hockley, his face grim. 'The sin of Cain, meted out by his son, or so the rumours say.'

'Tsar Paul was found dead in his bed, after a banquet at which he had shown considerable agitation,' said Clay. 'That is what is being reported.'

'You and Mr Vansittart were present at the palace that

night, were you not?'

'At the banquet, yes,' said Clay. 'But we were seated a long way from the tsar. I saw little of note.' Hockley stared at him for a while, and then shrugged his shoulders.

'"*All they that take the sword shall perish with the sword*", as scripture teaches us, captain,' he concluded, leaving Clay unsure if he was still referring to the tsar.

'A risk that must apply equally to all military men,' he said. 'But you astonish me, Mr Hockley. You seem quite unmoved at the prospect of leaving my ship at last. I thought that you desired it above all things?' His guest sighed before he replied.

'Oh, I welcome the opportunity to leave the *Griffin*, right enough,' he said. 'All has gone ill, since I set foot upon her. But I fear that I may be quitting your frigate alone.'

'Alone?' queried Clay. 'Why so?'

'You know there can be no secrets onboard a ship, Captain,' he said. 'I daresay you will have heard of my estrangement from my daughter.'

'I had not, in truth,' said Clay. 'I have perhaps been too involved with matters ashore, but your spirits do seem very low. What, pray, has occasioned your breach?'

'The folly of an old man, and the native stubbornness of a North Country lass,' explained Hockley. He twisted his hands together as he sat. 'It is as I feared; she has given her heart to your Mr Preston, and so is lost to me now.'

'I see,' said Clay, 'although I do not fully understand the nature of the problem. Why does her attachment to Mr Preston also mean she most forego your society?'

'Because the relationship is objectionable.'

'Does she have an understanding with another gentleman?'

'No, she does not,' said Hockley, rising from his chair and striding about the cabin, following the path that Clay had moments earlier. 'It is I that object to Mr Preston.'

'Hmm, well naval officers are not to everyone's taste, I grant you,' said Clay. 'I myself had some difficulties obtaining the hand of Mrs Clay. I do not want to be guilty of impertinence, but might I offer an opinion?'

'If you wish,' said Hockley, staring out of the cabin windows into the rain.

'I have served with Mr Preston since he was a young midshipman,' said his captain. 'I can assure you that he is from a good family, I am certain he is un-engaged and I know him to have great merits as an officer. He is in possession of a formidable character—the manner in which he has returned to duty after his injury is testament to that. To my mind, he makes a perfectly eligible match.'

'I know all this!' exclaimed Hockley, resuming his pacing. 'I just wanted something more for Sarah! She is my only child. And now I have said things in a passion that have driven her to him, and away from me.'

'Come and sit down, sir, and let me give you council, as one father to another,' said Clay. 'Do you mark that painting of my wife?'

'Aye, she must be a handsome lady. Your second lieutenant was the artist, was he not?'

'Just so,' said Clay. 'When I am troubled, or far from home and missing my wife, as I am now, I look upon her image and I find it soothes me. You see I am devoted to her above all things.'

'You are very fortunate, sir,' said Hockley, pulling out a handkerchief and dabbing at his eyes. 'I lost the support of my own wife many years ago.'

'I have never found the heart to be a vessel that holds a set amount,' continued Clay. 'I could not love her more than I do, and yet I find, to my surprise, I that I can also find much the same affection for another, now that I am blessed with a son.'

'That is very touching, sir, perhaps surprisingly so in a naval captain, but how does that relate to my daughter?'

'Because you speak only of choices in this matter,' said Clay. 'You think that if Miss Hockley admires Mr Preston, she must also be lost to you? But why can she not have affection enough for you both?'

'I have handled matters very ill,' said Hockley, his head bowed. Clay regarded the distraught father for a moment, then felt the familiar stirring of an idea.

'Mr Hockley, will you indulge me a little further,' he said. 'I need to go on deck presently, to attend to our preparations to depart. While I am gone, please make free to use the privacy that my cabin affords.'

'You hope for a reconciliation between me and my daughter?' said Hockley. 'I despair of achieving that.'

'No, I want you to oblige me by conversing with Mr Preston,' he said. 'Not as an aggrieved father, but in a civilised fashion. I fancy your opinion of that young man will change, once you are better acquainted with him. You may yet find it a route to not only regain the affection of your daughter, but perhaps also acquire that of a son.'

He watched Hockley as he wrestled with the idea, and then detected the briefest of nods.

'Harte there!' called Clay. 'Kindly bring me my oilskins, a fresh pot of coffee, and pass the word for Mr Preston.'

******

228

After several hours of labouring in the pouring rain to prepare the ship for sea, the crew of the *Griffin* were all thoroughly drenched. They flowed down the ladder ways and into the grateful warmth and comparative dryness of the lower deck, hungry and ready for their breakfast. As luck would have it, the first tubs of hot burgoo were being delivered to the mess tables from the galley. It was a noisy and boisterous lower deck that gathered around each mess table, the steam from the food mingling with that from the men's sopping garments.

'Your man Ryan Conway's a strange fecker, even for a Lobster,' remarked O'Malley to his fellow mess mates, once the edge had come off his hunger.

'That be Lobsters for you all over,' said Trevan, through his last mouthful of burgoo. 'They be neither fish nor fowl. If it was soldiering they was after, what's wrong with the army? Better vittles and no chance of drowning, I says. Ain't that right, Josh?'

'Not sure as there's much bleeding difference in the fare,' said Rankin, allowing the grey slop in his spoon to splatter back into his bowl. 'But the army can still be proper hazardous. Back in Madras it were sickness as did for nine men from ten.'

'Them ain't odds as I fancy,' said Evans. He took a pull from his cup and made a face. 'Bleeding hell, this small beer's getting sour! I reckon that brew'll poison nine from ten presently. We'll be moving on to Adam's Ale soon, lads.'

'What made you mention Conway, Sean?' asked Sedgwick.

'Me and O'Brian was sharing a pipe, hard by the galley last night, jawing about home and stuff, when your man comes off duty, like,' said O'Malley. 'So he sits down with us, and says as how he's just spent a watch guarding that fecking cut-purse Ludlow, down in the hold.' Rankin looked up from his bowl, and put down his spoon.

'"*Holy Mary, but I need a fecking breather,*" says Conway,' continued O'Malley. '"*If I've told that arse Ludlow to shut up once, I've told the fecker a dozen times. I had to tap him with my musket before he piped down.*"'

'What was the bleeder saying?' asked Rankin.

'Usual stuff you'd expect,' said O'Malley. 'That he's as innocent as half the saints in fecking paradise, and how some bastard's stitched him up.'

'That don't signify any,' remarked Trevan. 'I ain't heard tell of a lifter yet as didn't swear it weren't him as done it. He were caught red-handed, with the goods in his dunnage.'

'There could still be some truth in what he says, Adam,' said Sedgwick. 'I've felt in my bones that something ain't right with this whole thing.'

'What do you mean?' asked Rankin.

'Takes a bold cutpurse to try his hand at thieving on a ship as crowded as this,' commented Sedgwick. 'I wouldn't have marked Ludlow down as having the bottom for it.'

'Maybe he saw that Earnshaw ticker and couldn't stop his bleeding self,' said the valet.

'Perhaps,' said the coxswain. 'That clock's worth a king's ransom ashore, or so I heard Pipe saying, but how would a bloke like Ludlow have come to figure that out?'

'According to Conway, he only took it 'cause some arse had the fecking squeeze on him,' reported the Irishman.

'They squeal all manner of nonsense, once they got the leg irons on and can feel the noose a coming,' said Evans. 'I bleeding hate a cutpurse.'

'This bloke what dropped him in it,' said Rankin. 'Did he

name the bleeder?' O'Malley turned to look at the valet.

'Aye, Joshua Rankin, a name were mentioned,' he said. 'That was why Conway came to find me. See, just before he fecking belted him, he could have sworn Ludlow said something about Big Sam here.'

'Me!' exclaimed Evans. 'What's the little bleeder fingering me for? I ain't had nothing to do with any of this shit!'

'Ah, well, Conway's strong as they come, so Ludlow weren't really able to say much more after he tapped him, like,' said the Irishman.

'Something ain't right, lads,' repeated Sedgwick. 'Why's he bringing Sam's name up? I reckon we should have a little chat with Ludlow. See what he has to say when he ain't being cuffed around by a Lobster. When's your mate Conway due to be guarding him again, Sean?'

'How the feck am I meant to know that?' protested O'Malley. 'Am I after being Corporal Edwards now?'

'Steady Sean, only asking,' said Sedgwick. 'I'll find out myself.'

'Make way there!' ordered a marine private, as he came marching along the lower deck, carrying a tray set with a single bowl and mug.

'Speak of the fecking devil,' said O'Malley, pointing after the soldier. 'There goes the Lobster as is collecting Ludlow's vittles from the galley.'

'Aye, I dare say he is,' said Rankin, deep in thought. Then he looked up. 'His vittles...'

'You all right, Josh?' asked Trevan. 'You look as if you just sighted a spectre.'

'What? No, it were just Sean rattling on about the galley,' he said, rising from the mess table. 'Put me in mind of something I ain't done yet. His Nibs can have a proper temper on if I don't fetch his coffee. I better scarper, lads.'

'But you ain't finished your scoff...' protested Evans towards the fleeing back. 'Ah well. Pass over his bowl, Adam.'

Sedgwick drummed his fingers against the side of his bowl as he watched the valet go, his mind deep in thought. He was turning over the conversation they had just had in his mind. There was something out of place in what had been said, like a wrongly played note in a familiar tune, but the more he searched for it, the further it slipped away from him.

'You all right there, Able?' asked Trevan. 'Now it be you as has gone proper thoughtful, like.'

'He's had his fecking head turned, I reckon, what with all his rattling around in palaces of late, hob-knobbing with Dukes an' the like,' observed O'Malley.

'I were just thinking on Ludlow and this clock,' said Sedgwick. 'Not that the palace weren't a proper eye-opener, even from below stairs.'

'So did you see how their king got done over?' asked Evans. 'Throttled, weren't he?'

'I weren't there when it happened,' said Sedgwick. 'Rankin and Pipe were, although Rankin won't say nothing about it.'

'Rankin was fecking there!' exclaimed O'Malley. 'Your man as nearly strangled the Dane? It was never him, was it?'

Sedgwick shook his head. 'I don't doubt he could have, but remember Pipe was there too. I can't believe he would have stood back and let such a thing happen.'

******

While the sailors were talking, Rankin had already climbed up the main ladder way, taking the steps two at a time, and then rushed out onto the main deck. He hunched deeper into his coat, his hands buried in his pockets against the pelting rain, as he crossed a section of open deck to duck under the forecastle. Ahead of him was the glowing warmth of the immense black iron range that dominated the galley. He arrived just as the marine was setting down his tray on the counter.

'Breakfast for the prisoner, if you please, Mr Walker,' said the soldier, his scarlet back towards the valet.

'Sorry, mate, but can I have a pot of bleeding water first,' said Rankin, arriving next to him. 'Only Vansittart'll skin me if I don't get him his brew sharpish.'

'Bit of a bastard is he, the Hollander?' asked the marine.

'Ain't every Grunter?' said the valet. The soldier smiled at this.

'Aye, that's the truth,' he said. 'Fix him first, Mr Walker. Ludlow can wait.'

'My thanks,' said Rankin. He turned to slap the soldier on the back, and the trailing cuff of his coat caught the wooden bowl on the tray and sent it clattering to the deck. 'Oh, sorry there, mate!' he exclaimed, and stooped down to pick it up. He went to put it back on the tray, and then paused. 'Did you say Ludlow?'

'Aye, that's his dish,' confirmed the marine. Rankin bent over the bowl and spat noisily into it. Then he set it back on the tray. 'Give the filthy little cutpurse that from me.' The marine stared in surprise, and then laughed.

'I guess he deserves that,' he said. He glanced down at the bowl. 'Bleeding hell, did all that spittle come out of you kisser?' The cook came over to join them at the counter.

'Water for the wardroom,' he said, banging down a steaming can, 'and vittles for the prisoner.' With his other hand he slopped a ladle full of burgoo into the bowl. 'Help yourself to small beer from the firkin over there, Private.'

'God bless you, Mr Walker,' said Rankin, picking up the water. 'You've proper saved my life.'

******

Later that day the *Griffin* was underway once more, standing out from the narrow end of the Gulf of Finland, with St Petersburg astern and open grey water ahead. The lashing rain closed in around the frigate as she battled along, making her crew on watch crouch under the gangways and angle their tarpaulin hats into the wind. The dark, forested shores had vanished on either side, as had the last of the floating ice as she sped along with the wind on her beam, driving westwards.

After four hours on watch beside the wheel, Lieutenant Preston was soaked, in spite of the sea boots and oilskins that he wore. He was cold, hungry, and the stump of his arm ached, yet in spite of this he felt content. In his mind he ran through the events of this morning — the summons to come to the captain's day cabin, followed by Clay's departure that had left him in Hockley's company. The strange, stilted conversation they had had, awkward and heavy with leaden pauses, then the dawning realisation that Sarah's father was trying to be pleasant to him. After that had come his encounter with Sarah, close and warm, the taste of her lips against his, the feel of her cascading hair through his fingers. Full of sadness, and yet also promise. Laughter and tears in equal measure.

He opened his eyes to find that the rain was still pouring down, and the midshipman beside him had just turned over the glass and signalled to the belfry. Eight bells rang out, and with a squeal of boatswain's pipes the watch changed over. The quartermaster surrendered the wheel to his replacement and headed gratefully below deck. Around him the new afterguard came charging up to replace their fellows on the quarterdeck, followed by Lieutenant Blake, tugging his hat low against the driving rain as he came up to relieve him.

'What orders, Edward?' his friend asked, glancing down at the slate that hung beside the binnacle.

'Course is west by south,' replied Preston. 'You're to set topgallants if the wind moderates enough for her to bear them. Mr Armstrong says to watch for islands to the northward, and the captain wants to know the moment the wind should freshen.'

'West by south, topgallants, northward isles, captain if it freshens, aye,' repeated Blake, blinking into the driving rain and hunching a little deeper into his coat. 'Now get below, shift out of those wet clothes, and enjoy Britton's beef pudding in the warm, curse you!'

'As you insist, John,' said Preston.

Down in his cabin, Dray, his servant, had just brought in some towels that had been heated on the galley stove, and he rapidly stripped Preston of his wet clothes before helping him to dry himself.

'Bless you, Dray, but that does feel better,' said the officer, as his head emerged through a fresh linen shirt. He towelled his hair dry, while the youngster knelt down at his feet to buckle him into his britches and stockings. A comb through his hair, and Preston began winding his neck cloth about his throat and then tying it one handed, using his mouth to hold the other end. Then he smoothed it into place.

'Not quite as Beau Brummell would have it done, but tolerable nonetheless,' he commented to his reflection in the square of polished steel that hung over the washstand.

'Aye, you do that well now, sir,' said Dray, looking up

from his place on the deck. 'Here are your shoes.' Preston pushed his feet into them, and the youngster stood back up and held the lieutenant's coat out to him.

'Thank you, Dray,' said Preston, as he shrugged it on, before stepped through the cabin door and into the wardroom.

'A quorum at last!' exclaimed Armstrong, from the far side of the table. 'Poor some wine for Mr Preston, Britton, and then away and fetch your noble beef. I am famished.'

'Aye aye, sir,' replied the harassed steward. He filled the lieutenant's glass and Preston took a sip, then relaxed into his chair and surveyed the crowded table.

'Any sign of that damned Frenchman in the offing?' asked Taylor, from the head of the table.

'Not this watch, George,' reported Preston. 'Although a sighting of Noah's Ark might be more likely, should this rain persist.'

'You seem oddly content with life, Edward,' observed Macpherson, from his place beside him. 'I would have expected to find you melancholy in the absence of Miss Hockley.'

'What, have the Hockleys departed?' asked Corbett, his voice peevish. 'Why am I always the last to learn of such matters?'

'The captain's coxswain took them to St Petersburg in the longboat this morning, Doctor,' explained Taylor. 'They plan to take passage home from there.'

'Handsome filly, that one,' remarked Faulkner. 'I admire your taste, Edward, although I shall not regret the absence of that frightful old puritan of a father.'

'I find that he grows on one, upon closer acquaintance,' said Preston.

'Really?' queried Faulkner. 'You astonish me. Why, only yesterday you barely had a civilised word to say about the rogue. What can have occasioned the change?'

'The captain arranged for me to spend an hour in his company this morning,' explained the lieutenant.

'Goodness!' said Macpherson. 'What had you done to merit such punishment?'

'When he has a mind to do so, Mr Hockley can make his society very agreeable,' said Preston.

'What the devil did you find to converse about, Edward?' asked Armstrong.

'Mutual acquaintances back in Yorkshire, maritime matters, the state of navigation, how disagreeable the weather is at present,' listed Preston. 'Oh, and finding that he was so determined to be amiable, I took my opportunity and asked for his daughter's hand.'

'Mind your back there, sir!' announced Britton as he burst through the wardroom door with the steaming pudding held aloft.

'Not now, Britton!' exclaimed Armstrong, waving him away. 'So pray tell us. What did he say?'

'That if Miss Hockley will have me, he has no objections to the match.' There was a roar of approval from the assembled officers, and Preston found his back being pummelled from one side while Macpherson grabbed his hand on the other.

'Well done, laddie!' he enthused.

'Which it is hotter than brimstone, sirs,' supplemented Britton, juggling the dish he still held.

'So has an understanding been reached with the lady?' asked Faulkner.

'It has indeed, George,' said the lieutenant. 'I saw her

immediately after she was reconciled with her father. We shall make the arrangements when I am next on leave.'

'I can't answer for the consequences if it ain't set down soon, sirs!' added the steward.

'Oh quit your whining, and put it on the table, man, and let us drink to their health,' grumbled Taylor.

The steward banged the pudding down with a sigh of relief and stood back, wiping his hands on his apron. Meanwhile, Taylor rose to his feet and raised his glass aloft.

'Gentlemen! Let us drink to the engagement of Mr Preston and Miss Hockley, with a bumper, if you please.' The toast was drunk with considerable good cheer, and the meal got underway. But the first plate of food had only just been served when there was a knock at the wardroom door.

'Beg pardon, sir, but Corporal Edwards is outside,' reported Britton. 'He's asking for Mr Corbett. He says how the prisoner is poorly, an' having some manner of fit.'

CHAPTER 13

RETURN

The body of William Ludlow slid down the tabletop as it was tilted up by his messmates. His remains had been sewn into his hammock with, as was the custom, the last stitch passed through his nose in final confirmation that he was indeed dead. The eighteen-pounder round shot placed at his feet ensured that he vanished beneath the waters of the Baltic. Clay closed his service book and nodded to the boatswain.

'On hats!' ordered Hutchinson, leading the way by cramming his leather one down over his long grey hair.

'Dismiss the men, if you please, Mr Taylor,' ordered his captain.

'Aye aye, sir,' said the first lieutenant.

Clay climbed up the ladder way and emerged onto the quarterdeck, to be greeted by a triumphant crowing from the frigate's hen coop.

'An egg, by Jove, sir,' exclaimed Preston, who was officer of the watch. 'I had despaired of tasting one again this voyage. It would seem that our young ladies find longer days and milder weather more agreeable to them.'

'Quite so,' said the captain, smiling at the transformation in the lieutenant. 'I understand you are something of an expert on the preferences of young ladies more generally. Did that assist in gaining the hand of Miss Hockley?' He half listened to Preston's fulsome reply, but his mind was on the burial service. Fresh air, and a serious walk, he told himself, that is what I need.

'Excellent, Mr Preston,' he concluded, shaking the officer's hand. 'You have my congratulations and best wishes. I shall walk for a while. Pray see I am not disturbed, unless the ship is in peril.'

He began to pace up and down the windward side of the quarterdeck, his head bowed and his hands clasped behind his back. Although he was only in his thirties, Clay had spent two decades amongst sailors. This had given him an acute feel for their moods. He could sense when they were content, and when they were nursing a grievance. He could tell when they were rebellious and angry or when they were boisterous and playful. On one ship he had even witnessed the sullenness and indifference to authority that had preceded a mutiny. A line of soldiers drilled to stand stiffly at attention reveal nothing, but a row of jostling sailors could tell an observant commander all he needed to know. He had watched his crew just now, drawn up in their blocks and divisions, as they had witnessed the burial, and what he had seen surprised him.

William Ludlow had been a thief, and sailors had no time for such people. Thieving upset the harmony of a ship and was often dealt with ruthlessly by the men. Clay had little doubt that the same casual violence his crew showed the enemy could equally be turned onto those who broke the code of the lower deck. So when the ship's surgeon was unable to give him a cause of Ludlow's death, Clay's first thought was that his sailors were in some way responsible. But that was not what he had just witnessed. He had expected to see indifference. Instead he had detected boiling rage.

Up and down Clay paced, his path kept clear of crew and officers by Preston. His mind churned over the possibilities. Why were they so angry? He sifted through the facts, trying to think of a solution that would fit the various pieces into a whole. What were the crew of his ship thinking, and more importantly, what would they do next?

'Excuse me, sir,' said a tentative voice.

'Oh, what is it now?' demanded Clay, rounding on the unfortunate officer.

'Sorry to disturb you, sir, but the lookout is reporting a sail in sight,' said Preston, 'off the bow. He believes it may be the *Liberté.*'

'Thank you, Mr Preston,' said Clay. 'You were quite correct to draw my attention to it. How far off is this sighting?'

'Topsails just clear of the horizon, sir.'

'Very well, get the topgallants on her,' he ordered. 'Royals too, if she will bear them, and let us give chase.'

'All hands!' roared the boatswain's mates. 'All hands to make sail!'

The watch below came running up on deck, spreading out from the fore hatchway like ants teeming from a nest. The top men flew up the shrouds to loosen the sails, while the other seamen took their places at the sheets. Clay looked with satisfaction at the speed with which they ran to their stations now, with hardly any need for direction from the petty officers.

'They have the look of a tolerable crew,' he commented to Preston.

'Aye, the new have blended well with the former *Titans*, sir,' said the lieutenant. 'Do you think we will catch the *Liberté*?'

'Only if she is game,' said Clay. 'Even after the buffeting we gave her, I daresay she can give us royals, and yet prove the swifter ship.'

Sail bloomed above sail on the frigate's lofty masts, her speed growing with each one. By the time the main royal was sheeted home, high above Clay's head, the *Griffin* was leaning over at an angle as steep as that required to slide Ludlow's remains into the sea. Preston and his captain had both made their way up to the windward side of the deck, where they could hold onto the mizzen shrouds. Clay leant out over the side and glanced down. The *Griffin* had rolled a good foot of bright copper clear of the waves. Then he focused his telescope on the ship ahead.

'She is setting more sail too, Mr Preston,' he reported. 'Even on that fished yard we shot through. I don't believe she is anxious to renew our acquaintance.'

'Now here is a merry dance for you,' exclaimed Vansittart, struggling up the steep deck to join them. 'One moment I am playing at backgammon with Lieutenant Macpherson in the wardroom, the next the board is on the floor and the world is angled over like the deuced pyramid of a pharaoh! Probably for the best, mind, for he's a dashed fine player.'

'Apologies to have inconvenienced you, sir, but we have our Frenchman ahead,' said Clay. 'I wanted to come up to her, yet it seems she wishes to keep her distance.'

'If this is the same ship you thrashed some weeks ago, it

is hardly a surprise,' said the diplomat. 'I dare say it is a case of once bitten and twice shy. Does she lie between us and the fleet at Copenhagen?'

'At present, but we will be turning to the south once we have left the Gulf of Finland, sir.'

'Can you catch her?'

'Not without her carrying something away,' said Clay.

'Let her be, Captain,' urged Vansittart. 'You might chase her for a month and not catch her. The word we carry from Russia is of much greater significance than this Frenchman.'

'It goes against every instinct to allow an enemy to escape,' protested Clay.

'Nevertheless, that is what we must do,' said the diplomat. 'War with Russia has been averted. We must try and do the same for Denmark.'

******

It was breakfast once more, and the lower deck was full of noise. The previous day's brief chase of the *Liberté*, abandoned when it had barely started, was still being discussed. But there was also something else in the air, something more urgent. Drained mugs of small beer were banged down on mess tables, sleeves were dragged across mouths and hot burgoo was being shovelled down hungry throats.

'Bleeding hell, but that's better,' announced Rankin, letting his empty bowl drop back onto the table top. 'Filled a proper hole, has that.'

'You've changed your fecking tune,' said O'Malley. 'Time was when you didn't care for our fare at all.'

'Perhaps it's grown on me with closer acquaintance, my Irish friend,' smiled the Londoner. 'Although how you can eat them maggoty rusks is beyond me.'

'They be fine, once you knows how to drive the weevils out,' said Trevan, tapping away at his ship's biscuit.

'You seem in good spirits, Josh,' commented Sedgwick, who had hardly touched his breakfast.

'Maybe I am starting to relish the society of negros,' said Rankin.

'So you ain't missing your mate Ludlow, then?' asked the coxswain.

'I ain't sure where you got the notion as we was friends,' commented Rankin, his eyes watchful.

'Didn't you both come from Seven Dials?' continued Sedgwick. The rest of the table were silent now, watching the two men.

'Plenty of folk hail from there,' said the valet. 'Sam here, for one. Don't mean as how we are all acquainted.'

'That's true,' said Evans. 'An' I didn't recall the little bleeder either, at first. But now that Able has had me thinking upon it, I reckon I can place him. I am certain I saw that Ludlow hanging around with your sort, Josh.'

'My sort?' queried Rankin. 'What's that suppose to bleeding mean? You best go easy with your tone there, Sam lad. *My sort* has friends what you really don't want to go messing with.'

'So you was mates with him, then?' persisted Sedgwick.

'What of it?' said Rankin. 'I knew no end of folk, back in the day. Don't matter, now he's gone and died, does it?'

'Aye, but how did he come to die?' asked Sedgwick.

'What's all this about?' demanded Rankin. 'Speak plain! You trying to say as how I somehow had a part in his sickening? Coz that would take a bleeding miracle, seeing as I never went near the bugger the whole time the Lobsters

244

had him. Now, if you'll excuse me,' he concluded, rising to his feet.

'Sit yourself down, flunky,' growled a voice from behind him, and firm hands pushed Rankin back onto his stool. The valet glanced around to see that a crowd of sailors had gathered to listen. He looked across to the tables where the petty officers normally messed, but they were empty. Directly behind him stood Hibbert and Perkins, two of the watch's larger sailors.

'You are all going to be in such a world of shit, once I tell Mr Vansittart about this,' he said. 'He's mates with the bleeding Prime Minister! An' he plays cards of an evening with Prinny at the palace.'

'Ah, yes, the Hollander,' said Sedgwick. 'Funny you mentioning him. Have you noticed how he's gone right off his morning coffee? The day poor Ludlow was taken sick, you was in a perishing hurry to fetch his brew from the galley. Strange how you ain't done so since.'

'What has that got to do with anything?' demanded Rankin.

'Oh, I think it were proper revealing,' said Sedgwick. 'Sean here says how Ludlow's ready to tell all, then one of the Lobsters passes us to collect his scoff, and you can't get up to the galley fast enough. You even left the burgoo that you seem to be so fond of now.'

'Aye, Ludlow was singing,' snarled the valet, leaning forward and pointing. 'And the only name what he spouted was Sam here!'

'True, but I been thinking upon that an' all,' said the coxswain. 'So I had a word with Conway. Now he's had time to ponder, he ain't so sure as Ludlow was fingering the person what was squeezing him. He thinks he might have been trying to warn someone.'

'Why would he want to warn bleeding Sam?' demanded Rankin.

'Perhaps this clock he stole was going to be stashed in Big Sam's dunnage?'

'And why would I be after setting up Sam here?' scoffed the valet.

'Coz I lumped you back in that bar, Joshua Rankin,' said Evans. 'You always was a nasty shit, as hates them what stands up to you. I daresay Ludlow cheeked you, an' that's why you shopped him in the first place, and then snuffed him out when that didn't answer. I got a good mind to finish you now.'

'Easy, Sam,' said Sedgwick, placing a hand across the chest of the big sailor.

'Is this it, blackamoor?' said Rankin. 'All you got on me was how fast I scarpered to the bleeding galley, and how Sam here reckons I shopped Ludlow?'

'We saw you throttle that poor fecking Dane in Copenhagen,' added O'Malley.

'So are you saying you ain't never seen this big ticker what Ludlow lifted?' asked Sedgwick.

'Never.'

'Then how did you know it were an Earnshaw?' continued the coxswain. 'You said it right here, not three days ago. It sounded odd at the time.'

'W... what's that you're saying?' stuttered Rankin, fear knotting in his stomach. He began to turn on his stool.

'Belay that,' growled Hibbert in his ear. 'I'll stick you long before you can get clear.'

'You named it as an Earnshaw,' continued Sedgwick. 'And you was right, it is. I got the Yank to show me it. *Thomas*

Earnshaw of London, it says, writ across the face. Only you have to open the box it comes in to see any of that, an' you just said you never set eyes on it.'

'Must of heard it mentioned then,' said Rankin. 'Any road, you still ain't said how me running for coffee can kill a man.'

By way of answer Sedgwick held up a little polished brass bottle, the surface richly engraved. The light from the lantern overhead sparkled off the metal. Rankin stopped the involuntary movement of his hand towards his coat pocket, but all had seen it. There was a further growl from Hibbert.

'Where did you...' began Rankin.

'It ain't just Londoners as can lift stuff,' said Sedgwick. 'Every slave needs to thieve, to survive on the plantations. When you ran after that Lobster, like your arse was ablaze, you had no time to fetch nothing. I figured that whatever you put in Ludlow's scoff had to be on you that morning. A quick root in your pockets, and I found this.' The coxswain pulled out the stopper and sniffed cautiously. 'Smells rank,' he declared. 'What is it then? Some manner of poison?'

'It's just balm,' said Rankin, 'from out east, for my joints.' Sedgwick shrugged and handed the bottle back to him.

'Let's hope that's true.' The valet shook the bottle beside his ear

'What's going on?' he demanded. 'It's bleeding empty!' Sedgwick rose to his feet, along with the others and Rankin felt the prick of Hibbert's knife removed.

'Glad you enjoyed your burgoo, Josh,' said Evans, leaning close.

******

Nicholas Vansittart walked with care, avoiding the low beams overhead as he followed Corbett towards the canvas screen.

'I am most concerned about your servant, sir,' the surgeon was saying. 'He presented to me with much the same symptoms as that Ludlow fellow. Blood in his stools and vomit, a growing lethargy of pulse, and yet little sign of any real fever. I must confess to being most uncertain as to the cause.'

'Do you believe he will die?' asked the diplomat, coming to a halt.

'Very like that he will, I fear, sir,' said the doctor. 'Of course nothing is certain, but Ludlow succumbed within a matter of hours.'

'Rankin dead,' murmured Vansittart.

'He may yet surprise us,' said Corbett. 'His constitution is stronger than that of Ludlow, who was a rather inferior specimen. In any event, he is most insistent on speaking with you.'

The surgeon unfastened a flap and held it to one side. Vansittart ducked through the canvas screen and into the sick bay of the *Griffin*. An oil lamp swung to and fro just beside his head, sending yellow light and deep shadow running across the tiny space and the two patients it contained. The occupant of one hammock lay quiet, while in the other a sailor was having the dressing on his heavily bandaged foot unwound by the surgeon's assistant.

'I were just telling Tom here as how I can't be losing my foot, Mr Corbett, sir,' said the seaman, his face beaded with sweat. 'They'll throw me on the parish, and what will my Kate and the nipper do then?'

'Then you should have attended to where your foot was placed during yesterday's practice with the great guns, Morgan,' said Corbett, peering at his patient over the top of his silver-rimmed glasses.

'That larboard carriage wheel ain't never rolled true,' muttered the sailor, as the dressing fell open to reveal a blackened mass, encrusted with dried blood. The surgeon bent over the soiled bandages that his assistant held out and sniffed at them.

'Hmm,' he muttered, before advancing like a bloodhound across to the crushed foot. Some more sniffing and he stood back upright. 'There is no putrefaction. I dare say if that remains the case we may yet save the limb. But at the first hint of corruption, I shall be reaching for my saw. We do not wish Mistress Kate to be obliged to dress in widow's weeds, eh?'

'Fair enough, sir,' said Morgan, easing himself back in the hammock. 'Truss it up, and make all fast, if you please, Tom,' he said, to the sickbay attendant.

'Now then, Mr Vansittart, let us see if your man is still conscious,' said Corbett, moving across to the second patient. 'You will need to lean close, for the power of his voice is quite spent. Do you have a cloth to mask your nose and mouth? I do not think there is contagion, but while I am so uncertain about what ails him we had best take care. It would be a sad pass if we were to lose you as well.'

'Quite so,' said Vansittart, producing a large emerald green handkerchief from his pocket. The scent of cologne filled the tiny space as he scrunched it into a wad and held it over his lower face and then took Corbett's place beside the hammock.

The valet had been transformed in appearance since he had seen him earlier that day. The tanned face was grey and drawn, the lips blue and flecked with a dry white scum, and the hand that gripped the top edge of the blanket trembled uncontrollably. He had expected Rankin to be asleep, but found two fierce eyes staring back at him.

'How do you fare now, Rankin?' he asked, bending his ear close to pick up the answer.

'Shit... ' came the reply, just above a whisper. 'Done... for...'

'I am very sorry to hear that, Rankin. I truly am.'

'Owe... me...' stuttered the valet. 'Murder... tsar...' Vansittart glanced over his shoulder. The assistant was busy dressing Morgan's foot, while Corbett had moved away and was looking through his dispensary chest.

'Steady, Rankin,' he murmured. 'Let us not speak of such things, until you are mended.' The valet reached out with a trembling hand, and drew him closer by his lapel.

'Dying... poison...' he gasped. 'Bastards... burgoo...'

'You make no sense, Rankin,' said Vansittart. 'What poison? Who did this?'

'Sedgwick!' he whispered, with a final effort. 'Kill... him... tsar...'

'Very well,' said the diplomat. 'I believe I follow you. You think that the captain's coxswain is responsible for what has happened to you, and you wish to be avenged? Is that it?'

The huge effort made by the dying Rankin had washed past now, leaving him exhausted. His eyes closed and his chest heaved a little. A droplet of bright red rolled out from one nostril. Then his head faintly nodded, and was still. The diplomat pried open the hand that clutched his coat, and let it fall back onto the blanket.

'Did he have anything of import to recount, sir?' asked the surgeon, coming to his side and feeling for the patient's wrist. With his other hand he pulled out his watch and flipped open the cover.

'What?' queried Vansittart, still deep in thought. 'Oh, nothing of note. A sweetheart to whom he wishes to be remembered, and a message for his mother, that is all. Tell me, did you find a small metal bottle on his person?'

'With an oriental pattern, sir?' asked Corbett. 'I believe it is in the coat hanging there, together with a curious length of cord.'

'I had best look after those,' said the diplomat. 'How is he?'

'Ebbing fast, I fear,' said the surgeon, peeling back an eyelid.

'Good, good,' muttered Vansittart, his hands already deep in the pockets of his valet's jacket.

'I beg your pardon?' queried Corbett. 'What is it that you find to be good?'

'Eh, I meant that it is for the best that the poor man's ordeal is almost at an end. Would you excuse me now, Doctor?'

******

The frigate made good progress after her encounter with the *Liberté*, rushing ever southward and westward, with a northerly wind driving her on. The days ticked by, each spent crossing a Baltic empty of ice, and slowly beginning to fill with shipping once more. But all the sails they encountered fled before them, unsure whether the warship was friend or foe, till one afternoon she finally rounded Maklappen Point at the extreme southwest tip of Sweden and entered the approaches to Copenhagen. From the masthead, the green spires and trailing chimney smoke of the Danish capital was in sight, together with the distant masts of a large fleet that lay in the Sound. Almost within touching distance, if only the

ALLAN

wind would change direction. The sun had some spring warmth in it, but was steadily dropping towards the horizon.

'Can we not make more progress, Clay?' asked Vansittart, gesturing towards the north.

'Not at present, sir,' reported the captain. 'This wind is dead foul, and unless it should shift we can only advance by beating into it, as we are doing. Mr Armstrong believes those clouds there may indicate change.' He reached out to touch the rail with his hand as he said this, and the diplomat noticed the gesture.

'You don't seem very assured,' he observed.

'I have been a mariner for too many years to predict what the weather will do with any confidence,' said Clay. 'But I too am anxious to get up with the fleet. They are just off Copenhagen now, and if I know Lord Nelson he will not long delay getting to grips with the enemy.'

'Quite so,' said Vansittart. 'Can't you send one of those deuced signals you naval coves are always rattling on about? With flags and the like?'

'None that can be seen at dusk, from fifteen miles away, sir,' observed the captain.

'How vexing,' said the diplomat.

'I have yet to say how sorry I was at the death of your valet,' said Clay, after a pause. 'Mr Corbett is quite bemused as to what killed him and Ludlow. He did fear it might be some sickness, but the rest of the crew seem unaffected.'

'Ah, yes, most unfortunate,' said Vansittart. 'Thank you for your concern, but pray, have no anxiety on my part. Mr Taylor was good enough to furnish me with one of your volunteers, who makes a decidedly superior servant.' Vansittart was about to say something more when Clay held up a hand, and looked towards the commissioning pennant at the masthead.

'Do you feel that, Mr Taylor?' he called.

'Aye, sir,' replied the first lieutenant. 'Now blowing north-northeast, perhaps?'

'Maybe even further round, sir,' suggested Armstrong. 'Northeast by north, I should say. Change, just as I predicted!'

The diplomat looked from one naval officer to the next. 'I confess to not having the pleasure of understanding you gentlemen at all, with your this-this by that, but I am sure you know your business,' he sniffed. 'Does all this mean we may yet reach our destination?'

'The wind is shifting, sir,' said Clay. 'Should it continue to do so, we may come up with the fleet by nightfall.'

The wind did indeed continue to swing around until it settled in the east, with the promise that it might back further. Now the *Griffin* made much better progress, although Clay's prediction was a little off. It was after dark when they came sliding across the calm waters of the Sound once more, towards the mass of anchored warships, their bulky hulls and web of masts backlit by the glow of Copenhagen, spread along the shore.

'What is the current night recognition signal, Mr Preston?' asked Clay of the officer of the watch beside him.

'A red bengal and a blue light, displayed together from the foretop, sir,' replied the lieutenant.

'Have it made now, if you please.'

'Aye aye, sir,' said Preston. Soon crimson and blue shone out from high up in the rigging, while Todd, the teenage signal midshipman, watched the flagship through a night glass.

'Flagship has made the correct response, sir,' reported the

youngster. 'Oh, and now they're signalling!' There was a pause while a pattern of coloured lamps formed in the rigging of the lead ship.

'It's for us, sir. *Captain to repair onboard.*'

'Thank you, Mr Todd,' said Clay. 'Acknowledge, if you please.'

'Aye aye, sir,' came the reply.

'Mr Preston, kindly have my barge called away, and pass the word for Mr Vansittart,' ordered Clay.

'Aye aye, sir,' said the lieutenant.

Soon Vansittart was making his uncertain way down the frigate's side, breathing heavily in the dark. He was being hurried along by the barge crew, all anxious not to tarnish their ship's reputation by keeping the admiral waiting.

'Yes, yes, I am descending as quickly as I am able, unless you desire me drowned?' he said testily. Clay went after him, clutching his package of reports with everything that had occurred since the *Griffin* had left Great Yarmouth, seemingly an age ago. It had come as something of a surprise, when leafing through the log book earlier, to find that the frigate had been at sea for a bare few months. He settled himself in the stern sheets next to his coxswain.

'Give way, if you please,' he ordered. 'Far side of the flagship, Sedgwick. It is too late for ceremony.'

'Aye aye, sir,' said his coxswain. 'Push off in the bow, there! Give way larboards!' The boat turned in a tight circle towards the line of warships and quickly crossed the few hundred yards of sea between the side of the frigate and the two-decked ship of the line.

'Boat ahoy,' came a hail from ahead.

'*Griffin!*' replied Sedgwick, followed by an urgent hiss towards the boat crew. 'Pull handsomely in the bow there!'

The big hull towered above them like a cliff. Sedgwick rounded her stern and rowed into the pool of light that came from the double line of windows above them. Water sloshed and sucked against the big seventy-four's enormous rudder as they passed beneath the counter, and Clay glanced up to read the ship's name in the light.

'*Elephant*,' he mused. 'Surely that is Captain Foley's ship?'

'I daresay it is,' said Vansittart from out of the gloom. 'What of it?'

'I served with him in the Mediterranean a few years back,' said Clay. 'But my surprise is to find that his is a flagship. It was nothing of the sort when we left.'

'Easy there!' ordered the coxswain. 'In oars! Clap on in the bow!' The boat swept neatly up to the thin steps built into the warship's bulging side.

'Have a care on these, sir,' said Clay, looking at the diplomat. 'The lower ones will be slick and treacherous, and the side of a seventy-four is higher than you imagine.'

'Me and the lads will see him aboard, sir,' said Sedgwick, as Clay made his way to the side of the boat, grabbed hold of the hand rope, and climbed up to the entry port.

'Boyo! Now I know things are serious!' said the well-remembered voice, and Clay found his hand engulfed by the big Welshman's paw.

'Good to see you again, sir,' he smiled. 'My, but it's been a while.' There was a frantic scrabbling sound from behind, and his companion arrived, with a hand on his hat and his coat awry, having been boosted up the side with some force from below. 'May I name the Honourable Nicholas Vansittart? This is Captain Thomas Foley, who commanded the *Goliath* at the Battle of the Nile.'

'In truth, I just followed Clay 'ere,' replied the Welshman, giving his fellow captain a playful punch on the arm. 'Welcome aboard, Mr Vansittart.'

'Delighted, I am sure,' replied the diplomat, straightening his clothes before holding out his hand.

'Right, follow astern,' said Foley. 'Let's get a glass of something with his lordship.'

The great cabin of the *Elephant* was full of light and activity. Several midshipmen sat in a line along the dining table, like pupils at a school desk, copying out orders. Others stood beside them, waiting to take them away. At another table a group of officers were gathered around a sailing master, who was explaining something on a chart. In the corner, a tiny man lay on a cot, dictating fresh orders to a clerk sat beside the bed. Hanging on a peg near him was a heavily decorated coat. He looked over when Foley came in, then jumped up from the bed to patter over in his stockinged feet. The empty sleeve of his shirt reminded Clay of Preston, but there any similarity ended as he took in the familiar figure. The long brown hair was threaded with a little silver above the temples now, but the prominent nose and generous mouth were much as he remembered. Once again, he went through the uncertainty as to which eye he should focus on. He ignored the right, blank as a shark's, and looked instead at the one that sparkled with pleasure.

'Captain Clay, my dear sir!' exclaimed Nelson, his accent thick Norfolk. 'I felt sure that you would somehow contrive to be present for our battle! Did I not say as much, Captain Foley? There is no man in the service with a better nose for the scent of gun smoke.'

'I am truly delighted to see you again, my lord,' said Clay. 'If only so I can thank you properly for the invaluable letter you wrote for my court martial.'

'It was nothing,' said Nelson. 'Why such a drama was being made of a fighting captain losing his command is beyond me. If I had been censured every time I ran a ship into danger, I should have long ago been out of the service and never in the House of Peers! But I am uncommonly pleased that you are here. Now I shall have a good few of my Band of Nile Brothers with me. You and Foley of course, Tom Hardy too, Freemantle in the *Ganges* and Thompson in the *Bellona*. God help the poor Danes when we come at them, what?'

'I believe you know Mr Vansittart,' said Clay, bringing the diplomat into the conversation.

'Welcome, sir,' said the admiral. 'We received your dispatch from Copenhagen after the Danes refusal to comply with your demands. It was most welcome for getting the fleet away from Great Yarmouth at long last. Without it, I daresay Sir Hyde would still be hosting balls for his new wife! But now there is a battle to be won, he at least has had the good sense to leave the fighting to me.'

'That is reassuring,' said Vansittart. 'Concerning that, I wonder if we might speak with your Lordship in private. We have come as expeditiously as possible from St Petersburg, with intelligence of some importance.'

'By all means,' said Nelson. 'Pray come through to the coach. If we were on my flagship I could offer you more lavish hospitality, but the *St George*, along with the other larger rates, draw too much for these waters. Sir Hyde has given me most of the smaller ships for tomorrow.' He led the way through into the day cabin, and they took their places around the chart table.

'A glass of sherry wine, gentlemen?' asked Foley, bringing

over a ship's decanter and a fistful of glasses.

'Thank you, Captain, most kind,' said the diplomat, sipping at the dark liquid and grimacing slightly. 'Now, to business. I bring some excellent news. Tsar Paul is no more, and has been replaced on the throne by his son, Alexander.'

'He's dead!' exclaimed Nelson. 'How did such a thing happen?' Vansittart straightened his glass on the table and shot a warning stare at Clay, before replying.

'Reports are a little confused, my lord' he said. 'He seemed to have died in his bed, or at least in his bedchamber. Where the intrigues of the Russian court are concerned, I find it pays well not to inquire too closely into the particulars.'

'Still, that is excellent for us, my lord,' said Foley. 'Wasn't Paul behind all this wicked armed neutrality nonsense?'

'Those devils, the French, were the true instigators,' corrected Nelson. 'But it is welcome tidings, I don't doubt.'

'Indeed, my lord,' said Vansittart. 'When we left, Lord Whitworth was busy negotiating an end to Russia's participation in the pact of armed neutrality, and all British shipping seized under the orders of Tsar Paul had been returned. Furthermore, I understand from the ambassador that Sweden and Prussia are certain to follow the Russian lead.'

'And what of the Danes?' asked Nelson.

'That I do not know, my lord,' said Vansittart.

'Word of Paul's death cannot have arrived in Copenhagen any swifter than we did, my lord,' said Clay. 'I am sure they will acquiesce when they learn what has happened.'

'I dare say they might, Captain, but the situation is not so simple,' said Nelson. 'The Danes have chosen to defy us. Their Crown Prince refused to see you, did he not, sir?'

'That is correct, my lord,' said Vansittart.

'Our ambassador had his passport returned to him,' continued the admiral. 'That wretched Chief Minister Bernstorff is a virtual puppet of the damned French. Blows have been exchanged, too. Their coastal batteries fired on our ships as we passed through the Sound, and we responded in kind. They have chosen the path of war and defiance, gentlemen. So we shall still attack at first light.'

'But surely once they learn what has happened in Russia...' urged Clay.

'I have no doubt that they will want to make peace when they hear which way the wind is now blowing,' scoffed Nelson. 'But what of all the trouble we have been put to? Sending such a huge fleet out to the Baltic? The treasure spent, at a time when our country is fighting for its very life? What of the defiance offered to our king?' Clay looked to Vansittart for support, but the diplomat's face was stony. Then he felt Nelson's hand on his. He looked around, and found the single blue eye looking at him, the expression kindly.

'It is a noble thing to wish to save unnecessary bloodshed, Alexander, but in this you must trust me,' he said. 'We are fighting a war between reason and chaos. Between revolution and order, good and ill, the righteous and the wicked. All must choose their sides, and the Danes have chosen unwisely. They must be taught a sharp lesson, if only to prevent others from following that path. Consider when you order a seaman flogged. It does him some good, for sure, but it also teaches those who witness the punishment the folly of opposition.'

'I understand, my lord,' sighed Clay. 'What part would you have me play?'

'Good man!' enthused Nelson. 'I was certain I could rely on you. But you have been in Copenhagen already, and have viewed this line of ships and hulks the Danes have moored along the seafront of the city. What would you do, if you were I?'

'Their line is very strong at the northernmost end, my lord,' said Clay. 'That is where they have built that huge battery on piles. The southern end has no such protection. My coxswain had occasion to walk along that stretch of shore, and reported as much. I would sail around the shallows in the middle of the Sound, attack from the south and roll up the Danish line as if it were a carpet. Also the wind favours such a move.'

'You see, Foley,' said Nelson. 'Clay is exactly of my way of thinking. Your plan may be thought bold, but I am of the opinion that the boldest measures in war are always the safest, which is why I have been issuing orders for just such an attack. We will make peace with the Danes tomorrow evening, I don't doubt, but in the morning we shall fight them.'

CHAPTER 14

THE MIDDLE GROUND

'Two bells in the morning watch, sir,' reported Yates, holding a glowing lantern up with one hand, and a can of steaming water in the other. Clay groaned and tried to roll away from the light. 'Still dark, sir,' continued the servant's remorseless voice, 'but I reckon there's a little fog, and Mr Taylor says the wind is steady, south by east.'

Wind in the south. Wind in the south, repeated Clay to himself, as he drifted up from sleep, letting the clinging arms of his wife fade back into his dreams. For some reason, that seemed important. Then he sat up in his cot. It was the second of April, 1801, and today his ship was going into battle.

'South by east, you say?' he said as he rose from his cot. 'Thank you, Yates. That is most welcome.' He pulled his nightshirt off, dropped it into the young man's hands and wandered over to his washstand.

Ten minutes later he was clean, dressed and shaved and sitting before a fresh pot of coffee, re-reading the orders that had arrived from the *Elephant* in the early hours of the morning. They were strangely open, where his frigate was concerned. Having assigned a precise opponent in the Danish line for each of the ships under his command, Nelson had gone on to give the *Griffin* a much freer role. He was ordered to contribute to the battle "*as circumstances permitted*" and "*as he saw fit.*" Clay looked out of the window lights at the back of the cabin, onto the dark sea, as he considered what was really expected of him. Of course, the looseness of his instructions could be a simple reflection of his unexpected arrival, after the admiral had already finalised his plans. Or perhaps they indicated the relative insignificance of his frigate, amongst all the hulking ships of the line that made up most of Nelson's command, but Clay thought not. He fancied he detected something else at work here. What looked like flattering trust in his judgement might also be a test. Maybe Nelson was less sanguine than he had appeared about a captain whose last command had ended as a smouldering mound of cinders on a French beach, and wanted to see for himself how Clay would act when given freedom.

'Yates!' he called towards his sleeping cabin. 'Kindly pass the word for Mr Taylor, if you please. And tell Harte to lay another place for breakfast.'

Lieutenant Taylor was already prepared for action when he came into the cabin. He was in his best uniform, his silver Nile medal pinned to his lapel, his sword buckled around his middle, and Clay thought he detected the heavy bulge of a pistol in his coat pocket.

'With that much to do this morning, I wasn't sure if I should have time to shift garments later, sir,' Taylor said, a little apologetically.

'Pray make yourself comfortable now,' said Clay. 'Yates!

Come and relieve Mr Taylor of his sword and coat.' Once the two were seated, Harte came into the cabin, holding a large dish in his hand.

'Salt bacon, biscuit crumbs fried in molasses, and eggs, all hot from the pan, sir,' he announced, as he placed it down between the two men. 'Biscuits with two kinds of preserve on the side, and that Russian butter in the croc ain't too rancid. Shall I fetch more coffee?'

'If you please, Harte,' said Clay, helping his guest to food. 'I take it you have arranged substantial fare for the people?'

'Yes sir,' confirmed Taylor, as he accepted the plate. 'The galley is cooking it now. The men will have a meal early, after which we shall make ready to get under way.'

'Excellent,' said his captain. 'Would it inconvenience you to read our orders while we eat? You need to be familiar with them, in case I should fall.'

'By no means, sir,' said the lieutenant, accepting the document that his captain passed across. A period of quiet followed, while he read. 'They seem a little, eh... imprecise, with regard to our role, sir.'

'Ain't that the truth,' said Clay, through a mouthful of bacon. 'Lord Nelson has licensed us to carry on as we please. My intention will be to support Captain Lawford in the *Polyphemus*, in the first instance. He will be directly ahead of us in the line, and is tasked with attacking the southernmost Danish ship. Then we shall see how the battle unfolds.'

'I note we are ordered to be ready to anchor by the stern,' said Taylor, reading on. 'That is sensible, with a following wind. By your leave, I shall get Mr Harrison to have the kedge anchor moved and a cable prepared.'

'And a spring, too,' added Clay. 'I hope to lay across the

bow of the end-most Dane.'

'Aye aye, sir,' said Taylor, returning to the orders. After a pause he tapped the final section of them. 'I don't like the sound of this last part, regarding all the navigation hazards. Now the wretched Danes have pulled up all the buoys, it is treacherous hereabouts. Mr Armstrong says this Middle Ground we shall have to sail around is shallow as a dish, miles long, without a trace of it showing proud of the water.'

'Enemy cannons on one side, and an impassable mud bank on the other,' smiled Clay. 'What could possibly go wrong? Fortunately we shall be following in the wake of the larger ships, and Captain Hardy will have marked the southernmost end of the shoal during the night.'

'Hmm, I suppose if we follow where the *Elephant* and the other seventy-fours can float, there should be water enough for the likes of us, sir,' conceded Taylor.

'Pray God that is so,' said his captain.

'Amen to that, sir,' said Taylor. 'So what will be done about the enormous battery at the northern end of the Danish line?'

'We spoke of that last night on board the *Elephant*,' said Clay. 'Sir Hyde with the main part of the fleet will bombard it, while Captain Riou and his frigate squadron make a demonstration before it.'

'Riou?' queried Taylor. 'That name is familiar, sir. Isn't he the chap who should have been drowned on the old *Guardian*, back in eighty-nine?'

'The very same,' confirmed his captain. 'He struck a mountain of ice in the Southern Ocean on his way to Botany Bay. Most of the crew got back to the Cape in the boats, while he stayed onboard with a few of the bolder souls to try and save the ship. Every one believed him dead, and then two months later, the *Guardian* limped into port, with the sea washing over her deck.'

Both men fell silent, remembering their own desperate attempts to save their ship the previous year.

'Perhaps if we had been as determined as Captain Riou...' began Clay.

'Nothing more could have been done for the *Titan*, sir,' said the veteran lieutenant. 'Of that I am certain.'

'No, I daresay you are right, George,' said Clay, staring at his plate. Then he looked up more brightly. 'Now, let us eat, for goodness only knows when we shall have the leisure to do so again.'

******

Clay came onto the quarterdeck, just as the first light of dawn was growing in the sky. In the east was a thin line of rose, behind the dark wooded shore of Sweden. The waters of the Sound slopped against the sides of the British warships, the yellow bands on their hulls slowly resolving in the growing light. All were anchored with their long bowsprits pointing as one, like weathervanes, in the same direction. South by East, into the steady wind that would soon take them into battle. A little mist trailed across the cold sea, weaving its way between the ships and off towards the north.

Clay acknowledge the salutes of the officers who stood in groups dotted across the deck, all armed and dressed for battle, waiting for the day to begin. Standing a little apart from the others was Vansittart, immaculately turned out as always.

'Good morning, gentlemen,' said the captain. 'My glass, if you please, Mr Russell.'

The midshipman of the watch passed the telescope across, and Clay walked to the side of the ship that faced

Copenhagen. There was the city, sprawling along the shore, protected by its row of warships. Through a gap between two Royal Navy seventy-fours, he could see a portion of the Danish line. It was much as he remembered from his last visit, a motley collection of ships, moored bow to stern. Some seemed little more than floating hulks, with only a single mast left, like the flag pole above a fortification. Others were lofty two-deckers, fully rigged with yards crossed, as if ready to set sail. But every ship had two things in common. They bristled with cannon, run out already, and at the top of every mast fluttered the deep red and white flag of Denmark.

'The enemy seem well prepared to receive us, sir,' commented his first lieutenant from the rail beside him.

'So it would seem, Mr Taylor,' said Clay.

'No prospect of steering between them, as we did at the Nile, sir,' added the sailing master, from his other side. 'They are moored so close together, I doubt if anything above a longboat could pass through.'

'Captain Hardy surveyed their position two nights ago, in a launch,' said Clay. 'There is little prospect of coming between the Danes and the shore. They are anchored on the very edge of the deep water channel.'

'Flagship signalling, sir!' announced Midshipman Todd. '*All ships to prepare for battle.*' Clay slid his telescope closed, aware that everyone's eyes were on him.

'Acknowledge, if you please, Mr Todd,' he said. 'Mr Taylor, will you kindly have the ship cleared for action.'

'Does this mean that I shall be required to join Mr Corbett amongst the rats in the hold again?' said Vansittart, examining the smooth broadcloth of his coat.

'I fear so, once matters become warm, sir,' said Clay. 'But there is no occasion for you to go there directly. I daresay there will be some hours of manoeuvring for you to observe. I shall tell you when I require you to go below.'

'My thanks, Captain,' said the diplomat. 'Now that I have mastered my sea sickness, I find life on the azure main quite tolerable.'

'In spite of the limitations of the accommodation, sir?' asked Armstrong, provoking chuckles amongst the officers.

'Ah, there you have me, Mr Armstrong,' smiled Vansittart. 'I don't belief I shall ever be reconciled to that.'

A thunderous drum roll started on the deck beneath them, close to the base of the mainmast, the sound echoing back to the *Griffin* from the ships all around them. In response the crew of the frigate scattered to their stations.

Some climbed upwards, like the armourer and his mate, hauling aloft iron chain-slings to reinforce the hemp that held the heavier yards in place. They were followed up the shrouds by the marine marksmen, each one carrying spare boxes of cartridges, to help with them with their job of clearing the enemy's deck of opponents.

Some disappeared downwards, like the gunner, into the pink-tinged gloom of the magazine, safe below the waterline. The space was lined with sheet copper, hard enough to resist rats or damp, soft enough not to raise a spark from a carelessly dropped tool. With his mate, he started to line up the gun charges, stacking the serge bags, like bricks in a wall, close to the heavy cloth 'fear-nought' screen. Beyond it he could hear the expectant crowd of ship's boys, ready with their leather charge cases to bring the powder up to the guns.

Richard Corbett was below the waterline too, down in the stuffy dark of the cockpit. There was only five feet of headroom, and his assistants had to bend over double as they lashed the officers' sea chests together beneath a canvas cover, to form his operating table. Off to one side the surgeon lay out his instruments, the light from the lantern glittering from sharp edges and jagged teeth.

'Saw, lesser knife, probe, extractor, gag, chains,' he muttered as he lined them up. 'Pray God we have sufficient laudanum.'

But it was to the frigate's main deck that most of the crew of the *Griffin* went. While Clay was up on the quarterdeck, examining the line of Danish warships, all trace of his living quarters was vanishing from beneath his feet. Bulkheads were knocked down, furniture dragged away, possessions gathered up. Within a matter of minutes an uninterrupted space had been created, a hundred and fifty feet long and almost forty wide. This was Lieutenant John Blake's domain, and he stood at its very heart, revelling in all that was happening around him. He stepped aside as a pair of sailors rushed past, scattering sand over the deck to give the gun crews purchase on planking that might become slick with water, or worse. Around each of the big eighteen-pounders a crew had gathered, busy preparing for battle. Many were stripping off their shirts, others were winding their neck clothes into bandanas to protect their ears. Behind him a queue of men had formed to collect buckets of water from the ship's pumps. Ahead of him the tall figure of Evans was pulling his cannon's rammer from its place under the gangway, while beside him O'Malley blew life into the glowing end of a length of slow match. Tackles were being rigged and tested, cannons were being cast free, and seamen were rushing to-and-fro. And then people reached their places, or stood back from their completed tasks, and the confused, busy movement became a settled, familiar pattern. He saw nods exchanged between gun crews and their captains, captains and their petty officers, and petty officers and their midshipman. Across the crowded deck came Midshipman Russell, touching his hat when he arrived in front of Blake.

'The guns are ready for action, sir,' he reported.

'Thank you, Mr Russell,' said the lieutenant. 'Will you kindly give my compliments to the captain, and inform him of that.'

'Aye aye, sir.'

Russell strode to the ladder way and climbed up onto a quarterdeck that had suddenly filled with life. More gun crews here, clustered around the big carronades, with marines lining the gaps between them. He picked out the figure of his captain, obvious in his glittering uniform, where he stood by the rail with his telescope in his hand.

'Mr Blake's compliments, and the great guns are ready, sir,' he reported.

'Thank you, Mr Russell,' said Clay. 'Kindly report that we are cleared for action to the flag, Mr Todd.'

As Russell departed he heard the little midshipman's high falsetto behind him.

'Flag acknowledges, sir!' he cried. 'Now the admiral is signalling to all ships. *Form line of battle as previously ordered.*'

'Thank you, Mr Todd,' he heard Clay reply. 'Raise the anchor, if you please Mr Taylor. Our place is in the rear, directly behind *Polyphemus*.'

******

The battle line of two-decked British warships was gradually forming as they approached the southern end of the Middle Ground. Big seventy-fours, with masts that towered into the grey sky, were mixed with smaller sixty-fours and two little fifty-gun ships from an earlier age, valuable once again thanks to their shallow drafts. Ahead of the main fleet was a swarm of seven frigates and sloops, while bringing up the rear came the *Griffin*, swinging into position with the ornate stern of the *Polyphemus* filling the space beyond her long bowsprit.

'A cable length, no more and no less, if you please, Mr Hutchinson!' yelled Taylor towards the bow. 'Set some of your men to spilling wind from the foretopsail!' The grey-haired boatswain on the forecastle raised a hand in acknowledgment, and a group of crew ran to man the sheets.

'Those tubs ahead are slower than a gaggle of Dutch herring busses, sir,' supplemented the first lieutenant. 'We shall need to look sharp not to run ourselves onboard them.'

'Quite so, Mr Taylor,' agreed his captain.

'This is very engaging,' enthused Vansittart. 'The commencement of a genuine fleet action, all occurring before my eyes! Although I must confess to having little notion as to the significant parts. What, pray, are all these various groups of ships about?'

Clay looked around him and assessed the situation. 'As the ship is now prepared, and we have a little time before we shall be engaged, I daresay I can oblige you with an explanation, sir,' he conceded. 'But if Lord Nelson should signal, or action commence sooner...'

'Then I shall meekly withdraw to my little box amongst the rodents.'

'Very well, sir,' said Clay. 'Kindly take my glass, and I shall make haste to explain all. You shall need to close an eye. And for preference not the one engaged in looking through the apparatus. Just so. Let us start with the enemy, for his part is easily explained.'

'Yes,' said the diplomat, swinging the telescope towards the shore and causing Armstrong to step back out of its path. 'The row of sundry vessels, betwixt us and the city, that all show Danish colours. Mr Preston was good enough to point them out earlier.'

'Indeed, there are some twenty in all, with a very large gun battery on piles covering the far end of the line, together with sundry guns on shore that may serve to annoy us.'

'I think I can see some now,' said Vansittart, pointing the telescope towards the Danish coast. 'Some cannons over there, behind earthworks.'

'Very good,' said Clay. 'Then we have Lord Nelson's force, which is this line of ships we are part of. Captain Rioux commands the smaller craft in the van, but they need not concern us. They will sail away presently to engage the large battery with feints and the like, while the twelve larger vessels, including us, set about the Danish fleet.'

'Twelve against twenty,' remarked the diplomat. 'They don't seem the best of odds. I thought Sir Hyde commanded a rather larger force?'

'Indeed he does, and if you direct your gaze towards the north—no, sir, in that direction,' said Clay. 'Do you see the ships over yonder?'

'I do,' said the diplomat. 'They seem very distant.'

'That is the main fleet,' explained Clay. 'For the most part they are the vessels that are too large to come at the Danes in the narrow channel where they are moored,' explained Clay.

'How unfortunate,' mused Vansittart. 'And what pray are those small vessels anchored in a line, just over there. Oh, I see now, they are badly damaged. Why, every one of them has lost their front masts.'

'Not quite, sir,' said Clay. 'For they never had any *foremasts* to lose. They are bomb ketches. They lob prodigiously large exploding shells from out of a big mortar set in their bow.' The diplomat lowered the telescope and looked at Clay.

'That sounds decidedly better,' he said. 'Will they not make short work of these Danish ships?'

'Alas, no,' said Clay. 'For they are also prodigiously inaccurate, sir. But they may have a part to play in the battle, firing over our heads at the enemy. Once the Danish ships have been captured, they will be brought closer in to bombard the city, a target so large even bomb ketches cannot miss.'

'Bombard the city!' exclaimed Vansittart, before dropping his voice so only Clay could hear. 'And you thought my actions in St Petersburg were barbarous.'

'It is only the threat that will be required, sir,' said Clay. 'I am sure a talented diplomat, such as yourself, will be able to negotiate an end to this conflict with such powerful arguments to hand.'

As the two men contemplated the line of bomb ketches moored on the far side of the Middle Ground, one of them spouted a column of flame from its bow. A thin arc of white smoke was drawn across the sky, heading for the Danish ships, while the ketch itself bucked and pulled against its anchor with the force of the recoil. Moments later the dull boom of the shot echoed across the water.

'Now that firing has begun, sir, I must require you to go below,' said Clay.

'Very well, Captain,' said Vansittart, returning the telescope to its owner. 'I shall honour my undertaking and retreat into your hold to join Mr Corbett. My only regret is that I didn't choose to wear my third best weskit this morning.' He then leant forward and gripped Clay's hand. 'The very best of good fortune to you and your men, Captain. I shall see you presently, I don't doubt, when this day is done.'

******

All bar one of Nelson's ships successfully rounded the southern end of the Middle Ground. The lone exception was the leading sixty-four, which had turned too early and now lay at a strange, lifeless angle where she had run herself up onto the slick, gripping mud. Across the water came the sound of shouted orders as she launched her boats in an attempt to pull herself off. Beside her a painted red keg bobbed in the water.

'Shame not to have the *Agamemnon* with us,' remarked Taylor. 'Good fighting ship, that. I wonder why she missed her mark. The buoy placed to guide us seems plain to see.'

'Because she has a fool for a navigator,' snorted Armstrong. 'Heaven help any ship with John Ducker for a sailing master. Why, only last spring he had the poor *Agamemnon* up on Penmark Rocks, waiting for the next tide to lift her off. No, that man's failings are well understood in the service.'

'They calls him John Ducker, the Witless Fucker,' whispered Old Amos at the wheel, for the amusement of the teenage midshipmen stationed as runners beside him.

'No tide to lift them here,' continued Taylor. 'She looks to be firmly planted on the bank.'

'It's Captain Hardy that I feel sorry for,' added Armstrong. 'Dragging a plum line around for much of the night to find the shoal's end, and the lubbers still pass his mark on the wrong side.'

'Indeed,' said Taylor, in a distracted way as he looked over his shoulder towards the wheel. 'Mr Todd, is that you I hear, gasping and snorting? Kindly display the decorum to be expected of a King's officer. The eve of battle is no occasion for laughter.'

Clay watched the barrel pass the *Griffin*'s starboard side as she followed the *Polyphemus* around, the last pearl on the string of Nelson's ships. The pace of the line quickened as the wind settled behind them, and they headed northwards towards the first of their Danish opponents.

'It cannot be helped now,' said Clay. 'But pray do not tell Mr Vansittart that the odds have lengthened. He was worried enough when we were twelve against twenty.'

A series of explosions sounded from the line of bomb ketches, and the sky overhead was streaked with more trails of smoke. Tall columns of water rose up around the enemy's ships.

'Perhaps one hit, on that single-decker, near the end, sir?' offered Armstrong.

'Maybe,' said Clay. 'If so, it is the first.'

'They are wasting powder, if you want my opinion, sir,' commented Taylor.

'You have the truth of it there, I fear,' said his captain. 'They will be turning their attention to the battery soon. We shall have to settle this in the traditional manner, great gun to great gun.'

He returned his attention to the enemy. They were close now, a ragged looking line of disparate ships compared with Nelson's. The mix of different sizes gave the effect of crenulations on the top of a castle wall. Some hulls were painted plain black, others had gun decks picked out in red, yellow or white. He focussed on the nearest, the enemy he would help fight. She was a big, two-decked warship, with heavy cannon run out and ready. Her masts were bare, save for a huge Danish ensign that flew from the top of each. Through his telescope he could see a faint haze of smoke rising into the air, and he imagined the smouldering linstocks, held poised above every touchhole. On her forecastle there was a cluster of officers; tiny in contrast to the ship's carved lion figurehead crouched just beneath them. Sunlight glinted off gold braid and the brass of telescopes as they watched the approaching British fleet.

'That is our enemy,' he said to Taylor, pointing at the ship. 'We shall let *Polyphemus* come up alongside her while we lay off her bow and rake her.'

'Aye aye, sir,' said Taylor. 'We had best reduce sail for the turn, and I shall check that the anchor is ready to be dropped.'

'If you please, Mr Taylor,' said his captain. 'Mr Todd! Now you are yourself once more, give my compliments to Mr Blake, and ask him to run out the starboard guns.'

'Aye aye, sir,' replied the youngster. He scampered away, and Clay returned his attention to the enemy he would fight. The front of the British fleet was almost next to her, and the Danish officers had vanished back to their posts, leaving the grave-faced lion to watch their approach. The *Edgar* had replaced the *Agamemnon* at the head of the British line. As she drew level, the Danish ship erupted in fire and smoke, heaving away from her enemy as her cannon all thundered back inboard. The roar of the broadside had just reached him when the *Edgar* fired back.

'It has started at last,' exclaimed Preston, who had taken Taylor's place beside his captain.

'Yes,' said Clay, watching the unfolding battle. 'Kindly

have the time recorded in the log, Mr Preston.' Now the *Edgar* was sailing on, receiving a fresh broadside from the next enemy in line, while the *Bellona*, following the Edgar, fired into the leading Dane. Ships followed one another into battle, each pouring broadsides into the Danish fleet, and receiving the same in return. As the volume of firing steadily rose, and the frigate grew closer, the din of battle became something Clay could feel vibrating through his hand where it rested on the rail, as well as ringing in his ears.

'Mr Hutchinson has the anchor bent on its cable, and ready to drop when you give the word, sir,' reported Taylor, 'and we are sailing under foretopsail alone now.'

'*Edgar*'s dropped anchor, sir,' reported Preston, who was still watching the battle. 'I can see her top men gathering in sail. She is opposite the fifth Dane, as ordered. *Bellona* is turning to pass outside of her. Now, that's strange. What has happened?' Clay had his telescope to his eye in a flash, trying to pierce the clouds of smoke. He saw the big seventy-four, stationary now, with her sails flapping in the wind as she let fly her sheets. There was something familiar in the angle of her hull. A series of flags shot up her mizzen halliards.

'Distress signal from *Bellona*, sir!' announced Preston. '*Am aground!*'

'No!' exclaimed Taylor. 'Not another bloody one!' Preston had continued to watch the unfolding drama.

'Sorry to bring ill tidings, sir, but the *Russell* was following hard behind the *Bellona*,' he said. 'I believe she may be aground too.'

'Curse these damnable Danes, pulling up all the marker buoys!' exclaimed Armstrong, thumping the rail of the frigate.

Clay stared at the two grounded British ships in horror.

Over his shoulder the *Agamemnon* was still stuck fast. Twelve against twenty had seemed challenging odds at dawn. A few hours later, with the battle barely started, and they were down to nine ships. He felt despair grip his heart. Was he cursed, he wondered? Was the *Griffin* to be the second ship he would lose within twelve months? He felt the eyes of his officers on him, together with those of the sailors beyond them, standing at their posts. Sedgwick, his arms folded, patiently waiting to follow his captain into battle. Macpherson, immaculate in his scarlet tunic, with his grandfather's claymore by his side. The wooden-faced Amos, his gnarled hands on the spokes of the wheel as he kept the frigate precisely behind the ship ahead.

'The *Elephant* is passing inside of the *Edgar*, sir,' said Preston. 'She must have moored on the very edge of the deep water.'

Clay returned his attention to the battle, forcing his trembling hand steady as he focussed his telescope on the flagship. The *Elephant* was leading the line now, sailing boldly into battle as he watched. Then she vanished in a cloud of smoke as she fired. Somewhere on board, the little figure of Nelson would be pacing her deck, his single hand behind his back, with Foley by his side. He found the image comforting, calming. He lowered his telescope and smiled at his officers.

'At least we know where the deep water channel ends, gentlemen,' he said, raising his voice a little, so that those beyond his officers could hear him. 'What need have we of Danish navigational buoys, Mr Armstrong, when we have stranded ships of the line to mark our way? To your stations, for we need to make that turn. And let battle commence.'

CHAPTER 15

BATTLE

After all the dash and bustle of preparing for action, there came a period of calm for the men stationed on the main deck. They knew that the frigate was under way, through the stirring of the hull beneath their feet and the idle flap of canvas overhead, but with the gun ports closed they were isolated in an oak cocoon. Lieutenant Blake stood at his place beside the mast, rocking occasionally on his heels to ease his legs. The other officers stood at their posts too, while the gun crews sat around the cannons, waiting.

Evans traced his fingers over the flowing white letters painted on the eighteen-pounder's barrel, wondering again about the mystery of writing. All the guns had been named by their crews. Some had chosen famous prize-fighters, like Dan Mendoza or Jack Broughton; others had selected more traditional names, like Spit Fire and Dread Nought. Evans knew that the first letter was an "S", from its snake-like shape, which he recognised from his own name, but the rest was just loops and curves.

'Is Shango truly set down here?' he queried, not for the

278

first time.

'Aye, Sam lad,' said Trevan, from the far side of the gun. 'Leastways according to Able.'

'Why do you call it that?' queried one of the crew from the next cannon in line. 'Right peculiar bleeding name, if you ask me. Proper foreign, an' all.'

'Will you hear your man?' exclaimed O'Malley, the gun's proud captain. 'Is it sneering at the best handled piece on the fecking barky you're after doing? And what pray is the name of your cannon?'

'Brimstone Belcher,' said the seaman.

'Brimstone Belcher,' he repeated, in mock admiration. 'It must've taken you philosophers an age to come up with that. Why, there can't be above fifty of them feckers in the fleet.' He patted his own barrel with pride. 'Only the one Shango, mind, him being the God of fecking Thunder, back amongst the savages where Sedgwick hales from.'

A sound, not unlike the distant wrath of a West African thunder god, came from beyond the frigate's hull. Evans looked up as a number of dark smudges flew across the sky, trailing lines of smoke.

'You reckon them bomb ketches will be sorting the Danes out?' he asked.

'Don't you go heeding them,' warned O'Malley. 'They couldn't strike the side of McGinty's barn with a shovel.'

'It'll come down to us firing ball, fast and true, from a biscuit-toss away,' added Trevan. 'Be odd, mind, not fighting Dons or Frogs. Has he got much bottom, then, your Dane?'

'Them as are shipmates are game enough,' commented Evans, 'like Pedersen over there. Now that's bleeding odd! Where's he gone to?'

'Pipe ordered the Danes to go an' help the sawbones, so

they don't have to fight their kin,' explained O'Malley. 'Mind, I ain't sure as holding down folk being parted with their legs is how I would choose to spend a battle.'

'Look lively, Sean,' said Trevan, nodding towards the quarterdeck ladder way. 'Here comes one of the Snotties.'

Midshipman Todd's progress along the middle of the gun deck was accompanied by a wave of movement, as sailors spotted the youngster and rose to their feet in anticipation of what his arrival might portend. When he stopped in front of Lieutenant Blake, he was at the centre of an oasis of silence.

'The captain's respects, and can you run out the starboard-side guns, if you please, sir,' said the junior officer, touching his hat.

'Quiet there!' roared Blake, glaring around him to choke off the rumble of approval that had greeted this news. 'Thank you, Mr Todd. Please tell the captain that the guns are being run out now.'

The lieutenant waited till Todd had threaded his path most of the way back to the ladder before issuing his first order.

'Starboard side!' he called. 'Up ports!'

This was Evans's job. He leaned forward across Shango's barrel, unbolted the port lid, and swung it open. Through the square in the ship's side, he saw dull green water stretching away, choppy close to, swirling like molten glass over the shallowest part of the Middle ground. In the distance was the stricken *Agamemnon*, still gripped fast, with cables leading from her stern towards where her long boat lay in deeper water.

'Starboards!' yelled Blake. 'Run out the guns.' Evans stepped aside to allow the men at the tackles space to work. They leaned back in diverging lines, one each side of the carriage, like a pair of tug-of-war teams. The eighteen-pounder jerked into motion and then trundled forward until it thumped into place. The roar of carriage wheels in motion faded across the deck until it was quiet once more.

After a pause, Evans began idly spinning his rammer between his hands. Then he glanced across at Trevan, who was turning over one of the round shot in the garland. O'Malley checked the flint on the cannon's firing mechanism again, then puffed his cheeks out. Green water continued to slide past, taking the *Agamemnon* away and replacing her with the first of the bomb ketches. Through the open port came the sound of water slipping along the hull of the frigate, followed by a pair of muffled roars from ahead, deep and thunderous.

'Would them be thirty-two pounders at all?' asked O'Malley.

Trevan nodded. 'That be the old *Edgar*, I'm after thinking,' he said. 'Not long now, lads.' A couple of the crew tightened their bandannas, and Evans bumped fists with his friends across the breech of the gun.

More broadsides, louder and coming closer. They started to run into each other, blending from distinct explosions of noise into a more constant roar.

'Taking in sail now, lads,' said Evans, pointing aloft with his rammer. High above them the main topsail was vanishing as the row of sailors doubled over the yard gathered it in. Then he sniffed at the air. 'I bleeding know that smell, an' all.'

Faint at first, but growing all the time was the whiff of gun smoke. A wall of it rose up in front of the frigate like a bank of fog, flickering with an inner light. The sound of gunfire grew ever louder.

'Ready about!' Taylor's voice came from out of sight, distorted by a brass speaking trumpet. 'Is the anchor ready, Mr Harrison?'

'Ready, aye,' came the boatswain's reply, his voice deep and loud, clear above the sound of battle.

'I reckon old Harrison could holler up to the royal yard in one of them hurricanoes,' observed Trevan.

'Here we go, lads,' said O'Malley, as the frigate began to turn. Yards creaked around, volleys of orders were shouted, more sailors streamed aloft, and then the voice of Clay cut through it all.

'Mr Blake!' he yelled. 'Have your guns ready. The ship with the lion figurehead is your mark.'

'Aye aye, sir,' replied Blake. 'Ready, starboards?' O'Malley crouched down beside the gun and took up the slack in the firing lanyard. He glanced over his crew, then raised his left hand aloft.

Now the view through the gun port was changing rapidly as the frigate swung out of line and headed towards the shore to cross the bow of the leading Danish ship. For a moment it grew darker, as the stern of the *Polyphemus* towered over the *Griffin*. Windows and gilding, the name picked out in a curve of letters above where her huge rudder dipped into the water. The frigate sailed forwards, and now they could see the wall of enemy ships, curving away from them to vanish amongst the grey clouds of smoke. Tongues of fire darted out towards the British and were replied with in kind by Nelson's fleet, filling the space between them with sound and fury.

'Take in sail, Mr Taylor,' roared Clay. 'Let go the anchor, Mr Harrison!'

'Aye aye, sir!'

The frigate drifted forward, and the bow of a big warship

appeared, perhaps a hundred yards away. She had the broad beam and lofty sides of a ship of the line. The elegant sweep of her head rails joined behind her figurehead, an upright lion with a gaping mouth, holding a coat of arms between its front paws. Heavy cables led down to two substantial mooring buoys, both green and slimy with weed. Two chaser guns protruded from the front of her forecastle, the only cannon that could bear on the *Griffin*. Glancing up, O'Malley could see their crews, looking down and pointing at this unexpected arrival in front of them.

'Anchors holding!' announced the boatswain. A chorus of groans echoed through the ship from her bits as the strain came on, and the frigate slowed to a halt, rocking in the gentle swell.

'Rig the spring to hold us thus, Mr Harrison,' yelled Clay.

'Aye aye, sir,' replied the boatswain. The enemy's bow chasers both banged out together, and a line parted aloft, snaking down with a rattle onto the main deck behind O'Malley.

'Mr Macpherson, have your men shoot down those gun crews!' The captain's voice rang out.

'Aye aye, sir,' replied the marine.

'Mr Blake, you may begin engaging.'

'Starboard side, open fire!'

'Stand clear,' yelled O'Malley. He glanced along the barrel, but there was little need to aim. His whole view was filled with the bow of the enemy ship. He drew the firing lanyard towards him, and after a moment of resistance the flint snapped forward. A white spark, then a hiss of red from the touchhole like a roman candle, and the big cannon roared back into the frigate. Before it had halted Evans thrust the wet end of the rammer into the muzzle.

'Clean!' he announced as he pulled it free and reversed the end. The moment he did so, Trevan on the far side pushed the powder charge in, his whole arm vanishing down the barrel. Evans rammed it home, ball followed charge, and wad followed ball.

'Loaded!' said Evans, stepping back from the gun.

'Run her up!' ordered O'Malley, while Trevan threw the empty leather charge holder to the ship's boy stood behind him.

'Fetch us another, lad,' he said, and the boy sped away towards the magazine. O'Malley thrust a spike down the touch hole until he felt the barbed end burst through the serge of the charge bag. He pulled it free, filled the touch hole with fine powder from the horn that hung around his neck, then he snapped back the lock of the firing mechanism and took up the slack of the lanyard. Through the dispersing smoke of the first broadside he saw the bow of the enemy ship. Patches of torn white wood pockmarked it, and a section of head rail bobbed in the water.

'Stand clear!' he yelled, and the cannon roared out again. He glanced across at the Brimstone Belcher and noted with pleasure that they had only just run their gun up. Then he heard a heavy crash from the front of the frigate, and the deck trembled beneath his feet.

'That was fecking rowdy for one of them little chasers,' he muttered.

'Clean!' said Evans, as he pulled the rammer free once more.

******

'The shot came from that battery over there, sir,' reported Preston, pointing towards the shore. 'The one in front of those warehouses. I count only four pieces, but they are of

284

large calibre, to judge from all the water they are throwing up.' Clay looked where the younger man pointed. The coastline was at least a half mile away, and the smoke of battle lay heavy on the water in between. Then he saw tongues of fire, and a fresh cloud of smoke. Moments later columns of water rose up all around the frigate. There was a ripping sound as a shot passed overhead.

'They are as like to hit their own ships as ours at this range,' he decided. 'Particularly with all this damned smoke. I am sure it was pure hazard that they struck us. Have the carpenter repair the damage, if you please Mr Preston, and let the bow chasers throw the odd ball their way in return.'

'Aye aye, sir,' said Preston. Clay crossed to the other side of the *Griffin*. Beneath his feet the deck was trembling continuously as the guns hurled ball after ball into their opponent. Holes and gashes had been beaten all across the shattered bow, and one of the two chase guns now rested at a drunken angle. But there was still defiance. He could look along the side of the enemy ship from where he stood. Many of her guns had fallen silent, but others were in action, firing back at the *Polyphemus* opposite her. Around the wrecked bow chaser a group of sailors appeared armed with muskets. Two were quickly shot by the *Griffin*'s marines, but one in a battered straw hat aimed his weapon straight at Clay. He held his breath as the man fired, the old wound in his shoulder aching in sympathy. There was a sharp tap from the rail beside his hand, and looking down he saw the flattened hemisphere of a musket ball stuck in the oak.

The quarterdeck carronade next to him shot back on its slide with an angry bark, and its smoke obscured his view for a moment. When it cleared, the enemy ship seemed transformed. Clay searched for the reason, and then saw that the lion figurehead had been decapitated. A cheer made him look around. The crew of the carronade were slapping hands and pointing, before they broke off to reload when they realised he was watching.

'They will have been trying to hit that for a while, I suppose, sir,' commented Taylor, who had come across to join him.

'Load with canister and clear those marksmen away, O'Brien,' ordered Clay to the gun captain of the carronade.

'Right you are, sir,' said the sailor, knuckling his forehead. One of the crew rolled a big copper cylinder across to the gun, the hundreds of musket balls it contained chinking musically as he did so.

'Our opponent is named the *Provesteenen*, sir,' said Taylor from his other side. Clay raised an eyebrow at his first lieutenant, who continued. 'I know because when we were last here, Hibbert had a bout of arm wrestling with one of her boatswain's mates in a tavern.'

'Did he win?'

'He said that he did, sir.'

'A good omen, then,' said Clay. 'Whatever her name may be, she has an unusually resolute crew. Our balls will be passing along her whole length, and she has endured the broadsides of the *Polyphemus* much longer than I would have supposed possible. They must breed their seamen tough in these parts.'

'Shall I have Mr Blake elevate the guns, sir?' suggested the older man. 'Fire up through her decks, to bring things to a conclusion.'

'If you please, Mr Taylor,' said Clay. Another musket ball whined past his head, and then the carronade beside him fired, filling the air with a sound like swarming hornets.

When the smoke cleared, the Danish sailors had vanished. Farther back the enemy's foremast began to move, leaning away from him. The big forestay tightened for a moment, like a bar, and then gave way with a loud crack. Now the mast was moving faster, crumpling into its three parts and tumbling into the sea along side, taking much of the upper main mast with it. Clay looked towards the mizzen, where the one remaining Danish flag flew, wishing it would come down.

'Stop this slaughter, you fools,' he urged. 'Surrender, damn you!'

But still the *Provesteenen* fought on. Clay walked to the stern of the frigate, where he had the best view along the Danish line. The punishment the enemy ships were taking was obvious now. Several had masts down, the wreckage trailing across them, and all of those in view showed signs of the remorseless barrage they were under. The ship next to the *Provesteenen* seemed to be sinking, heeling towards the British line like a servant caught mid-bow. The hull beyond that was little more than a floating battery. Flames licked up its side, while thick black smoke rose above it. But still most of the Danish guns were in action, continuing to blast across at Nelson's fleet.

The British rate of fire was still good, noticeably quicker than the Danes, but many ships were battle damaged. Closest to him was the *Polyphemus*. Her battered side was riddled with shot holes, and a large section of her main chains had broken away. Beyond her the fifty-gun *Isis* had lost much of her mizzen, while farther away he could see a profusion of mast and hull damage.

A crash sounded from the front of the *Griffin*, and water rained down across the fore-part of the deck. Taylor hurried up onto the quarterdeck. 'That damned battery has hit us again,' he said. 'The carpenter says from the damage, he thinks they are firing forty-two pounders.'

Clay looked towards the forecastle and saw a wounded sailor being carried below by two others. 'Little we can do about that,' he said. 'Two holes in the bow are fair exchange for the damage we are inflicting.'

'Mr Blake has the guns at full elevation now, sir,' said Taylor. 'Let us see what difference that makes.'

'Anything that persuades them to yield,' said Clay in exasperation. 'The inside of your *Provesteenen* must be like a charnel house! How are they even finding the men to serve their guns?'

'I think I may know, sir,' said a voice from behind him. Both officers turned in surprise. 'Eh, permission to speak, sir,' added Sedgwick.

'Yes, of course,' said his captain. 'What is it that you suspect is happening?'

'Boats, sir,' said his coxswain. 'I reckon they're using them to ferry fresh gun crews across from the city.'

'How on earth can you possibly...' began Taylor, but Clay held up a hand.

'Why do you hold that to be so?' he asked.

'When we was here afore, an' you had me go fetch out Rankin, we was obliged to come along this section of coast to get clear of the tipstaffs,' explained Sedgwick. 'There was all manner of ships' boats pulled up on the shore. Must have been a good fifty of them. I thought no more about it, being concerned with getting back to the barky, but they came to mind just now.'

'I dare say ships moored in such calm waters don't need sailors to man their guns,' mused Clay.

'There was no end of Lobsters in the city, sir,' added Sedgwick. 'Perhaps they're taking the place of the tars as we knock them down.'

'Very well, my thanks to you, Sedgwick, let us put your theory to the test,' said Clay. He picked up a speaking trumpet and pointed it towards the top of the foremast.

'Masthead ahoy!' he yelled. 'Do you see any ship's boats?'

'Deck there! Plenty of the buggers, all plying with the shore!' replied Hoskins, who was lookout, in his West Country burr. 'Like skimmers on a pond, they be!'

'Mr Taylor, have the anchor pulled up, if you please, and prepare to make sail.'

'Aye aye, sir,' said the first lieutenant.

'And when this is all over, remind me to stop Hoskins's grog for a month.'

'Yes, sir,' smiled Taylor.

'Mr Todd, my compliments to Mr Blake, and would you ask him to join me on the quarterdeck. The guns may continue firing for the present.'

'Aye aye, sir,' said the midshipman, touching his hat before dashing off below.

'Now, Mr Armstrong, I want to advance the ship such that our guns are able to fire into the space between the Danish fleet and the shore,' explained Clay. 'To enfilade, if you will. I believe the enemy may be using ship's boats to reinforce their crews.'

'Advance the ship, sir!' exclaimed the American. 'Captain Hardy surveyed these waters and found there to be nothing but shallows between the Danes and the shore. We shall be aground for certain.'

'Good, then I can dispense with the need to anchor again,' said Clay. The sailing master stiffened at this.

'It is my duty to keep the *Griffin* from navigational peril, sir,' protested the American. 'I have to point out the hazards of running us ashore. Under fire from a battery, I may add.'

'I know it well, Jacob,' said Clay. 'Let us show no more than a scrap of jib, just enough to steer by. Then, should we be grounded, there will be little damage done, and we can haul off when we are finished.'

'All right, sir,' conceded Armstrong. 'If we advance gently, that may answer.' Clay turned to the second lieutenant, who had joined them. His face was grey with gun smoke, and his coat smelled of burnt sulphur.

'Now, Mr Blake, Sedgwick here tells me the enemy may be using boats from the shore to reinforce their line. I will advance to a position where the guns bear, after which I shall need those boats sunk. How would you best achieve that?'

'I will give them a mark, and a broadside for each should answer,' said Blake. 'The gun captains have practiced on empty casks as targets, so a big launch should present few problems. Once we have smashed a few, the rest may be less inclined to chance the passage.'

'Make it so,' said Clay. 'Have your guns readied while the ship gets under way.'

******

The shrill of Blake's whistle cut through the furnace heat and roar of sound down on the *Griffin*'s main deck.

'Ceasefire there!' yelled the petty officers. O'Malley let the lanyard drop from his hand and reached forward to un-cock Shango. Around him, the rest of the crew stood back from their tasks, some easing their backs, others wiping sweat from their faces.

'Buggers must have struck at last,' offered the Irishman.

'About fecking time, mind, with all the hammering we've been after giving them. These Danes fight fiercer than Moors.'

'Ain't sure as they have, Sean,' said Evans, peering out of the gun port. 'The bastards is still firing.'

'Gun captains to me!' ordered Blake.

'Right, get yourselves a drink from the scuttlebutt; I'll be after finding what we're about,' said O'Malley.

'Is it me, or be the barky underway?' queried Trevan. 'Real slow, like?'

Over by the main mast Blake gathered his gun captains together in a ring around him. Most were stripped to the waist, their torsos grimed with smoke, their arms inked with tattoos. All pulled their bandanas away from their ears to hear the officer.

'This fight is not over,' he cautioned. 'Not by a long stretch. The enemy is ferrying fresh gun crews from the shore to replace the fallen. We are to stop them. I shall give you a mark and range. Aim low and true, just as when we shoot for kegs. We shall revert to broadside fire once more. All clear? Good, then return to you pieces and await my signal.'

'Fecking boats we're after hitting now,' said O'Malley, returning to his eighteen-pounder. He wiped his hands on his trousers, then re-cocked the cannon. 'Places, ladies, and be lively with them handspikes.'

The crew crouched back down around the big cannon. O'Malley leaned forwards to sight along it and felt heat radiating from the heavy iron barrel beneath his bare chest. The frigate was drifting forwards now, creating the illusion that it was the shattered bow of the *Provesteenen* that was really moving away. O'Malley could see the shore-side of the line of Danish ships for the first time. Downed masts festooned many of them and smoke poured in trailing fingers across the green water. Now Copenhagen could be glimpsed at, a few towers and spires proud of the smoke of battle, as if seen on a foggy morning. And there were boats, plenty of boats on the water. Most were powered by oars, others with a mast and sails, all busy moving to and fro. Shouts of warning from the forecastle were followed by a loud creaking from under the bow as the whole ship trembled to a halt. Disturbed brown water swirled past, and the natural spring and movement of the deck under foot became inert and leaden.

'We're fecking aground,' announced O'Malley. 'I hope Pipe knows what he's about.'

'Quoins in fully!' ordered Blake. 'Observe that blue launch coming up, a cable off the bow, gun captains? That is your first mark.' O'Malley glanced down to check the elevation wedge was pushed all the way home, then searched for the target. She emerged from the smoke, a hundred yards from the frigate, a big boat with eight oars a side. Her pale blue hull was low in the water with the weight of her crew of sailors, and a double row of uniformed men sat along her centre line.

'To larboard there, a good foot,' he ordered, and the handspike men levered the gun around. 'Another inch,' he added, and then raised his hand to show he was ready. In the Danish launch faces were turning towards the frigate. He could see arms pointing, hear cries of alarm. 'Inch to starboard now,' he said.

'Open fire!' ordered Blake. A pause, as gun captains made sure of their aim, and then a stuttering broadside as some fired straightaway, while others continued to traverse their guns. O'Malley had a brief view of the water around the boat boiling up as he yelled a warning and jerked the firing lanyard. Thick smoke blotted out the target.

'Gun's clean,' announced Evans, as he completed swabbing it out. The smoke was dispersing now. The Irishman peered into it, trying to see the launch.

'Loaded!' continued Evans, stepping back.

'Got the fecker!' announced O'Malley, as a cheer rolled along the gun deck. A shattered bow appeared, riding clear of the water, with two men clinging to it. All around it were floating oars, bits of debris and struggling figures.

'Belay that noise, and get those guns loaded,' roared Blake and the cheering subsided.

'Run up,' ordered the gun captain, reaching forward to prime the cannon.

'New target!' announced Blake. 'Fishing boat with dark sails, two cables away, dead on the beam. Quoins out a half inch!'

******

Clay and Taylor looked out over a sea that was clearing of enemy boats. Three patches of floating wreckage and the upturned hull of a large pinnace marked where broadsides from the frigate had dashed away those trying to cross to reinforce the Danish ships. Through his telescope Clay swept the shoreline. He could see parties of troops standing near the remaining boats, reluctant to chance the frigate's broadsides. Only at the far end of the enemy's line was anyone still making the passage. Blake was now trying to sink these, allowing individual gun captains to fire when they thought they might hit. A small cutter loaded with red-coated Danes appeared from out of the smoke; three guns banged out, raising splashes all around the target but failed to hit it.

'The *Provesteenen* has hauled down her colours, sir,' reported Preston. 'I think I can see a boat putting out from the *Polyphemus* to take possession of her.'

'Starved of reinforcements,' said Clay, with satisfaction. He turned to smile towards his coxswain. 'Well done, Sedgwick.'

'Thank you, sir. I were only keeping my eyes open.'

'The ship in the centre of the Danish line is quite ablaze now,' said Taylor. 'And I believe two of the other Danish ships may have surrendered. The battle favours us at last.'

As if in response, a chain of splashes leapt from the water all around them and a hammer blow shook the frigate as something struck the side of the *Griffin*. Taylor went across and looked over the rail.

'Another gift from the shore battery, fortunately only a glancing blow, sir,' he said as he returned. 'Mind, it has left a gash a yard long and made a sad wreck of the chesstree. Might we look to kedge off this mud bank, before we are quite knocked to pieces?'

Clay was about to answer when the voice of Blake came from the deck beneath him.

'New target!' he yelled. 'Two launches putting out!' Clay returned his attention to the shore and found the boats, both leaving the same landing stage and rowing like fury.

'They look to overwhelm us,' he observed. 'One will pass while we deal with the other. I fear there is no question of withdrawing while the enemy is yet game, Mr Taylor. We shall just have to endure the odd ball from the shore.'

'By divisions!' ordered Blake. 'Guns one to eight, your mark is the nearer boat. The rest take the far one. Make sure of your aim, and fire as you bear.'

One by one the eighteen-pounders banged out, each

accompanied by its own plume of smoke as the guns bore on the target. Splashes rose up all around the two boats, mirroring in miniature the bombardment the frigate was under. The forecastle carronade crashed out, and figures in the larger boat tumbled like wheat before a scythe as the ball ploughed through those packed on board. She faltered for a moment and then turned around to return the way she had come.

'All guns on the far launch!' ordered Blake. The next shot seemed certain to have hit, the splash right alongside, soaking the occupants, but the boat pressed on. Then a cluster of cannons fired together, and when the smoke cleared the water was peppered with wreckage.

'They should all set off together, sir,' said Armstrong. 'Two we can cope with. But send six, and four might well survive.'

'Their crews will be reluctant to take to the boats now,' said Taylor, rubbing his hands.

'*Polyphemus* has weighed anchor, sir,' reported Preston, who continued to watch the rest of the battle. Clay looked towards the British seventy-four. She had sheeted home her big foretopsail and moved along the Danish line, seeking a fresh opponent. The Royal Navy ship ahead of her was already out of sight. Soon the frigate would be alone and exposed as Nelson's fleet advanced up the enemy line. More columns of water reared up around them, and high above his head a rope parted with a crack.

'Get that backstay spliced, Mr Powell,' he heard Hutchinson order, while Blake's guns resumed their attempts to hit the more distant boats.

'Deck there!' called Hoskins. 'Flagship be signalling!'

'Aloft with you, Mr Todd,' ordered Taylor. 'Tell us what

Lord Nelson requires.'

'Aye aye, sir,' said the youngster, hanging a telescope over his shoulder before rushing for the main shrouds.

'Mr Todd!' roared Taylor. The midshipman skidded to a halt. 'Have you committed every one of Captain Popham's multitude of signals to memory yet?'

'Eh... no, sir.'

'Then you had best take the signal book with you.'

'Oh, yes,' said Todd. 'I mean aye, aye, sir.' Clay watched the midshipman snatch up the book and scamper aloft, passing the boatswain's working party as they repaired the backstay. When he was in position he had a brief conversation with the lookout, then he pointed his telescope towards the north.

'Deck there!' he called. 'It isn't the *Elephant* signalling, but the *London*, sir.'

'The *London*?' queried Clay. 'Is the main fleet in action?'

'Not yet, sir,' reported the midshipman. 'They are continuing to beat up into the wind. General signal thirty-nine, sir. That is to discontinue the action.'

'Leave off the battle!' exclaimed Armstrong. 'How in all creation does Admiral Parker think we shall accomplish that, sir? Half the fleet are aground and the rest are caught between the Danes and the mud!'

'Shall I order preparations to kedge us off, sir?' asked the first lieutenant.

'A moment if you please, Mr Taylor,' said his captain. 'Mr Todd! What signal is the *Elephant* flying?'

'Still number sixteen, sir,' replied the midshipman. 'That is for close action.'

'The rest of the fleet are continuing to hammer away at the Danes, sir,' supplemented Preston. 'And I believe their flagship may have struck.'

'There is our direction, gentlemen,' said Clay. 'We take our lead from Lord Nelson. Our role is to keep the Danes on shore honest, until instructed to do otherwise.'

Now a lull followed in the action for the *Griffin*. The Danish ships at their end of the line had all surrendered, and the main battle had moved away from them. Looking that way Clay could see it was as fierce as ever, but now they were observers on the edge of the storm, rather than participants at its heart. Down on the main deck Blake had released some of his gun crews to get a drink of water. Clay watched Evans pouring a ladle down his throat, and ran his tongue over his own dry lips, realising that he had drunk nothing since his breakfast with Taylor. He glanced towards the south. The sun was visible as a patch of brightness behind the veil of cloud. Past noon already.

Once Clay had drunk from the quarterdeck butt, he looked back towards the enemy. He could still see boats on the move in the shallows, although none seemed to want to brave the frigate's guns. Farther back there were blocks of red-coated Danish troops, some marching, others standing. Mounted officers rode to and fro, or stood gesticulating as they gave orders. One cluster of horsemen in elaborate uniforms all stood facing towards the frigate. He had a strange feeling that they were discussing him.

'Gentlemen,' said Clay to his officers. 'Direct your gaze towards the enemy. What do you think these deuced Danes are about?'

'There's a deal of shifting boats,' commented Armstrong, after a while. 'Some to the north, doubtless to seek a crossing beyond our reach, but more are heading the other way.'

'And a considerable body of soldiers are forming up over

yonder,' added Taylor, pointing past the frigate's bow.

'Have you noticed that the battery has stopped firing, sir?' added Preston. Clay paused to listen. It seemed strangely calm, despite the continuing roar of battle taking place farther up the channel. Then he felt his stomach knot with anxiety as he realised what the Danes were up to.

'They mean to rush us with boats from the shore,' he said. 'They will come at us over the bow, where only our chasers can be brought to bear.'

CHAPTER 16

BOATS

Clay watched the approach of the lanky young officer as he hurried along the frigate's gangway all the way from the forecastle, certain already of the message he brought.

'Mr Preston's compliments and a dozen boats have put out from the shore, sir,' reported the midshipman.

'Thank you, Mr Sweeney,' he said. 'Kindly tell Mr Preston I shall come directly.' The youngster touched his hat and retuned along the side of the ship, leaving Clay with his thoughts. The frigate's two nine-pounder bow chasers both banged out together, the sound much sharper than the lusty roar of the bigger cannon on her main deck, and smoke drifted across the front of the ship. A dozen boats, he repeated to himself, each with between thirty and forty men on board. Such a force could overwhelm them if they were in any way ill-prepared. He looked over his frigate, making sure that all the measures he had ordered were in place. He would have liked to have rigged boarding netting, but this was a lengthy task, and time was short. Besides, at best it would hold for a short while before it was cut and wrenched free by a determined attacker. He stepped up to the front of the quarterdeck and looked down at the gun crews. Every cannon was manned and run out.

'Are you quite prepared, Mr Blake?' called the captain.

'Yes, sir,' replied the lieutenant. 'Both sides are loaded with canister over ball, depressed as low as possible and trained as far forward as can be.'

'And once you have discharged your pieces?'

'The crews will bolt the port lids tight and then come up to help repel boarders,' replied Blake. He indicated the open chests of arms arranged along the centreline of the deck. Clay could see rows of gleaming cutlasses, and the rounded butts of pistols in the two boxes immediately beneath him.

'Very good, Mr Blake,' said Clay, satisfied with what he saw.

'When they attack, I fancy they will come over the bow,' said Armstrong, beside him.

'With so many boats there will be a want of space,' said the captain. 'I daresay some may chance their arm alongside, but you are right, it is the forecastle that is critical, which is where I must station myself. Take charge here, Mr Taylor, if you please.'

'Aye aye, sir,' said the older man. 'Good luck.'

Clay walked past the big quarterdeck carronades and along the gangway, forcing himself to stroll calmly for the benefit of the crew. Behind him came Sedgwick, with a cutlass belt slung across his chest and a pistol thrust in his waistband. The side of the ship was thinly guarded with the ship's idlers, for once drafted in and armed with muskets and boarding pikes. They moved from his path as he approached, knuckling their foreheads in salute.

'Give those Danes what for if they come to take our

Griffin, shipmates,' he ordered.

'Don't you go a-worryin' 'bout them buggers, sir,' said Stephenson, the portly armourer's mate, shaking the musket he held in his fist. Clay smiled at this and walked on towards the forecastle.

The front of the ship had been transformed into a fortress. The forecastle rail had been augmented with baulks of timber and rolled up hammocks to turn it into a solid, waist-high barricade. Lieutenant Macpherson had formed his marines up into a block of scarlet in the central space between the two nine-pounders, both of which were in action. On the outside of the guns was a thick line of sailors, armed with muskets. Behind them stood another ten men, all armed with cutlasses and boarding pikes. At their head stood Lieutenants Preston and Macpherson, side by side. Just as Clay joined them, the bow chasers fired again. More smoke trailed across the deck, accompanied by a cheer from the watching seamen.

'Have you sunk one of them already, Mr Preston?' asked Clay.

'Not yet, sir, but we have knocked a file of soldiers down in one of the boats,' replied the lieutenant.

'Your arrangements seem excellent, gentlemen,' said Clay, looking around. On a grating near the foremast was a line of large round shot. 'What, pray, are those for?'

'Eighteen-pounder balls, contributed by Mr Blake,' explained Macpherson. 'We have men detailed to pitch them over the rail when the Danes come alongside. I fancy from this height they may knock down a few attackers, or perhaps drop through the bottom of even a solidly built launch.'

'Good. And what is your plan to repel the enemy?'

'Musketry combined with canister from the nine-pounders, in the first instance,' said Preston. 'If that don't answer, and the Danes get a foothold on deck, we shall drive them back with the men here that we hold in reserve.'

'You seem to have considered everything,' said Clay. 'Let us see what the enemy is about.'

Clay stood behind one of the bow chasers and was shocked by how close the Danish boats were. They were formed in a tight group, barely three hundred yards away. Big pinnaces, smaller launches and cutters, painted in various colours, but all packed with red-coated soldiers and rowing quickly towards the frigate.

'Clear!' shouted the sailor in charge of the chase gun. He yanked on the firing lanyard. A tongue of flame, a gush of smoke, and the small cannon shot back inboard.

'Got one!' exclaimed one of the crew, pointing with his rammer.

'Stow that, an' swab the bleeder out,' growled the gun captain. 'We ain't got no time for gawking!'

'Load canister now,' ordered Preston, 'and hold your fire till I give the word.'

Clay looked at the approaching boats. The one the nine-pounder had struck was listing badly. He could see soldiers bailing her out with their hats, the water flashing silver as it was pitched over the side. The boat slowly turned around and limped back towards the shore.

'One less to worry about, sir,' said Preston. Clay nodded, his attention on the rest of the flotilla, now a bare two hundred yards away. As they came on, more detail began to emerge. A blond-haired naval officer at the helm of the nearest cutter, his mouth a circle, as he bellowed encouragement to his oarsmen. The lines of soldiers seated in the boats shifted from anonymous figures into individuals.

There were tall ones and stout ones, small ones and thin ones. Some had fair hair and some were swarthy. There were those who sat calmly with their backs to the approaching frigate, and there were anxious ones, peering over their shoulders at the imposing ship, so much loftier when seen from the surface of the water.

When the flotilla was a hundred yards away, the sounds of their approach began to precede them: the rattle of oars against gunwales and the foaming drag of them through the water, the cries of encouragement from the coxswains as they urged their flagging crews to a final effort.

'Make certain of your targets, gun captains,' said Preston.

'Red cutter off to larboard,' said one. 'Lugger at the front,' replied the other.

Fifty yards, now. Clay watched as a sailor crouched in the bow of one boat started to whirl his grappling hook around his head, eyeing the frigate's bowsprit.

'Marines, present arms!' ordered Macpherson. 'Take aim, now.' With a smooth, precise movement the soldiers all brought their muskets up to their shoulders and then angled them down towards the enemy.

'Gentlemen, you may fire when you are ready,' said Clay. The nine-pounders fired first, blasting a swarm of musket balls towards the approaching flotilla. This was not the devastation Clay had witnessed the big quarterdeck carronades inflict on the crew of the *Provesteenen* earlier. The canister round for a nine-pounder could fit in his hand. One blast missed its target completely, producing a cone of foaming sea between two boats, but the second was better aimed. Soldiers and oarsmen tumbled down in one of the cutters amidst a chorus of screams, and they dropped back from the others. But the remaining ten continued to press home the attack.

'Marines will open fire!' ordered Macpherson, and forty muskets crashed out as one. Clay saw a sailor slump across his oar, the blade dragging in the water. In another boat two soldiers tumbled over. The frigate's crew spread along the sides of the forecastle were all firing as well, and more men fell in the boats, but still the Danes came on.

'Rapid fire!' ordered Macpherson. The marines were tearing off the tops of cartridges with their teeth and pulling out ramrods. On the sea, four of the attacking boats manoeuvred around until they were side on to the frigate, while the remaining six pressed on.

'What do you suppose the enemy are about, sir?' asked Preston.

'A well executed plan, I don't doubt,' answered Clay. 'There is no room for all of them around our bow at once. Some will stand off and pepper us with musketry, while the others press home the attack.'

The nine-pounders fired again, sending a fresh storm of canister towards the attackers. The flutter of a passing musket ball sounded close to Clay's head, and a marine staggered back from the rail, clutching his arm. Then one of the crew manning the nine-pounder in front of Clay dropped like a felled tree, crashing to the deck. The marines were leaning right out over the side to fire downwards. A series of bumps sounded against the hull, and then with a roar of noise the enemy came, a wave of fury scrambling up the side of the frigate.

A Danish soldier thrust his bayonet-tipped musket through the open port of the bow chaser and slashed at the legs of the gunners. One stepped back with blood pouring from his calf. Another soldier clambered above his comrade and swung his musket towards Clay. Before he could fire, a jab from a rammer sent him tumbling backwards. All along the rail of the forecastle little battles were being fought. Several Danish sailors had climbed up onto the frigate's bowsprit, where they sat astride the huge spar like riders on a horse. They battled with the nearest marines, their cutlass blades screeching and clashing on the bayonets thrust at them. Another party had climbed in amongst the frigate's head rails and were taking a steady toll on the defenders. They fired muskets passed up to them from the boats below in a steady chain, returning the empty weapons to be reloaded. Clay stepped back from the furious battle so he could see the broader picture.

Along the rail to his left, the attackers looked as if they were being contained. The fighting was fierce, but the initial assault had been held off. Into the centre of the defenders waded the bearlike form of Josh Black, the *Griffin*'s Captain of the Foretop and a veteran of a dozen fights. He had laid aside his boarding axe and instead held one of the eighteen-pounder cannon balls high above his head. He reached a portion of rail vacated by the enemy, took aim, and hurled the heavy sphere. A splintering crash came from over the side, and he retreated to find a fresh missile.

Another marine fell down, shot from below, to join the half dozen or so already killed or wounded.

'We need to clear away the enemy lodged on the frigate's beak head, sir,' said Macpherson. 'They're shooting my men like salmon in a tub.' He pointed down with his sword at the deck beneath them. 'I can take them with an assault through the door that lead to the heads.'

'No, Tom, I need you here,' said Clay. He turned to the midshipman who stood beside him, looking with wide-eyed horror at the carnage around him.

'Mr Sweeney!' he called. The boy turned slowly towards him, as if emerging from a trance.

'Sir?' he said.

'Listen with care. You are to find Mr Blake, and tell him to send a party of twenty to clear the beak head of the enemy, and then send the rest of his men up here.'

'Reserve men, follow me!' ordered Preston, drawing his sword. 'Clear those Danes from the deck.' Clay ignored the overwhelming urge to look where Preston had directed, and instead concentrated on the frightened thirteen-year-old in front of him.

'Repeat my order, Mr Sweeney,' he said.

'F... find Mr B... Blake, twenty men to clear the b... beak head and the rest to the f... forecastle, sir,' said the youngster.

'Good, now run, boy!' said Clay, looking around to see where Preston and his men had gone.

A fresh pulse of attackers had managed to force their way onto the starboard side of the deck. A dozen Danish soldiers formed a solid wedge, driving forwards and widening the breach in the frigate's defensive line. Exhausted sailors and marines were falling back, while more Danes clambered over the rail to join the attack. Others had climbed up onto the starboard cathead and were running along it to jump down into the melee. Preston was in the middle of the fray, his single-armed stance looking curiously unbalanced as he hammered at the guard of a Danish officer, while around him his little group of sailors desperately tried to contain the enemy. Out of the corner of his eye Clay could see the boats that had stood off getting underway to reinforce the attack.

He wrapped his hand around the hilt of his glittering sword, the same that had been returned to him at the end of his court martial. Not again, he told himself, I'll be damned before I lose another ship. He swept out the blue-steel blade. Beside him Sedgwick did the same with his cutlass. The crisis in the battle was at hand.

'Come on, lads!' roared Clay. 'Drive them back!' He dashed forward and threw himself into the fight. A soldier wrenched his musket towards him, but he deflected the blow, stepped close and drew his blade across the man's arm. The edge was as sharp as a razor, and he felt it slice deep. The Dane recoiled backwards, blood pouring from him, and Clay followed him as he retreated. Now he was in the press of the melee. Another bayonet thrust towards him, but Sedgwick appeared beside and smashed the hilt of his cutlass into the soldier's face before the blow could land. A space cleared before Clay and he stepped forward, leading with his sword. As he planted his front foot, he felt it slide from under him on planking that was slick with blood. An instant later he had crashed down on the hard oak deck, the wind driven from his lungs. Around him was a forest of legs, and for a moment he half expected to see the huddled figure of the murdered tsar, surrounded by conspirators. Then he glimpsed an onrushing boot, and knew no more.

*****

'Captain's down!' roared Sedgwick. 'Ahoy, *Griffin*s! To me! The captain's down!' The coxswain slashed around him with his cutlass in a frenzy, trying to dive the enemy back. The blade caught against the musket barrel of a soldier who stood in his way. With his other hand he swept out his pistol, shoved it against the man's stomach, and pulled the trigger. The gun crashed out, hot smoke singed his hand, and his opponent sank to his knees, but Sedgwick could still not advance. More and more Danish soldiers were pouring over the rail now. He used the empty pistol in one hand as a club while continuing to hack with the cutlass in the other, but the mass of men pressing him backwards was remorseless. Every enemy he cut down seemed to be replaced by a fresh assailant.

He had no recollection of having been wounded, but he could feel blood trickling from a cut on his left arm, and his shirt was torn and sodden from a painful slash across his ribcage. Sweat dripped into his eyes, and he gasped for breath. He could feel his limbs becoming stiff with exhaustion, and his cutlass felt as heavy as lead as he struggled to raise it for one more attempt to reach Clay. A surge in the crowd of fighting men brought him hard up against a young Danish soldier who had lost his hat. Unable to raise his arms, he ducked his head down and crashed it against the ash-blond hair in front of him. When he looked up the youngster had vanished, to be replaced by a cloud of tiny motes that sparkled in the air in front of his face. The battle around him became remote, and he felt his legs wobbling beneath him. A moment later, he too was slipping down between the struggling bodies. Waves of tiredness washed over him. If he could sleep for just a moment, he told himself, then he would be able to fight all the harder. His eyes closed and he slid further down, until the flat of one hand touched the wet planking.

'Holy Mary!' announced a familiar voice, from somewhere close. 'There's hundreds of the feckers!' Sedgwick opened his eyes to find he was on his hands and knees, being jostled and kicked by the legs around him. He shook his head to clear it.

'Drive them back, *Griffin*s,' ordered Blake, his voice loud.

'Up and at them, afterguard!' shouted Armstrong, from farther away.

'Marines will advance!' said Macpherson, calm as ever.

Sedgwick tried to heave himself back up, but found the legs around him pressed to close, so he sank his teeth into the nearest calf. There was a yelp, the limb was wrenched free and a little light appeared above him. He forced himself back to his feet, surfacing through the crowd of struggling bodies like a swimmer after a deep dive.

In front of him were at least fifty Danish boarders, standing amongst the dead and wounded heaped around the deck. Most were soldiers, dressed in deep red with white cross belts, the rest were sailors in clothes of a different cut to those worn by the *Griffin*s. They were penned into perhaps a third of the forecastle. The flow of Danes from over the side had slowed, with those clinging to the outside of the rail unable to find any space, and those still in the boats blocked by the ones above them.

Facing the boarders was Preston, leading the remnant of the original defenders. Beside them Macpherson had drawn up his surviving marines in close order. They slowly advanced, their bayonets a hedge of steel towards the enemy, thrusting at any one who came within range. Over Sedgwick's left shoulder Armstrong had arrived along the gangway with the grey-haired Taylor besides him. The American's wig was askew, and the grip of his small, thin sword was lost in his large fist. At their backs came all those whose posts were on the quarterdeck. The afterguard, the carronade crews, even the quartermasters who should have been manning the wheel, all armed with whatever weapons had come to hand. Then he felt more than saw a wave of men sweeping up behind him, as Blake led his gun crews streaming up the ladder way from the deck below.

'Come on, Able!' urged Evans. 'There ain't time for admiring the view!'

'You all right there, lad?' asked Trevan from his other side. 'You look proper beat, and that arm don't look so good. Can you find your way to the sawbones?'

'Captain's down,' gasped Sedgwick, waving vaguely with the hand that held the battered pistol. 'I... I... ain't sure where, exactly. It all happened that quick. I tried to reach him, but there were so many of them.'

'You go over to the rail for a rest,' urged Trevan. 'Big Sam will go an' haul him out.'

'Right,' said Evans, ripping out his cutlass and looking around him. 'Hibbert, Perkins, to me! Pipe's down, somewhere under these bastards. Follow astern. You too, Sean, and watch me bleeding back!'

Hibbert and Perkins were two of the frigate's better fighters, but neither was a match for Evans. The largest of the three, his agility never failed to surprise a new opponent who expected such a huge man to be slow. Where others relied on brute strength, Evans was an artist. He faced up to his first opponent, who stabbed at him with his bayonet only to find that Evans had twisted aside from the blow. As the Dane stumbled forward, the Londoner wrapped his left fist around the barrel of the musket and used it to guide his hapless adversary onto the point of his cutlass. The man slumped to the ground, and Evans moved on to his next victim. Hibbert and Powell followed in his wake, pushing opponents back on both sides and widening the wedge driven by Evans into the wall of enemies.

The Danish attackers had flooded onto the frigate like a wave across a beach. While the momentum had been with them they had been irresistible, but now they were checked. There was still fierce resistance, blows traded, and everything hung in the balance for a moment. Then the first few attackers began to fall back. Like the turn of the tide, the movement became irresistible in the other direction, and confidence grew amongst the *Griffins* as swiftly as it drained away from their opponents.

Sedgwick saw the change as he stood back from the fray with Trevan by his side. One of the Danish soldiers, who had stood waiting on the rail to join his comrades, quietly slipped back down into the boat alongside. Then the one next to him did the same, and another. A soldier already on the deck became aware that no one was behind him, and tried to clamber back over the side. He was seized by a bawling lieutenant, who grabbed hold of one of his cross belts to restrain him; but while the officer was distracted, others took the opportunity to flee. Across the deck the enemy was in retreat. Some fought bravely, like the group who withdrew steadily, led by a big sergeant with a half pike in his hand. Others turned and fled, dropping their muskets and vaulting over the side in their haste. Still more placed their weapons on the deck and raised their hands in surrender.

Cheering *Griffins* reached the rail to see the boats below them leaving the side of the ship in a wide fan. Some were overloaded, others almost empty, but all were being rowed in haste. All around the bow of the frigate, broken wreckage and discarded oars bobbed amongst a shoal of red-coated bodies. British sailors rushed to get the bow chasers back in action while others began to reload their muskets, but before they could fire a whistle sounded. All turned around to see Lieutenant Taylor standing in the middle of the forecastle.

'Cease fire!' he ordered. In answer to the grumble from the men, he pointed towards the lines of warships. Sedgwick followed where he indicated. The Danish ships were in a sorry state. Most had struck their colours, while others had come adrift from their moorings and run aground. Two were on fire and a third was sinking. Through gaps in the line the Royal Navy ships could be seen. Many had spars and masts missing, and their pockmarked sides were stained black with powder smoke. Then the coxswain realised the most significant thing.

'They ain't firing no more,' he said to Trevan.

'Aye', said Trevan. 'An' the old *Elephant* be flying some manner of signal.'

A Royal Navy launch with a large white flag held aloft appeared from between two of the Danish ships and headed for the shore. In the stern sheets, the watery light glittered from the uniforms of the officers seated there.

'I reckon the battle must be done, Able,' said Trevan.

'Mr Macpherson, kindly see those prisoners are disarmed and made secure,' ordered Taylor. 'Mr Preston, your men can carry the wounded down to the surgeon, if you please. And has anyone seen the captain?'

EPILOGUE

His majesty's frigate *Griffin* was afloat once more, her battered bow patched and the last of the blood holystoned from the planking of her forecastle. She swung at anchor in spring sunshine, amongst the other ships of the British fleet. Through the windows at the rear of the cabin another frigate and a ship of the line could be seen, rising from out of their broken reflections on the calm water. Behind them was the shoreline and spires of Copenhagen, now without any protective row of Danish ships moored between. Clay looked up from his desk as Harte came and stood before it.

'Mr Vansittart has returned, sir, and is waiting outside,' he said. 'An' Mr Corbett was asking when it would be convenient to come and change them dressings.'

'Do show him in, Harte, and bring us some of the sherry wine,' said his captain. 'The doctor will have to wait until I am at liberty to see him.'

Vansittart strode into the cabin, trailing a whiff cologne. He was dressed once more in the sky-blue coat and held the silver-topped cane that Clay remembered from his court martial. The captain began to pull himself up, wincing as he did so.

'Oh, my dear sir, do not inconvenience yourself on my part!' exclaimed the diplomat, fluttering his hands in agitation. 'Remain seated, I pray!' He quickly sat down in his chair, forcing Clay to do the same.

'And how are the hero's wounds this morning?' he asked, accepting a glass from Harte.

'There is very little heroic about falling on one's backside and spending most of the battle insensible beneath a pile of Danish casualties, sir,' said Clay. 'Mr Corbett was positively vexed when he removed my blood-sodden garments to find that I had barely a scratch.' He touched the fingers of one hand in turn to his black eye, cut scalp and the bandage beneath his shirt that kept his broken rib immobile. 'In truth, I am more battered than wounded. The victor of a tavern brawl could boast superior injuries.'

'No need for such modesty, my dear fellow,' said Vansittart. 'Lord Nelson speaks very highly of your intervention. Without you staunching the flow of reinforcements from the shore, the wretched battle might have gone on until all of Copenhagen had been ferried across, what?' Vansittart pealed with laughter at the thought.

'What word from the shore, sir?' asked Clay, when his guest had finished. 'Is it peace?'

'Indeed it is,' beamed the diplomat. 'Lord Nelson and myself signed the accord this morning. All agreed that our peoples ought never to have quarrelled, and the current melancholy situation should be resolved. The Danes have rescinded their membership of this Armed Neutrality nonsense, and agree that our Baltic trade can resume without any threat from them. But allow me to acquaint you with the best part. Do you recall that impudent pro-French rogue Count Andreas Bernstorff?'

314

'The Chief Minister who prevented you from seeing the Crown Prince?'

'The very same! He is dismissed! Sent packing! That will teach him to be so damned high-handed with Nicholas Vansittart, what? By Jove, I would give a hundred guineas to see Talleyrand's face when word of all this arrives in Paris.' The diplomat laughed again, and Clay tried to chuckle along but found it too painful for his rib.

'So what will happen now?' he asked instead.

'The French are thwarted, and the war is over, at least in this corner of the world,' said the diplomat. 'Admiral Parker will return home with the more battered parts of the fleet, including the *Griffin*, while Lord Nelson will stay on until the Swedes and Prussians fall into line. For my part, I must report back to the government. Of course, by the time I return home, I will have missed most of the London Season, but hey ho. The sacrifices one has to make in the service of the king, what?'

'Does this mean that you will be leaving the ship?' asked Clay.

'I think not,' said Vansittart. 'Sir Hyde did offer to accommodate me in his flagship but, astonishing as it may sound, I find that I have grown fond of my little cabin down in the bilges. I would also miss the society of your wardroom, so with your blessing, I thought that I might voyage home aboard the *Griffin*.'

'Astonishing is the word,' said Clay. 'We may make a sailor of you yet, sir.'

'Do not press your advantage too far,' laughed his guest. 'Now tell me, Clay, there is one aspect of this battle that I don't understand at all, although you will recall my view wasn't the best, what?'

'Mine was hardly superior, from beneath my pile of cadavers, but I will help you if I can, sir.'

'Most obliged,' said Vansittart. 'I had always understood that you naval coves had some regard to deference and rank.'

'I should say that we do,' said the captain. 'Without obedience the navy would come to a sad pass.'

'Then why, in all creation, did the fleet not break off the action when the commander-in-chief ordered it to?'

'The custom is to take you orders from your direct superior,' explained Clay. 'Mine was Lord Nelson, and he continued to wish his ships to engage.'

'And why, pray, did Nelson not follow the instruction?'

'According to Captain Foley, he was in a rare passion over the signal,' said Clay. 'He named Admiral Parker an old woman and said, *"Leave off the action? Well damn me if I do!"* or words to that effect. Then he took up his telescope, clapped it to his blind eye, and claimed not to be able to see the signal at all.'

'I trust he will not be censured for such a lack of obedience?' asked the diplomat. 'I am not sure how many courts martial a fellow can attend to keep you and Nelson away from the gallows, what?'

'Things might have gone ill for him if we had been defeated,' said Clay. 'Fortunately, we won.'

'And another deuced layer of veneer is added to the growing ego of Lord Nelson,' said Vansittart. 'He will be requiring larger hats presently.' Clay put his drink down and frowned at his companion.

'It is very easy to sneer at Lord Nelson, sir,' he said. 'He offers so many marks to aim at, what with his boastful character and shameful private life, but consider this.' Clay pointed towards the ships still visible through the windows.

'Nine from ten officers would have followed Parker's ridiculous order, lost the battle and sacrificed their men. Choosing to disobey, and risk the consequences, required true courage.'

'Bravo, Clay,' said the diplomat. 'Your rebuke is merited. It is those that go beyond convention who genuinely influence the world. You could almost say he took the harder path, just as I was obliged to do, not so long ago, much against your advice, if I recall. Which brings me to the, eh... events in St Petersburg.' He sipped at his sherry and looked towards the steward.

'Would you leave us, please, Harte,' ordered the captain. When they were alone, Vansittart resumed, leaning towards the captain and lowering his voice.

'You know, Clay, welcome as the prowess of the Royal Navy is, it will ultimately take an army to defeat Napoleon, and a deuced big one at that. We shall have need of the Russians to fight for us before this damned war is done. No hint of what happened that night at the palace can be allowed to escape. Paris would play Old Harry with such a tale, if they ever learned of it.'

'Agreed, sir,' said the captain. 'I will never mention it.'

'That is welcome, and we can trust the Russians present to stay silent, for they have more to lose from a full disclosure then anyone. As you and I are gentlemen, our word not to speak of it will suffice, but that will not cover that negro coxswain of yours.'

'Sedgwick?' said Clay. 'He was not even present. Do you not recall, you sent him from the room? Besides, he is wholly to be trusted. No word of this will come from him, I assure you.'

'Hmm, well, I suppose I am in his debt,' mused

Vansittart. 'He did save me a task when he dealt with Rankin.' Clay spluttered over his sherry.

'What did you just say?' he gasped. 'What is it that Sedgwick did?'

'I believe that he killed Rankin,' said Vansittart, calmly brushing a little dust from his britches.

'Sedgwick killed your valet!'

'Very like,' said the diplomat. 'Rankin told me as much, just before he died. But I daresay it was revenge for Rankin murdering that seaman of yours.'

'Who? Ludlow? How many damned murders have there been!' exclaimed Clay. 'But stay a moment, Ludlow was under armed guard. How did Rankin manage such a thing?'

'It was not just the use of the garrotte that he learned during his time serving the Madras Presidency,' explained Vansittart. 'He was also skilled with poisons, and carried several upon his person. As soon as I heard tell of this mysterious fit from your surgeon, I was sure that Rankin was behind it.'

'I am captain of this ship, and yet I seem to be the last to be acquainted with what is truly happening,' said Clay. Then he stared at the diplomat, as another thought came to him.

'You spoke of Sedgwick having saved you a task, sir,' he said. 'What exactly did you mean?'

His guest pulled one of his lace cuffs straight. 'I meant that there can be no loose ends in this affair,' he said. 'I have already sent Rankin's more incriminating possessions to the bottom of the Baltic in a weighted package. You may trust your coxswain, but I did not trust Rankin at all. I daresay, if he had lived, he would have found a way to turn his knowledge into cash, either by blackmailing the government or from selling the story of Paul's death to our enemies. Your coxswain's actions have saved me the unpleasantness of dealing with that situation.'

'What would you have done?'

'I don't personally attend to such matters, Clay,' said the diplomat. 'I would have sent him back to India, together with some confidential instructions for his superiors. They tell me the climate there is especially unhealthy for those of the white races, don't you know?'

Clay waited for Vansittart to say more, but the diplomat remained silent. The captain noticed, for the first time, that the master shared the same expressionless eyes his late servant had once had.

THE END

NOTE FROM THE AUTHOR

Historical fiction is a blend of the truth with the made up, and *In Northern Seas* is no exception. These notes are for the benefit of readers who would like to understand where the boundary lies between the two.

The frigates *Griffin* and *Liberte*, the privateer *Hirondelle*, and the brig *Fair Prospect* are all fictitious, as are the characters that crew them. That said, I have tried my best to make sure that my descriptions of those ships and the lives of their crews are as accurate as I am able to make them. All the other ships that I mention are historic, and were in the locations that I state at the time. As always, any errors I have made are my own.

The historical background to the campaign behind *In Northern Seas* is broadly accurate. In 1800, under strong French pressure, Russia, Prussia, Sweden and Denmark were encouraged to renew the Northern League of Armed Neutrality that had been formed during the American War of Independence. This threatened the supply of naval stores that were vital for both the Royal Navy and Britain's merchant marine. London's response was to send a large fleet under Admiral Sir Hyde Parker to the Baltic in the spring of 1801. In advance of the fleet, a trusted diplomat called Nicholas Vansittart was despatched on a mission to the Danish court in the hope that he could negotiate a peaceful resolution. When this failed he returned to the fleet aboard the frigate *Blanche*. There was no subsequent voyage to St Petersburg as portrayed in my novel.

Tsar Paul was murdered by strangulation on the 23rd of March 1801 in the Mikhailovsky Palace. Those responsible were led by General von Bennigsen and Count von Pahlen.

The conspirators obtained the support of the Grand Duke Alexander by showing him his arrest warrant, although at this stage their plan was just to force Paul to abdicate. After a tense banquet, the tsar retired to his private rooms. The conspirators were then let into the palace by the guards, and forced their way into Paul's bedroom using violence. When the tsar refused their demands, he was killed. No British citizens were present, although the change of regime came as a huge relief to London and effectively ended the Northern League of Armed Neutrality. Some historians have suggested that the British Ambassador, Lord Whitworth, may have encouraged the plotters. The murder of his father was to haunt Alexander for the rest of his life.

The scene on the eve of the Battle of Copenhagen in which Nelson receives news of Tsar Paul's death is my invention. In reality, word of the change in the Russian regime only arrived in Denmark after the battle was over, where it helped to bring the two sides to a swift peace agreement. My portrayal of the battle itself is mostly correct. The ships I show as running aground did so, and the Danish defenders fought with the tenacity and bravery I portray. With the help of a constant flow of reinforcements from the shore, ferried across in a variety of boats, the Danish ships resisted for much longer than the Royal Navy had expected. Nelson came closer to defeat at Copenhagen then in any of his other major fleet actions.

As with my account of the Battle of the Nile in *A Man of No Country*, I wanted my characters to serve as the eyes of the reader, witnessing history. To this end I substituted the *Griffin* for the frigate *Desiree*, which placed herself across the bow of the Danish ship *Provesteenen* during the battle. The *Griffin*'s subsequent intervention in the flow of boats from the shore, and the Danish attempt to board her are both fictitious.

The Battle of Copenhagen is best remembered for Admiral Parker's notorious signal ordering the fleet to break off the action, which was flown at the height of the fighting. At the time he was too remote to have made such a decision, and although he could see that three of Nelson's ships were aground, he undoubtedly should have trusted the judgement of the commander in the thick of the battle. Nelson is reported to have held his telescope to his blind eye and claimed not to be able to read the signal, an incident from which we get the expression "to turn a blind eye." Sir Hyde Parker later claimed that his signal was meant simply to give Nelson permission to break off the action if he wished to, rather than a definite order. This explanation lacks as much credibility today as it did at the time. After the battle, Parker was recalled by London, and command of the Baltic Fleet passed to Nelson.

About The Author

Philip K Allan

Philip K. Allan comes from Watford in the United Kingdom. He still lives in Hertfordshire with his wife and his two teenage daughters. He has spent most of his working life to date as a senior manager in the motor industry. It was only in the last few years that he has given that up to concentrate on his novels full time.

He has a good knowledge of the ships of the 18th century navy, having studied them as part of his history degree at London University, which awoke a lifelong passion for the period. He is a member of the Society for Nautical Research and a keen sailor. He believes the period has unrivalled potential for a writer, stretching from the age of piracy via the voyages of Cook to the battles and campaigns of Nelson.

From a creative point of view he finds it offers him a wonderful platform for his work. On the one hand there is the strange, claustrophobic wooden world of the period's ships; and on the other hand there is the boundless freedom to move those ships around the globe wherever the narrative takes them. All these possibilities are fully exploited in the Alexander Clay series of novels.

His inspiration for the series was to build on the works of novelists like C.S. Forester and in particular Patrick O'Brian. His prose is heavily influenced by O'Brian's immersive style. He, too, uses meticulously researched period language and authentic nautical detail to draw the reader into a different world. But the Alexander Clay books also bring something fresh to the genre, with a cast of fully formed lower deck characters with their own back histories and plot lines in addition to the officers. Think *Downton Abbey* on a ship, with the lower deck as the below stairs servants.

IF YOU ENJOYED THIS BOOK VISIT

PENMORE PRESS

www.penmorepress.com

The Captain's Nephew

by

Philip K.Allan

After a century of war, revolutions, and Imperial conquests, 1790s Europe is still embroiled in a battle for control of the sea and colonies. Tall ships navigate familiar and foreign waters, and ambitious young men without rank or status seek their futures in Naval commands. First Lieutenant Alexander Clay of HMS Agrius is self-made, clever, and ready for the new age. But the old world, dominated by patronage, retains a tight hold on advancement. Though Clay has proven himself many times over, Captain Percy Follett is determined to promote his own nephew.

Before Clay finds a way to receive due credit for his exploits, he'll first need to survive them. Ill-conceived expeditions ashore, hunts for privateers in treacherous fog, and a desperate chase across the Atlantic are only some of the challenges he faces. He must endeavor to bring his ship and crew through a series of adventures stretching from the bleak coast of Flanders to the warm waters of the Caribbean. Only then might high society recognize his achievements —and allow him to ask for the hand of Lydia Browning, the woman who loves him regardless of his station.

PENMORE PRESS
www.penmorepress.com

A Sloop of War

by

Philip K.Allan

This second novel in the series of Lieutenant Alexander Clay novels takes us to the island of Barbados, where the temperature of the politics, prejudices and amorous ambitions within society are only matched by the sweltering heat of the climate. After limping into the harbor of Barbados with his crippled frigate *Agrius* and accompanied by his French prize, Clay meets with Admiral Caldwell, the Commander in Chief of the island. The admiral is impressed enough by Clay's engagement with the French man of war to give him his own command.

The *Rush* is sent first to blockade the French island of St Lucia, then to support a landing by British troops in an attempt to take the island from the French garrison. The crew and officers of the *Rush* are repeatedly threatened along the way by a singular Spanish ship, in a contest that can only end with destruction or capture. And all this time, hanging over Clay is an accusation of murder leveled against him by the nephew of his previous captain.

Philip K Allan has all the ingredients here for a gripping tale of danger, heroism, greed, and sea battles, in a story that is well researched and full of excitement from beginning to end.

PENMORE PRESS
www.penmorepress.com

On the Lee Shore

by

Philip K.Allan

Newly promoted to Post Captain, Alexander Clay returns home from the Caribbean to recover from wounds sustained at the Battle of San Felipe. However, he is soon called upon by the Admiralty to take command of the frigate HMS Titan and join the blockade of the French coast. But the HMS Titan will be no easy command with its troubled crew that had launched a successful mutiny against its previous sadistic captain. Once aboard, Clay realizes he must confront the dangers of a fractious crew, rife with corrupt officers and disgruntled mutineers, if he is to have a united force capable of navigating the treacherous reefs of Brittany's notorious lee shore and successfully combating the French determined to break out of the blockade.

PENMORE PRESS
www.penmorepress.com

A Man of No Country

by

Philip K.Allan

In 1798, the Royal British Navy withdrew from the Mediterranean to combat the threat of invasion at home. In their absence, rumors abound of a French Army gathering in the south of France under General Napoleon Bonaparte, and of a large fleet gathering to transport them. Alexander Clay and his ship, Titan, are sent to the Mediterranean to investigate. Clay verifies the troubling rumors but is unable to learn where the French fleet and the army will be heading. When Admiral Lord Nelson arrives from Britain with reinforcements, Clay and Titan join Nelson's fleet heading for Southern France. But on their arrival, they discover Bonaparte's fleet is gone, and Nelson, aware of the dangers of an ambitious and ruthless general, orders an all-out hunt for Bonaparte's armies before it is too late.

As the Titan searches for Napoleon's forces, another threat has already gained passage on the ship. After engaging and destroying a Russian Privateer, the crew capture a mysterious stranger, claiming to be an English sailor who has been serving from childhood on Barbary ships. Shortly after he joins the ship, there begins a rash of thefts followed by the murder of another sailor. With the officers baffled as to who is behind this, it falls to Able Sedgwick, the Captain's coxswain and the lower deck to solve the crimes.

PENMORE PRESS
www.penmorepress.com

The Distant Ocean

BY

Philip K Allan

Newly returned from the Battle of the Nile, Alexander Clay and the crew of the Titan are soon in action again, just when he has the strongest reason to wish to abide in England. But a powerful French naval squadron is at large in the Indian Ocean, attacking Britain's vital East India trade. Together with his friend John Sutton, he is sent as part of the Royal Navy's response. On route the Titan runs to ground a privateer preying on slave ships on the coast of West Africa, stirring up memories of the past for Able Sedgwick, Clay's coxswain. They arrive in the Indian Ocean to find that danger lurks in the blue waters and on the palm-fringed islands. Old enemies with scores to settle mean that betrayal from amongst his own side may prove the hardest challenge Clay will face, and a dead man's hand may yet undo all he has fought to win. Will the curse of the captain's nephew never cease to bedevil Clay and his friends?

PENMORE PRESS
www.penmorepress.com

THE TURN OF THE TIDE

BY

PHILIP K ALLAN

Freshly back from a year in the Indian Ocean, it is not long before Alexander Clay and the crew of the *Titan* are in action once more. This time they are sent on a secret mission across the Channel. Amongst the forests and marshes of Southern Brittany, a Royalist rebellion is building and the Government at home is keen to support it. But as the uprising grows, Clay finds himself being drawn into a world of deception, intrigue and treachery. Who is the charismatic rebel leader, Count D'Arzon, and what is the secretive Major Fraser really up to? Meanwhile the settled community of the frigate's lower deck is disturbed by the arrival of a new recruit who appears to have strange mystical powers

PENMORE PRESS
www.penmorepress.com

Midshipman Graham and the
Battle of
Abukir

BY

James Boschert

It is midsummer of 1799 and the British Navy in the Mediterranean Theater of operations. Napoleon has brought the best soldiers and scientists from France to claim Egypt and replace the Turkish empire with one of his own making, but the debacle at Acre has caused the brilliant general to retreat to Cairo.

Commodore Sir Sidney Smith and the Turkish army land at the strategically critical fortress of Abukir, on the northern coast of Egypt. Here Smith plans to further the reversal of Napoleon's fortunes. Unfortunately, the Turks badly underestimate the speed, strength, and resolve of the French Army, and the ensuing battle becomes one of the worst defeats in Arab history.

Young Midshipman Duncan Graham is anxious to get ahead in the British Navy, but has many hurdles to overcome. Without any familial privileges to smooth his way, he can only advance through merit. The fires of war prove his mettle, but during an expedition to obtain desperately needed fresh water – and an illegal duel – a French patrol drives off the boats, and Graham is left stranded on shore. It now becomes a question of evasion and survival with the help of a British spy. Graham has to become very adaptable in order to avoid detection by the French police, and he must help the spy facilitate a daring escape by sea in order to get back to the British squadron.

"Midshipman Graham and The Battle of Abukir is both a rousing Napoleonic naval yarn and a convincing coming of age story. The battle scenes are riveting and powerful, the exotic Egyptian locales colorfully rendered." – John Danielski, author of *Capital's Punishment*

PENMORE PRESS
www.penmorepress.com

Penmore Press

Challenging, Intriguing, Adventurous, Historical and Imaginative

www.penmorepress.com

Lightning Source UK Ltd.
Milton Keynes UK
UKHW040724271219
355981UK00001B/190/P